NOVELS BY

BROWN MEGGS

———

THE WAR TRAIN   1981

ARIA   1978

THE MATTER OF PARADISE   1975

SATURDAY GAMES   1974

THE WAR TRAIN

THE WAR TRAIN

A Novel of 1916

BROWN MEGGS

\\\

New York **ATHENEUM** *1981*

Library of Congress Cataloging in Publication Data

Meggs, Brown.
    The war train.

        1. Mexico—Frontier troubles—1910—Fiction.
    2. United States. Army—History—Punitive
    Expedition into Mexico, 1916—Fiction.   I. Title
    PS3563.E34W3   1981   813'.54   79-55612
    ISBN 0-689-11052-9   AACR2

DEDICATED TO THE MEMORY OF MY FATHER

Charles Winfield Meggs

artist & gentleman

MAY 18, 1902—JULY 3, 1980

AUTHOR'S NOTE

The War Train is fiction based on fact. Much of the story was told to me by my late grandfather, Frank Leo Moore—"Moe"—who, in March 1916, as a young man fresh out of baseball and then employed by the Pullman Company, escorted elements of the 12th Cavalry from South Dakota to New Mexico in support of the Punitive Expedition against Pancho Villa.

As a novelist, I have chosen to embroider Moe's account, inventing scenes and characters where it has suited me to do so. Thus, the resulting novel is fiction in the true sense of the word.

I am particularly indebted to Mary Jane Alexander, Vincent Atchity, Ned Brown, Ted Calleton, Herman Gollob, Nancy Meggs, Brook Meggs, Marye Myers, M. J. Snyder, and Tom Stewart, each of whom contributed generously to the manuscript. I also wish to thank the staff of the National Archives, Washington, D.C., for making available War Department records, including *Returns of the 12th Cavalry, October 1915–July 1916*.

Brown Meggs

PASADENA, CALIFORNIA
JANUARY 1981

CONTENTS

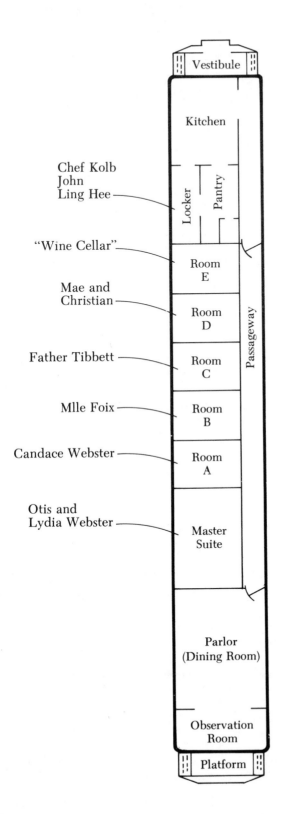

THE
MOTHER LODE

Vestibule

Kitchen

Chef Kolb
John
Ling Hee

Locker

Pantry

"Wine Cellar"

Room
E

Mae and
Christian

Room
D

Passageway

Father Tibbett

Room
C

Mlle Foix

Room
B

Candace Webster

Room
A

Otis and
Lydia Webster

Master
Suite

Parlor
(Dining Room)

Observation
Room

Platform

MAKEUP OF PULLMAN'S NO. 3

1st Section

- Baldwin locomotive No. 506 & tender
- 3 supply wagons (40' boxcars for heavy equipment)*
- Squadron Armory (baggage-express car for weapons & ammunition)*
- 3 flatcars (horse wagons, water wagon, and Red Cross ambulance truck)*
- *The Mother Lode* (Webster party's private Pullman)**
- Headquarters Car (Pullman drawing room/stateroom car; accommodations for 9 officers & civilian veterinarian)
- cook car (boxcar fitted for messing of enlisted men)*
- 4 Pullman standard parlor cars (33 enlisted men each)
- 6 horse wagons (40' boxcars, 18 horses each)
- caboose No. 1865

2d Section

- Baldwin locomotive No. 799 & tender
- 4 flatcars (2 Jeffrey "quad" motor trucks each)**
- 4 parlor cars (enlisted men)
- 9 horse wagons
- caboose No. 333

*added at Fort Meade
**added at Omaha

Route of the WAR TRAIN
March 11–16, 1916

I

DOUBLING OUT

Lincoln, Nebraska
March 10, 1916

Children are travellers newly arrived in a strange country, of which they know nothing: we should therefore make conscience not to mislead them. They are strangers to all we are acquainted with; and all things they meet with are at first unknown to them, as they once were to us; and happy are they who meet with civil people, that will comply with their ignorance, and help them to get out of it.
JOHN LOCKE, *Some Thoughts on Education* (1693)

Such was the male line, as far back as anyone could remember:

William McGill, born 1816, Ballinascarthy, County Cork; tenant farmer.

In 1846 came the blight, in 1848 the Great Famine. In fall of the latter year, Billy McGill set sail aboard **Endymion** *from Skibbereen on Roaringwater Bay, landing at Boston on 12 December. Accompanying Billy were his wife Hannah O'Hea of Clonakilty and their three sons, Padraig, Denis, and Michael. Boston being then crowded with refugees, Billy removed his family to Chicago, where they found shelter with Hannah's kin, the Connaghtons.*

Padraig McGill, born 1840, Ballinascarthy; laborer.

Eight years of age during the voyage to America, Paddy McGill reached manhood in Chicago, taking for his bride Mary Ellen Moore of Knockcroghery in County Roscommon. Their issue were sons Leo, Chester, Benjamin, and Joseph.

Benjamin McGill, born 1866, Chicago; farmer, merchant.

Bent on seeking his fortune in the West, Ben McGill left Chicago at age eighteen, going first to Omaha, thence to Hastings, Nebraska, where, by means of the Homestead Act, he acquired 160 acres of land. Vida May Foley of Grand Island became his wife, she and Ben being distant cousins through the O'Briens of County Donegal.

On 9 October 1897, Vida May produced the first of five children, a son. He was christened **Cassius James Patrick.**

1

THE STEEL DOOR to the caboose clanged open like a great church bell, scaring Cassie half to death.

"*Watchin' good are ye, mister?*"

It was old Stokes again, mean and blustery as the storm then blowing. Cassie caught his breath and replied:

"Sure am, Captain Stokes! Oh, yes, sir!"

The senior conductor gave a snort. His raspy black tones cut through the clickety-clack of wheels on rail joins like a steam saw ripping pine:

"*Yard's comin' up! Look sharp, boy, or ye'll dance on the carpet afore the super hisself!*"

The captain disappeared inside. He was headed back to the Franklin stove, Cassie expected. Vans on the Red Eye Line offered all manner of comforts, including—to judge from the captain's generous breath—occasional drafts of sweet corn liquor. This despite the Railroader's Rule G: Thou shalt not drink.

Cassie looked back to the door and shouted aloud, knowing the captain could not hear a word of it:

"Oh, thank you, sir! It's good o' you to invite the likes o' me to your little party! Only I much prefer it out here, sir, in all this fine fresh air!"

He was eighteen years of age, a helper conductor—"student," in the lingo of the line—in Pullman's Palace Car Company. Just now he was close to freezing. Cursing under his breath, he hunched down on the van's front platform, balancing on his hindquarters like a circus acrobat. He had been riding outside since Captain Stokes put him there at Waverly, five miles back. He had no business in the cold, but Captain Stokes was top master on the Red Eye Line and permitted no argument or complaint.

"*There's no sayin' what's behind us and runnin' late!*" the master had said. "*Keep yer eyes open and yer lamp at the ready!*"

So it was Cassie's job to protect the rear of the train against another outfit that might not have its signals straight. This was properly the duty of Mac Simpson, the flagman. But Mac was as partial to the blessed Franklin as old Stokes was. Mac had known Captain Stokes for twenty years, or maybe forty. Cassie had known the same gentleman two days.

Cassie fished out his timepiece: 5:17. A skyful of snow clouds made for fast nightfall. March 10 it was and not a hint of spring. It had been zero degrees at Omaha around midday. Now, as they approached the yards at Lincoln, the peekaboo sun dropped down behind the grain elevators to the west and the temperature dropped with it. Deep black canyons of shadow showed ice in every nook and cranny. Snow had not been off the ground since Thanksgiving.

It was not even Cassie's run. This knowledge hurt him worse than the cold. The train was the Chicago & North Western's *No. 9*. She ran Chicago, Grand Island, and return twice a week, hauling grain and livestock mostly. Today she added a solitary wood-sided varnish—what civilians called a day car. Her few passengers were farmers and drummers, by their looks. Cassie was nothing but a passenger himself, or supposed to be. He had been out ten days this time and was deadheading back from Hammond, Indiana, where his last run had taken him. He had doubled out twice in a row—three nasty runs all together, with no break between. Deadheading was always bad—no pay for your time—but it was especially bad now, on account of Captain Stokes.

"*So what's yer name, boy?*" the master had said to him their first morning together.

"McGill, sir. Cassius McGill."

"*'Nother damn mick, is it! An' how old would ye be, boy?*"

"Eighteen, sir."

"*An' one o' Mr. Lincoln's wee students, are ye? Well, don't let us catch ye a-doggin' it, laddy boy! 'Cause not even Mr. Lincoln hisself is gonna save yer hide!*"

Captain Stokes was referring to Mr. Robert Todd Lincoln, who was boss of Pullman's and son of Abraham. When Mr. Pullman died in '97—the year Cassie was born—Mr. Lincoln, who had been the company's lawyer, took over the top job. It was Mr. Lincoln's idea to hire students. These were youngsters who were supposed to learn railroading in a dignified way, as a true profession.

Captain Stokes did not appreciate students. Most conductors in Captain Stokes's time started out as brakemen. This was back in the days before Mr. Westinghouse's air brake, when stopping a freight meant climbing up top and screwing down the brake wheel by hand. That was the most dangerous occupation in the world, next to working the old link-and-pin couplers. Captain Stokes and most other senior men that Cassie had come up against saw red at the idea that Cassie and a few others had the great privilege of donning a master's blue serge right off instead of learning their trade from the bottom of humanity's ladder.

Knees about to break, Cassie lowered himself to the platform, sitting flat this time, Indian style, one leg hooked around the brake rod. Between his thighs, for safety, he cradled a genuine Handlan Patent Engine & Train Lamp. This was Cassie's to use till he earned his own. The lamp was solid brass throughout, weighed seven pounds, boasted a crystal lens set in a ruby-red globe, and could be seen five miles or more in clear air. Etched into the globe was the legend: PROPERTY OF L. B. GUMP, LODGE 32, BENEVOLENT ORDER OF RAILWAY CONDUCTORS. L. B. Gump was a famous master from olden times. Cassie had toted that lamp for nine months now with proper respect and some fear, too, should something happen to it while it was in his care. Captain Stokes and Captain Gump had worked the same roads for fifty years, and Captain Stokes did not believe that any student was fit to carry so honorable a lamp. Cassie might have agreed with this sentiment, but his boss, Mr. Hebb, the Pullman agent at Lincoln, had supplied the lamp and ordered Cassie to carry it.

"Oh, gentle Jesus!" Cassie shouted for the wind to hear, "I'm about froze out!"

"Whoooooooooooooooosh!" answered the wind.

Cassie doubled up, making himself into a tight ball so the yellow slicker he was wearing would give maximum cover. His troubles had begun two days earlier when he lost his overcoat and gloves. He had not "lost" them exactly; they had been snatched from under his nose in the Chicago yardmaster's office. The smart clerks on duty there pretended to be ignorant of the crime, but Cassie knew better. It was hard to swallow. He would make fifty more runs before he could save up enough cash to buy new goods. He was not eager to explain the loss to Ma.

The weather had gone bad soon after Joliet. That was when Cassie grabbed the slicker off the peg in the buggy. Borrowing that slicker had brought him to the notice of Captain Stokes. By Moline, Cassie was doing all the captain's chores. This meant hooping up train orders set out along the right of way, carrying messages forward to the hoghead, and even working the flag some when they went in the hole to let another train pass. It also meant dropping down to the platform at every stop and suffering the cold. Cassie's hands had turned numb by Davenport. There was not an extra pair of mittens on the whole rig; Cassie had asked every trainman aboard.

His physique offered little resistance to the cold. "Awful skinny fer a spitballer, ain'tcha?" Jake Moriarty, the manager at Falls City, had once said to him. Cassie guessed he was. He had got his full growth at age fifteen: a hundred forty pounds scattered over a six-foot frame. Mr. Pullman's uniform did not help much, either. Underneath the slicker Cassie wore the better of his two sets of trainman's harness. The suit was blue serge with a long-skirted, five-button tunic and trousers that draped over his shoe tops. His shoes were official black dress trainman's model, ankle high and worn with black cotton stockings held up by garters.

The rest of the outfit was BVDs, suspenders, vest lined in real China silk, starched white shirt with high round collar, and a black silk tie stuffed down inside the vest. It was a smart outfit when fresh. Stretched across where his belly would have been if he had had any was a gentleman's vest chain in 10-karat gold, $4.18 from the Sears, Roebuck catalog. Tethered to the chain was a Special Railway Model pocket watch manufactured by the Hampden Watch Company in Canton, Ohio. It had been a gift from Pa when Cassie signed on with Pullman's. It cost $24.90 and was warranted "to pass inspection of any railroad in the United States or your money back." It had twenty-one ruby and sapphire jewels, was damaskeened in green and copper, and boasted fleur-de-lis hands. It kept fine time.

On his head, Cassie wore a trainman's box cap with chin strap and brass strip across the front stating his duties: SPECIAL SERVICE. After three years' apprenticeship he could hope for CONDUCTOR. Adorning the lapels of his tunic was a pair of brass emblems, "P" for Pullman. In his breast pocket he kept an array of pencils; in his hip pocket his "first reader" or train book; in the right-hand trouser pocket $1.50 for emergencies. Hooked to his belt in a cowhide holster was his nickel-plated ticket punch. This instrument put out the "M" which was his official signature in the brotherhood. No two punch holes were exactly alike, so a division super or other brass collar could tell which conductors were passing over their roads just by the way a pasteboard was punched. Cassie's M was flowery like handwriting; it might be taken for an upside-down "W" unless a man knew his business. Cassie liked it a lot.

All together, Cassie found his harness most agreeable. He gave considerable thought to his dress. This was not idle vanity, he believed, but good business. If a young man was to get ahead in his chosen line of work, he had best see to his appearance: this lesson had been taught Cassie early on by his favorite uncle, Leo. Leo also taught him to play poker, draw pleasing tones from a Jew's harp, and sing the ballads of Erin. Cassie wished he had the benefit of Leo's advice just now; Leo would know how to handle Captain Stokes.

Wet snow swirled in all directions, blew down his neck. The icy blast plucked at his eyes; only a steady stream of tears kept the lids from freezing shut. His lips had gone crusty and hard; he felt them only now and again when a warm substance dripped down. This was blood, he figured, spilling through purple cracks. His nose might have fallen off, for what he could sense of it. He could see what looked like a stump if he crossed his eyes; otherwise he could not tell. His ears were icicles, pointy sharp and brittle: no room for them under his cap, though he wore it as low down as regulations of the Pullman Company permitted.

He was in steady pain now. To improve his spirits, he shouted back at the gale, which had become his good friend and loyal companion:

"Oh, ain't this railroadin' grand! Oooooooooooo-eeeeeeeeee!"

He laughed at his own nonsense. The cold was making him crazy. Whistling through the wind came the words of Mr. Terry O'Toole of the Boston Brownies, Cassie's last manager ever in baseball:

"Fate has smiled her prettiest smile at you, me boy! Be grateful for her kindness—she coulda broke yer head an' not yer arm!"

Cassie wondered. To his mind, there was little but pain and humiliation to be got from certain tricks of fate. One mean trick is to be kicked out of baseball when you are seventeen years of age because you are horsing around in the shower room between games of a doubleheader and an ignorant Yahoo from Dade County, Florida, of the name Willie Soddy, tosses you on the cement floor and busts the elbow of your throwing arm. You are a prime spitballer with two no-hitters to your credit in the Nebraska Cities League, and fate srtikes you out just when you are called up to the Brownies. This is what your Uncle Leo will pass off as "luck of the draw," while Pa says, " 'Tis sure to haunt you all the days of your life."

Still, Cassie supposed he had little cause for complaint, cold as he was. Lots of fellows his age had no work at all. And what better occupation was there in these modern times than the railroad? From what Cassie had seen, it sure beat farming, which had occupied most all McGills since anyone could remember. And it beat the coffee and spice trade, too, Cassie was thinking—this being Pa's occupation these past two years since the family moved up to Lincoln from Hastings. In Pullman's the pay was not large but it was regular. For Pa, pay came whenever a customer might feel up to it.

The only thing that came close to spoiling Pullman's for Cassie was the notion that he had got his job through connections and not on merit. "Kissing arse," Mr. Hebb had called it. After Cassie hurt his arm, Mr. Terry O'Toole had put the matter to one of the Brownies' owners, a fellow on close terms with Mr. Lincoln. That was all it took; Cassie did not know of it till it was done. Next thing he knew, he was invited to be a student in Pullman's. Cassie was not proud of how he got his job, but he did not turn it down either.

He put his mind on pies.

Steaming hot pies as big around as a Texas cowboy's hat.

This was his last best trick for staying alive in such circumstances: thinking hard on pies. Pies such as Ma made—double crusted, deep sided, stuffed with butter—could defeat any amount of cold. Cassie had carried one on the outbound run and finished it before Des Moines. That one was beef and lamb both, with plenty of lard in the crust for flavor. Ma wanted him to carry two, but he already had his valise and lunch pail and Captain Gump's lamp, and so had declined. This proved a serious mistake, as the eating house in Hammond, Indiana, where Cassie took his next meal, was not home cooking or anything like it. He intended to recover himself that evening at supper. He was hoping for one of Ma's juicy dessert pies made from raisins and dried apples off the farm down at Hastings. This gave him something pleasurable to think on. Bad as the run had been, it was nearly over and then he would have two whole days off—Mr. Hebb had promised it to him—with nothing to do but enjoy Ma's cooking and stay by the fire and sleep in a bed.

Meanwhile, he still had Captain Stokes's work to do and never mind the hog law that said all crewmen had to tie up after twelve hours' steady service. And never mind that conductors were to work no more than seventy hours a week. Or maybe such laws did not apply to Mr. Pullman's lads—at least not to what the pay vouchers called a Special Service Helper, which meant you had all the pains but none of the privileges of a regular smart aleck for $1.87 a day and no end to bad grub from the caboose.

The ride got rough. Cassie figured it for roadbed broken up by frost. The hogger up front throttled back, but there was still a chance of Cassie's being bumped off and snagged by a wheel; so he clamped one hand to the brake wheel. He knew he would lose some skin getting it off again, but it was better to freeze a finger than lose a leg, as many yardmen did.

He tugged a chaw of Red Devil from his vest pocket, hoping to work some feel into his frozen jawbones. The chaw was hard as stone. He worked at it till it softened some, then spit, hitting the striker plate of the boxcar ahead. He watched the spittle slide down the icy metal, slow, freeze right there, brown and hard. Cassie opened his mouth wide and let the rest of the wad drop down to the trackbed. He did not like tobacco much anyway. It seemed a fine. habit, but one he had not so far been able to acquire.

The train slowed to a walk. There was little traffic in the yards, but the hogger displayed a good supply of caution—he could see no better through the snowflakes than Cassie could, probably.

They stopped altogether. Cassie leaned out and peered into the murk: red board ahead. Ten seconds later, the caboose door again clanged out its alarm.

"*What are ye waitin' for, boy? Climb down! Do yer duty!*"

"Just going, Captain Stokes!"

Cassie let go of the brake wheel. Sure enough, bits of his palm and fingers stuck to the metal. Sucking at his wounds, he unfolded his limbs and climbed down, swinging Captain Gump's lamp in a broad arc to warn off other rigs.

He had hardly hit the trackbed when the board went green and *No.* 9 began to roll again.

"*Well, boy? Git aboard, why don'tcha! I swear, the lad's deef and dumb both!*"

Cassie pulled himself aboard again, cursing and asking forgiveness of the Lord all in the same breath.

Soon there was sweet music from the locomotive: one long blast for APPROACHING STATION, followed by one medium and three short: PUT OUT THE FLAG.

"*Well, boy? Sleepin' agin, are ye?*"

"No, sir, Captain Stokes!"

"*Work yer lantern then, damn scamp! See ta yer customers!*"

"Yes, sir, Captain Stokes!"

The rig was traveling at a slow trot now, platform dead ahead. It was Cassie's job to signal the engineer when the day car was lined up with a certain marker so that the customers might march off in perfect comfort and safety. The rig would then be backed out into the freight yard for switching.

Mac Simpson, the true flagman, showed his face at last, yawning and scratching like an old cat. Without uttering a word, he dropped off to protect the rear of the train, which was his job. Cassie, too, wanting to escape the chatter and boom of the cars' taking up slack, swung down like an old hand. But his knees, stiff from the cold, betrayed him, and he went sprawling on all fours, to the disgust of the captain.

"*Dint I jest know it! Ha, he is sure some 'student' and no railroader atall!*"

Cassie scrambled to his feet and sprinted forward, sighting down the track as he went, trying to figure out which marker was theirs. It was not easy to know. The snow was falling thick and wet now, and the gas lamps along the platform gave off no more than a dim yellow glow.

"*Well, boy?*" the captain shouted down at him. "*Show yer lamp, can't ya?*"

Cassie never did see the marker, but it was as noticeable to Captain Stokes as a boil on the behind. Quick as he could, Cassie flashed the signal forward to the eagle eye at the throttle: STOP TRAIN. The hogger backed off not a yard too soon. With a great belch of steam, *No.* 9 eased to a stop.

Cassie ran forward to the day car and lowered the steps at both ends, seeing his passengers off—the few who had been ignorant enough to ride a slow rattler like this one—with a proper Pullman smile and a pleasant

"Thank you, sir!" There were eleven such riders by count and not a smile—or tip—among them. Cassie did not wait for any blessing from Captain Stokes either. He grabbed up his lamp and valise and followed his passengers directly on toward the station.

"Ho, boy! I'd be havin' a word wit ye!"

A gnarled little trainman came shuffling along the platform, banging his paws together for warmth. Cassie had seen the old fellow around the yards, knowing him by what others called him, Mr. Fingers. Mr. Fingers had been a switchman in past days, which included standing between cars and dropping the pin to couple up. Under his mittens the old gentleman missed two fingers off each hand, and the thumb off his right.

"What is it, then?" Cassie replied. He feared delay, should Captain Stokes be gaining on him.

"Would ye be knowin' a smart aleck of the name McGill?"

"Who's asking?"

"Mr. A. O. Austin, is all!"

Mr. A. O. Austin was division superintendent for the Red Eye Line at Lincoln. "Then you found him," Cassie admitted.

"Ye be McGill?"

"That's me."

Mr. Fingers appeared to doubt this claim. "And how old would ye be, then?"

"Old enough to do my job."

"Tsssssk! They call it railroadin' but it ain't, not no more!" The old trainman spat out his words in a dry croak. "Bless me, boy, ye're wanted over't the super's office. Best git yer wheels a-turnin'!"

"Who is it that wants me? Can't be Mr. Austin—he wouldn't know my name."

"If yer name's McGill, he knows it, boy! Him and Mr. Hebb both!"

Mention of Mr. Hebb, the Pullman agent, brought Cassie up short. He did not like the sound of it, not late of a Friday.

"I'll just go by the pay car and pick up my time for the week," Cassie said.

"I'd skedaddle, boy, I was ye! Super ain't much for waitin'!"

Cassie reconsidered. "I'll stop by the lockers and put up my lamp."

"Hee-hee-hee, boy! It's yer lamp ye'll be needin' most!"

Cassie went along, his aching hands barely able to grip his valise and Captain Gump's lamp both. *Another stinking run.* He would be told to shine at daybreak and go straight back to Omaha or Des Moines or someplace worse. It was not fair, but it was orders, most likely.

There was nobody at the desk outside the super's office. Cassie waited for a clerk to appear, but none came. Finally, hearing muffled talk inside, Cassie hitched up his trousers, applied his frozen knuckles to the door and admitted himself.

"Begging your pardon, sirs—but is it *me* you're wanting to see?"

Mr. Hebb jumped up from his chair. "Thank God, it's the boy hisself! Don't hang back, lad—come forward!"

The other gentleman remained silent. Cassie had never before set eyes on Mr. A. O. Austin but knew him at once for the super. He was squat, sour-faced, and fidgety and looked about as easy to manage as a keg of nails. Cassie figured him no older than Pa but lacking Pa's easy smile and kindly manners.

Nor did Mr. Hebb, tall and bent like an old tree, seem the sweetest of men on this occasion:

"What the devil you got on, boy? Why, it's nothing but a *slicker!* On a night like this? Have you lost your *reason?* Remove it at once! Stand over there by the fire till you get some color to you. You'll die of pneumonia and then what am I to tell your ma? Drop your valise, boy—we've business to tend to, important business. And for the love of Jesus, set down that lamp! Ain't no signals to give in this office but what the super and me choose to give!"

Cassie obeyed Mr. Hebb's various instructions. There was a roaring wood stove in the middle of the office. Cassie stood as close to the glowing metal as he dared. The bottoms of his trousers began to steam and drip.

Mr. Hebb shook his head, clicked his false teeth. "Truly, A.O., the lad is generally smarter in his conduct!"

"I should like to believe so," the super said. He looked Cassie up and down with sorrowful eyes. It did not seem to Cassie a friendly inspection. "Well, boy?"

"Sir?"

"Explain your costume. Or maybe you're an Eskimo and happy in the cold."

"Lost my belongings, sir. Went for supper in the Chicago station and found my goods missing when I got back."

The super turned to Mr. Hebb and said in a sad voice, "The boy has no coat." He spoke as though Cassie were not present.

"He will secure another," said Mr. Hebb. "Find one quick, Cassius—mittens, too. Help yourself to the coffee, boy—you're looking a mite peaked."

There was a large tin pot churning and spitting on the stove top. Cassie wrapped his kerchief around the handle and poured himself a cup of the scalding brew.

"Hold up, boy," said Mr. Hebb. The Pullman agent came forward with a bottle of whiskey from the super's desk.

"Thank you, sir, only—"

Mr. Hebb did not wait for objections, splashing a finger or so of the dark liquor into Cassie's cup. "Be silent, boy, and drink up. You'll be the better for it, take my word."

Cassie sipped the beverage and found it comforting. Mr. Hebb poured more coffee for himself and the super, adding liberal doses of whiskey to both cups. The two men had been working over some papers on Mr. Austin's desk. Cassie took note of a spread-out copy of *Busby's Universal Railroad Atlas & Gazetteer*. Also a stack of train orders and waybills and the late edition of the *Lincoln Citizen-Dispatch*.

The super tilted back in his chair and spoke to the ceiling. "I remain of the opinion she's too much train for this boy."

Mr. Hebb responded sharply in Cassie's defense. "He is not taking her to the moon, A.O., but to Omaha!"

"You are leaving out the fort," said the super, "and the nature of the customer."

"You do not know this boy as I do, A.O.!"

"I surely do not."

"He is a strong boy!"

"I hope he is stronger than he appears."

"He is a boy of some schooling and great resource!"

Cassie had the feeling that Mr. Austin was being sold a bill of goods he was not anxious to buy. The super's eyes narrowed. "Bet you got your diploma, huh, boy?"

Cassie's stomach knotted up. He wished he could answer differently. "Not exactly, sir," he admitted, his voice down a notch or two. "It's only the one more term I'm lacking, though, sir."

Cassie felt his face go red, as it always did when the subject of his education came up. He preferred not to explain how he had run off from the Christian Brothers for the sake of the Major Leagues; there had been quite enough discussion of it around the McGill dinner table. Pa liked to quote another Irishman, Finley Peter Dunne, who wrote in the *Chicago Herald* under the guise of "Mr. Dooley's Opinions":

"In me younger days 't was not considhered rayspictable f'r to be an athlete. An athlete was always a man that was not strong enough f'r wurruk. Fractions dhruv him fr'm school an' th' vagrancy laws dhruv him to baseball."

Cassie felt that Mr. Dooley got it wrong in this one instance. It was not fractions that drove him from the Christian Brothers, but Latin grammar.

"Still," Mr. Hebb was then saying, "he is a heady lad, A.O., and can read and write both. I told you he is a top baseballer and tough competitor, too. What was it they used to call you, Cassius, over there to Falls City? 'Sidewinder,' was it?"

"Some did, sir."

Cassie wished people would leave off of nicknames. He had already owned a string of them: "Speed" for his fast ball, "Lefty" because he was a southpaw, "Sidewinder" for the way he delivered his big breaking curve. With the Christian Brothers he had been "Kid McGill"; with Nebraska City, "Slick."

". . . Why, Cassius was as good a thrower as you'd ever care to see, A.O., and that was just the smallest part of it! With the bat he was another Daubert, a Hornsby—a Lajoie, even!" The Pullman agent turned to Cassie and addressed him sternly. "Tell what you done, Cassius. Now is not the time to hold back."

Cassie let out a sigh, then admitted his sins. He had been an outfielder until '14, when the Girard Indians of the Nebraska Cities League sent him to the mound. The next year he went to the Falls City Falcons, where he was the top left-hander with sixteen wins, four losses. His .377 led the league in batting, too. After that he got called up to the Boston Brownies for a tryout in the exhibition season. He threw a pair of one-hitters back to back and looked a sure bet to make the club when he suffered his accident. When the pain finally went away, he could no longer come sidearm with his fast ball, and no amount of spit would fool the batters. So he was out of baseball.

"But you ain't out!" objected Mr. Hebb. "Pullman's will field a team in summer, A.O., and Cassius here's our first base. Ain't that right, boy?"

"Yes, sir. Guess I forgot."

Cassie had wanted to forget. He meant to accept fate's decree, but Mr. Hebb would not hear of it. Pullman's was set on fielding a scratch team to go against the Rock Island and Burlington and Missouri Pacific and the other outfits in Lincoln, with the best of the locals to move on to Omaha and play the champions of the railroad league there. Cassie had known lots of sore-armed first basemen in his time and figured he could get by. There was no pay in it, but Mr. Hebb said a good batting average might be rewarded when it came to making up the duty rosters.

The super reached for the whiskey bottle again. He did not seem much impressed by Cassie's credentials. Cassie guessed the railroader did not follow the game. "So tell me, boy, do you miss it at all? Playing a game for your livelihood? Or do you"—the super's gravelly voice turning sarcastic on the words—"maybe prefer the railroad?"

Cassie blushed at the idea. Who wouldn't miss it, having Ma and Pa come out to watch him play on a real diamond with wood bleachers? Getting to visit cities like Boston and New York and Chicago with plenty of spare time to enjoy?—not a bit like passing through with Pullman's! Having some burly catcher hug the breath out of him when he got the last out for a no-hitter? Seeing his name in the newspaper box scores? Making a good salary—ten *times* what he could ever earn in Pullman's—

for playing a game he had played for free since the fifth grade? What fool wouldn't miss it!

Cassie lowered his chin. "I guess I do miss it, sir—sometimes."

"'*Course* the boy misses it!" Mr. Hebb stuck in. "But he's a sensible lad and there's no point to dwelling on misery. Ain't that right, Cassius?"

Cassie nodded. He would always remember what Mr. Terry O'Toole said to him that last day in Boston, when Cassie learned he was to go back down:

"So there it be, laddie. Lady Luck's called strike three on ye and ye're out. No use to deny it or curse it. You wuz anutter Mathewson, I do believe. You wuz anutter Johnson—even quicker maybe. Ain't never seen a fast ball quicker'n yers, never in me life. But she's gone fer good, laddie, an' no use to spill yer tears over't neither. Y'are a brainy lad and kin make somet'in' o' yerself if ye want ter." Eighteen years old and washed up for sure.

The super's unsympathetic grunt brought Cassie back to Lincoln.

"*Listen* to us, Calvin. Talking 'bout this boy's baseball when the true and proper question ain't baseball but railroadin'. Boy? Yes or no? You ever rode even one mile by your lonesome? Or always in some true master's shadow?"

"Take a train on my own, sir? No, sir, sure haven't."

"There! The boy's said it for himself."

Mr. Hebb did not back off an inch. "But you rode some with Billie Sparrow, dint you, boy?"

"Yes, sir, three trips."

"And with Mr. Liberty?"

Cassie paused to think. "Yes, sir—four trips or maybe five."

"Then you worked helper with the best—ain't *that* the truth!"

Mr. Austin gave another loud grunt, came out from behind his desk. "Dammit all to hell, Calvin, give the boy his orders if that's what you're of a mind to do, and let's get on home. Sun's long set and ain't none of us gettin' rich on talk."

"My very intention, A.O.!"

The two brass collars again passed the whiskey bottle between them. They spiked Cassie's cup, too. He saw his brew grow lighter and thinner as the whiskey began to crowd out the coffee.

"Take a seat, boy," ordered Mr. Hebb.

Cassie took a chair by the work table.

"Seen the newspaper, boy?"

"No, sir, sure haven't. Meant to get me one at Des Moines, only—"

"Never you mind. Set your eyes on this."

Mr. Hebb handed Cassie the *Citizen-Dispatch* off Mr. Austin's desk. Cassie scanned the headlines:

SEVENTEEN AMERICANS SHOT DOWN ON U.S. SOIL

COLUMBUS (N.M.) PUT TO THE TORCH

WILSON ORDERS ARMY INTO MEXICO TO PUNISH VILLA'S RAIDERS

9 Civilians, 8 Soldiers of the 13th Cavalry Lose Lives in Reign of Murder and Arson Perpetrated by Frenzied Gang of Villistas Led by the Bandit Himself

TRAINS CARRYING MEN AND MUNITIONS ORDERED TO BORDER WITHOUT DELAY

"*Well*, boy?" growled Mr. Hebb impatiently. "Know what this means?"

Cassie remembered reading in January how Villa's men had pulled seventeen Americans off a train near Chihuahua and gunned them down just for the pleasure of it. But that was Mexico; this was the United States. "Well, sir—"

"It means *war*, boy—honest-to-goodness war! And you're to have yourself a front-row seat!"

"Sir?"

"He *can* read, can't he?" inquired Mr. Austin.

Cassie thought maybe the super was only joking, but he spoke up for himself anyway. "Yes, sir, I sure can read."

"Read some more!" Mr. Hebb ordered.

Cassie read on:

Washington, March 10—President Wilson has ordered that Francisco Villa must be captured or killed at any cost. The United States Army will undertake the task. The American expedition, under direct command of Brigadier General John J. Pershing, brilliant Indian fighter and hero of the Philippines, will go to Mexico as soon as possible. A decision to this effect was reached at this morning's Cabinet meeting.

"Oh, to be this boy's age again!" Mr. Hebb was saying. "What a fine opportunity for a worthy lad!"

"There's all kinds o' fools on the railroad," pronounced Mr. Austin.

Mr. Hebb drew his chair close to Cassie's. "Now, pay attention to what I tell you, boy. You're to get home, climb into fresh harness, and report back to the yards at ten o'clock sharp."

"Excuse me, sir, but would that be in the morning?"

"Why, yet tonight, lad, o' course! It's Emergency Rules from here on. By nine in the A.M. you'd best be in South Dakota. This very minute there's a special making up. You're to ride part way as master, *Captain* McGill, so get out your first reader and write down what I tell you."

Captain McGill. Cassie gasped at the idea. He hated the thought of another run so close on the heels of the one he had just finished, but he had strong appetite for that word "captain." Of all the names given to conductors—smart aleck, brains, big ox, grabber, swell head, skipper, king, master—he liked "captain" best.

"Well, boy, are you listening?"

"Yes, sir, sure am!" Cassie sat up straight, ears burning. He slipped his train book from his hip pocket and prepared to write.

Mr. Hebb continued. "I'll tell it to you straight. This is rightly Mr. Liberty's run, only he is feeling poorly and cannot shine. Only other master close by is Captain Stokes, but he is outlawed. There is nobody fresh for duty on short notice excepting yourself. I know you are not one to disappoint folks who have been mighty good to you."

"No, sir."

The Pullman agent opened *Busby's Atlas* to a map showing the Central States from border to border. "At daybreak you are to meet the Army here—Fort Meade. Nearest railhead is Sturgis. Don't expect you've ever been up Dakota way."

"No, sir, sure haven't."

"It is hard country, take my word. You will meet your customers, load up, and make for Omaha at full throttle. War won't keep, boy—you'll have a green board the whole way. At Omaha you will pick up extra cars—munitions and the like. After that you will highball it south and west till you reach El Paso. Near as the super and I can figure it, the run is eighteen hundred miles. It is a goodly run, boy."

Eighteen hundred miles! Cassie traced the route with his fingers. It was three times, easy, any run he had had before.

"You are on your own up to the fort and back down to Omaha. At Omaha Mr. Liberty will come aboard and take the train. From there to the border you will work helper to him and skipper the second section."

Cassie took some relief from the news but felt disappointment, too. He liked Mr. Liberty well enough; the master was near to seventy years of age and easy in his ways. But after swallowing the idea of Captain McGill, Cassie regretted stepping down again to helper.

"Well, what do you think, boy?"

"I believe I can manage, sir."

"Of course you can. You see, A.O., he is a responsible lad and not afraid of work!"

"Unh!" grunted the super. He did not look up as he spoke. "I shall reserve judgment till the run is made." The super was busy sorting through stacks of paper that littered his desk top. Being as short as he was, he had trouble reaching to the farthest regions of it. Cassie had the idea that Mr. Austin was readying himself to leave the station; he made rumbling and hissing noises, like a Baldwin getting up steam.

"Well, now, boy," said Mr. Hebb, "best acquaint yourself with the flimsies." He handed Cassie the train orders, pounded out by machine on green tissue. Cassie guessed there were maybe twenty extra copies on Mr. Austin's desk, one for each hogger and division super along the right of way.

Cassie studied the orders. His customer was to be the War Department, United States of America. Passengers were the 4th Squadron, 12th Cavalry Regiment. The rig would total thirty-nine cars made up in two sections and bear the name *Pullman's Special Service Train No. 3.* Rolling stock was leased from the Chicago & North Western, the Red Eye Line, which was the road Mr. Austin worked for. This accounted for the super's interest in who the master might be. Provision was to be made for nine officers, 280 enlisted men, and one civilian, a doctor by the name of Rose.

Mr. Hebb continued. "You'll be needing a helper to ride the second section far as Omaha, then do chores for you on to 'Paso. Allowance is two dollars a day and grub off the caboose. No pay, o' course, on the home leg. Who you get is your business, but if I was you I'd get me a fella handy 'round animals."

"Animals, sir?"

"Horses, boy! It's cavalry you're carrying, ain't it?" Mr. Hebb consulted the waybill. "Of horses—two hundred seventy head. The Army's wranglers will see to 'em mostly, but there's no sense in getting yourself a helper who's shy o' the beasts. Off the farm yourself, ain't you?"

"Yes, sir. Down by Hastings."

"Rode horses all your life?"

"Yes, sir, guess I have."

Mr. Hebb turned back to the super. "You see, A.O.? Could we ever *hope* to find a better master for such a rig!"

The super gave another grunt: it seemed neither yea nor nay to Cassie. Mr. Austin had stuffed most of his papers into drawers and was now locking up the desk.

Mr. Hebb kept on with business:

"Thanks to the super here, the hog law is waived for you and your crew. You'll carry the same boys all the way. Hoggers and firemen is different. They must obey. Your brakies can get their shut-eye on the move, hoggers and firemen can't—this is the reason for it. Reliefers for the cabs will come from the roads you're passing over. The Company is arranging for it now from Chicago. See that those fellas sign your book good and proper. And see they are discharged afore twelve hours is up." The Pullman agent paused. "You getting all this in your book, boy?"

"Yes, sir, sure am!"

Cassie's wet cuffs kept wiping across what he had written, making the ink run. He hoped he could read his words when he needed to.

"For top George," Mr. Hebb said, "I been able to get you old Nelson. He's a high-type Negro and will look after you in case of trouble."

"George" was what the Pullman Company called porters, after Mr. George Pullman. "Yes, sir," Cassie said, "I traveled with Nelson once before, and like him fine."

"He's out rounding up the best boys he can find on short notice. You're entitled to eight, so you shouldn't none of you want for shut-eye—leastways, not after Omaha. Can't say it'll be a joy ride, boy, but these customers is easier to please than some. Being soldiers, they're a rough lot and not used to Pullman comfort."

"We'll sure handle them, sir," said Cassie. "Me and Nelson." He was in fine humor now; he could feel the whiskey in his cheeks.

Mr. Hebb seemed to share Cassie's good feelings. The agent's long thin face broke wide in a smile. "Your own rig to Omaha, and you so tender in years. Won't your ma be proud."

"I believe she will, sir. Pa, too."

The Pullman agent rose. "Them's your orders, then."

Cassie stood. Under his chair, a large puddle of melted snow now stained the parquet.

"No time for lallygagging, boy," said Mr. Hebb.

"No, sir."

"Step smartly and be prepared for business."

"Yes, sir, sure will."

"You're a mighty lucky boy."

"I know it, sir."

"Highballing it to Mexico with nary a red board twixt here and there." Mr. Hebb stuck out his hand; Cassie took it.

"You'll do us proud," said the Pullman agent. "You'll do honor to the Company."

"I'll try my best, sir."

Mr. Hebb turned to Mr. Austin. "The boy is going now, A.O. Got any words to give him?"

"I do," said the super. He was just then dragging on a large bearskin overcoat. He had finished stuffing his portmanteau with whatever papers he could not fit into drawers or the wastebasket. He had downed his fill of whiskey and now kept one hand on the desk to steady himself. He was about as drunk as he meant to be, Cassie figured, or perhaps a drop more. The railroader fixed Cassie again with sorrowful eyes. "I have three words for you, boy."

"Sir?"

"First word is *coat*. Find one."

"Oh, yes sir, I sure aim to." Cassie was thinking of his late Uncle Chet's mackinaw, which was up in the attic last time Cassie looked.

"Second word is *galoshes*. 'Cause by the wire there's four foot o' snow on the ground at Sturgis an' more fallin' by the minute."

"Yes, sir. Got a fine pair of galoshes, sir."

"Third word—most important, boy—is *longjohns*. 'Cause she's ten below up there, Dakotas bein' the devil's own icebox."

"Yes, sir. Got plenty of longjohns, too, sir."

"You are well advised then. Now do your duty—nothing more, nothing less."

"Yes, sir! Thank you, sir!"

The super sank back into his chair. Maybe he had downed one drop too many, Cassie was now thinking. He did not wait to find out. With Mr. Hebb's help, he put on his slicker, gathered up his valise and Captain Gump's lamp, and backed out the door. The last thing he heard was rough laughter from inside—as though someone had told a fine joke.

Oh my, yes, ain't this railroadin' grand.

2

HIS OWN TRAIN.

The thought of it pleased Cassie greatly—pumped fresh energy to his tired limbs, gave him second wind. To save time, he rode the electric trolley up O Street till it crossed 16th. This cost a nickel but put him only six blocks from home. Climbing down, he consulted his Railway Special: 6:40. Immediately, he set off with a long and purposeful stride. He had much to do before reporting to the yards at ten: get supper, ask Ma to see to his soiled uniforms, pack his valise for ten days on the road, go searching for a helper.

The sky was now a great black moonless cloud. A light shower of silver snowflakes drifted down, dusting roofs and tree limbs. Cassie liked Lincoln best under a sprinkling of snow. It was prettier than life, like an engraving in *Collier's*. He had gone only a block when he noticed a dark figure coming his way. The fellow was short and compact and wrapped in a muskrat coat about five sizes too big. A red wool muffler covered his face up to the nose.

By gas lamp, Cassie could not be sure, but the oatmeal cap and rolling gait looked painfully familiar. Cassie pushed on, shoulders hunched against the cold, head bent low to conceal his features. Maybe the fellow would pass by.

It did not work. The fellow stopped and waited for Cassie down the path, unwrapping his muffler and puckering his fat lips into a friendly whistle. The tune was none but "The Bard of Armagh," which the whistler knew to be among Cassie's favorites.

Cassie stopped in his tracks. It was the shortstop all right—Riley McAuliffe, called Rocks. For an instant Cassie was almost happy to see him again. But then he remembered their last association; this cured him of any Christian feelings. Cassie started up again. He passed straight by the interloper without uttering a word.

"Ho, Professor! Don't ya *know* me? Ain't ya even gonna say *hullo?*"

Cassie called back over his shoulder, "Got no time just now." He kept on.

"Well, *sure* ya do, Professor! An' who'd ya be wantin' to see more after so long a spell o' winter?"

Cassie kept on.

"Well, you're glad to *see* me, ain'tcha?"

Cassie kept on.

"Dint I *tell* ya Boston'd take Philly in the Series? *Dint* I? Dint I say Cobb'd win the battin' crown again? Picture a shortstop hittin' three sixty-nine! He's likely to top four hundred again, too, like in '12. Wanna bet on it?"

Rocks had always fancied himself another Cobb, the shortstop for Detroit. Like the loud-mouthed Georgian, Rocks was built on the small side, maybe a hundred twenty pounds, standing five three in his stocking feet. Rocks had Cobb's build but lacked the Georgian's skills on the basepath or at the plate. He had Cobb's temper, though, and Cobb's flashing spikes; he could be as dirty and underhanded as Cobb ever was.

Cassie kept on.

"I'm fresh from the Florida League, Cass! You ain't never seed nothin' like it in yer life! Oh, it was grand! I hit about three hundred meself and dint have an error in twenty games! It was close to Paradise, sure it was!"

Cassie called back over his shoulder: "Then how come you're here in Lincoln? That's snow falling, 'case you didn't notice. There's no snow in Paradise, that I ever heard of."

Rocks stayed on Cassie's heels. "Friends, Cass! It's no use bein' away from yer *friends*. I'm back to make my way here in Lincoln. Maybe in the railroad, don'tcha know!"

"Hah."

"Sure it's true! Could ya give me a letter, do ya s'pose? Maybe to one o' the bigwigs at Pullman's? Sayin' as how I'm a good worker and dependable?" Rocks put a smile on it, smiles being the sole currency in his purse.

"Not on your life."

"It's only a favor you'd be doin' me, Cass. It ain't like money or nothin' o' value, but only what one brother does fer another."

Brother! Cassie laughed at the nerve of it. Still, Rocks was the only "brother" he had known till he was nine years old and the twins, Dwight and Dewey, came along.

Cassie paused to inspect the plain face that now beamed up at him, a face he had not seen since last spring. Irish it cried out, but not handsome at all. Silly grin frozen on, lily-white Irish skin, hair black and rough as coal, impudent chin, flapping ears, queer button nose. Cassie blinked hard. It was as though he had never seen such a face before. What an unlucky creature that face belonged to! Rocks had first come to them down at Hastings when he was five years old. He lived with them on and off, depending on his ma's health, till the McGills removed to Lincoln. His ma was called Aunt Kitty in the McGill household, though she was not blood kin. She and Ma had grown up together in Grand Island; they were close as sisters. Aunt Kitty had named her only child after her proud family; she was cousin to the Chicago alderman, Patsy Riley. The name Rocks had been bestowed by Hugh fitzOsbern, manager of the Hastings Bees, who told Rocks, "Ye must have rocks fer brains!" for the way he played shortstop.

Rocks never knew his pa. The fellow ran off before Rocks was born. About all Rocks knew of him was his name, Liam McAuliffe. Liam McAuliffe had set up his family on a hard patch of ground out by Hastings town limit; it was good for nothing but raising hogs. "We might as well abin back in Ireland!" Rocks said of that farm. Rocks had never been to Ireland, of course, but his family, like Cassie's, had lived there till the Famine.

Rocks had no education to speak of: Aunt Kitty needed him around the place. "Got me schoolin' in pig shit," Rocks would say. He started out with Cassie at the Blessed Sacrament School in Hastings but never went past the third grade. He could write his name but scarcely read it. Rocks had got his full growth, what there was of it, by twelve. From then on, he was too much for Aunt Kitty to manage. He would stay put till spring, then be off, looking to play ball. He was close to twenty now and had not changed his ways. Cassie supposed he never would.

Cassie got over his daydreaming and started up again. The shortstop stayed right with him. "I been to the house a'ready. Cass. Ma says you're on a run t' Chicagy and ain't expected."

"You see me, don't you?"

"And a treat 'tis! Here now, Professor, gimme yer lamp. Gimme yer fine grip. No mittens? No greatcoat? Ain't ya freezin' yer nuts?"

Cassie kept on, clinging tight to the lamp and his valise. *Rocks McAuliffe*. Here was the author of a hundred grand schemes—"grand" being the word Rocks loved best—like joining up with the Foreign Legion to fight the Germans in Africa, or walking up to Alaska and prospecting for gulch gold on Anvil Creek, or following after Perry to the North Pole, or a hundred other dandy propositions sure to bring them to ruin by the shortest route.

"Besides, I brung ya a present, bein' so glad at the notion o' seein' ya again! Here, we can share. You go first."

Cassie pushed the bottle away. It was a half-empty pint of rye whiskey, warm from riding on Rocks's hip. "There's no drink allowed on duty," Cassie said back.

"You ain't got no duty that I can see, Professor! 'Cept enjoyin' yerself, that is!" Rocks helped himself to a swig of Cassie's present.

Cassie kept on. So did Rocks. The shortstop managed a side-legged skip step to keep abreast. "Here, gimme that," he said. He made a grab for Mr. Gump's lamp.

Cassie smarted at the idea of Mr. Gump's lamp suffering even momentary possession by Rocks McAuliffe. He wheeled and swung his valise as hard as he could.

The shortstop's feet went out from under him and he crashed to the icy path in a heap. "Now why'd ya go and do *that,* Cass? Me tailbone's broke, sure 'tis! I can't rise!"

Cassie pulled him up. "Now out o' my way, damn you! You and me are quits, that's the truth." Cassie marched on again.

"Ya don't mean it, Cass."

"Bastard."

"I ain't no bastard, Cass. Call me anything you want, only not bastard."

Cassie wasn't proud that his temper had led him to say it. Rocks, never knowing his own pa, was touchy on the subject. "Damn thief, then," Cassie said.

Rocks's pained countenance turned to mock surprise. "So it's *that* what's makin' you sore! Gosh darn! Dint ya get me letter? Dint ya get the money I sent ya?"

"I didn't get it 'cause you never sent it."

Cassie kept on. Rocks fell silent, but Cassie could still hear the shortstop slogging through the snow behind him.

"Okay then," called Rocks, "ya caught me out, same as always. I was gonna send it to ya, Cass. I had that much and more tucked away in me cap, only these fellas I was travelin' with got me in a crooked game o' spit-in-the-ocean. They took me whole stake, Cass, every nickel. God's own truth!"

"You can't open that big mouth of yours without telling a lie, can you?"

"Aw, Cass."

Cassie marched on.

"It's drink, Cass. That's what done it. It's drink that's brought me low."

"Lord Jesus, a confession!"

"It don't mean I can't mend me ways, Cass. See here—I'm off the drink!"

Cassie turned around in time to see the shortstop pitch the whiskey bottle into a far snowbank. Cassie figured the bottle was empty by then anyway. He resumed his pace. It was always dangerous to hear Rocks out. Rocks could make a body do things he ought not to do. This talent had accounted for the trip Cassie and Rocks had made up to Canada, and for the loss of Cassie's money. They went to Winnipeg in the West, where "the pickin's is easy," Rocks had said. What he meant was there were more ladies than men in that town. Cassie had just come home from his tryout with the Brownies and was at loose ends; this was before he received the telegram from Mr. Terry O'Toole telling him to report for work at Pullman's. Cassie felt uncomfortable hanging around Lincoln: it was a hard thing being sent down from the Major Leagues and having everybody know about it. So he agreed to Rocks's scheme, bankrolling the expedition, too, as Rocks was always cleaned out. The minute they got to Winnipeg, Rocks disappeared from the boardinghouse where they put up, taking along Cassie's stash—something close to twenty-five dollars—and leaving Cassie to make his way back to Lincoln as best he could. This meant bumming on the Canadian Pacific, which wasn't the same as buying a plush seat in a parlor car.

"Hey! Hold up, can'tcha?"

Cassie kept on. The shortstop was out of breath. He looked to be in poor shape if he meant to report someplace by summer.

"So what's yer hurry all of a sudden? Supper's been et a'ready, 'case yo're rushin' fer that!" Rocks kept close track of people's eating times, especially the McGills', where he had taken meals all his life. " 'Course Ma'll fix you somethin' without yer askin'."

"I know about eating in my own house," Cassie replied. He could feel his mean streak coming to the fore. "I'm off to war, is all."

Rocks grabbed hold of Cassie's arm again, this time dragging him to a stop. The shortstop's eyes glistened with excitement. "You're gonna *do* it, Cass? You're joinin' up? You're goin' after the Kaiser?"

"Lord Jesus," Cassie swore without thinking, "never read the papers, now do you!"

"Ain't seen one in a dog's age, tell the truth."

It was a mean thing for Cassie to say, knowing that Rocks couldn't read. Cassie backed off—softened his tone of voice. "It's not the Germans," he explained. "It's the Mex."

Rocks squinted back. His cold-blushed features became a rosy puzzle. Whereupon Cassie told of Pancho Villa and the raid on Columbus and the lucky job that had come Cassie's way, delivering the 4th Squadron to El Paso. "The Army's aiming to capture the bandit dead or alive," Cassie declared, "and I expect I'll be witness to the better part of it."

By the time Cassie had finished, Rocks was near to tears. The shortstop tore the cap from his head and slapped it across his knees. "Don't that beat all! You sure do run to luck, Professor!" He was jumping up and down, showering Cassie with hot whiskey breath. "It never fails, ain't that right—me wantin' so bad the very riches that falls in yer lap!"

They had reached the front gate to the McGill house. Cassie was glad to see it. "You'd best be off now, Riley. I can't be talking to you now—there's my bag to pack and crew to round up and such as that." Cassie was too intent on making it sound official and important to realize his mistake.

"Why, ain't that grand!" cried the shortstop. Again he slapped his cap across his thighs. "Already yo're a boss yerself! And what crew would ya be roundin' up then?"

"Well, there is this and that," Cassie said. "Fellows to do the dirty work along the way. Such as that."

"Why then, yo're in the best o' luck, ain'tcha! 'Cause for starters ya got the best fella you could ever want, an' you knowed him yer whole life!"

Cassie took a quick step backward. "It's not handy work but proper railroading. You're not cut out for it."

Cassie meant to break it off then and there, but the shortstop would not permit it. "Cut out *perfect* is the holy truth! All them horses? An' who sits easier'n me on a horse's back!"

Rocks had once been a fairgrounds jockey, Cassie recollected. He could ride a horse, all right. Cassie thought some more. "There's no horse riding to be done," he said. "I told you it's proper train work. It calls for fellows who are dependable and sober. You're neither one."

Embarrassed by the harshness of his own words, Cassie turned his back on the shortstop and went through the front gate. But Rocks was as hard to shake as a summer cold or a case of poison ivy. "It'll be *different* this time, Cass, I swear it! Swear it on Ma's Bible, ya want me to!" The shortstop looked to heaven, then crossed himself.

Cassie shook his head. "I learned my lesson. Learned it up in Winnipeg, if I didn't know it before."

"You *gotta* take me this time, Cass! 'Cause I got no place else to go—God's own truth!"

Cassie detected a strange, fearful note in the shortstop's usually stout voice. "So what about spring practice? I suppose you're not about to report to some low-down club in the Toledo Commercial League?"

Rocks tugged at the rumpled cap in his hands. "I ain't been able to catch on so far, Cass. I'm on the outs, I guess. It's not like when you and me was bummin' together."

Cassie was not surprised. He and Rocks had played together from the time they were big enough to swing a broomstick and pitch a corncob. The first team they played on that had proper uniforms was the Elks Lodge Peewees back in '10. Cassie was twelve, Rocks almost fourteen. After that they played for Hostetler's Emporium All-Stars, the Shenandoah (Iowa) League Team, Hunt's Livery & Boarding, and the Nebraska City Cyclones. They split up in '14, when Cassie signed on with the Girard Indians and Rocks went off to try his luck in Ohio, where he had a cousin of the name Hodder. Rocks had no love for Ohio, but he could not find another team in Nebraska to take him on. Managers generally went for him on sight, but none would go two seasons with him. He was clever as any Irishman but too full of tricks—like hiding away the top pitcher's shoes before a championship game or dosing the waterbag with saltpeter. Now, in the modern game, what club would suffer the manners of a Cobb without Cobb's booming bat? So here he was, back to Lincoln, tail between his legs, no prospects and probably not the price of a meal in his pocket.

"I'm sorry for your hard luck," Cassie said, "but I've got my own job to look after."

"'Course ya do!" Rocks exclaimed. 'An' that's how come I'm offerin' me services! I'm goin' along fer *free*, Cass! Can ya beat that? 'Course ya can't!"

"I can't do it."

"I'm off the drink, Cass—you *saw* it, dint ya?"

"There's no use talking."

The shortstop put on a false smile. "Heck, Cass, I'm sure to catch on somewheres afore league opens. Did ya know there's a *thousand* teams up Mich'gan way? I mean to go there and find me one. Only I'm needin' this li'l job o' work to keep me straight, ya understand, till summer. 'Member when we was back in the 'Braska Cities League t'gether? It can be like that fer me again, sure'n it can!"

Cassie sighed in disgust. "You know what?" He stared Rocks in the eye till the shortstop had to look away. "Your league days are over, same as mine. Only you're too ignorant to see it."

Rocks put on a look of terrible pain. "Now why would ya say somethin' so mean as that, Professor? I'm still quick on me feet, ain't I? You doubt it? Looky here!"

Rocks did his best hook slide into second base—second base being a tree stump ten paces off. He got to his feet spitting snow. "You still doubt it? Dint I show ya?"

"You dumb Irishman!" Cassie declared. "It's not *me* you got to show. Where are you going to find a manager to put up with you? You think managers are different up in Michigan?"

Rocks came right back at him. "Hugh Jennings puts up with Cobb, don't he? Detroit's up in Mich'gan, ain't it?"

It was useless to argue with the shortstop. Cassie braced himself, then spoke in a quiet voice: "I'm going to give you some free advice. I'm not charging you for it because you'll surely not take it and I'm not aiming to cheat anybody if I can help it. I give it to you for old time's sake and then we're quits."

"I always listen to you, Cass. Sure ya know—"

"*Listen*, can't you? Don't talk. What I have to tell you is this:

"We can't pretend to be kids anymore, 'cause we're not. It's past time for us to go funning from town to town, pretending summer's all that counts. It's time to think grown-up. It's time to get *work*, Riley. Not baseball, which is just a stupid damn game, but real work, with a paycheck every Saturday and a chance to settle down, maybe start a family—make something of ourselves, if we ever mean to.

"That's all the advice I can give you. Let's shake on it, and then you be off."

Rocks's face lit up like a child's. "But ya said the very words I was hopin' to *hear*, Cass! I aim to take yer advice to heart, sure do!"

"That's good," Cassie said. He set down his valise and came back to the gate and offered his hand to the shortstop.

Rocks grabbed hold with all his might. "You said it yerself, Cass! Baseball's just a stupid damn game! It's real work I'm needin', ain't that the truth!"

Cassie backed off again. "I can't do it. I told you why. I need somebody I can count on in the tight spots, and you're not him. I'm going inside now."

The shortstop dropped down to his knees in the snow. "I'm *beggin'* ya, Cass. It's life and death now, sure 'tis!"

Rocks looked about to cry real tears this time. Cassie was not moved. "I'm going inside now," he repeated.

Finally, he did.

Pa was down cellar doing his roasting: Cassie could tell from the rich scent of coffee that flowered the air. He left his belongings in the front hall and went looking for the others. The first he met was his dog, Flag. She was fourteen now, fat, blind in one eye, with bare patches in her shaggy coat. He knelt down to pat her head and accept her fond licks in return. She could barely wag her tail anymore, but Cassie loved that old dog—she had come to him as a puppy, the gift of Uncle Leo.

Ma appeared next, her light blue eyes sparkling at the unexpected sight of him. "Darling boy, home at last! Such a rare treat it is these days to see my own son. You've only just missed Riley—ate supper for two, he did! Well now, won't you be kissing your mother?"

He kissed her ample cheeks and gave her a hug besides. "It's sure good to be home, Ma, only I'm due back to the yards by ten sharp. It's a long story—like the ride I'm going on!"

He told of his orders, of meeting up with Rocks, of needing to rush out again and find himself a helper.

"Such a grown man you've become," Ma said with a sigh. "And won't your father be pleased. He's tied to his roaster or he'd be up to greet you himself. There's ten sacks fresh from Brazil."

Brazil. The very sound of the word sent shivers down Cassie's spine—filled his head with jungle pictures. Pa's business was to import coffee and spices from far-off places, then sell the goods to local merchants west to Denver, south to Oklahoma City, east to Des Moines. There was a stack of wood crates in back of the house stenciled with magical names—Paramaribo, Barranquilla, Kuala Lumpur. Cassie longed to see such places but supposed that the border of Mexico was now as close as he would ever get.

"I'd best go down, Ma, and lend a hand."

"Not a bit of it—your father can manage. If you're meaning to catch that train, off to the kitchen with you—you'll be wanting supper. Quick now, out of those dirty rags. How is it a student's expected to get along on two outfits when the one's always filthy and the other's on the way to being so?"

"It's not ladies and gents I'm to carry, Ma, but roughriders and their mounts. Neither one's likely to notice a dirty uniform."

"Well, *I* surely notice it, Cassius McGill, and so should you."

"Oh, I noticed it, Ma. I been living in it the week now—I guess I noticed it!"

He put on his robe and slippers. Ma set him down at the kitchen table over a steaming hot plate of lamb stew, a dozen biscuits, and half a mincemeat pie. The children gathered around and he told them of his great adventure to come. The twins, Dwight and Dewey, aged nine, had been doing catechism for their Saturday morning First Communion class at St. Jude's; they were glad of an excuse to quit it. The family already knew of the war Cassie was bound for: it was spread all over the front page of the *Nebraska Combine*, the farmers' paper that Pa still preferred. There was even a picture of Pancho Villa, mustachioed and fierce.

"You gonna bring him back dead or alive, like it says, Cass?" asked Dwight.

"It'll be dead for sure, won't it, Cass?" asked Dewey.

"One way or the other," Cassie agreed.

"Oh, big brother!" cried sister Ada, drowning him in hugs and kisses. "Ain't you the luckiest one!"

Ada was just turned fourteen. The excited way she talked made Cassie think of Rocks, who never looked at the underside of anything but always accepted the world at face value. The same could not be said for Cleo. Being sixteen and sophisticated—and vain, Cassie could tell, as to her blossoming figure—Cleo pretended no interest in the war, but kept on with her practice of the Gregg shorthand system. She was enrolled at Miss Barlow's Secretarial College in anticipation of obtaining a good position in one of the commercial concerns down on Omaha Boulevard. She set aside her practice tablet only long enough to judge that any war with such lowly creatures as the Mexicans would be over long before Cassie got to it. "And I do believe it's sinful to send the *Army* to chase after a few low scoundrels—and traveling by Pullman at that!"

"Hush up, Cleo!" Ma said. "It's a matter far beyond you."

Ma had taken up the *Combine* again: it suddenly made her short-tempered. The newspaper gave over a good many words to the sorrowful fates of the seventeen dead Americans at Columbus. An artist no closer to the battle than Omaha had drawn his idea of the corpses and the violent manner of their deaths. One poor fellow had his head chopped off with a sword. The legend beneath the drawing said: CUT DOWN ON AMERICAN SOIL!

There was an item touching on Cassie's orders; he read it aloud, thinking to calm Ma's fears:

U.S. SOLDIERS FROM THIS DEPARTMENT ORDERED TO MOVE AGAINST VILLA

Omaha, March 10—Everything indicates that within hours the regular soldiers of the Department of the Missouri will be en route to the Mexican border to take a hand in avenging the death of the American citizens killed by Pancho Villa and his murderous band. Earlier today officials of the Pullman Company here received from the War Department instructions to assemble equipment at Fort Meade, S.D., and Fort Robinson, Neb., preparatory to moving the troops at these two points on short notice. At the same time, Union Pacific officials received instructions for the movement of the regulars from Fort Russell, near Cheyenne. It is asserted that from the three forts some 1500 men will be sent to the front.

"So you see, Ma," said Cassie, "there's no danger to it. I'm not going there alone but am taking the whole Army to protect me. Besides, I'm aiming to get back in a hurry to get more stew as good as this!"

It did no good; she refused him her smile. She went on with her chores, tight-lipped and solemn, worrying over his uniforms, sponging off the dirt where she could and applying a hot iron to the load of wrinkles he had collected in his travels. He had been away from home a hundred times—maybe a *thousand* times—since he was twelve years old, first for baseball, then for Pullman's; so Ma was well accustomed to his comings and goings. But he had never before gone off to the scene of a true massacre. He guessed this made the difference.

When he could put it off no longer, he told Ma how he had lost his greatcoat and gloves. She didn't even scold him for his carelessness, but went straight to the attic and brought down Uncle Chet's mackinaw and a pair of fur-lined gloves that had once belonged to Pa's baby brother, Uncle Joe, who died of the smallpox before Cassie was born.

"Ain't they swell, Ma!" said Cassie.

"Aren't," said Ma.

"*Aren't* they swell," said Cassie. Ma preferred the children to use correct language in the house; Cassie had let down his guard for an instant. "They're ever so much better than what I lost. Thank you again, Ma."

But still she would not speak more than she had to, or show even the hint of her regular smile.

At last, Pa came up from his work and heard the news.

"Your own *train*, Cass." Pa spoke in hushed tones. "And you nowheres near to nineteen!"

Cassie admitted that Mr. Liberty would be taking the train after Omaha, but this did not seem to lessen Pa's pleasure.

"You've proved yourself to Pullman's, lad, or they wouldn't think to put you in charge. It sounds a man's job all right, and you're surely the man for it!"

Pa went to the larder and brought back a bottle of the elderberry wine that Leo had put up the summer before. Everybody was permitted a full glass including Dwight and Dewey, though Ma made them take theirs cut half with water. Pa made the toast:

"May all the Saints in Heaven love and preserve our son Cassius on his fine trip!"

"Amen," said all.

Ma shed a tear or two, as Cassie knew women were wont to do, then excused herself and talked on the telephone to Father Terwiliger, the McGill family's confessor from Hastings. Father was visiting two streets away at the Naughtons's—Grandpa Naughton was close to passing on— and Ma asked him to stop by the house and bestow on Cassie the Church's special Blessing for Travelers. This would petition St. Christopher to bring Cassie home safe and sound.

Father came directly. Ma settled him in the parlor with a glass of Leo's elderberry while Cassie got into one of the uniforms Ma had freshened for him.

"Well now, Cassius, look at us," said Father, taking note of Cassie's best blue serge. "But for this collar o' mine, there's little to choose 'tween our handsome outfits."

Ma spoke right up. "There's *much* to choose, Father, twixt your callings. So don't go stuffing this boy's head with fanciful apologies for bad behavior."

Ma pretended impatience with Father, but Cassie could tell that she was as happy as he to have Father in the house again. Ma set the wine bottle on the sideboard and then withdrew so Father and Cassie could be by themselves.

Father at once pulled a fat black stogie from a gleaming silver case and proceeded to light up. "Will you share with me some good Havana leaf, Cassius?" Father said, extending the case in Cassie's direction. "Vida May will not approve, but you are old enough now to taste of such worldly pleasures and thus know firsthand the temptations which the Prince of Darkness has set before us—and which, of course, we must stoutly resist."

"Thank you, Father. Only I believe this wine is temptation enough for now."

"Such moderation is rare at any age—I commend you. Indeed, let us tend to business while I am yet sober enough to conduct it."

Cassie knelt down and Father applied the blessing. It was *so* good to see Father again. He was as much a member of the family as Ma or Pa or the children. Cassie, when he was an altar boy at Blessed Sacrament, had served Mass for Father many times. Father was a handsome man, tall and spare, with two patches of pink skin for cheeks and the longest white fingers Cassie had ever seen. He looked the way the Saints must have, Cassie supposed. Being a Jesuit, he spoke three languages besides Latin. He had taken Holy Orders at Rome and served as a priest at Notre Dame in Paris while a young man. When the McGills were back in Hastings, Father would come by the house two or three times a month at suppertime. He had a hearty appetite for Ma's biscuits and especially liked the peach brandy that Pa put up each August following harvest of the fruit trees that Leo now tended along the banks of the Little Blue River. The Terwiligers were moneyed people from Indianapolis, and Father was their only son: he traveled about in his own automobile, a bright blue KisselKar. Cassie glanced out the parlor window: there it sat by the front gate, a queer ghostly monster, its color and shape disguised by the ice and fresh snowflakes it had collected.

Cassie rose and Father poured more wine.

"I shall spare us both the confessional just now, Cassius. Yet I sense that you are not entirely at your ease. Is it that Vida May's been poking your ribs again in the matter of the seminary?"

Cassie thought: It's no confession but seems mighty close to it! "She's not mentioned it of late, Father, but I expect she's still disappointed. I can't even finish in the prep school, so what's the use of hoping for the seminary?"

Father nodded easily, puffed on his cigar. "Since your baptism, Vida May's wanted the collar for you. Simple man that I am, I suppose I've encouraged her in her aspirations. Now, perhaps she and I had best apply our wiles to the twins instead."

It was hard for Cassie to think of Dwight and Dewey as priests. "Yes, Father," he said anyway.

"With only your senior year remaining—can you not bring yourself to return to the Brothers?"

"I would do it, Father, but for the Latin. There's two make-ups on my record already and Cicero still ahead."

"You're a bright lad, Cassius. Perhaps with tutoring—"

"I can't seem to get the hang of it, Father. I cannot do it, or I would."

Father made a church steeple of his fingers and nodded again. "Then we must assume the Lord has other plans for you. There's no disgrace in it. If God had meant you to help Him inside the Church, He would have provided passing marks in Latin."

"I'm awful glad to hear it, Father."

"Besides, a steady diet of fasting and deprivation can make a fellow dismal and stupid." Father gave a wink and waved his Havana in the direction of Leo's elderberry. "To wear the collar is no guarantee of quick admission to the Kingdom of Heaven."

"I don't suppose it is, Father. But it couldn't hurt either, do you suppose?"

"I shall know the answer to that question soon enough—but too late to help you out!"

It was time for Father to go. He had other families yet to visit in Lincoln. He promised to come back in the morning to hear Ma's confession; she was most grateful for the promise of it.

"Can I ask for a ride in your automobile, Father?" said Cassie. "I'm bound for Main Street, if it's not taking you out of your way."

Cassie's mind was on finding the helper he needed for the run ahead. Father was pleased to be of service. Cassie bundled up in Uncle Chet's mackinaw and Uncle Joe's mittens and his own galoshes.

"Be back in twenty minutes, Ma, or quicker even. Could you fill my dinner pail in the meantime, do you suppose? Another slice or two o' that mincemeat sure would help fight off the cold!"

They reached Main Street in a fraction of the time any buggy might take. This gave Cassie a high opinion of the KisselKar. "Come down to Hastings in summer," Father told him, "and learn to operate her for yourself. In the modern world, every man must learn to do so—there'll naught be a horse to find except behind a plow. This is the gospel according to Saint Henry Ford."

"I'll be happy to, Father. Thank you most sincerely!"

"*Bon voyage* to you then, my son. And *pax vobiscum.*"

"Thank you, Father!" Cassie figured this was more of Father's Jesuit wit and good humor: "Peace be with you," just when he was off to war!

Turning east, Cassie aimed for the two best billiard parlors in town, Robard's and Yule's Pool. He was disappointed both places. Nobody at the tables looked to be the dependable soul needed in railroading. He moved on another half block and scouted the Odd Fellows' Hall, without success. Finally, he made his way among the vagrants and drifters who put up at the YMCA. It was not a promising lot; the cold weather had reduced their number. The best of the bunch appeared to be Skeets O'Dwyer, who had worked one summer as a gandy dancer on a section gang for the Rock Island. He was known more for his ability to avoid blisters than to lay track. Still, Cassie put the proposition to him.

"That's it then, Skeets. It's two dollars a day and meals. No pay on the home leg, 'course."

"And *you're* to be master?" The drifter's close-set ferret eyes showed contempt at the idea.

"That's it."

"Well, now, it's a strange world, ain't it? I'd go fer ya, only the pay ain't sufficient. What say ya ta three bucks a day and half that on the way home? Bein' as I don't eat much, you'll make yer profit on grub."

"I can't do it. The terms I told you is all I'm authorized by the Company."

Skeets gave a nice smile. "Well then, stick yer job up yer ass, why don't ya?"

The other men within earshot offered like sentiments. Cassie took leave of their company with pleasure. He went on toward home at a dog trot. He had played his best card and gone broke on the hand. Now he prayed he could sign on some fellow at trackside. Otherwise, he would have to handle the two jobs himself, or maybe ask Nelson, the head porter, to help out. Either way was bad. Nelson, being a Negro, had no say in the matter; he would do it if Cassie asked. But a head porter had plenty of duties of his own. And Cassie could not be in two places at once.

Out of the blue, he snatched a fresh idea. He thought of Laws Beemer, who had been a classmate at the Brothers, and who lived nearby with his parents on 14th Street. Laws was the only fellow Cassie could think of from the Brothers who was not still in school. Like Cassie, Laws had had his fill of it; he dropped out about the time Cassie went off for his tryout with the Brownies. Laws had been a true friend—honest, strong, hard-working, too. Cassie scolded himself that he had not thought of Laws Beemer before.

He received a shock. There were two hacks sitting alongside the house with the words LAWS BEEMER—DELIVERIES & EXPRESS painted on the sides. Cassie hesitated, but Mrs. Beemer saw him through the sitting-room window and beckoned him to come. She met him with a gracious smile and showed him back to Laws's room. "And got yourself a job with Pullman's. Weren't you always the fine boy!"

Laws, too, displayed a warm smile. "Well now, I do believe it is Mr. Pullman himself." He gave Cassie's hand a powerful squeeze.

"And you be kin, I do believe, to Mr. Rockefeller," Cassie replied in kind. He mentioned seeing the hacks out front.

"If business keeps going, Cass, I'm thinking to get me one o' them motor trucks by summer's end. It'd be quicker than any hack, cheaper to run, and it'd never foul the city's streets with horse dung neither."

Laws revealed that he was in the business of making deliveries for merchants around town. He was not yet the size of Wells Fargo but seemed on the way to it.

"It sounds a fine business," Cassie said.

"I believe it is. I have an eye to grow. There's no proper service in Nebraska City nor in Grand Island—I have studied them both out. The merchants there all run their own hacks. It's not economical to them, their customers are sore on account of the time it takes to receive their goods once they've paid their money, and here is Laws Beemer to save the day."

Laws had changed a bit since he and Cassie sat beside each other at the Brothers. Bull-necked, with the arms and back of a blacksmith, Laws had always worn overalls or other rough clothing both winter and summer. Now he appeared in suit, vest, and starched collar.

"It's a 'convenience' business, you know, Cass. People today is lazy as cats—won't do nothing for themselves if they can pay somebody else to do it for 'em. And that's me. Laws Beemer will save you getting dirt on your hands or mud on your boots."

Cassie could see at once that this Laws Beemer was far above the job of helper conductor for Pullman's. "I'm looking to hire a fellow," Cassie said, "and wonder if you know of anybody I can get on short notice." Cassie told of the run ahead. "I've been down to the Y and the Odd Fellows both, only there's no one suitable."

"I might have told you so and saved your time. I've been looking for fellows to work my routes, but there's no one to hang your hat on. It's tough to build a business nowadays—country's gone soft in the belly. It's your Mr. Debs and his Social Democrats, I'm thinking—anarchists is a better name for 'em. Look at Henry Ford. To get men, he's paying five dollars a day in wages. Ain't never met a fellow worth five dollars a day —present company excluded! No, it's bad times ahead—watch if it ain't."

Cassie used silence as his reply. He knew nothing of politics, so had nothing to say. Pa was much the same; he had gone for Taft in '12 and didn't think much of Wilson yet. As for Debs, Debs was the locomotive fireman who had led the Pullman strike in '94, before Cassie was born. Now he was leader of the Industrial Workers of the World—"Godless radicals and sinners," Uncle Leo called them.

"There's no men to be had," Laws went on, "so I'm taking my pa in with me."

"Are you now?" said Cassie. The idea of a fellow's giving work to his own father made Cassie uneasy. "Well, it seems a fine thing to do."

"I believe it is."

Laws's pa was like so many thereabouts: he had quit the farm when the wheat crop went bad in '07. Some, like Ben McGill, held out a few more harvests, but it was slow going and life in town soon called them off the land.

"Well, my thinking on it is this," Laws said. "You can stick to the land and eke out your crop every year and hope to keep the bank at arm's length. This is a losing proposition most of the time, though people are too dumb to notice it till it's too late.

"Or a fellow can sign on with some big outfit, like you've done, and hope to find himself a place. There's maybe even riches in it, if you don't get yourself killed falling under a train.

"Or there's my way. I could never see being another fellow's slave. Take my word—there's money to be made, using sweat for capital. Already I've put a dollar or two in the bank, I own two rigs and four horses outright, I can see down the road a stretch, and my time's my own—I'm free to waste it or spend it as I see fit."

Envy twitched in the far reaches of Cassie's brain. Here was a fellow no older than himself who already had his own enterprise and was prospering at it.

"By the by," said Laws, "I came upon Father O'Kane some weeks back. He moaned as how the varsity is sure to miss your good left arm again this spring. Did you ever think o' going back, Cass?"

"Only tonight I've had this same talk with Father Terwiliger!"

"Then you'll excuse me asking. But you was always seminary prep, wasn't you? There was talk you might take the collar."

"Ever see a Father without his Latin?"

Laws indulged himself in a loud guffaw. "Not likely!"

Cassie looked again to his Railway Special: already 9:00. "I'd best make tracks if I'm to catch my ride."

"Catch it you will, then—courtesy o' Laws Beemer's express."

Easy as talking about it, Laws obtained a sprightly mare from the barn behind the house, hitched her up to one of the hacks, and moved them off at a smart pace toward 16th Street.

"If ever you tire of the railroad, Cass, you come see me, hear? I'm always on the lookout for an honest partner."

"Do you mean it?"

"I do. I told you I'm aiming to take on Nebraska City and Grand Island both. It's only the start. What's to say I can't do business even into Kansas? Or Iowa?"

"I sure will think on it," Cassie replied.

"Do so. We're already in the same business, you and me—only I'm more partial to shoveling oats than shoveling coal!"

Cassie went off shaking his head. Laws Beemer had shown that a bold fellow could make himself a capitalist in short order, and no Latin in him either. It was indeed something to think about.

3

BACK HOME, Cassie went to his closet and brought out his treasure chest. This was a steel box in which he kept his cash and valuables; only he and Pa had keys to it. He unlocked it and counted out its present holdings. The cash came to $61.40. He was owed better than fourteen dollars in back wages from Pullman's but would be unable to claim it until he returned from the run. He took fifteen dollars from the box to have in his pocket. This sum, plus the $1.50 he had brought home with him from Chicago, would bankroll the new trip and allow him plenty extra for meals now and again in an eating house, and the buying of souvenirs for the children.

He inspected his account book from Turners Savings Bank of Lincoln. It showed a balance of $174.30, which was drawing interest of three and one-half percent per annum. The better part of it—$100—was money Uncle Chet had left Cassie in his last will and testament. Pa had named the savings account Cassie's grubstake, meaning that Cassie was to hold it back and not touch it until some fair opportunity came his way, like buying a good piece of land. "It's your ticket to freedom," Pa once told him, "should things ever get too stiff for you where you're at."

Pa would not even borrow on it himself to finance his coffee trade, though Cassie had repeatedly offered it. Now Cassie thought of what Laws Beemer might do with such a sum; $174.30 would put delivery vans in both Nebraska City and Grand Island with plenty to spare, Cassie figured. It might entitle him to a partnership in Laws Beemer— Deliveries & Express. No, it would entitle him to a partnership in *Beemer & McGill.* That had a better sound to it.

He returned the book and extra cash to the box, locked it, and returned it to its hiding place. From the stand by the bed he took his Bible; Ma would expect to see it in his valise. He inspected his bookcase. There would be opportunity for reading on such a run. Cassie had built up a good collection of tales by the writers he liked best—Jack London, O. Henry, Booth Tarkington, Mark Twain, Zane Grey. He decided on Grey's *Riders of the Purple Sage.* He had read all the best parts of it five or six times, never expecting to see real sage in his lifetime. Now it appeared that he would.

He decided to take his telegraph key, too, to practice along the way.

When Cassie first came aboard Pullman's, Mr. Hebb gave him the key and encouraged him to take up Morse as a means to advancement. No man could hope for a sit-down job on the road until he learned his code. The key traveled in its own mahogany box. Cassie opened it on his desk and rapped out an urgent message, his quick wrist producing a rhythmic tattoo that might have been the envy (he imagined) of any stationmaster:

. . . AMERICAN FORCES MOVE TO CAPTURE VILLA . . . RESISTANCE FIERCE . . . PERSHING'S SWIFT CAVALRY VICTORIOUS IN FIRST BAT- TLE . . . PULLMAN COMPANY CONGRATULATED ON PROMPT DE- LIVERY OF ARMY TO BATTLEFIELD . . . TRAINS IN CHARGE OF MASTERS LIBERTY AND MCGILL . . . SERVICE EXCELLENT, SAYS GENERAL PERSHING . . .

He collected his baggage downstairs by the front door. Cleo and Ada and the twins stood by and marveled at his *impedimenta*—one of the few Latin words Cassie remembered from his Caesar. Besides his well-stuffed valise, he had Captain Gump's lamp to carry, the telegraph key in its box, a small leather satchel containing his books and razor, and the dinner pail that Ma had put together for him. Some pail! There were two kinds of pie, pork and mince, some hunks of yellow cheese, rutabaga cooked with molasses, a loaf of fresh-baked pumpkin bread, a handful of dried apples, and a bag of roasted peanuts. Also a jar of Cassie's favorite baked beans, which would make a nice breakfast.

Ma was back in the kitchen; Cassie went there to say his farewell. "And thank you specially, Ma, for the victuals. I'll surely not starve!"

She was a big handsome woman. Five children in nine years had spread her some, but she kept her smile and she could still run the house without raising her voice. "You're to take this," she said. "On so long a journey, there'll be times when only a book will do."

Ma did love her books. Pa seldom touched one, except the Bible, but Pa was a farmer through and through; he'd only learned to read when he was full grown. Ma kept her own private library of several hundred volumes. Cassie believed she had read every one. She had been to school with the Sisters of Mercy and had taken her lessons to heart.

Cassie accepted the volume Ma now held out to him. It was titled *The Nigger of the "Narcissus."* The author's name, Joseph Conrad, was unknown to him.

"You may think it a curious choice for a journey by rail," Ma said, "being that it's a tale of the sea. But you'll enjoy it, I do believe, and learn from it. It's a man's story true enough, and well told."

"Thank you, Ma. I expect I'll like it a lot."

"There's something else for you to carry," Ma said.

He did not know what to think at first. From around her neck she removed her rosary, a beauteous object of rosewood beads with a silver crucifix. It had belonged to Great-grandmother Hannah O'Hea and was brought straight from Ireland aboard the sailing ship *Endymion* in '48. It was the greatest relic on Ma's side of the family and might well have been made from bits of the True Cross for the respect Ma's family showed it. As a small boy, Cassie had sometimes tiptoed into his parents' room to look at it, even touch it, where it lay on Ma's dresser. The beads were long and thin now, instead of round, from having been rubbed so often by its owners. It had never known a day without prayer in a hundred years or more.

"Oh, but I couldn't take it, Ma!"

"It would please your mother greatly if you could. You've such a long way to go, Cassius—it cannot hurt to have it along. Won't you please an old woman?"

"Oh, Ma! You're no old woman! Such a thing to say!"

"I'd feel ever so much better knowing it was around your neck."

"But what if I lost it, Ma?"

"Then it's God's will."

"I won't lose it, Ma."

"Of course you won't."

She placed it around his neck, sighed, then collected herself. "Well now, Cassius McGill—running off again, are you? Might as well be back with that wretched team in Falls City, for the little we see of you."

"It's my job, Ma."

"There's jobs to be had in town, I do believe. Under this roof, even."

She meant helping out with Pa's business. "I like Pullman's, Ma."

"I suppose you must. And who am I to speak against it?" She took his hands in hers. "You're grown up for your years, Cassius. What might bring another boy low cannot even touch you. You hold clean thoughts and carry yourself as a good Catholic. I've no cause for complaint, I know it."

"I'm sorry when I disappoint you, Ma." Cassie was thinking of the Brothers—of leaving school early.

"Now who's talking about disappointment? What a silly notion!" She reached up to him for a kiss and a hug. "Be off with you now, and know that you take our prayers with you."

Tears brimmed from her eyes, so Cassie excused himself, tucking the rosary down inside his tunic and barely avoiding tears of his own.

He carried Flag down the steps to the cellar. The old dog was stiff in her joints and liked best to settle beneath the high stool that Pa occupied for his roasting. This put her but inches from the cast-iron grate of the oven.

"I sure miss the smell of fresh coffee, Pa, when I'm on the road."

"Here, I've ground you a sackful. Take care how you fix it. You want it scalding, remember, but never on the boil."

"Yes, Pa. I'm always careful how I do it."

Sitting there on his high stool, Pa seemed bent and weary, as though he had spent all day in the fields as he used to down at Hastings. Skin wrinkled and gray, eyes red-rimmed and watery, brow furrowed from the cares of the day. Being a merchant in town was no easier than being on the farm, Cassie guessed, especially when a man had put on years. Pa was three months from being fifty.

Pa spread a shovelful of green beans over the wire-mesh shaker of the big wood-burning stove. Cassie stepped forward and lent a hand. The shaker had to be jiggled every so often or else the beans would scorch and turn bitter.

"You'll not do all this tonight, will you, Pa?" Several hundred-pound sacks of the green beans lay by the cellar door.

"Another batch or two, maybe. Gettin' a jump on tomorrow, is all."

Whenever a fresh shipment arrived, Pa could hardly wait to get it roasted up so he could get on with the bagging and selling. He had borrowed from the bank to pay for his orders when he first started up the business, and now he was anxious to pay off the debt.

Pa sacked up the batch just done and toweled off his sweat. "Well now, Cass, can we share a sweet melody or two afore you're off?"

Pa liked nothing better of a cold winter's night than a little musicale. He had a high pure tenor voice and could sing the songs of the old country as well as anybody except John McCormack himself.

"I've only the five minutes or so to spare, Pa," said Cassie. "I can't be tardy on this run, being as I'm master."

"Well, then, a bit o' 'Skibbereen,' nothing more."

"That'll do fine, Pa," Cassie said.

Skibbereen was a seaside town close by Ballinascarthy, where Grandpa Padraig McGill had come from. Pa obtained from the cupboard Grandpa's own psaltery; also a bottle of good Irish whiskey, from which he poured them each a small tumblerful. Pa preferred this beverage for moistening the throat between verses; Cassie had learned the same habit. Likewise, Cassie preferred the gentle accompaniments of the psaltery, with Pa strumming the chords he knew so well, to the stronger tones of the piano upstairs in the parlor.

"Well now, won't you take the first verse, boy?"

Cassie proceeded:

"O father dear, I oft-times hear you talk of Erin's Isle,
   Her lofty scenes and valleys green, her mountains rude
    and wild.
They say it is a pretty place wherein a prince might
   dwell.
And why did you abandon it, the reason to me tell."

Whereupon Pa answered in his sweet high tones:

"My son, I loved our native land with energy and pride,
Until a blight came on my land, my sheep and cattle died.
The rent and taxes were to pay, I could not them redeem.
And that's the cruel reason why I left old Skibbereen."

They each added a new chorus, and then Cassie spun out the final verse:

"O father dear, the day will come when vengeance loud
   will call,
And we will rise with Erin's boys to rally one and all.
I'll be the man to lead the van beneath our flag of green,
And loud and high will raise the cry, 'Revenge for
   Skibbereen!' "

"She went awful quick, don't you think?" said Pa.

"I was rushing it a bit," Cassie admitted. He was sad to quit: Pa was feeling himself and singing like an angel through the whiskey. "I'll be home in ten days' time, Pa. Then we can have a proper musicale, and give the twins a lesson too."

"Sure we will," Pa said. "Well, you be off, then. Don't hold back on my account."

"Pa?"

"Yes, boy?"

Cassie pulled the rosary outside his tunic. "Ma gave me this to wear."

"Did she now? Well, isn't that a fine thing for her to do."

"I'm pleased to have it, o' course. Only—I believe she's worried some harm will come to me on the run."

"Well, that's the way of women. Your mother will be glad of her rosary around your neck, to provide the Lord's protection. It's nothing to be troubled over."

"I suppose not, Pa."

"You've been away from home plenty before now, so I'll not lecture you."

"No, Pa."

"You've known the temptations of the world, and come through un-tainted. Still, the Army is not baseball, nor is it the railroad. Soldiering is a peculiar kind o' man's work. Your uncle Chet, God bless him, suffered a spell of it when he was hardly older than you, and it took him a while to put the soldier's life behind him."

"Yes, sir."

"Men living on their own—with no family women to look after them— they can be a mean lot. Mean as to their speech, mean as to morals."

"I've seen lots of mean ball players, Pa."

"Sure you have. Carry yourself as a true Christian and you'll come through in one piece."

"I expect I will, Pa."

"Read your Bible, be respectful of your elders, remember the teachings of the Brothers. This is all the advice any boy needs."

"Thank you, Pa."

Pa looked again to the roaster. "Well now, I'd best get on with one more batch, lest I waste this good fire." He spread a shovelful of beans across the shaker and stirred up the embers.

Cassie turned and started up the steps.

"Cass?"

"Yes, Pa?"

"As for them women who sometimes go following after soldier boys—"

"Yes, Pa?"

Ben McGill kept his eyes on his roasting as he spoke:

"You'll be keeping your pecker in your pants, now won't you, son. . . ."

Cassie went along to the yards. *Captain McGill.* Only one thing kept him from full enjoyment of his newfound glory: knowledge that he had failed to find himself a helper for the second section. Now he wished he had taken Skeets O'Dwyer for the job, paying from his own pocket the extra wages that Skeets had demanded. Even showing up with a bum like Skeets would be better than showing up with no helper at all.

Cassie began to sweat. His failure to find a body could earn him Brownie points, if ever Mr. Hebb learned of it. These were demerits on a trainman's record for bad conduct or poor performance of his duties. Three points cost a day's pay, five meant a week's suspension, ten brought discharge. An old-time super of the name Brown had invented the system and gone into the history books by so doing.

Cassie made straight for the dispatcher's office. Sometimes in winter a spot man got hungry enough to sign on for most any run at two dollars a day and grub.

But not today. What Cassie found today was Mr. Hebb himself.

"Well, boy, from the look on your face, I'd say you wasn't glad to see me!"

The elderly Pullman agent was fitted out in a division man's traveling leathers; he appeared ready to board. Cassie let out a sigh. The super had had the last word after all. Mr. Hebb might trust a lowly helper to take a run on his own, but not Mr. A. O. Austin.

"Then you'll be riding master yourself, sir?" Cassie replied glumly.

"Now don't go turning hangdog on me," Mr. Hebb scolded. His thin gray cheeks had turned pink in the cold. "It's only to Sturgis I'm going. Government's calling for another special, and I'm to write the order. Lord bless Pancho Villa! If this keeps up, there won't be a free stick o' rolling stock west o' the Pennsy. But I ain't planning to do your work for you, youngster. *No. 3's* your rig, Cap'n McGill, and nobody else's."

"Yes, sir. Thank you, sir!"

"Now where's that helper o' yours? It's time we was making steam."

Cassie never expected his sins to catch up with him so promptly. Telling a lie or telling the truth was all the same: either way it would cost him money, or maybe his job.

"About that helper, sir—"

"He sure ain't much to look at, I'll say that for him!"

Cassie thought maybe he had heard wrong. "Helper, sir?"

"Land o' Goshen, boy!" cried the agent. "Sometimes I think you get your sleep standing up. *Helper,* lad. The fella who belongs to them goods."

Cassie looked over to the far corner of the shed where Mr. Hebb pointed. *What the devil!* There lay a brown cardboard box wrapped with a shabby belt. Cassie recognized it at once. Mr. Riley McAuliffe could fit all his worldly possessions into that one sorry space. Slipped under the belt, where it would be available at a moment's notice, was the shortstop's meal ticket, a scuffed, rosin-stained mitt.

"Oh, yes, sir," said Cassie. "*Him.*"

"Yes, boy, *him.* He's some talker, that fella. Says he done spot work on the Burlington, but I'm thinking he's never been on the road afore."

Without wanting to, Cassie found himself defending the rascal. "Yes, sir, he sure has worked the Burlington—I can vouch for that."

They had once caught on as callboys over at Nebraska City. This meant chasing after fellows to work fireman on runs nobody wanted, or making a sweep of the saloons in search of some wayward mechanic, or smoking out a lazy engineer who had slept past his shining hour and so kept the express stuck down in the station. It would not be counted as true railroading to Mr. Hebb, so Cassie did not spell it out.

"You're saying you can trust him, then?" asked the agent. "Riding back there all by his lonesome?"

Cassie crossed his fingers behind his back. "I expect I can trust him, sir."

" 'Cause carrying the Army, son, is no job for drifters or scalawags."

"No, sir. He'll do fine, sir."

"That's good, 'cause it's your neck if he don't. . . . Now I'm gonna settle in the van and have me a little snooze. Wake me afore Broken Bow, if you please. . . ."

Moments later, Rocks showed himself. He had been to the passenger station to enjoy the pleasures of indoor plumbing. With his nappy muskrat open down the front, he seemed a puny, pathetic creature, his wrinkled and soiled businessman's suit—secondhand and never cleaned by its various owners—hanging loosely off his small frame.

"Dint find nobody, did ya?" said the beggar, his mouth cracked wide in a jack-o'-lantern grin.

"That's my business and none of yours," Cassie replied.

"Is so! Why, me an' yer boss is close as bees and honey!" Rocks tried to put up a brave front, but his hands shook so badly he finally stuffed them in his pockets.

"My boss says I'm to hire any fellow I want," said Cassie, "and that's sure not the likes of you." Cassie began working the buttons to his mackinaw, as though about to leave.

"I *seen* 'im, Cass—the Mex bandit! I seen his pitchur in the paper! It's war, sure 'nough!"

Cassie gathered up his gear and headed to the door.

"You *gotta* take me, Cass," wailed the shortstop. "I'll never ask ya fer nothin' agin in me whole life! I'm *beggin'* ya, Cass!"

Cassie set down his baggage again. "It's a bad bargain," he said in a quiet voice, "but I guess it's the only bargain I can make."

"You *mean* it, Cass?"

"No liquor the whole time."

"I swear it, Cass!"

"Not a drop between here and the border."

"Nary a drop!"

"Dollar a day and meals and no pay on the return leg. Can you swallow that?"

"Swallow it? I kin grow fat on it!"

Cassie had in mind to save up the other half of the helper's allowance and make Rocks a gift of it when they got back to Lincoln. In this way the shortstop couldn't dribble away his earnings along the route. Even five or six dollars in a lump sum was more of a bankroll than Rocks was likely to come by in any other honest manner.

"Then I guess you're coming along," said Cassie.

They shook on it. The shortstop jumped with glee. "We're goin' west, Professor! Ain't life grand!"

"Collect your goods and follow me. There's no time to waste."

They marched up the line, Cassie in the lead, Rocks trailing along, whistling and showing off his fresh good spirits. At the second-section van, Cassie gave the shortstop his instructions:

"Settle yourself up there in the cupola and stay awake, hear me? Keep one eye on the air gauge—needle should hang around the seventy mark. If ever it falls below fifty, you're to signal 'emergency' to your hogger—that's five quick tugs on the pull cord. Your brakies will watch out for hot boxes, so don't concern yourself over that. Keep looking back over your shoulder, especially when you're slowing or stopping for water. If you can make out another rig's lamp, then she's too close and you're to give three tugs on the cord—the hogger'll know he has company.

"Got all that?"

Rocks had been hanging on Cassie's every word, nodding solemnly at each instruction. He seemed on his best behavior. "I'll do it, Cass—what you said. You'll see—I'm cut out for railroadin'!"

"If anything bothers you after we're running, come see me at the next watering stop. The first section will wait up ahead while your hogger tops off, so you'll have plenty of time to get forward, see me, and get back again. That's it, then. I'm counting on you, Riley."

"You're countin' on the right man, too, Cass!"

"We'll both know the worth of that claim soon enough."

Cassie went back down the line and showed himself to the other trainmen. He could see in the eyes of some a disregard for his youth. But after so many runs as student, he was accustomed to malice and envy.

He surveyed his rig. The two sections, standing side by side on adjoining spurs, made an imposing sight by moonlight. The train now comprised fifteen boxes, eight varnish, one Pullman snoozer, and the two cabooses. Another eight cars would be added at Fort Meade, five more at Omaha. Cassie checked his orders and made some rough calculations in his train book. Before *Pullman's No. 3* reached the war zone, she would weigh out at better than 1,300 tons and—with the bare minimum thousand feet of running room between the sections—occupy over a half mile of track.

Cassie moved forward and took a closer look at his rolling stock. He was taken aback by its nature and condition. Mr. Austin had not seen fit, in Cassie's opinion, to supply the Pullman Company with the top stock in the Red Eye Line's inventory. For the most part, the cars were ancient, filthy, and dilapidated. Maybe war called for nothing better.

Such locomotives! Only once or twice before had Cassie seen hogs of this vintage. They had birth certificates far older than his own. They were a pair of heavy-breathing old girls, big double-domed Baldwin ten-wheelers, Atlantic "4-4-2" in Whyte's official classification. They seemed to be sisters despite the gap in their numbers—No. 506 and No. 799—and had similar appetites for coal and water, each tender holding ten tons of the one and six thousand gallons of the other. Neither engine sounded in the best of health, suffering noisy asthma. They were handsome in their way, but their beauty was skin deep. Close inspection revealed they were leaking steam from every pipe and tube and join. Even a greenhorn could see that it would take a heap of shoveling to keep up steam in these lovelies.

Cassie sought out the head porter, Nelson, and shook his hand. He was a clean Negro, fifty years of age, more gray than black, regular in his habits and smooth as to manners. He was a bit stooped and noticeably splayfooted from working on his feet all his life. He had already done twenty-five years for the Pullman Company; his father had done twenty years before him. Cassie told the colored man:

"I'm counting on you, Nelson, to set me straight when I go wrong."

"You jes ask, Cap'n. It'll be my pleasure to serve you!"

Cassie felt some relief on hearing it. "If you'll sign my book, then."

Cassie's first chore was to get the crews' marks in his book, together with the lodge number of each man's brotherhood, time he reported for work, and, later on, time he quit. Before they reached the border, Cassie's book would crawl with trainmen's scratchings: there would be ten or more changes of engine crews along the way. More than one railroader would sign with an X, as Nelson did now. Reading and writing were skills not demanded for making up a bunk or throwing a switch or firing a hog.

Cassie got the rest of the crew into his book in good order, leaving the locomotives for last. He climbed up into the cab of No. 506 and introduced himself. The engineer was Mr. Ira Parker, the fireman Mr. Ham. Mr. Parker was a white-haired gentleman in greasy railroader's cap with overalls to match. He offered neither a smile nor a frown. Mr. Ham was a younger man, slope-shouldered and blunt of aspect. His forearms were as big around as most men's thighs, and he made the coal fly into the firebox with no more effort than a boy pitching hay.

They signed the book. Both men could write their names.

"She sure looks a fine old engine," Cassie remarked.

"She looks no such thing," replied Mr. Parker. "And she ain't, neither!"

Mr. Parker told her history, and that of No. 799 too. These high steppers had been built to order for the Baltimore & Ohio and used for express passenger service on that line. They had been tinkered with in recent years but still bore the 70-inch drivers and big 23-by-28-inch cylinders that allowed them to earn their keep running all day at sixty or better. They were designed to pull nothing more than a half-dozen parlor cars and provide fast commuter service between Philadelphia and

Washington, where the grades never rose or fell twenty feet in a mile. For such work they were probably the best on rails. "But for haulin' heavy freight—an' thet's what them troopers an' their horses add up to— why, boy," said Ira Parker, "mebbe you'll be wantin' somethin' different from these black beauties in yer harness a-time you git where you're goin'—if you ever do!"

Cassie could only smile in reply; he had no arguments to make in the matter. Smarter fellows than Cassius McGill had made up this rig, so who was he to question it?

Cassie went on to the cab of No. 799. Being the quicker of the two locomotives, No. 799 had been assigned to the second section. In this way she could not run away from her slower sister. Cassie prayed her brakes were as good as her boiler. The cab was so hot that neither crewman there wore even an undershirt beneath his coveralls. In those narrow steel confines, the air reeked of sweat more than coal dust or lubricating oil. The hogger was Mr. Amos Birkenhead, the fireman Mr. Dingle. Mr. Birkenhead's deeply lined face was framed by pure white muttonchops, and he showed hands that were as callous as any fireman's. Cassie speculated that the engineer helped fire the hog just for the fun of it; he looked to be a man who had no fear of hard work.

The hogger gave Cassie the same curious stare that most old trainmen did. "You, boy. *You're* to be brains on this run?"

"Yes, sir. McGill's the name."

"Well, don't that beat all. They is recruitin' children, Dolly. See fer yerself!"

Dolly was Mr. Dingle's nickname. He was a burly fellow with a bald head painted in coal dust stuck on by sweat. "He's a sweet one, 'Mos! Ain't he ever!"

Cassie did his business, getting their names in the book. "Soon as I get back to the van, we'll be off," Cassie said. "So please to get up a good head of steam."

"Oh, yes, sir, Cap'n!" cried Dolly Dingle. "'Twill be our pleasure, sure 'nough!"

Cassie could hear their laughs a good way down the trackbed.

As dubious as Cassie had been on first seeing the locomotives, he took heart from his van. It was No. 1865 and had once done service on the Mohawk line—that proud name could still be seen in faded white script through a fresh coat of the Chicago & North Western's barn red. What kind of caboose a trainman had to ride often decided how good or bad the whole run was to be. Cassie liked the looks of this one. He went over it now with the care and pride of a real captain. It would provide his bed and board for the next ten to twelve days.

No. 1865 was a sturdy eight-wheeler built by American Car & Foundry. It boasted a steel frame, which was the modern method of construction. Steel could come in handy in any sort of rear-end dustup. The van offered plenty of sitting-down room and other comforts: five good wicker chairs, four clean double-tiered bunks for reliefers and off-duty crewmen, even one semiprivate guest bunk surrounded by draw curtains. This latter accommodation was reserved for division supers or other brass collars who might want to come aboard and ride a piece on company business. It was now occupied by a snoring Mr. Hebb.

In the center of the cabin stood a generous coal-burning stove for heat, in one corner a wood-burning stove for cooking. Abundant supplies of both fuels were provided in handy bunkers. The coal stove was now surrounded by the five colored boys Nelson had been able to round up for porters. They were called Waldo, Jesse, Dan, Tobias, and Milo. They sat on the wooden floor and crowded the fire, which Milo built up at intervals. Cassie found the heat excessive, but the others enjoyed it mightily. Sitting back a bit was the rear brakeman, an old-timer called Legrand. He was a solitary sort, pinch-faced and somber. He made a sucking noise with his mouth; maybe his plates bothered him.

Along one wall stood a good-sized work desk with pigeonholes arranged overhead to hold train orders and other paperwork. On the wall opposite where Cassie would be sitting was a big air-pressure gauge to let him see at a glance what kind of brakes they might have. One of the desk drawers had a strong lock to it for securing his valuables while he slept. Cassie paused to unpack and stow his belongings. In the locking drawer he placed Ma's rosary, his Bible, and his telegraph key. He stored his dinner pail in the small warming oven over the cook stove. He kept on his person his wallet and timepiece and of course his train book; that stayed in his hip pocket night and day.

He climbed the ladder and had a look around the angel's nest. There was glass on all four sides so the master could see where he was going and where he had just been. The windows had steel frames and solid locks. There was an air-pressure gauge, too, smaller than the one downstairs but hooked onto the same line, so the master could mind his business without relying on the brakie down below.

Back downstairs, Cassie finished his tour of inspection. There was a private saloon with toilet and basin, an icebox, lots of closet space, and, outside, a great possum belly chest under the car between the trucks to carry tools and the crew's extra baggage. There was another big locker at the rear end for lanterns and the fusees that switchmen lighted up whenever the train stopped as a warning to unwelcome traffic that might be contesting a piece of track.

The chimneys from the two stoves seemed watertight where they passed through the roof. There were four ventilators in good working order to keep a crew from being asphyxiated on cold nights when they might be sitting in the hole or otherwise stopped and the men tended to become overly fond of the fire. There was also a goodly supply of fresh drinking water in a tank close enough to the stove to keep the water from freezing up.

Cassie rejoiced in his good fortune. No. 1865 was equipped with anything a body might require on a run, whether it be for ten miles or a thousand. This was as good a monkey house as he had come across since getting his first Pullman pay envelope.

The draw curtains to the super's bunk suddenly parted, revealing the night-shirted Mr. Hebb. "Well now, are we sitting out a red board, Cap'n McGill? Else why ain't we moving?"

"Just now preparing to give the signal, sir!"

"Be at it, then, boy. War won't keep."

The colored boys hid their faces; Cassie knew they were grinning at his discomfort. "We're off then," Cassie said in a loud voice. He was talking for his own benefit. He yanked on the pull cord twice for SLOW RUNNING and was soon rewarded by two blasts on the whistle of No. 506, then two more from No. 799.

Not a minute later, *Pullman's No. 3* was off to war.

I I

MAKING STEAM

Fort Meade / Dalhart
March 11–14, 1916

The sight of human affairs deserves admiration and pity. And
he is not insensible who pays them the undemonstrative tribute
of a sigh which is not a sob, and of a smile which is not a grin.
JOSEPH CONRAD, *A Personal Record* (1912)

1

THE RUN UP TO STURGIS was something to talk about. Cassie knew that when he was an old man he would be telling about it to his grandchildren—like seeing Halley's comet in '10.

Loaded and traveling in the regular way, such a trip might have taken two days, even longer. Instead, riding empty with no passengers to concern them and no ordinary schedules to stick to, they covered the 581 miles in less than twelve hours, most of it over tracks of the Chicago, Burlington & Quincy. On the long straights between Broken Bow and Alliance they touched seventy miles an hour. Steam never fell below 185 pounds; pistons and valves sang a happy tune behind acetylene headlamps. Division points and depots up and down the line were alerted to their progress by telegraph. Coal clattered down chutes, water splashed from fill spouts. No stop lasted over ten minutes. "Green board to Mexico!" became their motto.

Mr. Hebb slept through much of it, but Cassie stayed wide awake. This was a side to railroading he had never seen before and could not now resist. This was true highballing, and he yearned for a steady diet of it. Traveling empty did not make for an easy ride. After a hundred miles or so, Cassie found himself beginning to get sore, the way he had after first day of baseball practice in spring. With only the string of empties out back and no freight to hold her down, *Pullman's No. 3* danced like a drunken farmhand and threatened to shake herself to pieces. Cassie marveled that the couplers held. On curves the rig appeared about to go whipping off into eternity, only to come crashing back to the rails at the last possible moment. The first time Cassie got down—at Little Platte Junction, where they took on water—he could hardly keep his feet.

Cassie kept a sharp lookout for the beam of No. 799 riding behind. The hogger, Mr. Birkenhead, crowded the first section now and again but not so as to put them in peril: he knew his business, as Cassie had figured. There was no sign of Rocks at the first watering stop, and none thereafter. Cassie assumed the shortstop was getting along all right or he would have called for help; no such call came. The porters and brakies continued to worship the glowing red coal stove. Cassie stayed at his desk for an hour or so, going over orders; afterwards, he climbed up into the angel's nest and enjoyed a close-up view of the blue-black Nebraska sky with its splash of icy stars. It was not until they crossed the state line into South Dakota that the stars disappeared and snow began to fall again.

It stayed bitter cold. Every river they crossed was sheeted in ice. Shattered floes jammed against the railroad bridges over the Platte and Elkhorn and Niobrara and Oglala. Cassie did not mind the weather. He was snug in his fine van, his mind occupied with thoughts of the great adventure ahead. It would take more than ice and snow to spoil his ride.

Halfway along, about four in the morning, Mr. Hebb arose and called for an early breakfast. This was cooked up in no time by head porter Nelson: eggs, ham, potatoes, biscuits, coffee. While they ate their fill—coffee sloshing dangerously in the cups from the constant lurch and sway of the van—the Pullman agent lectured Cassie on his future duties:

"By War Department regulation, you'll be stopping one hour in four to detrain your animals and give 'em exercise. Obey orders, Cassius, but take care you find yourself a free siding so as not to tie up the tracks you're crossing over."

Cassie entered this instruction in his book. It would mean stopping the two sections time and again, letting off 270 horses, watching them find their legs for an hour, then boarding them again—all without confronting regular traffic on the road. It would take some doing.

"I couldn't help noticing, sir," said Cassie, "there's only one snoozer."

"It's the Army's wish. That'll be for the officers, o' course. Troopers will occupy the day cars."

Cassie nodded. This seemed a peculiar arrangement, but he did not say so. It meant that the plain soldiers would find little sleep, sitting up like department-store dummies all the way—more than a thousand miles—to the border.

"I was wondering, sir," said Cassie, "about their meals."

"Messing, boy. The Army calls it messing."

"Yes, sir, messing. I was just wondering how they'd go about it, sir—being as there's no diner?"

Mr. Hebb explained. Like any regular customer, the War Department was renting the entire train from the Pullman Company at so many dollars per day. The sleeper, for example, was costing the government fifty-five dollars, and that included the colored boys and linen and toilet supplies and heat and hot water. Usually a customer would include commissary service in his order. A few customers preferred to stop at eating houses in train towns along the right of way, where a person might obtain a good meal for twenty-five cents. But more often than not Pullman's would be asked to provide dining cars, including cooks and waiters and tableware and utensils and the food itself.

Mr. Hebb had proposed a pair of diners, each seating forty passengers at a time. Food would be provided at cost, plus fifteen percent for preparation and service. Even with two such cars, it would take four sittings to feed the Squadron one meal. But the Army was no regular customer. It believed it could supply meals cheaper still. The Army intended to give the troopers only one hot meal per day. To do so, they would take a forty-foot boxcar and make a kitchen out of it, setting up their field stoves inside. The train would stop at dinnertime—11:45 A.M., according to regulations—and the enlisted men would line up at trackside and pass by the mess car, collecting their grub in the tin plates and cups kept tied to their belts. For the rest of their meals, the soldiers would eat cold rations; each man carried five days' worth in his pack. This consisted of hardtack, bacon, "canned Willie," which was what the Army called corned beef, and chunks of "war baby," their name for soft bread. Naturally, this scheme did not apply to officers; they would take proper meals in the comfort of the snoozer.

"So you're beginning to know your customer, eh, boy?" said Mr. Hebb.

"They seem a tough lot, sir—the troopers." Cassie was thinking of the one true meal per day, and no berths for five nights.

"*Tough?*" exclaimed Mr. Hebb. "Why, you defame 'em, son! We carried the outfit up to Sturgis when they transferred from Fort Robinson. Got under my skin, they did—I made a study of 'em. The Twelfth Cavalry Regiment is the nastiest bunch o' jungle fighters ever there was—heroes o' the Philippines and *awful* mean. Why, one o' them would as quick cut out your liver as tell you his right name!"

The Pullman agent paused to accept fresh coffee from Nelson and light up a pipe, then continued his description of Cassie's customers-to-be. The outfit had been born in '01 at Fort Sam Houston, Texas; on its shield appeared a green cactus and the legend *Semper Paratus*. The regiment now consisted of four squadrons totaling 65 officers, 1,250 troopers, and some 1,200 horses. The 1st Squadron was doing duty in the Hawaiian Islands, the 2d was guarding the Isthmus Canal, and the 3d was preparing to follow the 4th into Mexico. The 4th was chosen to go ahead, Mr. Hebb suggested, because it was the meanest.

"Hellions and misfits, they are. Veterans, mostly, with only a sprinkling of greenhorn recruits. A good many served with Pershing back in '02 and '03—you're too young to remember it—doing battle against the Moros. These fellas fought at Zamboanga and so fancy themselves the 'Zamboanga Brigade.' They're the hardest men alive—and not afraid to die!"

Cassie could only think of the coffee crates out back of the house in Lincoln. He was sure he had seen "Zamboanga" on one of those.

"Trouble is," Mr. Hebb went on, "they're bored to distraction just now and itching for a fight. They've been at peace too long, laboring in bivouac, doing their burdensome maneuvers. What they crave is battle— so don't be standing in their way of it, boy!"

"No, sir, I sure won't."

"One in five is himself a Filipino who's joined up with the aim o' buying his citizenship thereby. So don't you be afraid, Cassius, first time you cross the path o' these dark-skinned gentlemen with their Spaniard's machete!"

Visions of bloodthirsty cannibals flashed before Cassie's eyes. What a great adventure he was now embarked upon!

They made their way up through the Buffalo Gap, riding the valley between the Black Hills on the west and the Badlands on the east. South Dakota gave little relief from the elements. Snow turned to dense fog, which made for nervous riding. What if some wayward slow freight were occupying the tracks meant for *Pullman's No. 3?* Yet Engineers Parker and Birkenhead refused to back off their throttles even a notch.

South of Rapid City they ran out of the fog into snow again. This was Sioux country in olden days, close by the Pine Ridge Indian Reservation and Wounded Knee, where an earlier trainload of horse soldiers had taught the savages a lesson in '90. Cassie kept his nose to the glass but saw neither Indian nor white man till they reached the outskirts of Sturgis. There, a lone figure bundled up in furs like a trapper gave them the yellow light for slow running, then, with a kick of his boot, switched them off onto a spur leading to the yards. Cassie flashed the high sign but the yardhand never saw it. He was already running for cover from the bloodsucking cold. It was then coming on to ten o'clock in the morning, but seemed to Cassie more like dawn, or maybe midnight. Snow clouds blotted out the sun.

They rolled to a stop. Cassie followed Mr. Hebb out onto the trackside. Wisps of steam and fog swirled in all directions, buffeted by icy blasts from the north. Cassie, wearing Uncle Chet's mackinaw and a set of Pullman Company sealskins over that, even so shuddered and ached from the cold. He thought to whistle an Irish tune to keep up his spirits, but his half-frozen jaws would not work sufficiently to allow it.

Sturgis was where the first engine crews finished up and the second crews were to come aboard. No reliefers were yet to be seen at trackside. Sturgis was also where the switching was to be done. The two sections had been made up at Lincoln backwards to the way they would be riding loaded; this because there was no way to turn a train around at the fort. The locomotives and cabooses now had to be moved to the opposite ends of the rig. *Pullman's No. 3* would then back up the spur leading to the fort and would thus be headed in the right direction for the run south.

Off in the distance, Cassie could make out Sturgis itself. It did not appear to be the last word in comfort or hospitality, being mostly weathered wooden shacks along a single dirt street. Sturgis had once been a mining town, during the Dakota gold rush of the '70s; it looked anything but prosperous now. According to *Busby's Atlas,* the Fort Meade siding was another mile or so down the track.

The second section made its arrival, chuff-chuff-chuffing to a stop inches short of Cassie's van. No. 799 looked about done in from the run, leaking water and steam like a teakettle with a hundred spouts. Everything behind the boilers was crusted over with a thick layer of ice, including the windows of the cab. Cassie wondered how Mr. Birkenhead had ever stayed his distance, especially in the fog. One look at Dolly Dingle told Cassie it had been all the craggy little fireman could do to keep No. 799 cooking. Dolly's BVDs were soaked through with sweat that would surely have frozen stiff but for the blast from the firebox. Now he was covering himself up in furs and galoshes, cursing the cold with each breath.

There was no sign of Rocks. Cassie thought of going back to look for him in the second-section van, but it was snowing harder now and he decided against it. Mr. Birkenhead and Dolly Dingle were soon joined by Mr. Parker and fireman Ham from the first section. They had little to say to each other. The outlawed crews, dog tired after a dozen hours in their cabs, gathered up their personal belongings and trudged off into the gloom, pausing only long enough to sign off in Cassie's book. Cassie did not expect he would ever see them again. Railroaders were common as flies, and a Pullman student seldom did duty twice on the same line.

The two locomotives sat dead still, spewing steam in smaller and smaller puffs, their boiler pressures falling fast in the bitter cold. A pair of sullen yardmen finally showed up, taking their own time about it, and reluctantly accepted orders from Mr. Hebb. It was not a difficult chore the yardmen had to do—switching the locomotives and cabooses—but they acted as though it were the toughest job of work ever to be asked of a human being.

There was still no sign of Rocks, and no sign of the reliefers either.

"What do we do, sir," Cassie inquired of Mr. Hebb, "if the new hoggers don't show?"

"They'll show, son," said Mr. Hebb. "You can bet on it. None of these fellas can stand a month's suspension, which is the least they'd get. But to hurry things up, where's that helper o' yours?"

"I expect I better go get him, sir."

"You do that."

Cassie sprinted up the track, letting his galoshes pound hard on the gravel to instill some heat into his aching toes. He swung up the front steps of the van and called Rocks's name. There was no answer.

Cassie went in. Rocks was there all right. He was fast asleep in his bunk, an empty bottle of corn spirits by his side. The fire in his coal stove had nearly died, but there was heat aplenty for Rocks. The short-stop had been smoking one of his prized stogies, and the blanket that covered him was now smoldering and about to blaze up.

"*Son of a bitch!*" Cassie shouted.

He grabbed up the shortstop, blanket and all, hauled him to the van's front porch, and tossed him off into the snowbank.

Feeling considerably better, Cassie marched back toward his own van, searching for head porter Nelson along the way. He meant to appoint Nelson as helper conductor in the second section and to discharge Rocks then and there, in Sturgis.

Rocks soon caught up to him. "So what's this place, Cass? Don't look like no fort to me!"

Cassie reached in his wallet and pulled out two dollars. "That's your pay. Take it. How you get yourself back to Lincoln is your business."

But then Mr. Hebb arrived. "Ah—Mr. McAuliffe."

"The one and only, sir!"

"Got a chore for you, boy. Listen to what I tell you."

Mr. Hebb gave Rocks instructions. The shortstop was to walk into the town and come back with the reliefers, whose wayward habits were well known to the Pullman agent.

"I'm on my way then!" Rocks replied. He was still clutching the two dollars that Cassie gave him.

"Seems eager, don't he?" Mr. Hebb said when Rocks had gone.

Cassie did not reply. Mr. Hebb was only seeing Rocks's good side. Rocks was at his best when given something special to do. He was not one for steady work or anything that smelled of it. But there was no one better for the occasional odd job, especially if it meant pleasing some bigwig.

Sure enough, the shortstop returned in triumph not ten minutes later, trailed by four growly-looking bearded gentlemen in sealskins and arctics. As Mr. Hebb suspected, the reliefers had been enjoying an early dinner at Miss Ton's Chinese Cafe. They now toted armloads of sandwiches and buckets of tea. Apparently they trusted Army cooking about as much as Cassie did.

Mr. Hebb pointed a finger at Cassie and announced to the crewmen: "Boys? This here's McGill, master o' this rig. Don't be fooled by his years —he knows his Rules & Regs better'n you and can pass out Brownie points quick as any master on the road."

Cassie put on his kindest smile, but this failed to soften the hard looks that came his way from the reliefers. As pleasantly as he could, he asked them to sign his book. Hoggers in the West generally sported fancy names like Blue Line Dick or Ol' Windy Baum or Smokey This-or-That or One-Eyed Paxton. The new pair called themselves "Quick-Step" Burroughs and Orrin "Pop" Yates. They were a couple of tough old souls off the Rapid City, Black Hills & Western. What talking they did was confined to "Yup" and "Nup." Under their greatcoats they wore rawhide vests over striped coveralls, had their pantlegs tucked into cowboy boots, and showed the engineer's badge of office, a red-checkered kerchief, at their necks. Quick-Step Burroughs moved in a sudden, jerky manner as though he suffered an awful tic. Cassie guessed it was nerves, not fast running, that gave him his nickname. Pop Yates wore his gray-streaked hair long in back from wood-burning days, when that manner of grooming served to keep hot cinders off an engineer's neck. He printed just "Pop" in Cassie's book. Mr. Burroughs wrote out his full name, George Edward Burroughs, in proper handwriting. The new firemen went by the names Ewald and Hogeboom. They were sad-looking and downhearted even for firemen. Immediately they voiced strong complaints, in rising tones, against the hogs they were taking over, and especially against the supplies of coal that were then filling the tenders.

"Ain't no way to keep yer pressure up on such poor crud as this!" declared Ewald.

Hogeboom said the same. It did not take either of them ten seconds to notice that the old Baldwin racers had been weaned on a diet of hot-burning Pennsylvania anthracite, which was the hard coal favored by the original owners, the Baltimore & Ohio. The smelly stuff now banging down the chutes was soft bituminous. This latter fuel, filled with tar and pitch, produced tons of smoke and ash but little heat. Worse, the supplies on hand in Sturgis, obtained from bunkers belonging to the Chicago, Burlington & Quincy, were half lignite and shale.

Cassie thought he saw a chance to show himself as captain of the rig, even there in Mr. Hebb's presence. He knew something about coal himself. During his first month with Pullman's, he had been introduced to the science of combustion when, like all students, he did time as a mechanic's helper in the Lincoln roundhouse. So now he scaled the ladder on the side of No. 506's tender and had a look for himself.

It was poor stuff all right. Not only that, it had been wet at one time or another and was now frozen into great chunks too heavy for any shovel. It could hardly be broken apart with a sledgehammer.

"It's poor stuff for sure!" Cassie called down to Mr. Hebb. "It'll take better than this to get us to Omaha!"

The yardmen who had done the switching stood below and lent support to Cassie's argument. "Oh, you'd best count on three, mebbe four coaling stops to the hour!" said the one. "If yo're meanin' to get there atall!" said the other.

Mr. Hebb called up to Cassie: "Come down, boy, and watch your footing! Them rungs is slick with ice!"

Cassie slid back down, using his gloves as brakes on the ladder's side rails. He felt his chest swell out with pride. The other trainmen had seen with their own eyes that he was no fat-assed master tied to a Franklin stove, but a captain who could take a hand in the running. "What shall we do then, sir?" he said to Mr. Hebb.

The Pullman agent spoke in measured tones. "Thank you, boy, for your kind assistance. Only now get yourself back to your office and set this train in motion."

"Sir?"

Mr. Hebb had already turned away to address the hoggers. "That's it then, boys. Take to your cabs and make steam. Time's a-wasting."

Everybody jumped at the sound of Mr. Hebb's order.

"But, sir," pleaded Cassie, "what about the *coal?*"

"You're running in reverse, McGill," said the Pullman agent sternly. "Flags out and plenty of whistle in this damned fog!"

Meanwhile, the happiest fellows in the world were the firemen Ewald and Hogeboom. Being true railroaders, they expected the worst and were never disappointed when they got it. Cassie thought he might well learn a lesson from them.

The arrival at Fort Meade was not what he had expected or hoped for. In Cassie's daydream, *Pullman's No. 3* pounded down the track at better than fifty, putting on a real show for the troopers. Instead, Rocks's van led the way, backing at a snail's pace, Rocks himself taking the flag and walking them up the spur through drifting snow, biting wind, and gray Dakota fog. Rocks had volunteered for the job, cold and wet as it was, with the idea of impressing Mr. Hebb by his devotion to Company business. In this he succeeded. The Pullman agent told Cassie: "By God, Cassius, you've got yourself a fine helper there. Ain't much for size, but he appears to be hardworking and dependable both. That's more'n can be said for most o' these young fellas. Count your blessings."

Cassie gave back a weak smile, then followed Mr. Hebb and Rocks down the trackbed. There was little to see but dense fog and swirling mists until—heads bowed to keep snowflakes from their eyes, boots sliding perilously on icy ties—they got within twenty paces of the Fort Meade platform. There, magically, the gray curtain parted, and they looked up to find themselves surrounded by troopers of the 12th Cavalry.

"Step lively, Cap'n McGill!" said Mr. Hebb. "Them's your customers!"

Pop Yates kept backing the second section until the draw bar on

Rocks's van kissed the bumper at the top end of the spur. Quick-Step Burroughs eased Cassie's own van to a stop just short of No. 799.

The 4th Squadron, nearly three hundred strong, had been paraded out from the fort and now waited impatiently—the troopers mounted and carrying their bedrolls and weapons and other equipment—in neat formations on both sides of the track. Cassie supposed that the yard-master at Sturgis had alerted the Army by telephone to the arrival of *Pullman's No. 3.* He hoped that the soldiers had not been waiting long in the cold, though snow on their caps hinted they had.

Small red-and-white flags atop cavalrymen's lances told what each unit was. On the east, closest to the fort, stood Troops A and B and Headquarters Platoon; across the way were Troops C and D and the 12th Regiment's band and color guard. The troopers wore yellow kerchiefs at the neck to show that they were not plain soldiers but cavalry. Many looked to be no older than Cassie; some were younger even. Not a few were the dark Filipinos. Whether foreigner or American, all tensed and shivered in the cold despite special winter gear: blanket-lined canvas overcoats, fur caps and gloves, felt socks, rubberized arctics. Under-neath, the troopers wore their regular khaki uniforms. These were suited, said Mr. Hebb, to the Philippines and would serve equally well in the hot climes of Mexico. But even two sets of uniforms were on the light side for Dakota winter. "Such fools!" said Mr. Hebb. "No man born of woman travels to the Black Hills in winter if he can avoid it!"

Troopers were like horses, Cassie supposed: they went wherever they were made to go. Still, the Dakotas seemed a mean place to settle an Army on horseback. The animals obviously agreed with him: they com-plained loudly and pawed the frozen ground with icy hooves. It was a question of which was more miserable, the men or the animals.

Off to the east, the bare outlines of the fort gradually emerged from the mists and fog. Roofs of the low barracks squatted down behind rough-timbered ramparts built at the time of the Indian Wars. At the first sight of *Pullman's No. 3,* a bugler high up in the sentry tower had let go a blast from his horn. Now the front gates swung slowly open and a small band of horsemen passed through, making for the troopers at trackside.

Rocks, finished with his official duties as flagman, came back to where Cassie and Mr. Hebb were standing. "Did ya ever see such a sight, Cass? Ain't it *somethin'?*"

Cassie was thinking the same thing, but did not say so. Mr. Hebb explained for their benefit the ceremonies that were now taking place. The approaching horsemen were led by two colonels. The one—white-haired and stiff-backed—was Horatio G. Sickel, commander of the entire 12th Cavalry. The other—younger but just as august—was Miles An-trobus, commander of the 4th Squadron. The colonels had been smart enough to wait for *Pullman's No. 3* in the warmth of Regimental Head-quarters. This was a privilege of high rank, said Mr. Hebb.

"That second fellow—Antrobus—he's your top customer, Cassius. You're to see to his satisfaction and pleasure at all times. Don't be fooled by his pretty manners. He's known for his strange ways and foul temper, so stay clear of him 'cept to do what he tells you."

In a week's time, the other officer, Colonel Sickel, would be heading to the border himself with the 12th Regiment's 3d Squadron. Seeing to their accommodation was Mr. Hebb's business in the fort. For now, Colonel Sickel had come out to the siding to bid farewell to Colonel Antrobus and the 4th Squadron, which would serve as the regiment's vanguard to Mexico.

The band began to play. Cassie recognized the tune at once; it was Meacham's "American Patrol," which Cassie knew from his days as piccolo player for the Christian Brothers Symphonic Band.

"Rest your eyes on them tubas, Cass!" Rocks bounced up and down like a little boy at his first Wild West show. A splendid band it was, with more slide trombones and cornets and big snaking tubas than a person could hope to count. Cassie marveled that the mouthpieces did not stick to the lips of the bandsmen. The temperature was down to zero, or close to it.

"Watcha think, Cass? Makes ya want to go and join up, don't it!"

Cassie made sure Mr. Hebb was out of earshot before replying: "Don't suppose they'll be wanting any drunks—not with war around the corner."

"I'm off the stuff for good," Rocks said, his expression as severe as a priest's. "Tell the truth, Cass, that damn moonshine made me sick as a dog. Sure do 'preciate yer puttin' out the fire, too—yes, I do!"

Cassie found it hard to stay mad at the shortstop for longer than five minutes at a time. Drunk or sober, Rocks was about the least likely candidate for Army service that Cassie could think of. Still, Rocks was about the size wanted for the cavalry. The horse soldiers had strict rules, Mr. Hebb told them: no more than five feet ten inches tall and not an ounce over a hundred fifty pounds. Smaller than that was preferred, on account of the small ponies the Army favored.

"Boys," Mr. Hebb said, "the proper trooper is small, close-knit as to bones and build, light on his feet, easy in the saddle, spry as a monkey, and skilled enough to leap off at full gallop, spin his pony down to the turf, and use the animal as his shield, firing over its belly, and the pony trained not to jump up or even flinch at the carbine's report!"

It seemed a piece of exaggeration to Cassie. Rocks took it for gospel, but countered it in his own way: "Ho, this ain't work fer the like of us, Cass! You're too big, and me, I'm too smart!"

The band stopped playing and the senior officers came forward on the platform. Colonel Antrobus's saber flashed skyward, reflecting the dull glint of leaden skies. *"Fourth Squadron all present or accounted for, sir!"*

"You may parade the colors, sir!" replied Colonel Sickel.

"Fourth Squadron! Aaaaaaaaaatennnnnnnnnn—shun! . . . Preeeeeeeee-sent . . . arms!"

A mounted trooper made his way forward and performed a bugle call. Cassie, following Mr. Hebb's example, removed his cap and held it over his heart till the bugler was done.

"Fourth Squadron! . . . Prepare for inspection!"

The two colonels and their staffs moved their animals at a walk, passing up and down the lines, taking a careful look at each man, sometimes speaking to a trooper in sharp terms, sometimes not. While they did this, the band across the way started up again, performing Victor Herbert's "President McKinley Inauguration March" and "Columbia, the Gem of the Ocean."

When the inspection was done, the colonels returned to the center of the formation, and Colonel Sickel delivered a brief talk. From where Cassie stood, he could not hear every word, but he got the gist of it. Eight of the poor victims murdered by Villa at Columbus had been troopers of the 4th Squadron's sister outfit, the 13th Cavalry. So it was now the 4th Squadron's duty to take revenge on Villa.

". . . Do not return, gentlemen, until your sabers have been drenched in Mexican blood!"

At these words, the troopers let out a great cheer. The band then played "Santa Anna's Retreat from Buena Vista," a march by Stephen Foster. Colonel Sickel judged it particularly suited to the departure of men who were presently to inflict another great defeat upon the Mexicans. The ceremonies were thus concluded.

"Come on, boy," said Mr. Hebb, "time to beard the lion!"

Cassie fell into line behind his boss, hitching up his trousers and wiping the toes of his boots across the backs of his pant legs as he went.

"How 'bout me, Professor?"

Rocks wanted to tag along but Cassie would not hear of it. "Back to the van and prepare to earn your wages!"

Colonel Antrobus was not hard to find, being one of only three men still mounted; the others were his top aides. Colonel Sickel had already returned to the fort.

"Colonel Antrobus, sir? Good morning. I'm Calvin Hebb, acting for the Pullman Company. It's a pleasure to be of service again to you and your fine outfit. This here is Cassius McGill, who'll be your conductor till Omaha."

The three officers swung down from their mounts. "How do you do," said the colonel. "This is Captain Bowles, deputy commander of the Squadron. And this is Lieutenant Van Impe, my adjutant."

Cassie took a close look at the three officers who would soon travel in his care:

Colonel Antrobus was a lieutenant colonel, to be exact about it; he wore a pair of silver oak leaves on his collar, whereas full colonels boasted eagles. Off his horse he was shorter than average, like most horse soldiers, wiry and hard, with steel-gray hair cut tight to his skull and a small but full mustache of the same metallic color. In place of trooper's canvas, he wore a smart, tight-cut buffalo-skin coat. Similarly, he avoided the soft fur cap of the soldiers, preferring a wide-brimmed cavalry hat with chin strap. He made a smart figure against the rest. Under his coat he wore a khaki tunic, stiff and tight at the collar, a glistening Sam Browne belt, riding breeches and high riding boots in place of arctics. He seemed a man who followed his own path. His face was longer than wide by double, and his skin looked thin and tightly stretched over the bones. The one thing that did not suit him, in Cassie's opinion, was his voice, which was high-pitched and raspy, though his lips were pleasingly sculptured and on the delicate side.

The second-in-command, Captain Bowles, seemed far easier in his manner. There was nothing jerky or nervous about him as there was to the colonel. He was the colonel's height but stockier in build and blond in his coloring. Even his mustache was the shade of straw. When introduced by the colonel, Captain Bowles showed a warm smile, extended his gloved hand first to Mr. Hebb, then to Cassie, and said in friendly tones, "Delighted to meet y'all." Cassie marked the captain's accent as that of a southerner.

The third officer, Lieutenant Van Impe, was a different breed altogether. He was even shorter than the colonel—not more than five feet two inches by the measure of Cassie's eye—and pink-cheeked, with reddish hair cut so short it was nothing more than a prickly fuzz. He looked to be about Cassie's own age but must have been twenty-two or twenty-three. Cassie knew the name Van Impe to be Dutch. There had been an outfielder named Teo Van Impe with Grand Island one year. Cassie remembered what a hardhead that other Van Impe had been. He hoped this one was different.

The colonel noticed that Cassie was studying out the young officer. "Lieutenant Van Impe will serve as train commander during the movement, Mr. McGill. You will wish to brief him regularly as to our progress."

"Yes, sir, I sure will!"

The colonel turned back to Mr. Hebb. "My staff and I shall board immediately."

"At your pleasure," replied Mr. Hebb. "Mr. McGill, if you will lead the way."

Cassie started off down the trackbed toward the first section's snoozer, with Mr. Hebb and the three officers close on his heels. The troopers and their animals still lined the trackbed, breathing hard in the frigid air. Loading up would not be easy, Cassie could see; the Fort Meade platform was long enough to handle only three or four cars at a time. The regimental band was then marching off toward the fort, instruments silent but for the snare drums, which provided a beat the men could march to.

Over his shoulder, Cassie could hear the colonel and Mr. Hebb talking.

"Be aware, sir, that Villa's army is making mischief," said the colonel, "every second that we remain at this siding. We travel with highest government priority—that you know—and must demand all possible speed to the front. We shall brook no delay, sir."

"Rest easy, Colonel," said Mr. Hebb. "Our boys know their business the same as your boys know theirs."

"*Correction*, sir!" said the colonel. "'Resting easy' is a luxury none of us can afford in this campaign. Beyond this, be aware that our 'boys,' as you call them, are men through and through, tested veterans for the most part, and all as anxious as I to get to the front. Do you take my meaning, sir?"

"Ah, indeed I do," replied Mr. Hebb without fuss. "Figures of speech only, sir. Our boys are men, too, I can promise you that."

"And yet this lad," said the colonel, "seems excessively youthful for the great responsibility he bears."

Mr. Hebb, too, spoke as though Cassie were out of earshot. "My, yes, youthful. But you'll have no cause for worry on his account. Our Mr. McGill's a stout lad of good education and upbringing. Beyond which, he has been a top baseballer in the major leagues, and knows the world better than many of his elders."

"I shall rely upon your assurances, sir," said the colonel.

Cassie was so busy eavesdropping that he almost walked them past the snoozer. "This is it then, sirs," he said belatedly.

Mr. Hebb led the party up into the car. "There's no finer accommodations to be had, gentlemen. See for yourselves."

The Pullman was seventy feet in length, contained ten compartments seating a pair of customers each, and featured a drawing room and two staterooms. It slept ten in comfort without resorting to the swing-down upper bunks provided. The car had two toilets, six washbasins, hot and cold water, steam heat, and illumination by both electricity and gas. The body of the car was finished in vermilion, elaborately carved, with the compartments painted in ivory and gold. The upholstery and draperies were of the finest materials and in perfect harmony with the overall design and finish, which was Pullman's best.

The colonel looked into every nook and cranny of the car. He was accompanied by Lieutenant Van Impe, Cassie, and the colonel's "body servant," a Filipino boy called Francisco. When the colonel moved to sit upon one of the bunks, the dark little monkey—or so the Filipino seemed to Cassie—sprang forward and relieved the colonel of his saber. Cassie had never seen anything to match it: a "body servant"!

They concluded their tour in the drawing room, where Mr. Hebb and Captain Bowles had waited. The drawing room was small but luxurious; here the officers would take their meals, in two sittings. Cassie made a note to have Nelson attend personally to the colonel's sitting. The senior officer did not seem long on patience.

"Well now, Colonel," said Mr. Hebb, "does she live up to your expectations?"

The colonel pronounced himself satisfied. He chose Stateroom A for himself and assigned Captain Bowles to B. Lieutenant Van Impe, being of lesser rank, would occupy a regular compartment.

"Henceforth, gentlemen," said the colonel, "this Pullman shall be designated Headquarters Car. Lieutenant Van Impe, you may proceed with boarding of the Squadron."

"At once, sir!" snapped back the adjutant. He wasted no time in turning to Cassie. "Well, mister? You heard the colonel!"

This was the moment Cassie had half dreaded, half yearned for: the troopers ready to climb on board, Mr. Hebb set to disappear inside the fort to do his business with Colonel Sickel.

"If you will allow us just the odd moment," said Mr. Hebb to the lieutenant, "I'll be having a brief word with Mr. McGill before I go."

"Two minutes, no more!" said the lieutenant.

Cassie could tell the young officer was acting more for the colonel's benefit than his or Mr. Hebb's.

The colonel nodded approvingly. "Indeed, gentlemen, make haste. *Tempus fugit.*"

Cassie followed Mr. Hebb outside and down the track a short distance.

"She's all yours now, boy."

"Yes, sir."

"Your first division point is Chadron. Get on the wire there and give your expected time of arrival to the stationmaster at Valentine. When you reach Valentine, do the same for Omaha."

"Yes, sir, sure will."

"From Omaha to the border, you'll take orders from Mr. Liberty. Till then, you're on your own. Keep your nose clean and don't go looking for trouble—trouble will find you soon enough all by itself."

Cassie knew that Mr. Hebb was referring to the matter of the bad coal at Sturgis. "I expect I'll be able to manage all right, sir," Cassie stated.

"Sure you will. But if trouble comes your way, don't be too intelligent to ask for help. Go straight to your hoggers—there's nothing like a cab jockey for giving advice."

"Yes, sir."

"Here—take this."

"Sir?"

The Pullman agent handed over his copy of *Busby's Atlas.*

"Thank you, sir. I'll take real good care of it and bring it straight back."

"It's yours to keep, boy."

The only trainmen Cassie had ever known to carry their own *Busby's* were regular conductors and division supers. "I sure do thank you, sir!"

"Best get a move on, son. Army don't like to be kept waiting by mere civilians."

"Yes, sir."

"Good luck to you. You're a fine lad to take on this load—sure you are!"

They shook hands with their gloves still on. Then Mr. Hebb turned abruptly and started his climb through drifting snows toward the warmth and hospitality of Fort Meade.

Cassie thereupon turned back to something quite different.

2

Lieutenant Van Impe paced the platform, waiting for him. "Don't hang back, man! *Move!*"

Cassie approached, taking careful little steps to keep from slipping on the ice. He was still clutching *Busby's* to his breast.

"McGill, is it?"

"Yes, sir, McGill. Cassius McGill."

"Do you suffer some acute physical disability, McGill?"

"Sir?"

"Your feet. You seem to have trouble moving them at a smart pace."

"Nothing wrong with my feet, sir, that I know of."

"Understand me, McGill. As train commander, I am responsible for the expeditious movement of this squadron to the border. I will not tolerate slovenly civilian ways. Do you know what 'expeditiously' means?"

"Not exactly, sir."

"I thought not. It means that when I give an order, I expect you and your crew to carry it out *now*, this very instant, without hesitation or delay or excuse. I shall accept no excuses for substandard performance. Do I make myself clear?"

"Yes, sir. I didn't mean to be tardy, sir. Only—"

"Enough. Work, not talk, is now required."

Cassie felt anger and resentment at the lieutenant's haughty manner, but took some amusement from it, too. Van Impe shaved no oftener than Cassie did, yet fancied himself already the top general in the Army.

The lieutenant motioned for three troopers who had been loitering nearby to come forward. "Men, this is Conductor McGill. He will be your liaison with the Pullman Company. McGill, you will work with these noncommissioned officers in the loading-up."

"Begging your pardon, sir," said one of the troopers, "but I'm only now a lowly private, you'll recall."

"So you are, Snivey, and so you shall remain."

The lieutenant proceeded to introduce the troopers:

"This is Sergeant Major Jacko Mudd, senior noncom of the Squadron. He will assign the men to each car by troop and by squad.

"This is Corporal Romero, company clerk. He is in charge of inventories, paperwork, and general housekeeping.

"And this—this is Trooper Snivey, *acting* quartermaster. He will see to the loading of equipment and supplies."

Cassie acknowledged each introduction with a hopeful nod and smile. Jacko Mudd was the oldest of the three, close to bald, with a fat belly that spilled over his web belt. Corporal Romero was a Filipino, dark-skinned with a mouthful of pearly white teeth. Most imposing was Trooper Snivey, tall for a cavalryman, big-boned and coarse in his features, with a broad-edged scar that ran down one cheek and across his jaw. Cassie supposed this great red welt was the work of a machete and won in battle. But the scar was so straight and neat that a razor might have done it. Dark patches on the sleeves of the trooper's faded overcoat showed where stripes had been, three for sergeant.

"In addition," said the lieutenant, "the Squadron veterinarian, Dr. Rose, will oversee loading of the mounts. Sergeant Major, where is Dr. Rose?"

Jacko Mudd's fleshy face eased into a broad smile. "Sittin' up with a sick horse, I believe he said, sir."

"An' taking somethin' for that awful cold o' his!" added Trooper Snivey with a crooked grin.

The lieutenant was not amused. "He is, is he? We shall soon see about that. Meanwhile, you've got your orders. Proceed with loading *on the double!*"

"*Yes, sir!*" the troopers shouted all together.

When Van Impe had gone off a short distance, Trooper Snivey turned to Cassie and spoke in a most earnest way: "Oh, he's a swell young fella, the lieutenant. He's Class o' '12 from the Academy and bound for the General Staff afore he's done."

Cassie looked back toward Van Impe, who was already bossing another gang of troopers. "He seems a hard officer," Cassie replied.

"Oh, he's that," said Snivey. "Still, he can be as pleasant as you'd want—only you've got to put your nose down there to his tiny wee asshole to bring out the best in him. . . ."

They set to work on the loading up. Jacko Mudd produced a table of organization for the Squadron:

Unit	Officers	Enlisted Men	Horses
Headquarters	2	2	—
Troop A & HQ Platoon	2	68	68
Troop B	1	66	67
Troop C	2	72	68
Troop D & Machine Gun Squad	2	72	67

"How many cars you brung us, boy?" Jacko Mudd demanded.

"There's the Pullman, sir, and—"

"Don't go callin' me 'sir,' boy. It's 'Sergeant Major' to you."

"Yes—Sergeant Major. Well, there's the Pullman, and eight of the day cars, and fifteen boxes."

Cassie thought to explain that the special had been put together on short notice at Lincoln, but decided against it. Jacko Mudd, like Lieutenant Van Impe, did not invite excuses.

The officers were taken care of first. Corporal Romero posted their berth assignments in the vestibules of the snoozer:

Headquarters Car

Stateroom A:		Lt. Col. Miles Antrobus, CO, 4th Squadron
"	B:	Capt. Lonnie Bowles, CO, Troop A
Compartment #1:		Capt. Ellis Dodd, CO, Troop C
"	#2:	Capt. Galen Sanderson, CO, Troop D
"	#3:	1st Lt. Abel Peaks, Acting CO, Troop B
"	#4:	1st Lt. Noah Canby, 2d-in-command, Troop C
"	#5:	2d Lt. Wallace Armstrong, 2d-in-command, Troop A
"	#6:	2d Lt. Harley Withers, 2d-in-command, Troop D
"	#7:	2d Lt. Tom Van Impe, Adjutant
"	#8:	Dr. Olan Rose, Veterinarian
"	#9:	vacant
"	#10:	vacant

Taking on the enlisted men would be a different matter; there were no vacant compartments to concern them. Corporal Romero performed the arithmetic. Each of the day cars seated thirty-three men. This gave a total of 264, yet 280 troopers meant to board—leaving sixteen men without chairs.

Jacko Mudd did not seem bothered by the calculations. "Troops A and B to the first section, C and D to the second, and bottom sixteen men on Punishment Detail to ride with the horses."

Instructions were quickly passed along to the sergeants and corporals down the line. Cassie thought maybe the sixteen culprits on Punishment Detail were the lucky ones. They could catch forty winks in the straw, whereas the troopers in the day cars could expect no sleep at all. The cars boasted steam heat and Pintsch-gas lights and rich Pullman upholstery and fittings, but, as the name said, day cars were meant for passenger runs lasting eight or ten hours at most. They were never intended to carry troopers to a war five days' distant.

The horses promised to be as great a problem as the men. There were

270 head to be carried in the fifteen boxes, meaning eighteen to the car. Twelve seemed to Cassie a more comfortable number. Cassie had never before worked a freight that carried horses in boxcars, but he supposed that Mr. Hebb and Mr. Austin, being old-timers, must have figured it right at eighteen.

"What about all them mules, Jacko?"

This point was raised by Trooper Snivey, who seemed a close friend to the sergeant major. Nobody else called the sergeant major Jacko. The sergeant major asked no officer for advice, but decided for himself on the spot. "Back to the stables with 'em. They can follow along next week with the Third. Maybe by then these pukin' railroaders"—his scathing remark aimed straight at Cassie—"will know their business."

Cassie heard from Corporal Romero that matters might have been worse. The Squadron was now well below strength, lacking a surgeon, assistant surgeon, chaplain, three regular officers, thirty enlisted men, and forty more horses. *Pullman's No. 3* could never have carried the full complement.

Cassie excused himself and went off on his own; he had switching to see to. Work gangs had already loaded up eight cars that belonged to the Army; these stood along a pigmy spur leading to the gates of the fort. There were three boxcars for heavy equipment and provisions; a steel express called the Squadon Armory for weapons and ammunition; another box fitted out as cook car; and three flats bearing the outfit's horse-drawn supply wagons, motorized Red Cross ambulance truck, and five-ton water wagon. Cassie instructed Quick-Step Burroughs to move the first section forward sufficiently to allow the Army's cars to be tagged onto Cassie's own van for the short ride back into Sturgis. There, the cars could be broken up and distributed fairly between the two sections. For now, the first section would pull nineteen and caboose, while the second pulled but thirteen.

Cries and shouts echoed up and down the siding: the troopers had begun to board. They first tied their ponies to a picket line, then filed by the Squadron Armory to surrender their weapons. They had been paraded out with pistols and carbines, which would not be needed until they reached the border. Nelson and the other porters stood by the steps to the day cars and welcomed the troopers aboard as if they were paying customers on any top passenger run in the East. The only difference was that these passengers answered the Negroes' politeness with bad humor and foul language.

Seeing the mood of the troopers, Cassie went down the line and sought out Rocks. "Minding your own business, are you?" Cassie asked him.

"Bet on it, Professor!"

In truth, the shortstop had been snooping about. By offering a chaw of his best Red Devil to a fellow in the armory, Rocks had obtained full particulars on the Squadron's hardware.

"Ya never seen such a mess o' swords and guns, Cass! Me, I wouldn't give ya a nickel for the life o' one single Mex—not after these boys have their fun!"

Besides the cavalrymen's favorite old Krag-Jorgensen carbines, the armory held crate after crate of modern Springfield rifles, as well as three hundred of the spanking new Colt .45 automatic pistols. The Squadron was also equipped with six of the French Bénét-Mercié machine guns, murderous brutes like those being used in the European war. But Rocks was most taken with the .45 pistol. "Kicks like a damn mule, she does, Cass! This ol' boy's promised fer me to try his out, soon as we hit desert!"

According to Rocks's new pal, the fiendish Moros of the Philippines had skulls so hard—and suffered pain so easily after smoking their hashish and other devilish drugs—that regular .38 bullets bounced right off. So the Army put the famous inventor John Browning on the job, and he delivered the .45. "Killed them Moros like a scythe cuttin' wheat!"

"Sounds like dime-novel stuff to me," said Cassie. "All made up for your benefit, too, I expect."

"It's God's own truth, Professor! Why, these fellas eat human flesh and drink blood fer their breakfast! Took them Philippine gals like they was no more'n Injuns! There's one fiercer'n all the rest—want to see 'im? Look there—by all them mules."

The shortstop was pointing to Trooper Snivey. "I know him," said Cassie. "He's the quartermaster."

"See how big he is, Cass? That's on account he came over from the field artillery in the Philippine wars—real cavalry boys is generally on the puny side. He was a sarge, only they busted him down."

"How come?"

" 'Cause he maimed a fella. Happened down to Rapid City, in the best fancy house in town. Cut this fella's hand off with one o' them Filipino axes! Cut it off so clean it hardly bled a drop!"

Cassie looked across to the scar-faced trooper with new respect. "You stay clear of him, hear me?" said Cassie. "There's little call for one-handed shortstops."

"Me? Wouldn't go near that fella fer nothin' on this earth!"

Lieutenant Van Impe now approached at high speed. "Who is this?" he asked Cassie, pointing at Rocks.

"He's Riley McAuliffe, sir—helper conductor in the second section."

"That I am!" said Rocks proudly.

The lieutenant looked Rocks up and down. Cassie had the idea that the officer disliked Rocks on sight. The two men were about the same size and shape and high pink color: maybe this was the reason for it. "Shouldn't this man be in uniform?" the lieutenant asked crossly.

Even to Cassie's eyes, Rocks's muskrat coat and bright red muffler looked sorrowfully out of place among the strutting military men and well-disciplined Pullman employees. "We expect to get him one, sir," Cassie said.

"See that you do," said the lieutenant. "And see that he obtains a shave and haircut."

Cassie quickly agreed. The shortstop's ideas on grooming did not fit Pullman Rules & Regs any better than the Army's. Rocks's last haircut was several seasons back. "He'll be getting all spruced up, sir, soon as we're loaded and rolling," Cassie promised.

"I shall hold you personally responsible," said the lieutenant. "Now then—see that man over there by the Troop C guidon? . . . *There*—the small white flag with the red C on it? For God's sake, man, don't play dumb—*there!*"

Cassie finally saw where the lieutenant was pointing. "Yes, sir?"

"That is Dr. Rose. He has questions for you concerning the animals. Report to him at once and satisfy his requirements."

"Yes, sir, sure will."

Cassie moved off, taking Rocks with him.

"Is that right, Cass? I'm to be gettin' me own *uniform?*"

"You heard the lieutenant."

"Ain't he the friendly one! So what kind o' funny talk would ya call that, then?"

Rocks was referring to the lieutenant's nasal, pinched manner of speaking.

"Never heard a New York accent before?" Cassie said confidently. He had played a week's worth of exhibition games up Albany way during his tryout with the Brownies and thus recognized the peculiar accent of the region.

Rocks spit out a juicy wad of tobacco. "New York, is it? Well, sounds to me like them fellas don't get out to the shit house as much as they ought!"

Cassie chewed on his lip to keep from laughing out loud. Rocks's analysis seemed close to the mark. "I was you," Cassie said earnestly, "I'd stay clear of the lieutenant, too."

"So far ya got me stayin' clear o' the whole damn Army!"

"Wish it were so."

Cassie sent Rocks back to the van to keep him out of mischief, then presented himself to Doc Rose, the Squadron's vet.

"And you're him, boy? Conductor of this train?"

"That's me, sir. Cassius McGill is the name."

"Olan Rose, horse doctor. Pleased to know you, son. Well now, isn't this splendid—meeting up with a young lad who's earned himself such a position of responsibility. I'm sure you've earned it, too—it's written on your face. But for the moment, Mr. McGill, I must express to you my displeasure over your company's arrangements for our animals. Not proper, sir—not proper at all. And I find that your engineer, Mr. Burroughs, shares my opinion. Come along, lad, he will tell you himself. . . ."

On appearance alone, Doc Rose might not have counted among mankind's finest specimens, but Cassie liked him just the same. He was an older man, gray-haired and stooped, with a long bent nose full of hair, nostrils that furled into sagging cheeks, and eyes faded to a glassy blue. His wizened mouth was buried beneath a dirty gray mustache and full beard. He wore bifocals and liked to stand near to the person he was addressing so as to bring his glasses into play. He pronounced his words in a curious way, but not like Lieutenant Van Impe: the vet's accent was that of Massachusetts. The vet talked as though he had lost all his teeth, though they were still with him, cracked and yellow and repaired with some base metal—tin, maybe—like something used in horses' mouths.

Cassie noticed something else about Doc Rose. He was drunk, or close to it. His breath told the story. So did his nose. Drink had turned his skin shiny and red-splotched and made him itch at regular intervals.

Cassie followed him over to where Quick-Step Burroughs was standing by the open doors to one of the boxcars.

"Ah, Mr. Burroughs," said Doc Rose, "would you be so kind as to repeat for young Cassius the various points you've raised with me?"

The engineer drained a mug of coffee before speaking. "Well now, boy—just how you plannin' to carry all them ponies?"

"Sir?"

"The *horses*, boy. How you gonna carry 'em?"

"Why, there, sir—in the boxes."

"Not likely!"

"Sir?"

"Hell, boy, you won't git half of 'em to Mexico alive. Them's *freight* cars, mister. Horses ain't freight—even a greenhorn like you ought to know it. Those ponies'll kick theirselves silly the first hour out."

"This is the way we were outfitted at Lincoln, sir," Cassie explained weakly.

"Then it was sure some jackass who did the outfittin'. If you was to make five miles an hour and let them ponies out ever' couple o' miles, you might—I say *might*—git where you're goin' with most o' your stock. But not with us runnin' flat out like the colonel wants. Hell, boy, them's *box-cars!*"

Cassie took a closer look at the cars. They were in poor state of repair. They had been without caulk or pitch for a dog's age, and were slat-sided besides. They might have given good service in summer but were ill-suited to the snow and freezing rains of a Dakota winter.

Quick-Step Burroughs was not finished. "What's needed, boy, is proper stock cars with swing-motion trucks. Why, these boxes o' yours has got *diamond* trucks. They'd shake the eyeteeth out of a buffalo, much less these delicate little ladies' mounts you see here about us. I'm warnin' you, boy—you'll not reach Mexico with half your animals, and that's a fact. Hell, these boxes ain't got *stalls* in 'em, maybe you noticed!"

"Mr. Burroughs raises valid objections, son," said Doc Rose. "These cars lack proper feed boxes and watering troughs. What's wanted, I'm afraid, is a Burton. Or, better still, a Keystone."

Cassie was acquainted with such rolling stock. The Keystone Palace Horse Car Company manufactured true livestock cars with all the niceties. Eighteen horses could be carried in the best of health in one of those. But what Mr. A. O. Austin had seen fit to provide was forty-foot boxes off the Red Eye Line, not Keystones.

"Without meaning to create unnecessary difficulties," said Doc Rose, "I must urge you to delay our departure until proper livestock cars can be obtained. Otherwise, I cannot take responsibility for the condition of the animals."

Cassie gave a wistful glance over to the fort, which sheltered the wise Mr. Hebb, who, in Cassie's opinion, might better have been there at trainside fielding the hot grounders that were now coming Cassie's way.

"I suppose the Company'd have sent Keystones or Burtons, sir," Cassie reasoned, "if there'd been any available on short notice."

"Surely a great company like Pullman's has such resources at its fingertips," said Doc Rose. "Why, I'm certain the yards at Chicago, or even Omaha, are fairly swimming in Keystones. There'll be the very devil to pay, Cassius—this I can assure you—should our animals suffer on account of inferior equipment."

By this time, a gang of troopers had gathered around to witness the argument. Among them was the scar-faced Trooper Snivey. "Here now, boy—lieutenant says why ain't we loaded up and steamin'?"

Cassie blushed from the embarrassment of it. "There's a problem over the cars," he told the trooper. "Do you suppose the lieutenant could come see for himself?"

"Oh, he'd be most happy to oblige!" Snivey laughed, and the other troopers laughed with him.

The lieutenant was summoned. "What is it now, McGill? Why this dawdling and delay?"

Cassie explained about the horses, ending with Doc Rose's idea that *Pullman's No. 3* should stay put until proper livestock cars could be brought from Chicago or Omaha.

The lieutenant glared at the silent vet, then barked out to the assembled troopers: *"Be at ease until I return!"*

The officer marched off to Headquarters Car, reappearing almost immediately in the shadow of Colonel Antrobus.

"It's Cassius, isn't it?" asked the colonel in a pleasant voice.

"Yes, sir. Cassius McGill."

"What seems to be the matter, son? Quickly now—time once lost can never be regained."

Cassie began to explain, then realized that Quick-Step Burroughs was close by, and so made the hogger tell the story for himself.

The colonel proved to be a poor listener. Before Quick-Step Burroughs was half done, the colonel roared, "Nonsense, man! One's equipment is not always what one wants. Why, many a time the Squadron has resorted to makeshift methods to transport men and animals. Had you been witness to our campaigns in Luzon Province, you would understand the need to *improvise*—to use one's God-given *brain!*"

Quick-Step Burroughs stood his ground. "So how you gonna get them animals up into them boxes in the first place—tell me that?"

Cassie saw what the engineer meant. Livestock cars came equipped with ramps; boxcars did not.

The colonel was not at all troubled by the engineer's objection. "Mr. Adjutant?"

"Sir!" cried Lieutenant Van Impe.

"Send for the carpenters!"

"Sir!"

The troopers had obviously learned to accommodate the colonel's wishes without question or hesitation. A work party was quickly sent into the fort to bring back the necessary quantity of oak planks. The Squadron's carpenters, assisted by a large number of regular troopers, thereupon ran up a batch of sturdy ramps while the colonel surveyed the activity with evident pride and satisfaction.

"Maybe so," said Quick-Step Burroughs when all this was done, "but how you gonna keep them ponies on their feet *after* we head out? Ain't no *stalls!*"

"Mr. Adjutant!" cried Colonel Antrobus again.

"Sir!" replied Lieutenant Van Impe.

"Let the cars be rope-rigged!"

"Yes, sir! . . . Mr. Quartermaster!"

Trooper Snivey came forward, saluted, took his orders from the lieutenant with a loud "Sir!" and ran off, followed by his work gang. What the colonel had in mind was to make stalls out of thin air by tying off ropes from side to side and floor to ceiling in each boxcar. Cassie judged this would take a bit of doing and a bit of rope!

Minutes later, Snivey and his men returned, bringing with them two enormous reels of stout Manila hemp from the Squadron's supply wagon. "Set to it, boys!" sang out the colonel. "Villa will not wait!"

The troopers did as ordered, using their machetes to hack the rope into ten-foot lengths and knotting each section into grids and squares like the cargo nets Cassie had seen on barges along the Hastings Canal in summer. Meanwhile, the shivering ponies stood tethered in uneasy strings along the trackbed, their nostrils festooned with muzzles of ice, breath erupting like dragons', the animals whinnying and neighing and complaining as loudly as their wranglers might have done if the colonel and the other officers had not been standing nearby.

"So you see, Cassius," said the colonel at last, "one must be resourceful above all. Learn a lesson from what you have witnessed here this day."

"Yes, sir. Thank you, sir."

"Now then, I have a question for you."

"Sir?"

"What is this train called, son? What is its name?" There was a twinkle to the colonel's eye, as though he were posing a riddle.

Cassie tried to think. "Well, sir, in my work orders it's *Pullman's No. 3.* That's the only name it's got, that I know of."

The colonel shook his head. "Insufficient. Functional, but lacking in wit. A war train must have a proper name—one that contributes to high morale and *esprit de corps* among the men."

Cassie remained silent. He had no ideas on *esprit de corps* or other military considerations.

"*Pancho Villa Express,*" said the colonel. "How does that strike you?"

"*Pancho Villa Express,* sir?" Cassie liked the sound of it well enough, but worried about what Mr. Hebb might say. "Yes, sir. Well, it sounds fine to me, sir—only on the telegraph I believe I'd best stick to *Pullman's No. 3.*"

The colonel laughed good-naturedly. "Of course, of course. We would not wish to confuse the railroad. But for military purposes—*Pancho Villa Express* it is, then."

"Yes, sir."

"We shall require appropriate signs, handsomely painted, one for each car. At your earliest opportunity, please inform the Squadron quartermaster. He will see to the necessary preparations."

"Yes, sir, the quartermaster."

"Each car must have its sign in place prior to our arrival at Leavenworth."

"Leavenworth, sir?"

"Fort Leavenworth, Kansas—where I once had the honor to serve as deputy commander. Of course, you are not acquainted with our history and reputation—why should you be? Suffice it to say that the Fourth Squadron has been called to battle by none other than my dear classmate and friend, Black Jack Pershing. You will have read his name in the newspapers."

"Yes, sir. He's from Lincoln, sir, where my folks live."

"That is correct, Lincoln, Nebraska. Jack and I have served long and often together—Cuba, the Philippines and, before that, here in the Department of the Missouri, during the Indian Wars. So you see, Cassius, it's only natural that Jack should now send for the Fighting Fourth."

"Yes, sir, I see."

"And thus you will understand why speed is of the essence."

"Yes, sir, I do."

"Hence, that word *Express*. Let nothing deter you or your colleagues from delivering the Squadron to Fort Bliss with all possible dispatch. *Tempus fugit!*"

"Yes, sir. You can sure count on us, sir."

The colonel's eye no longer showed its twinkle. "I fully intend to," he said.

The invisible sun, westering behind fresh banks of snow cloud, had climbed as high as it would that day. Despite the colonel's love of *tempus fugit,* the *Pancho Villa Express* was already running late.

Cassie went looking for the quartermaster, Trooper Snivey, to tell him about the signs the colonel wanted. The trooper was then occupied with the horses and could not talk. Cassie stood to one side and witnessed the loading up. A string of mounts had been led to the foot of a ramp, but there the animals balked. Snow was falling in great clumps, and there was a glassy, big-eyed look to the ponies and awful fear in the sounds they made. A sleek black gelding was sent up, but it slid right down again on the ice that had formed when the ramps were set in place. The troopers tried to coax the animal with kind words, then harsh shouts. In the end, they had to use their riding crops before the animal would try again. "Look sharp there!" the soldiers kept yelling at each other.

A pretty little roan got herself halfway up, then slipped to her knees and slid down to the trackbed, kicking and thundering with fright. The troopers moved on her, pushing and pulling and beating her with their crops. Her eyes bulged, her teeth shone yellow and menacing. The sounds she made were terrible to hear. Cassie pulled a wool cap down over his ears and wore his Pullman cap on top of that. Still he could hear that pony's fearful cries.

He moved on to another car. It was the same there. The boxes were freezing cold and wet and gloomy black inside except for narrow beams of light made by the electric torches the Army's wranglers carried. Horses emptied themselves in fear. Soon the cars reeked of urine and manure, which added to the sweet odors of hay and oats and the stink of troopers' sweat. The lowest-ranking privates were set to shoveling out the boxes; they dumped the manure straight off onto the siding. Cassie was now wishing he had forgone the pork pie he had gobbled for his breakfast. He had gas on his stomach and a green taste in his mouth.

"Step lively, sodbuster, or git stampeded to hell!"

Cassie jumped aside as a string of ponies passed. Anybody not dressed in khaki was taken by the soldiers for a lowly farmer. Cassie moved down the line until he met Rocks again. The shortstop pulled a paper sack from the pocket of his muskrat coat and raised it to his mouth. He had obtained a fresh bottle of spirits—won off a trooper in some risky bet, Cassie figured.

"Jesus save us, Cass! These fellas don't give a damn for horses nor men neither!"

The troopers were just then flogging the hide off a horse that refused to go up the ramp no matter what. Blood froze solid on the animal's back where they had beat it.

"You there—lend a hand!" came a harsh cry. It was Lieutenant Van Impe, calling to Rocks.

"Ain't my job!" Rocks shouted back.

The look on Van Impe's Dutch face! The lieutenant stopped what he was doing and approached Rocks in an arrogant manner. "It's customary to address an officer as *sir*, mister."

"Well, it ain't so cus-to-mary back where I come from," replied Rocks. Anybody could see that the shortstop had been drinking; he swayed and lurched and rocked back on his heels.

Cassie feared the worst. The trooper closest to Rocks, a corporal named Daguerre, grabbed the shortstop by the front of his muskrat coat and was about to throw him down when the lieutenant intervened:

"*Easy, soldier!* We'll deal with this troublemaker when we've finished boarding. Continue with your work."

The trooper let Rocks go. The shortstop smoothed himself out, then took another swig of his liquor. His hands were so palsied he could hardly manage the bottle. "Want some, Cass? It'll help ya fight off the chill."

Cassie declined.

"Shit!" said Rocks. "I can't watch no more!" He meant to go back to his van and drink himself to sleep. "It's sure better'n standin' out here freezin' yer ass and lookin' upon such poor beasts as these!"

Cassie offered no objection. Straight spirits mixed with Rocks's hot Irish temper had more than once made for a bad "sitsiation," as Mr. Terry O'Moore liked to say when his team was about six runs short and down to its last out. If the shortstop were gone from sight, Cassie figured, maybe the lieutenant would forget about him.

It did not work out that way. Before Rocks could take his leave, a badly spooked mare ran herself off the ramp and fell hard under one of the boxes. She scraped some hide off her rump and raised blood from one shank. The injuries did not look serious to Cassie, but the animal bellowed in pain. Rocks let out a great string of curses, which, together with the animal's piteous cries, served to recall Lieutenant Van Impe.

"What's the trouble here? Who is responsible for this animal?"

The animal's regular rider, a trooper called Tarbell, succeeded in getting the mare to her feet. "She's lost a bit o' hair is all," said the trooper. "See, sir? She'll heal up good as new."

The animal would not put one leg down; there was considerable blood coming from it. Van Impe had already unsnapped the flap to his holster. "Stand away!"

Trooper Tarbell spoke up in a tearful voice. "No, sir, it's not come to that—"

Craaaaaaaaaaaaaack! . . . Craaaaaaaaaaaaaack!

The men closest to the animal flinched at the first report, staggered back at the second. Trooper Tarbell dropped to his knees; others held him there, lest he go for the lieutenant. The mare sagged straight down and lay with her head on one rail. No animal ever died quicker.

The lieutenant holstered his .45 without looking down, as though he had practiced the trick time and again. Cassie felt his skin go crawly. Despite the snow, hot flashes rose in him and brought sweat to his brow. He thought of the time back at Hastings when he and Pa had to shoot the milk cows after they came down with anthrax.

Rocks suffered worst of all. He was struck dumb for an instant, then let out a piercing scream: "*Aaaaaaah!* Oh, ya awful bastard! I seen *lots* o' ponies hurt worse'n that! You had no call to do *murder!* Oh, ya great pile o' horse shit! Ya fuckin' awful Dutch bastard! It's *you* that needs the murderin'!"

Rocks went for Van Impe's throat but a pair of troopers grabbed him and pulled him back. One of them was Trooper Snivey. "Easy, boy, or you'll be hurtin' yerself."

Snivey had Rocks's arm pinned behind him and was lifting on it. Rocks screamed from the pain but kept his bloodshot eyes on the lieutenant. When Rocks was riled up, not even a broken arm would stop him: Cassie had witnessed his foul temper more than once on the diamond. Given half a chance, Rocks would kill the officer with his bare hands.

"Sergeant Major!" shouted the lieutenant.

Jacko Mudd sprang forward. "Sir!"

"Place this man under arrest."

Rocks laughed. "Ya can't arrest *me,* ya damn skunk! I ain't no asshole trooper!"

Trooper Snivey lifted up on the arm again until Rocks begged for mercy.

"Confine the prisoner to the guardhouse!" ordered Van Impe.

Jacko Mudd looked puzzled. "Back to the fort, sir?"

"Not the fort, Sergeant Major—*there*." The lieutenant pointed off in the distance to the second-section van. "For the duration of our journey, let that caboose serve as Squadron guardhouse and punishment barracks."

"Yes, sir!" Jacko Mudd turned back to Rocks. "You want to go easy, boy, or you want to go hard? Makes no difference to me."

"Easy then," said Rocks in a sly voice. Trooper Snivey let go of his arm. The shortstop spent a few seconds rubbing his elbow to get the feeling back. Then he lurched forward and threw his best punch at the sergeant major's jaw.

Rocks came up inches short. Trooper Snivey reached out and cold-cocked him with one easy blow. Cassie started toward the fallen shortstop, but the troopers kept him away.

Van Impe motioned toward Rocks's unconscious form. "Sergeant Major! Remove the prisoner to the guardhouse!"

Several privates came forward and carried Rocks off, holding him under the arms and letting his feet drag in the snow.

"Proceed with the boarding!" stormed the lieutenant. "No further delays will be tolerated!"

The loading resumed. Doc Rose, who had hidden himself away in his compartment, came out to trackside again. He was no steadier on his feet than Rocks had been. He knelt down to examine the dead mare and uttered a single word: "Butcher!"

About half the troopers who had already boarded came out of the train to help with the mounts. Nobody wanted Van Impe to have another excuse to use his .45. Ponies still balked and reared at the ramps; some fell and lost hide. But none needed shooting. In the end, 269 animals were taken aboard.

It was nearly 1:00 P.M. when an orderly from Headquarters Platoon found Cassie and delivered Lieutenant Van Impe's order to move out. Cassie went down the line with the other trainmen and made a check of car doors and air-hose connections. Along the way, he instructed head porter Nelson to take over from Rocks as helper conductor in the second section. The Negro did not seem pleased by his promotion; he had already acquired a low opinion of his customers.

Finally, Cassie went back to the van, sat at his desk, and gave two quick tugs on the pull cord. Moments later, Quick-Step Burroughs and Pop Yates answered him on their whistles and began dropping sand to help the Baldwins' drivers find traction on icy rails. The two sections soon jerked forward, spilling troopers in the crowded aisles and spreading panic among the animals.

Car by car, the cavalrymen cheered their escape from garrison life, but

Cassie found no such satisfaction. He had expected his first ride as master to be far different from what it was. Thinking on Rocks's sad fate, he suffered a spell of dizziness and got out to the van's platform in the nick of time: vomited his breakfast off the back steps. One of the brakemen, Mr. Legrand, saw him do it but made no comment, for which Cassie was most thankful.

3

THE TURNAROUND of locomotives and cabooses at Sturgis took less than twenty minutes. After that, the first leg was to Rapid City, a distance of twenty-eight miles over tracks of the North Western, working south along one slope of the Black Hills. The way up from Lincoln had been on the Burlington, so Cassie now found himself running on tracks he had never seen before and already had no desire to see again. Snow and fog abounded; there was nothing to see anyway.

Cassie unlocked his desk drawer, obtained Ma's rosary, and draped it under his shirt. He took pleasure from the feel of it against his bare skin: the warm rosewood beads, the cool silver cross. He got out *The Nigger of the "Narcissus"* and climbed up top to the angel's nest, where he was unlikely to be disturbed.

> Mr. Baker, chief mate of the ship *Narcissus*, stepped in one stride out of his lighted cabin into the darkness of the quarterdeck. Above his head, on the break of the poop, the night watchman rang a double stroke. It was nine o'clock. Mr. Baker, speaking up to the man above him, asked: "Are all the hands aboard, Knowles?"

Though the story told of another long journey at its start, Cassie could not seem to keep his mind fixed on the printed page. He would read a sentence to himself, lips following along, only to have the sorrowful image of a prostrate Rocks cross before his eyes.

The author's spell was soon broken altogether by a shrill voice from down below:

"*Please, suh! De co-lo-nel—he want you bad!*"

It was Francisco, the colonel's boy. Cassie returned Ma's rosary to the desk drawer, then followed the wiry Filipino forward. Besides six horse wagons, they had four day cars and the cook car to pass through. It proved a hard trip. Francisco offered what protection he could, but passing through the day cars was like running the gantlet: the troopers showed no respect for a Pullman uniform.

"Oh, ain't he the pretty one! Come here, boy—I ain't had me a woman in ever so long. . . ."

Cassie was pleased to reach Headquarters Car. The sentry on duty showed him straight into Stateroom A. Cassie doffed his cap and tried to keep his voice steady:

"You wanted to see me, sir?"

The colonel had been lecturing to Lieutenant Van Impe while the porter Milo served coffee. The windows were already fogged up from the steam heat, and the compartment smelled strongly of the officers' cigars.

"Come in, Cassius," said the colonel. "Tell us, son—what will our next stop be?"

"Next stop, sir?" Cassie reached into his hip pocket and pulled out his train book. "Well, sir, the next stop is—Buffalo Gap."

"Distance?"

Cassie referred to his book again. "It's forty-nine miles the other side of Rapid City, sir—which is maybe twenty miles from where we are now."

Lieutenant Van Impe entered the conversation: "Purpose of the stop at Buffalo Gap?"

"Yes, sir. Well, that's to take on water and maybe some coal if they've got any that's better than what we have now in the tenders. Which, to be honest, sir, is pretty poor stuff."

"And at what time," asked the colonel in a voice softer than Van Impe's, "do you estimate we shall arrive in Buffalo Gap?"

Cassie consulted his Railway Special. "It's hard to say, sir."

"Hard to *say?*" blustered Van Impe. "Surely you know our present rate of speed, man. Can't you simply calculate time of arrival?"

Cassie did not know their rate of speed for sure, but it could not have been much because of slow running for the horses. "I'd best ask Engineer Burroughs, sir," said Cassie.

"Please do so, Cassius," said the Colonel. "Supply the information to Lieutenant Van Impe as quickly as you can. Meanwhile, Lieutenant, let us tentatively plan to dismount at Buffalo Gap. By so doing, we shall avoid the necessity of a separate stop for the horses and thus make better time."

Cassie approved of this scheme. At Buffalo Gap there would be a proper siding, which would make unloading of the animals a safer proposition than doing it out on open track.

"When you see your engineer," said the colonel, speaking to Cassie again, "kindly reiterate to him our requirement of maximum speed throughout the journey."

"Yes, sir, I sure will."

"Very well. You may go."

Cassie started to turn but caught himself. He wished Van Impe were not present. "Sir?"

"What is it, Cassius?"

"I was wondering, sir—if we could talk about Mr. McAuliffe. My helper in the second section?"

"Not now, Cassius," said the colonel. "We shall speak of your friend in due course."

The two officers went back to their business, leaving Cassie to go about his.

He continued forward. He meant to see Quick-Step Burroughs without delay. He opened the vestibule door, jumped the coupler, and made his way across the three flatcars bearing the Squadron's wagons and ambulance truck. The howling gale all around him made him thankful for his mackinaw and gloves. Leaving the flats, he climbed the icy steel rungs to the roof of the express car. Up top, he crouched low, legs spread wide for balance, and staggered on, suffering a faceful of hot embers and oily black smoke from the hog. He came to the first of the three supply cars; leapt across; danced over the swaying roofs; climbed down again, this time to the tender; felt his way along the slippery catwalk; finally reached shelter in the cab of No. 506. At this point, he figured he was a thousand feet or more—nineteen cars—from his van.

Quick-Step Burroughs and fireman Hogeboom were drinking coffee and making steam.

"Colonel wants to know how fast we're going," said Cassie through half-frozen lips, "and why aren't we going faster?"

Quick-Step Burroughs laughed; Mr. Hogeboom did not.

"You tell the colonel for me," the engineer said, "that we're goin' as fast as we ought to go with this load. Maybe we're goin' *too* fast. Maybe I'd best back her off a notch, now as he brings it to mind."

Cassie accepted a mug of scalding black liquid from Mr. Hogeboom, then searched around, hoping to locate the speed gauge and prepare an answer for Van Impe. However, Baldwins of this vintage apparently lacked instruments other than the big glass that showed pressure in the boiler. "I'd guess," said Cassie, trying to act happy about it, "we're doing twenty easy—maybe twenty-five. Am I right?"

The trainmen refused to answer. Even so, Cassie decided to tell the lieutenant twenty-five. This would sound slow enough to Van Impe, but any further stretching of the truth was more than Cassie would dare.

He bade the trainmen farewell and made his way back to Headquarters Car. There, the sentry turned him away: Lieutenant Van Impe was attending the colonel's staff meeting and could not be disturbed. Cassie was pleased to leave a message: MAKING TWENTY-FIVE AND HOPING FOR MORE.

He headed back toward the van, climbing again to the roofs of the cars and remaining up top until he reached the first of the horse wagons. He might have descended to the warmth of the day cars along the way, but he preferred the wet and cold to the gibes of the troopers.

In the first horse wagon, Cassie came upon Doc Rose.

"Ah, Cassius, how timely. We have just now sent a runner to fetch you."

"Sir?"

The vet did not have to explain; Cassie could see for himself. The floor of the box was awash in straw and horse droppings and blood. Half a dozen troopers were battling a frantic gelding: the animal was trying to regain its feet despite a broken leg. The animals around it were panicked, too, some with legs caught in the rope netting, others free and kicking out at their neighbors. The rope stalls had largely come apart, the knots failing, the animals free to roam. At the far end of the car, Cassie could make out another animal on its side, that one dead.

"We had no choice but to destroy her," said Doc Rose, "and now must do the same for this one. You must stop the train, Cassius. Similar conditions prevail in the other cars. We must stop at once and detrain the animals."

The vet reached into his bag and brought forth a flask, which he put to his lips. He offered it to Cassie, but Cassie, remembering Rule G, declined.

Cassie knew what he had to do. Lieutenant Van Impe and the colonel would be against it, Cassie figured, knowing their great desire for speed. But the black gloom and the stench around him overcame any doubts. He gave five quick pulls on the emergency cord. In short order, Quick-Step Burroughs repeated the signal on his whistle and stood on the brakes. Cassie prayed that Pop Yates had been wide awake at his throttle and was now able to take similar measure in the second section.

They screeched to a safe stop. Cassie climbed down and made his way forward, accompanied by Doc Rose. It was not long before they met a furious Van Impe.

"McGill! What's the *meaning* of this?"

Before Cassie could attempt an answer, the lieutenant took notice of Doc Rose, who was having another sip from his flask.

"Medicine for a heavy cold," said the vet. His watery eyes seemed to beg for sympathy. "May I direct your attention, sir, to the grave condition of our animals?"

"Regardless," said Van Impe, turning back to Cassie, "you will *not* stop this train again without my prior authorization. Is that understood?"

"Yes, sir. Only—"

"Oh, let us not argue while the animals suffer!" cried Doc Rose. He headed back toward the horse wagons. Cassie and the lieutenant had no choice but to follow along.

They climbed up into the first of the boxes. The injured gelding, still pinned down by desperate troopers, thrashed and bellowed in its unsuccessful attempts to rise.

"Please!" begged Doc Rose. "The leg is broken."

Lieutenant Van Impe went for his pistol. He fired two rounds in close succession and the animal found peace.

The vet wiped tears from his eyes. "At our present rate of travel, Lieutenant—and given the abysmal condition of these cars—you will be well advised to draw extra rations of ammunition!"

The young officer's usually pink face reddened noticeably. Holstering his pistol, he addressed the vet in savage tones. "You, sir, may consider yourself under house arrest. The charge: drinking on duty. Until I make my report to the colonel, you are to remain at your post and give aid to the animals."

"With the greatest of pleasure!" replied Doc Rose.

Sergeant Major Jacko Mudd now arrived from the second section, where he was in command, accompanied by his friends Corporal Romero and Trooper Snivey.

"It's much the same out back, sir," said Jacko Mudd. "We've three dead and a dozen hurt bad."

The lieutenant had already made up his mind. "Detrain the animals at once, Sergeant Major, and set work details to repair the rope stalls where necessary to ensure safety of the mounts. Be quick about it!"

Van Impe went forward to make his report to Colonel Antrobus. While Jacko Mudd and his men began the tedious chore of setting the ramps and leading out the animals, Cassie went back to the second section and instructed Nelson and the rear shack, Mr. Coffin, to set out fusees and add torpedoes to the rails a quarter mile up the line to slow down any ignorant hogger from the north who might suppose he had the green light into Rapid City. This done, Cassie ordered the other brakemen in both sections to inspect the journals and bearings on each car, keeping an eye open for hot boxes that could slow their pace even further.

With his crews thus set in motion, Cassie repaired to the second-section guardhouse. He expected to find sentries, but there were none: Jacko Mudd had required all troopers to report at trackside to help with the animals. The van's only occupant was the prisoner, Rocks McAuliffe.

The figure on the cot hardly moved as Cassie approached. "'You dead or what?" Cassie asked.

The figure turned Cassie's way. "Mostly dead, Cass."

"What happened to your eyes?" The shortstop's eyes were puffed almost to a close.

"Had to teach a couple o' them soldier boys a lesson!"

"You were teaching *them*, were you?"

The shortstop raised his head an inch or two to see out the window, then fell back. "So why are we stopped, Professor? We ain't already to Mexico, by chance?"

Cassie described the plight of the horses.

"Well, ain't they the most ignorant ones you'd ever care to meet!" said Rocks, talking about the troopers. "Lord above, they make *me* look smart, swear to God!"

"I tried to see the colonel about you," Cassie said. "So far no luck."

"I knowed ya would be tryin'," Rocks said in a quiet voice. "Like old times, ain't it?"

Meaning like half a hundred past disasters on one team or another, mostly in the Nebraska Cities League.

"You can get into trouble quicker than any fellow I ever met," Cassie said.

"What do ya s'pose they mean to do with me, Cass? Shoot me, I guess— which ain't such a bad idea, 'cause I'm near to the Lord just now. Look what I done. I ain't good for many more miles, I can tell ya that."

Cassie saw that Rocks had tossed up his breakfast behind the cot. It made a foul mess. Cassie did not mention his own misfortune off the back steps. Rocks was sick from all the alcohol he had drunk—that and the stomach-tossing whiplash of slack action, which the caboose took worse than any other car.

"They don't generally shoot people for sassing back and drinking corn whiskey," Cassie said.

Rocks did not reply. He had fallen asleep.

As soon as he could, Cassie obtained another audience with Lieutenant Van Impe. "He's *awful* good around animals, sir, and a help in running the train, too. I'll be responsible for him, sir. There'll be no more sassing back to you or your men. He's not a bad fellow underneath it all—else I wouldn't be asking you the favor."

Cassie could see that the lieutenant had more on his mind than Rocks McAuliffe. All together, Van Impe had come across five more horses that needed shooting. This was even before the loading up of the animals started again.

The lieutenant poked a stubby digit into Cassie's chest. "The problem's *yours*, McGill. Any more trouble from your friend and *you'll* answer for it. Understood?"

"Yes, sir. You'll have no cause for regret, sir."

"Very well, I accept your assurances. You've been fairly warned, so don't come crying to me or the colonel if your friend acts up again. Now get on with your duties. The colonel is *exceeding* angry over this delay."

"Yes, sir. Thank you, sir."

Cassie secured Rocks's release from the guardhouse and set him to work at Doc Rose's side. The animals were boarded again. Every last inch of rope in the Squadron's supply wagons had been used to shore up the stalls in the fifteen horse cars. After a stop of some forty minutes, Cassie was able to give the START TRAIN signal. They left the car-casses of ten dead animals there at railside in fresh snow, a flagrant vio-

lation of Pullman Rules & Regs. Cassie could not help wondering what
Mr. Hebb would have said, had he known.

The next horse that needed shooting came just inside the yards at
Rapid City.

"These jury-rigged contraptions are simply *insufficient* to the task at
hand," lamented Doc Rose. He had finished with the bottle in his bag and
now had the shakes.

"You'd best grab hold o' that cord and pull fer all you're worth, Cass!"
cried Rocks. "Or ain't none o' these poor brutes gonna get off alive!"

Cassie signaled SLOW RUNNING, then STOP. "Rocks, go find the
lieutenant and tell him to come back here and shoot this horse. Say we've
stopped to coal up—that'll hold him till I get back."

Cassie visited both engine cabs and gave orders to top up with water,
then wait for further instructions. Quick-Step Burroughs stated his intention to go looking for a better brand of coal than they were now burning. "The way we're goin', boy, Omaha's about a week away!"

Cassie found his way to the North Western's passenger station and
presented himself to the man in charge of the telegraph room:

"I'm McGill, master of *Pullman's No. 3* out there in the yard. I need to
make use of your line."

The fellow behind the desk eyed him with suspicion. "Got your
brotherhood card, do you?"

"That I do." Cassie flashed the pasteboard under the fellow's nose.

"Write out your message and I'll get to it when I can."

"I'm a brass-pounder myself," Cassie said. "I'll send it off now, if you'll
let me."

"Suit yourself, mister. The key don't care who's workin' it."

Cassie sat down at the keyboard and pounded out his message. He
addressed it: MR. LIBERTY, C/O PULLMAN'S, UNION STATION, OMAHA. The
message said:

BOXCARS UNSUITED TO HORSES. HORSES DYING. REQUEST PROPER
LIVESTOCK CARS OMAHA. THIS IS SERIOUS SITUATION. YOURS. CAS-
SIUS MCGILL.

"I count that twenty-five cents' worth," the clerk told him when he
finished. Cassie tossed two bits in the fellow's direction and felt so good
about taking action against the woes of his run that he left the place
without getting a receipt—meaning that livestock cars sent to the rescue
at Omaha would be compliments of Captain Cassius McGill.

He went back to the rig and sought out Lieutenant Van Impe. "Sir, I
know I'm not supposed to stop the train, only—"

"Not now, McGill. . . . Remove that animal!"

The officer had dispatched another horse with his smoking .45. Cassie backed away. The yardmaster had switched *Pullman's No. 3* to a remote siding, and the animals were now being coaxed down the ramps and led away at a trot, to be confined in pens normally used for cattle. A light snow continued to fall, but the animals preferred this discomfort to the black terror of the boxcars.

Much had happened in Cassie's absence. At Doc Rose's behest and with Van Impe's approval, Jacko Mudd had taken a work party into Rapid City to fetch civilian carpenters and proper supplies of lumber and nails. It was Doc Rose's idea to build up individual stalls for the animals even if this took till doomsday.

Cassie watched awhile but did not take much heart from the results. Boxcars were just that, boxes, and a bunch of boards suddenly thrown up inside them was no remedy for the way the cars rode the rails. Quick-Step Burroughs had said it at the start: the trucks under the horse cars were wrong for living creatures, being rigid and hard as stone and not giving a bit to the swaying and lurching and jumping about of wheels on steel. Beyond which, the roadbeds were largely warped off the level by deep ground frost. The animals in their fear and ignorance thus froze up stiff and yearned to die. And so they died.

It was well past three o'clock, so the colonel agreed to Lieutenant Van Impe's request that messing commence. The troopers lined up at the cook car and obtained a late dinner of beef stew and hard biscuits, which they ate under snow showers turning to rain. The evil weather had its good side, however, for the colonel generously added spirits to the ration. Each man who passed by the cook car was given a quarter-cup of government-issue New England rum, dark in color, fiery in taste. Rocks and Doc Rose immediately jumped into line to share this unexpected bounty. Cassie held back.

"Come on now, Professor," cried Rocks, "ain't no prize fer stayin' sober on this voyage!"

Still Cassie refused. He lacked the taste for food or drink so close to seeing animals slaughtered and left to rot.

"Drink up," he called out to Rocks. "You'll be needing Dutch courage to get you through this run, that we know!"

He had meant to insult the shortstop with this sarcastic remark, but Rocks did not seem half so insulted as Van Impe, who glowered nearby.

A trooper shouted across to him: "Colonel's hollerin' for you, McGill!"

Cassie hurried to Headquarters Car buoyed by the knowledge that Mr. Liberty at Omaha would soon supply true relief from their troubles. The colonel would no doubt be furious over the death of so many animals; yet Cassie would now have a proper response.

To Cassie's amazement, the colonel made no mention of horses. "Are you aware of today's date, Cassius?"

"Yes, sir. The eleventh of March."

"That is correct. I now wish to share with you a military secret."

"Sir?"

"I must first take your oath, under the Articles of War. Raise your right hand and swear after me."

"Yes, sir."

" 'As provided in the United States Code of Military Justice, I hereby swear not to divulge what I am about to be told to any person, military or civilian, under the penalties prescribed by law.' "

"I swear it, sir."

"Very well, then. Today is the eleventh day of March. Not later than the sixteenth—*Thursday*—General Pershing's forces shall cross into Mexico. What this means, Cassius, is that the Fourth Squadron must be at the border not later than evening of the fifteenth—Wednesday."

"Yes, sir, Wednesday."

"Then you have your orders."

"Sir?"

"We shall undertake exercising of the animals and messing of the men *solely* in conjunction with normal stops for fuel and water."

"Yes, sir."

"Not a *minute* is to be lost during these stops."

"No, sir."

"In short, Cassius, you will not concern yourself with the Army's needs. The Army will gladly adapt itself to the needs of the Pullman Company."

"Thank you, sir."

"That is all."

"Yes, sir."

"Except—"

"Sir?"

"Except that I must admit to being sorely disappointed in you, Cassius."

"Sir?"

"The *signs*, Cassius."

"Sir?"

"Surely you've not forgotten the *Pancho Villa Express*? Yet in discussing the matter with Acting Quartermaster Snivey, I find to my great distress that you have not conveyed to him my instructions."

"Sorry, sir. What with the horses and all—"

"Such forgetfulness would earn you *fifty* demerits at the Academy."

"Sir?"

"You have the makings of a good soldier, Cassius. But you must learn to apply yourself single-mindedly to the task at hand."

"Yes, sir."

"I trust you will not give us further cause for disappointment."

"No, sir, I sure won't."

"You are excused then."

"Thank you, sir!"

He had hardly recovered from his chagrin when Nelson came to get him:

"Goshalmighty, Cap'n, you'd best come quick! There's a ter'ble ruckus out back!"

The Negro gave his explanation as they ran along the siding toward Rocks's van. While Cassie was off pounding out his message to Mr. Liberty, a gang of troopers led by Trooper Snivey had slipped into town, visited a boardinghouse known to them, and come back with three young ladies. It was the troopers' idea to keep the ladies stowed away in the guardhouse for the pleasure of Snivey, Jacko Mudd, and their pals all the way to Mexico.

Then Rocks had showed up. Surprised to find three young ladies, he introduced himself and began to make friends with them. The troopers objected; they wanted to get on with their business. Rocks tried to interfere, but the troopers were too strong for him.

"He's in bad trouble now, I 'spect, Cap'n!"

They reached the van's front steps. "I'm going in," Cassie said. "Go back and find an officer and bring him straight here. Tell him there's murder being done. Hurry, now!"

"I'll do it, Cap'n!" The Negro ran off.

Cassie took deep breaths, then flung open the van's sliding door. "So what's this?" he cried. Immediately he found himself hurled to the floor and held there, pinned by a brace of troopers he had not seen before.

"Well now, 'tis th'other one!" Jacko Mudd shouted. "Ain't they the best o' friends!"

Against one wall was a bloody Rocks, held upright by Trooper Snivey. The shortstop was sure to fall if the trooper let go. Snivey and Mudd were dressed in nothing but their longjohns. The three ladies appeared to wear no clothes at all. They were huddled together in a far corner, covering their nakedness with Pullman Company blankets. Cassie looked away. He had never before seen females so naked, except his sisters, when they were younger, in their baths.

"Let him be!" Cassie demanded of Snivey, wrestling hard with the two troopers who had him pinned. "There's an officer just outside!"

Snivey let Rocks collapse to the deck and turned his attention to Cassie. "I knowed this'un was the better o' the two!" Snivey said to Jacko Mudd. "I'd best break his neck, ain't that right?"

Jacko Mudd pulled Snivey off. "You—McGill! You ain't seen nothin', understand? Same goes for him," pointing to the fallen Rocks.

Cassie's chest was heaving, his voice hoarse. "You had no cause to beat him like that!" Rocks was bleeding worse than the horses. "I'll see you *hang* for it," Cassie spit out.

"You gonna be smart?" Jacko Mudd asked. "Or you gonna be like him?"

Rocks was beginning to stir and make noises. Cassie worried that the shortstop might drown in his own blood. But Rocks was hard to kill. Through broken teeth, the shortstop said, "Gonna teach 'em a lesson, Cass! Watch me!"

Trooper Snivey delivered a kick to Rocks's ribs. The shortstop fainted. "*You son of a bitch!*" Cassie hissed.

The trooper turned on him but was interrupted again, this time by a call from outside:

"Sergeant Major? Are you there? This is Lieutenant Withers. Report at once!"

Nelson had come back with Lieutenant Harley Withers of Troop D. He was an officer scarcely older than Van Impe.

"At your pleasure, sir!" shouted Jacko Mudd. He was already pulling on his trousers and jacket and knotting his kerchief. Before departing the van, he bent low and whispered harshly into Cassie's ear:

"One word o' this"—gesturing toward the three ladies—"an' you an' yer pal is dead as them ponies we been tossin' off!"

With this benediction, Jacko Mudd and Snivey and their fellow troopers made their escape.

The girls seemed too frightened to move, so Cassie and Nelson left them where they lay and applied their efforts to reviving Rocks. Finally, they were able to haul him back down the line to Cassie's van, where there was a Red Cross emergency kit and plenty of hot water and a good supply of adhesive tape for the damaged ribs the shortstop had acquired in the melee.

"They ain't chippies or nothin'," Rocks declared while Cassie worked at the taping. "They're o' good family and educated, too. Rita's eighteen —she's the strawberry blonde. Naomi's twenty and half Sioux—s'pose ya guessed it from her face. The littlest one's Jolene Potts. Can't be more'n sixteen, Cass, an' Irish as you or me! Didja ever know Tommy Potts over ta Indianapolis? Though he's no relation, I'd say."

"Glory be!" said Cassie. "You learned all this while Jacko Mudd and his boys punched your teeth out?"

"There's more important things than yer teeth," the shortstop gushed between mouthfuls of blood. Rocks had always been able to take a good beating and come back for more. He liked Ty Cobb's famous saying: "You may whip me today, but you got to do it again tomorrow!"

"Jolene, she sure worries me," Rocks went along in his painful singsong. "I'm gonna fix that fella Snivey fer what he done to her. They made me watch while that damn bull took his pleasure in her. That's how come they beat me so good—they knowed I was gonna take revenge on 'em!"

The shortstop sputtered a while longer, then slipped off, snoring through a nose that was most likely broken. Cassie taped over the bridge and then sagged himself to the floor. The smell of fresh blood finally brought him low.

It was five o'clock by the sun before they cleared the Rapid City signal board. Cassie no longer cast an eye to his Railway Special—it had been smashed during the scuffle.

They paused only briefly at Buffalo Gap to take on water. The colonel had decided the next horse stop would be Chadron, across the Nebraska line. This would take another four hours' steaming and a dozen more visits to the water towers and coal chutes along the way. It was snowing harder than ever now, and the Army's wranglers still had their hands full with the animals, the new stalls notwithstanding. Of the 269 horses taken aboard at Fort Meade, 258 were now alive.

After sundown, Doc Rose came back to Cassie's van to check on Rocks. "A tough lad," was the vet's judgment. "I suspect he'll live."

The nose was indeed broken. Of the two big teeth in front, one was missing and the other broken off, leaving a stump. This produced pain whenever Rocks opened his mouth to breathe.

"Take a swallow o' this med'cine and open wide," the vet told Rocks. The shortstop enjoyed a swig of the liquor. The vet then pulled out the stump with a quick yank on his horse pliers. Rocks screamed, then accepted another swallow and soon fell back asleep. He was pale as a corpse. They closed Rocks off in the super's bunk, where he could sleep undisturbed by the comings and goings of the trainmen.

"I sure do thank you, Doc," Cassie told the vet.

"It's my pleasure," said Doc. "It's not often I get to practice on human beings. Here now, don't make an old man drink by himself."

Cassie reluctantly accepted two fingers of peach brandy. The vet's satchel was again deep in spirits; there was scarcely room for his tools. They sat side by side on one of the window boxes close to the stove and enjoyed the fire. The porters, Milo and Tobias, who were off duty, napped in their bunks overhead.

"To your good health and future fortune," said Doc.

Cassie took a large swallow of the brandy, which brought a torrent of tears to his eyes. Only their first day on the run—and that not over yet—

and already so much had happened that he was not prepared for. The steady rhythms of a hard-pounding freight now served to steady him a bit—that and the brandy and Doc Rose's easy manner.

"And where might you be from?" the vet asked him.

"I'm from Hastings, sir—in Nebraska. Though it's Lincoln we now call home."

"Spent some happy days in the fine city of Omaha when I was younger. Wonderful people, Nebraskans."

Doc Rose told something of himself. He continued to sip brandy as he talked, but he did not seem to get any drunker from it. He could hold more liquor than Cassie had thought possible. Cassie listened and nodded and had another sip or two himself.

He was born, Doc said, in Chicopee, in the western part of Massachusetts. His father was a vet, too, but not with the Army. Doc Rose took his medical degree from the Springfield College of Veterinary Science and practiced for a short time in Chicopee. But failure of the banks during the panic of '93 made it impossible for a young man—he was then hardly older than Cassie—to earn a livelihood doctoring to farm animals. Thus it was that Doc signed on as a Department of War civilian vet assigned to service a squadron of the 2d Cavalry that went off to fight in Cuba during the Spanish-American War in '98. After that, Doc saw service in the Canal Zone and then the Philippines. This was how he got to know the troopers so well.

"They're not a bad lot, Cassius, no matter what you may think of them now. You're not seeing them at their best, I can assure you. It takes a real fight to bring out the best in these boys."

Cassie was tempted to remark on the treatment dealt out to Rocks by Jacko Mudd and Trooper Snivey, but he held himself in check.

Doc Rose had had a wife once, but she died of the typhoid while they were stationed in the Canal Zone. They had no children. "So I been footloose and fancy-free ever since, and it gets to be a habit."

"Yes, sir, I imagine it does." Doc Rose fell into silence. When the time seemed right, Cassie started up again. "Sir? There's something I'd like to ask you about—if you wouldn't mind."

"Mind? Why, I could hardly mind, talking to a fine lad like yourself."

"It's something awful private, sir. A hard secret to keep, but one that's got to be kept for now."

"Ah." The vet's usual soft red-eyed expression turned even softer. "Would you like me to guess at what this secret might be?"

"I don't suppose you'd guess it, sir."

"Perhaps not. But let me try."

Cassie could see that Doc Rose was having some fun with him. "You're sure welcome to, sir."

"Could this secret have three parts to it?"

"Three parts, sir?"

"Such secrets travel faster among troopers than any bullet, lad!"

"I don't believe we're talking about the same secret, sir."

"Well now, let's see. Does part of your secret go by the name—Naomi?"

Cassie was shaken. "You guessed it then, sir!"

"I'd be a poor horse doctor, son, if I didn't keep my eyes and ears open. It bothers you, does it?—what's going on back there in the other section?"

Cassie remained silent.

"Yes, of course it does. It would bother me, too, if I weren't so old and used up as I am. You're a good Christian lad, I suspect."

"I'm Catholic, sir."

"Well, then, you'll not have come face to face with it before. What we're talking about here, Cassius, is no stranger to the military. What we're talking about here is hookers."

"Hookers, sir?"

"Hookers, boy."

"I'm afraid I don't know that word, sir."

"Time you learned it. Named for Fightin' Joe Hooker, they are—general on the Union side. Old Joe was a practical man, much like a good doctor of veterinary. To keep his troops interested in the war—food and pay being even worse then than they are today—Joe Hooker would furnish 'ladies of the night.' Whores, boy. Know the word *whore*, do you?"

"Yes, sir. I was in baseball, sir."

"So I'm told—and a top-notch player too, I believe. Well, Joe Hooker would travel these ladies of his in government wagons and pay them with government funds. It's no different to what's happening out back in your caboose."

Cassie accepted another offering of Doc Rose's peach brandy. "And it's all right then, sir? With Colonel Antrobus?"

"Antrobus? Hah! I should think Colonel Miles Antrobus is the one trooper in this caravan who would *not* approve. But Jacko Mudd is the equal to any officer in the Squadron when it comes to stealth and deception. The colonel will never learn of the ladies—nor of their customers."

"I wasn't thinking of it in that way, sir."

"'Course you weren't. But can't say as much for myself! Being as I am already under house arrest for my drinking, I figure I'm likely to visit the guardhouse any time now—no longer the wretched and forbidding prospect it once was!"

Onward steamed *Pullman's No. 3*. Chadron came into view at a few minutes past 9:00 P.M.: a water tower, some livestock pens, and a weather-beaten freight station belonging to the North Western. Waiting on the platform were the relief crews: engineers C. B. Detweiler and

Curtis J. Bucklebock, firemen J. Foxe and Billy Rosecrans. There was little to distinguish these fellows from others of their kind on the road. Quick-Step Burroughs and Pop Yates gladly climbed down and headed off into the darkness, bent on hot grub and blessed sleep.

The men and animals were allowed to stand down. The temperature remained well below the freezing mark, which entitled the troopers to another ration of government rum. Cassie thought to wake Rocks so that he might line up with the troopers at the cook car, but the shortstop refused to stir. Doc Rose checked him over to make sure his condition had not worsened. "He's only drunk," was Doc's verdict.

Cassie did his business on the telegraph, informing Valentine and Long Pine of *No. 3*'s progress. Before they pulled out, Trooper Snivey and his wranglers dropped off the corpses of another half-dozen animals. The North Western's agent, when he saw what they were up to, came out from the warmth of his shack and demanded a "burying fee" of two dollars per horse. Snivey's boys threatened to remove the agent's clothes and toss him down a steep snow-covered ravine, where he would most certainly die. The fellow was all sweetness and light after that. He would see to the disposal of the corpses on his own, he told them. Cassie figured this meant butchering for food. There were people in this world who would eat horse meat. Cassie was not one of them.

Trooper Snivey knew how to please the colonel. Headquarters Car received the first of the *Pancho Villa Express* legends during the stop. The paint was still wet when they pulled out. Cassie was obliged to notice that Trooper Snivey was not exactly the foolish brute he sometimes pretended to be.

They pushed on, reaching Valentine after midnight and Long Pine in time for Sunday breakfast. The animals were let off at Long Pine and made to trot up and down the siding in the freezing rain for the good it would do their stiff limbs. Bales of hay were tossed down and the animals permitted to feed for ten minutes. What breakfast the troopers obtained came cold from their packs; the colonel would not take time to set up chow lines at the cook car.

The colonel and his officers lived another kind of life. They suffered fried eggs, ham steaks, corn bread, canned figs, and hot coffee, all served on well-starched linen by the porters Milo and Tobias in the comfort of Headquarters Car. Cassie knew the menu because Milo snitched a good mess of ham and hot corn bread and brought it back to the van for the other trainmen to enjoy.

Rocks seemed much improved since his surgery at the hands of Doc Rose. He ate a hearty breakfast over swollen gums, then persuaded Cassie to amble back down the line with him as far as the second-section caboose. They pretended to be on the lookout for hot boxes and bad air-hose connections.

One of Snivey's gang, a muscular trooper of Polish origin named Tor Przewalski, stood guard on the van's front steps. He was armed with pistol and carbine both. The windows of the van had been covered over with blankets; there was nothing to see.

"So what do ya s'pose is happenin' in there, Cass?"

"Oh, hell, Rocks, how should I know?"

"You know the same as I know!"

"If you know," Cassie replied with impatience, "why ask me?"

"Ravished!" Rocks said, like a curse. "Ev'ry hour o' the night and day —ravished by them buggers! Poor li'l thing. She'll be bleedin' worse'n me by now!"

Cassie knew Rocks was speaking of Jolene Potts. The shortstop had already talked himself into a particular fondness for her, not the least for her Irish family. Cassie sweated at the shame of the girl's fate but remained silent. It was like the bad coal or the dying horses: it was the conductor's business, all right, but it was not his business either.

Engineers Detweiler and Bucklebock and their firemen climbed down and departed. They had come and gone before Cassie ever got their names and faces straight. The fresh crews went by the names French and Sturdevant, hoggers, and Marmaduke and Tree, firemen. Cassie expected to become no better acquainted with them than he had with the others. Riding back in his van, he seldom saw the same faces more than twice, when they got on and when they got off.

All the healthy horses were loaded up again. Four more of the sorrowful beasts did not require loading: the lieutenant's pistol shots rang for miles in the icy wet Nebraska air. Long Pine, having a steady population of eleven souls, had no use for horse flesh. The carcasses were left to freeze along the roadbed east of town. The *Pancho Villa Express* had come three hundred miles since the new stalls were erected at Rapid City and lost eighteen head over that distance. This was one animal for every sixteen and two-thirds miles, Doc Rose calculated, meaning they would lose another ninety head or so before reaching the border. The stalls were coming apart now at a quicker and quicker rate, "so better make it an even hundred, Cassius! Now that's a pretty thought, don't you agree?" After trying to drink away his sorrows, the vet could barely stand up without assistance.

"I expect matters will improve after Omaha," Cassie replied. Something told him to resist the temptation to boast of his message on the wire to Mr. Liberty. He was learning something about the road. He preferred to see the quality of the livestock cars at Omaha before crowing over his good deeds.

They chugged on across the northern plains. The countryside was white and flat as far as the eye could see. They steamed all day Sunday without incident except for the dropping off of more carcasses. That had become routine now. The new hoggers, French and Sturdevant, showed they could burn coal as fast as the worst rawhiders on the road while eating up the map in *Busby's* like a pair of snails, an inch to the hour.

For their noon meal, the troopers were again directed to their packs while the officers ate chicken and dumplings. The scheduled supper and horse stop at Nickerson, fifty miles northwest of Omaha, was canceled by the colonel, who sent word through Van Impe that "the demands of war must perforce run roughshod over polite dining or the stretching of unused limbs. Pancho Villa will provide us with exercise soon enough!"

So it was cold rations again for the troopers. The Filipino boys were particularly bitter. Their taste ran to rice, whereas field rations were hard biscuit and beef jerky. Cassie and Rocks aimed to do better. There was plenty of cheese, pork roast, beans, and pumpkin bread still to be had from Cassie's dinner pail.

Cassie pulled open the door to the warming oven over the cook stove and found his dinner pail gone. He checked the storage cupboard above his bunk, thinking maybe he had hidden the pail on himself, but that was empty too. Breathing hard now, he checked the closets and then various drawers in his desk.

No luck.

Then he saw that the locking drawer had been jimmied. Hardly daring to look, he slid the drawer open and checked its contents. His Zane Grey and his *Nigger* were still there, also his Bible.

But not Ma's rosary.

"Hurry, can't ya, Cass? Me, I'm starvin', sure am!"

"Dinner bucket's gone," Cassie replied in a strange voice.

"Oh, them dirty bastards!" cried Rocks. "You know who done it, o' course. Tobias told me he saw that big scar-faced Snivey comin' out o' this very caboose durin' the stop at Long Pine. Pretended to be lookin' fer likker, he did! Damn thieves and cutthroats! Damn murderin' sons o' bitches!"

Cassie did not mention the loss of Ma's rosary. He was too ashamed of himself—and too scared—to admit it. For suddenly anger and resentment, the slights and insults, the sins and vileness of his customers, all welled up in him, and he swore a true blood oath between himself and God:

He would recover Great-grandmother Hannah O'Hea's sacred beads or, failing that, he would spill the blood of Trooper Snivey and every other bastard in Snivey's whole gang.

4

I T W A S N I N E O' C L O C K Sunday evening when *Pullman's No. 3* entered the yards at Omaha. Cassie breathed a great sigh of relief. The
train had been his for close to two full days; now Mr. Liberty would
shoulder the burden. The Squadron's men and animals seemed to share
Cassie's joy: they had been confined twelve hours straight. Not since
Long Pine had a trooper's boot or pony's hoof touched solid ground.

There was no sign of Mr. Liberty by the order board. A gaunt, cross-
eyed yardman provided instructions:

"Ho, boy-o! Y'are to ride her on out to Track Thirty-two. Th'are
a-spectin' ya thar."

"Thank you, sir. And would you know where I might find Mr. Liberty?"

"Him? Gone straight to hell, f'r all I care!"

Thirty-two tracks. Omaha was getting to be more like Chicago every
day. Track 32 was the farthest out, Cassie supposed, where a ton of horse
manure might be tolerated. But what of dead animals?

Pullman's No. 3 found her spur and the troopers began to set the
ramps. There was nothing in the way of livestock cars to be seen nearby,
but it was a big yard. Cassie had no doubt that a fleet of dinkies was
even then preparing to switch in the proper rolling stock. He decided not
to wait for Mr. Liberty. "Stay put," he told Rocks. "I'm hiking over to
the Pullman office to pick up orders. If Mr. Liberty comes looking for
me, tell him where I've gone."

"Ain't leavin' this bunk," Rocks mumbled. He was not a pretty sight.
His lips and cheeks and eyes were puffed out of shape, the skin dark and
swollen. He said he was starving for solid food but refused to take anything over his bloody gums.

"I'll bring you back something soft to eat," Cassie told him. "Maybe
they'll have some cooked eggs back in the station, or milk toast."

Cassie's own reflection flashed back at him from the van's window
glass. He jumped at what he saw. His eyes were deep burning holes from
want of steady sleep; his upper lip showed the meager beginnings of a
mustache. He had gone about a thousand miles in the outfit Ma had
ironed for him; this was now clotted with horse blood, manure, and axle
grease. He gathered up his spare uniform from one of the closets and
hurried on his way. He would obtain a bath and shave and put on clean

clothes and appear before Mr. Liberty in prime condition, like the master of some top commuter run. He figured he had a good thirty minutes before people started yelling for him.

Cassie liked Omaha. After Lincoln, Omaha was his second home. It was a great rich city with miles of macadamized thoroughfares, grand buildings, three fine ball parks, and acres of pens for all the cattle and hogs that might ever want to go to market. Cassie especially liked Union Station, where he now stood: a granite palace of modern design with countless ticket windows, a splendid Marconi room, the finest of accommodations for a weary traveler, and the best eating house west of Chicago. Society people from all over the Midwest traveled to Omaha for a meal in that eating house.

Cassie went straight downstairs to the Immigrants Room. This offered toilets for men and women and tubs where newcomers to the city could do their washing. A separate room provided the latest in naphtha "dry-process" cleaning. A fellow could take off his suit and they would clean and press it for him while he waited.

The place was in charge of a large German woman called Frau Tannenbaum. She greeted each customer with two questions:

"Vut you vant? How qvick you vant it?"

He gave his order. She ran him a scalding bath and waited till he climbed into it before snatching up his clothes. She promised to have them back in twenty minutes, wrapped for carrying, price twenty-five cents. The bath was another nickel, including soap and use of a razor. She went off holding his suit and underwear at arm's length.

The bath soon robbed him of his aches and pains and great ripe aroma. He whistled and sang a bit as he shaved—"The Bard of Armagh" and "Kathleen Mavourneen"—and then caught forty winks, soaking in the tub. He gave himself a good rough toweling off and dressed in his spare outfit. His cap showed some wear and tear, but the rest of him was close to Pullman standards. He left a nickel tip to show his satisfaction.

He arrived back upstairs weak from hunger. There was a small lunchroom on the mezzanine overlooking the splendid marble-decorated passengers' gallery. He sat down to the counter and obtained a quick meal: roast chicken, side dishes of sweet potatoes and beets, a basket of corn muffins, and all the coffee he could drink. He took his meal to the accompaniment of the *Omaha Sunday World-Herald*, which a previous customer had left behind. On the front page was a picture of Colonel Antrobus's friend Black Jack Pershing, under the heading FORMER LINCOLN MAN IN COMMAND. The caption said:

Brigadier General John J. Pershing, former commandant of cadets at the University of Nebraska and brother of Mrs. D. M. Butler and Miss May Pershing of Lincoln, will be in command of the punitive expedition into Mexico.

Cassie tore out the picture and folded it and put it inside his tunic to give later to the colonel, who likely would not see it otherwise. Most of the front page was given over to items on the war:

U.S. SOLDIERS READY FOR MEXICAN EXPEDITION

FUNSTON SECRETLY MOVES U.S. TROOPS ALONG BORDER

REGIMENTAL BANDS PLAY AS MEN WAIT
ORDER FOR CHASE

Columbus, N.M., March 11—Troopers of the Thirteenth Cavalry, which beat off Villa's raid on Columbus Thursday, were fully prepared today to move into Mexico at a moment's notice, and men and officers chafed at the delay in orders to begin a chase of the Mexican insurgent chief.

HAND VILLA TO CARRANZA
FOR PUNISHMENT, SAYS TAFT

Glens Falls, N.Y., March 11—"If I had my way, I would not try to bring Villa under the protection of the United States, but I would turn him over to Carranza, who would know how to deal with him," declared former President Taft at the first annual dinner of the Glens Falls Chamber of Commerce this afternoon.

It seemed the whole country was up in arms over Villa's treacherous raid. Cassie pondered the matter. Perhaps he had been too quick to think bad thoughts of the colonel over the business of the dying horses. Maybe war would not wait.

He paid up and took his leave. The meal cost him fifteen cents. He went downstairs to the offices of the Pullman Company. A weary clerk in eyeshade and suspenders sat outside the door to the super's office. On seeing Cassie, the fellow jumped to his feet. "You wouldn't be—*McGill?*"

"That's it, McGill," Cassie replied. "I was wondering if Mr. Liberty—"

"Hush up, boy! Prepare to meet thy maker!"

"Sir?"

"Through that door, boy! It's Mr. Cosgrove hisself who's waitin'—and remove that cap if yo're hopin' to collect yer last pay envelope on this road!"

Mr. Laurence Cosgrove. General Superintendent for the West. Cassie's scalp tightened at the idea. He smoothed his hair down a bit—it was still wet around the fringes from his lying too low in the tub—and opened the door.

"Mr. Cosgrove, sir? I'm Cassius McGill, off *No. 3.* I was hoping to find Mr. Liberty, only the fellow outside—"

"Glory be to heaven! The wonder boy of the railroad! So he's shined at last!"

"Sir?"

"Sit down, McGill, 'fore I *knock* you down! I have cherished the idea of this meeting for some hours now!"

Clutching his cap to his bosom, Cassie settled himself into a leather armchair.

"Oh, isn't this splendid! All by his lonesome he's decided to put in an appearance, while we've got half the Division out making a search of the yards!"

Mr. Laurence Cosgrove, with dozens of agents like Mr. Hebb under his thumb, was a man of formidable bearing and manner. He dressed like a deacon and sat a desk bigger than that of the President of the United States. His face, sharp-chiseled and brightly colored, bespoke a man of great powers, which he possessed in full measure. This was Mr. A. O. Austin one better. This was the difference between city, Omaha, and town, Lincoln.

Mr. Cosgrove took a deep breath and lowered his voice. "I won't waste time inquiring as to your whereabouts."

"Been getting a bath, sir."

"Don't *interrupt*, boy! Haven't you a proper coat?"

Uncle Chet's mackinaw looked rough for the great metropolis of Omaha. "Had mine stolen, sir, to tell the truth."

"Never mind. Let me see your hands."

"Sir?"

"Don't be dense, boy! Remove your mittens!"

Cassie pulled off Uncle Joe's fur-lined gloves.

"Umph. Fingernails will pass." The general superintendent referred to his timepiece, gold with diamonds in the face. "It is now ten minutes past ten. You are to clear the yards not later than eleven o'clock."

Cassie reached for his own Special Railway Model, forgetting for an instant the smashed crystal, the hands turned lifeless by Jacko Mudd's boys. "Eleven o'clock, yes, sir." Cassie squirmed in his chair. "That'll be cutting it close, sir, but I expect we can make it."

"See that you do!"

"Anyway, sir, I expect the livestock cars are already switched in by now. Mr. Liberty will have seen to it."

"Livestock cars?" Mr. Cosgrove spoke as though he had never heard the words before.

"For the horses, sir? Oh gosh, I sure hope my message got through!"

Mr. Cosgrove rose. Cassie started to follow, but the general superintendent knocked him back with a heavy hand. "My, yes, we are in receipt of your message, McGill. We have given it close study, you may be assured. And we have determined that you will proceed on to the border *with precisely those cars which are presently at your disposal.*"

"But, sir—"

"Understand me, McGill. You are acting conductor on *Pullman's No. 3* —you are *not* president of the road! The number and nature of cars required for this charter are not your concern. You will make do, McGill, with the equipment provided. Do you take my meaning, sir?"

"Yes, sir. Only it seemed to me, sir—"

"*Enough!* Let me give you some sound advice, boy. If you value your position with this company, I would advise you to mind your P's and Q's and not interfere in business that doesn't concern you. You are a well-intentioned young man, I have no doubt of it. But selection of equipment is not in your bailiwick. Our customer has willingly accepted the equipment presently available, and I see no need to delay this customer, do you, when considerations of war and peace are at issue? No, I should think not."

Cassie sat in silence.

"As for Mr. Liberty," continued the general superintendent, "Mr. Liberty remains incapacitated. He is ailing and not expected to report for duty again this month. He suffers the gout, truth be told, and cannot walk. Therefore, McGill, *you* will continue on as master of *No. 3*."

Involuntarily, Cassie rose from his seat. Immediately sat back down again.

"Well, boy, can you handle it?"

Again Cassie's reflexes, not his brain, went to the fore. "Yes, sir. I believe I can." He likened himself to the reliever who was sent in, bottom of the ninth, to get out Wagner or Cobb or Daubert and thus nail down the victory. He knew he could do it, and only waited his chance.

"'*Course* you can," said the general superintendent, smiling for the first time. "Let us get down to business, shall we?"

Cassie pulled out his train book and prepared to write.

"For your crews, we have succeeded in obtaining the services of two very fine engineers, senior men both, Dandy Bob Biddle off the Chicago & Western and J. L. Edwards off the Central Indiana. They'll take you as far as Lawrence, Kansas."

Cassie wrote down the names. But his mind was still on dead horses. "Sir, about the livestock cars—"

Mr. Cosgrove discarded his smile slowly and laboriously, the way a snake sheds its skin. "Mention livestock cars—mention *horses* again, McGill—and you will get the sack this very night."

"No, sir," Cassie said. "Yes, sir," he corrected.

"The world is running over with horses, boy. Horses are cheap as dirt. Let your concern be for your passengers, and for one passenger in particular."

"Sir?"

"You are familiar, I presume, with the name Otis Webster?"

Cassie thought hard. "No, sir, can't say as I am."

"Astonishing! Perhaps you don't read the newspapers. Mr. Otis Webster is president of Webster's Machine Lubricant Company of Chicago and Webster's Mining and Mineral of Denver, among other enterprises. He is a close personal friend to Mr. Lincoln, and he held the same relationship to the late Mr. Pullman. He is a millionaire and a gentleman of the greatest importance. His every wish is to be taken by you as a *command.*

"Mr. Webster has today chartered the fairest creation of our shops at Chicago. I refer to *The Mother Lode.* Have you carried her before?"

"No, sir, sure haven't."

"Well, you soon will. She is at this moment being added to your first section."

Cassie wrote again in his book. A private car added to a war train. It seemed a strange business—or perhaps it was a strange kind of war they were steaming toward.

"Let me see your order of makeup," Mr. Cosgrove demanded.

Cassie produced the desired document from his book.

"*The Mother Lode* will be tied on here—behind the flats and ahead of the DR&S. Mr. Webster will wish to consult with the Army commander from time to time, and this location is most convenient. Be aware that Mr. Webster has contracted to provide motorized transport to the Army. This equipment is now being loaded aboard four flats—they will be added to the second section. You are to carry Mr. Webster and his party to the Fort Bliss siding at El Paso. Should Mr. Webster require transport elsewhere, you will arrange that, too, through MacAdoo, our agent on the border. Here, take these and add them to your book." Mr. Cosgrove turned over to Cassie a pile of dispatch slips and freight manifests and the names and call letters of all Pullman agents along the right-of-way as far as Mexico. "Whatever Mr. Webster requires, you are to provide. He is one of the Pullman Company's most valued and best-satisfied customers. We intend that he should remain so. Do you *understand?*"

"Yes, sir."

"Kindly bear in mind that Mr. Webster is also a close personal friend to Newton D. Baker, former mayor of Cleveland and now secretary of war. Mr. Baker himself will no doubt request a full report from Mr. Webster as to the Pullman Company's assistance in the war effort. We intend that his report shall be favorable—*highly* favorable. You *do* understand?"

"Oh, yes sir, I do."

"Mr. Webster's wife is herself of prominent eastern family. Their daughter, Candace, has recently returned from finishing school in Switzerland. She, too, is most charming but of delicate constitution. Her health may well demand special attention from yourself and your porters.

"Hear me well, McGill. Your appointment to this run constitutes an exceptional opportunity for an ambitious young man. Perform your duties with diligence and dispatch and who's to say what exceptional benefits you may reap from a grateful Company? But I can promise you this: perform to *less* than complete satisfaction and your career with the Company will meet a quick end. Now you may go."

Cassie stood.

"I shall be trackside shortly to introduce you to Mr. Webster."

"Thank you, sir."

"Conduct yourself with dignity. Never mumble. Remove your cap, speak distinctly, and *jump*, boy, when the customer gives an order."

Mr. Cosgrove extended a generous hand in Cassie's direction. Cassie wrestled off the glove he had just put on and gave back a firm handshake.

"I envy you, McGill. Ah, to be witness to hostilities!"

"Yes, sir. Thank you, sir. I'll do my best, sir."

"The Company is counting on you, boy. You *shan't* let us down."

But it seemed to Cassie that Mr. Cosgrove's penetrating blue eyes mirrored certain misgivings, certain doubts. Cassie removed himself from Mr. Cosgrove's presence. So this was "dancing on the carpet" before the General Superintendent of the West. What a great pleasure, sir!

A foreign voice echoed across the broad reaches of the waiting room: "*Vell! Don't chew vant dis?*"

It was Frau Tannenbaum from the Immigrants Room. She carried the package containing his freshly cleaned outfit. He had left it in the dressing room.

Poor simpleton, he called himself under his breath. He offered another nickel tip, but Frau Tannenbaum refused it. She watched him go, a doubtful look on her broad German face. She obviously held the same misgivings about him that Mr. Cosgrove did.

Cassie found *Pullman's No. 3* moved to Track 6, where there was a proper platform. The horses had already been ramped up; many of the troopers were fast asleep.

Cassie went down the line to check on the new cars that had been switched in. He was not alone. Colonel Antrobus and Captain Bowles and Lieutenant Van Impe were there ahead of him, studying the new engines of war.

There were eight of the olive-colored Jeffrey "quads," two to a flatcar. They resembled overgrown delivery wagons and were self-propelled by gasoline engine. The Army called them quads because all four wheels were driven by the engine, not just two, as in automobiles. They stood high off the ground atop massive leaf springs and offered a single leather-upholstered bench for the driver and his relief. The steering wheel was a yard in diameter and horizontal to the floorboards so the driver could get a strong grip on it. A canvas top and side curtains kept out the rain. The wheels were spokeless iron disks with solid rubber tires; lengths of chain had been added to improve traction in desert sands. There were no running lights. Instead, a large acetylene spotlight was fixed to the firewall, to be aimed by the relief driver.

No Mexican bandit was likely to stand up to such modern vehicles, in Cassie's opinion. He had read about them in *Scribner's Weekly*. Each quad was capable of carrying three times the load of any horse wagon and doing so at thirty miles an hour, up hill and down. They cost over eight thousand dollars apiece and would be used to chase Villa deep into Chihuahua, if it came to that. However, most troopers believed that Villa would be strung up to a telegraph pole long before the first gasoline engine was fired up in the desert.

Colonel Antrobus soon noticed Cassie's interest in the quads. "Well now, Cassius, what do you think of the mighty Jeffreys?"

"They look mean, sir. And mighty quick!"

The colonel turned to the round-faced southerner, Captain Bowles. "You hear that, Lonnie? Spokesman for the new generation is our Mr. McGill. He holds the modern opinion, no doubt, that horses may soon be dispensed with—sent out to pasture in favor of such as these. May I never see the day!"

"I do believe the boy's gotten to the heart of the mattah, suh," replied the captain. "Mean an' quick! P'raps you'd be taking a ride yourself in one o' these beauties when we reach the border, eh, Mistah McGill?"

"Can't say I'd mind it, sir!"

"Well now, count on it, you hear?"

"I shall, sir!"

But Lieutenant Van Impe would not let it rest at that. "The captain's only making a joke, McGill. No civilians allowed in government vehicles."

The colonel soon took his officers off toward Headquarters Car. Cassie followed along at a safe distance, hoping to have himself a good look at the private Pullman, *The Mother Lode,* which was now coupled on ahead of the officers' snoozer. He was in luck. The private party had not come aboard yet, and Nelson, who had once served in the car himself, was there to show Cassie around.

She was some Pullman! Cassie had never seen anything to equal her. She was a palace on wheels, all right. No, she was greater than that: she was Queen of the Rails, being eighty feet in length, fourteen feet high, and ten feet wide at the eaves. The beauty of her outside finish—fine inlaid woods trimmed in gold and varnished against the elements—argued loudly against removing her from the safety of the train shed. According to Nelson, she had cost $50,000 to build in '06. She looked every penny of it. It would be an honor for any porter to serve in her—for any loco-motive to *pull* her.

The central portion of the car was devoted to six private compartments opening off a long passageway finished in glossy Mexican mahogany. Each compartment offered a separate toilet room, commodious wardrobe, floor-to-ceiling mirror, and built-in chiffonier. The toilet rooms boasted onyx washstands, bronze light fixtures, and tiled floors with wainscoting. The double-sized master suite contained a stationary brass bedstead with space below for a steamer trunk. There was even a cast-iron bath-tub with roll rim and claw feet. A person might travel for months at a time in such a suite and never know deprivation. There were endless supplies of coal-fired hot water and steam heat. An array of cooling fans in the ceiling supplied comfort in summer. Both electric and Pintsch-gas lighting were available, depending on the circumstances of travel.

At the rear of *The Mother Lode* came the parlor and, beyond that— separated by sliding glass partitions etched with scenes of the California gold rush—the observation room. The parlor also served as dining room; an extension table sat a dozen guests with ease. There were large bay windows on both sides, a variety of sofas and settees, a writing desk and secretary, tables for playing cards and dominoes and checkers, a pump organ, and a Victor Talking Machine. Several dozen disks were provided for the "Victrola."

The observation room was decorated in East Indian style with white wicker chairs, rattan davenports, and vivid paintings of elephant-borne hunters stalking wary tigers through dense Indian grass. An elegant buffet, its legs carved to resemble bamboo logs, stood ready to serve sandwiches and other delicacies for travelers who might fancy a light re-past between meals. A library of some five hundred volumes provided food for thought. The observation room was also the smoker, where considerate gentlemen could retire with their cigars after dinner so as not to disturb the ladies.

The Mother Lode fed her guests from her own kitchen, situated at the front end of the car, complete with gas stove and ovens, electric refrig-erator, walk-in food locker, spacious pantry, three sinks, and private toilet room for the staff. When a customer chartered such a Pullman, he obtained everything he might require for his comfort at mealtime—Havi-land chinaware of special design, cut glassware and elegant silver service handwrought in Europe to Pullman's order, Irish linen, a great supply of comestibles, the very kitchen pots themselves, plus the services of a chef, a cook, and a wash-up boy. The kitchen crew had already come aboard. The chef was short, round, and dressed all in white—trousers, jacket, apron, cook's high hat, kerchief knotted at the neck—except for his shoes, which were black and pointed. His name was Hans Kolb and he spoke no better English than Frau Tannenbaum:

"*Gut effenen, Kapitan! Velkum to 'Die Mutter Lodt'!*"

Cassie could imagine the fun Rocks would have with Chef Kolb's accent. The cook was a Negro called John, as cheerful and black as any African Cassie had yet met. The wash-up boy was an old Chinaman called Ling Hee. At Nelson's suggestion, Cassie offered Chef Kolb a bunk in the first-section van, but the German declined, saying he would prefer to stay close to his larder. Accommodations for the kitchen crew were provided in the form of pull-down berths in the pantry.

Cassie watched as the victuals were stored away. These included beef and venison steaks, turkeys for roasting, spring lamb, chickens and squabs and guinea hens, sacks of potatoes, all manner of fruits and green vegetables, a mess of fresh-caught lake trout on ice, two kinds of oysters, half a smoked salmon, and three earthenware jugs of heavy cream. There were so many cases of wine and spirits that the lockers would not hold them all. The surplus was stored away in a spare compartment not required for Mr. Webster's party; Chief Kolb called this his *Weinkabinett*.

Such luxury did not come cheap. Cassie figured *The Mother Lode* would be costing Mr. Otis Webster maybe $100 a day plus fifteen first-class fares for the roads traveled, fifteen fares being the usual minimum charged by railroads west of Chicago. His bill at the end could be $3,000 or more—a true fortune! Still, from what Mr. Cosgrove had said, such an amount was unlikely to disturb the millionaire.

"Ho there, McGill! Step lively, son!"

Mr. Cosgrove's brass-lined voice resounded along the platform. The general superintendent seemed less comfortable out of his lair. He was better suited to the comforts of a Pullman office than to the soot and grime of the train shed. He remained quite at home with customers, however.

". . . Mr. and Mrs. Webster, may I present your conductor, Cassius McGill. He is the young man I mentioned. Mr. McGill will be at your service throughout the journey. Don't hesitate to call upon him at any hour of day or night. . . ."

Cassie removed his cap and bowed in respect.

"You are too kind, Larry," said the millionaire. "I am sure Mr. McGill will prove most helpful. . . ."

The general superintendent stuffed a sheet of paper into Cassie's gloved hand. It gave the compartment assignments for *The Mother Lode,* together with Mr. Cosgrove's identification of each passenger:

Master Suite	Otis Webster, Esq., Founder & Pres. of Various Enter-prises; Industrialist & Millionaire; his wife, Lydia
Pvt. Rm. A	Miss Candace, Their Daughter
" B	Mlle Camille Foix, Companion to Miss Candace
" C	Father Paul X. Tibbett, Spiritual Adviser to Mrs. Webster
" D	Christian, Negro, Manservant to Mr. Webster; Mae, Negress, Wife to Christian, Maid to Mrs. Webster
" E	(unoccupied)

The Webster party had arrived by horse carriage, four vehicles being required to handle them and their baggage. The way they dressed and carried themselves made Cassie think of newspaper photographs of the first-class passengers on the Cunard Line's docks at Southampton before the *Titanic* sailed. The millionaire was tall, stout, and gray-haired. At a distance, he might have passed for the former President, Mr. Taft. He wore a Prince Albert frock coat and sported a beard made famous by the same gentleman. Mrs. Webster was a matron lady dressed all in black, plump as to figure, stern of aspect. Together the Websters made a formidable pair—fussy in their wants, Cassie expected, and about as dangerous to the plain workingman as aces dealt straight up.

Behind the Websters came the two Negroes, a respectable couple in middle age. After them, arm in arm, the French lady, Mademoiselle Foix, and the priest, Father Tibbett. The lady might have been thought pretty by some; she was thirtyish and proud of herself. She was not to Cassie's taste. The priest showed a rosy complexion, jowls that lapped over his collar, and a tiny bow mouth that was deeper pink than the lady's. He seemed fat under his gown and made Cassie think of an overripe peach, with the same fuzz to his cheeks. He was no Jesuit; Cassie would bet on that.

Finally, the whole pack was trailed by the solitary daughter. *Oh, such a daughter!*

"Come, McGill—see to the baggage."

"Yes, sir, Mr. Cosgrove—right away, sir!"

Nelson and Milo and Tobias bent to the task without Cassie's having to say a word. Suitcases began to fly. Cassie grabbed up the biggest case for himself, leather with solid brass hardware. It bore Mr. Webster's initials, so Cassie hauled it up into the master suite. This was not properly conductor's work except at small country stations where porters were lazy or lacking. But in Mr. Cosgrove's presence, Cassie would not stand on ceremony. He returned to the platform in time to hear Mr. Cosgrove say:

". . . He's an honest and reliable lad and may be counted upon to remedy any insufficiency with authority quite beyond his years. . . ."

"We travel Pullman in complete confidence, Larry, as always."

"And so you should. But now you will be weary after your arduous journey from Denver. Perhaps a hot drink before bed? Simply let McGill or one of the porters know your pleasure. . . . Come, I shall see you to your suite. . . ."

The general superintendent accompanied Mr. and Mrs. Webster inside *The Mother Lode.*

"*Well,* boy? Must I carry my own bags?"

Miss Candace Webster!

"Oh, no, ma'am! Excuse me, ma'am! Let me help, ma'am!"

Her golden hair, parted in the middle, streamed down her back like the finest silk. Almond-shaped eyes of hazel brown, lips soft and full, ears small and close to her head—the lobes adorned by delicate pearls. Cheeks naturally pink, nose straight with aristocratic furled nostrils, neck slender and creamy like an alabaster statue. Her fingers were buried in a fur muff. She could not have weighed a hundred pounds and was tall for a girl. Her skin was perfection—she might have been Irish despite her high birth and rich family. She was a true beauty.

". . . Well, porter, are you *asleep?*"

He awoke, staring. "Oh, no, ma'am, I'm not asleep! Excuse me, ma'am, I'm not the porter, but the conductor."

She gave a sudden high laugh. "*Conductor?* Are you now?"

"Yes, ma'am. But I'm pleased to get your bags all the same."

"Come along, then, Mr. Conductor. I'm beginning to take a chill."

"Maybe you'd like a hot drink, ma'am?" he asked, parroting Mr. Cosgrove's offer to her father.

"Ovaltine," she replied instantly. "Made with cream, please."

She had two large cases, leather like her father's, a half-dozen hat boxes, a smaller case like a carpetbag, and a steamer trunk. Cassie borrowed a handcart from Nelson and loaded it up. Nelson offered to take on the work, but Cassie preferred to do it himself.

"If you'll follow me, please, ma'am . . ."

He pushed the cart to the rear steps, then lugged the two large cases up through the observation room and parlor and down the corridor leading to the bedrooms. She stayed close behind, taking small rapid steps in her ankle-length traveling gown. He slowed often so she would not have to hurry. The bags almost tore his arms from their sockets. She was apparently planning an extended journey, judging from the weight of her cases.

He found her compartment by referring to Mr. Cosgrove's paper. "It's right here, ma'am." He slid open the door and allowed her to enter ahead of him. Her room was as luxuriously furnished as the master suite.

Though smaller, it provided two berths—the porters had already made up the lower—as well as armchairs, dresser, and wardrobe. A row of crystal vases filled with fresh-cut flowers decorated the window ledge. He made a note to ensure that those vases never wanted for fresh blossoms. "One more load should do it!" he told her.

She did not bother to acknowledge his announcement. He ran out the way he came and grabbed up as many hat boxes as he could. He instructed the Negro boys Milo and Tobias to follow him with the trunk and carpetbag. "Hurry!" he said impatiently. "Mustn't keep the lady waiting!"

He had the boys stack everything in the corridor. He would see to final delivery himself. "Got it all!" he said to her proudly.

Still she said nothing. He dragged the bags in. The trunk occupied a sliding shelf beneath the lower berth. He showed her how the device worked.

"I'm sure I can manage," she said.

She was no more than sixteen or seventeen, he judged. While he was out getting the bags, she had taken off her furs. He could now admire her flower-print dress, blue and white with a million folds to its cut. Her figure was as slim and delicate as he had imagined, yet womanly, and she carried herself with fineness and grace, ladylike in her every gesture.

"Well, that's the lot, ma'am!"

"Thank you," she said. She met him head on with a one-dollar bill.

"Oh, no, ma'am!" he said, backing away. He hated the idea that she had offered him money.

"Then divide it as you think best among the Negroes," she said.

"Yes, ma'am!" He folded the bill and slid it into a vest pocket.

"I shan't need anything else tonight."

"No, ma'am.'

"I take my breakfast at eleven o'clock."

"Yes, ma'am."

"And you won't forget my Ovaltine?"

"Oh, no, ma'am!"

"What is your name?"

"McGill, ma'am. Cassius McGill."

"*Cassius?* My, how very classical."

His face burned with embarrassment.

"Won't you be needing this?" She offered him his cap, which he had left on one of the chairs.

"Sorry, ma'am. Thank you, ma'am."

She closed the door after him. He stumbled down the corridor, put his cap on, took it off again, finally found his way out to the platform.

Snow had begun to fall again; the cold night air made him realize how flushed his face was. He went looking for Nelson, but found Lieutenant Van Impe instead.

"So there you are, McGill. How soon do we depart?"

"Any time now, sir."

"The quicker the better. Meanwhile, which compartment is Miss Webster's?"

Cassie returned with the officer to *The Mother Lode* and pointed to her window. "That one there, sir."

"Be on your way, then."

"Yes, sir, just going."

He went off, red-faced and short of breath. He could imagine Pa's words on the subject:

"We're talking here about two kinds o' uniforms, and the West Pointer's is sure to win the day every time."

Cassie gave Nelson Miss Webster's dollar bill and asked the porter to fix her Ovaltine and take it to her. Then he went forward and introduced himself to Dandy Bob Biddle in No. 506. "Got up steam, have you, Mr. Biddle?"

Dandy Bob gave him a sour look. "So what do you suppose that white stuff is that's leakin' out o' this teakettle?"

Cassie took it that Mr. Biddle was called "Dandy Bob" on account of his clean seersucker trousers and well-manicured fingernails. His sarcastic manner did not suit him, in Cassie's opinion. "Watch for my signal," Cassie replied sharply.

He made for No. 799, passing slowly by the window of Miss Webster's compartment. She sat in one of the armchairs and smiled brightly, laughing from time to time at Van Impe's remarks. The lieutenant stood over her, hand on hip, proud in his fancy tunic and Sam Browne belt.

Cassie stuck his hands into his pockets and kept on moving. By the time he put his nose into the cab of No. 799, it was nearly eleven thirty. They had already missed Mr. Cosgrove's deadline by half an hour. "You got up steam, Mr. Edwards?"

J. L. Edwards, thin and sickly, with cauliflower ears that stuck out from under his engineer's cap, looked to his pressure gauge. "Short thirty pounds, son. Ten minutes more should do it."

"We'll head out on your whistle," Cassie told him.

The ailing hogger called across to his fireman: "Hear that, Ollie? Bend to it, boy—got the whole damn load waitin' on us. . . ."

Cassie went back to the van. Rocks had stayed awake to see him. "Forgot your soft-boiled," Cassie confessed.

"Don't matter none," Rocks said. "Ol' Nelson stole me some fine bean soup left over from the colonel's supper. Listen to me—already fartin' like 'crackers on the Fourth!'"

"We're off in ten minutes," Cassie said.

"So whatcha been up to?" the shortstop asked him.

Cassie told about the private party, and about Miss Candace.

"So what's she like then? Put lead in yer pencil, dint she? Even a blind man can see it!"

Cassie was sorry he had spoken of her. "She's a lady, is all. Beautiful to a fair degree."

Rocks, who had been lying flat on his bunk, came up to one elbow. "An' she went fer ya, I 'magine."

"Oh, she did that," Cassie replied.

Rocks went on pestering him. "So she'll be droppin' her bloomers fer ya, s'pose?"

"That's for sure. Any time I ask."

"By God, Cass, I'm *pleased* fer ya!"

"Moron!"

"So what's yer trouble then?"

"She—she's different from us."

"O' course—she's got tits, don't she!"

Cassie held his temper. "I've got work to do," he said, flipping through the pages of his train book. "Mr. Liberty's taken sick. We'll not see another master on this run."

Rocks showed no surprise. "Nelson knowed it all along."

"What?" said Cassie.

"Knowed yer ol' geezer wasn't gonna show his face. It's cause o' no tips, o' course."

"What about tips?" Cassie didn't mention the dollar that had already come his way.

"Ain't no tips to be had from them soldier boys. That's how come none o' the reg'lars is gonna take this ride."

"Nelson told you that?"

"Sure did. Hell, Professor, this trip ain't no prize fer the league champeenship, now is it!"

Damnation! So that was it. Just the faintest suspicion of it had already crept into Cassie's brain. It was a general rule of the Company that conductors on overnight runs got ten percent off the top of the porters' tips, but there would be no pool to share when your customer was the War Department of the United States of America. No old-timer like Mr. Liberty was going to shine for a trainload of horse soldiers when there were plenty of good runs to be had to Chicago and Kansas City and St. Louis. For a run like this, the Company needed a true sucker—and that's what Mr. Cosgrove had got himself.

The whistle from No. 799 sounded its mournful tune.

"Here we go then," Cassie announced for the benefit of the other train-men in the van. He yanked on the pull cord, and seconds later they could hear the distant clank of the couplers as No. 506 took up slack. Cassie leaned off the back steps and gave his "*All a-boarrrrrrrrrrrrrd!*" long and loud, realizing for the first time that *Pullman's No. 3* was nobody's train but Captain Cassie McGill's.

5

CASSIE SETTLED into the angel's seat. This was the part of railroading he liked best, riding alone at night, the world outside asleep and only his train roaring through the dark, sounding its whistle now and again, pounding the rails, doing its business while others slept. There was no greater pleasure than a smooth ride with all signals green and only the whispering wind to keep a body company. But not this night. Thoughts of the still-suffering animals, the Rapid City stowaways out back, Ma's lost rosary—and now Miss Candace Webster, with damned Van Impe sniffing at her skirts—conspired to weigh him down.

He got out *Busby's* and studied the maps. They had come 578 miles from Fort Meade and would cover 1,137 more before touching the border. They were headed due south along the west bank of the Missouri. They faced heavier traffic now; their pace slowed. Dandy Bob Biddle and J. L. Edwards could coax no more speed from the laboring Baldwins than the other crews had—less even, because of the extra cars they were now hauling. No. 506 had twenty in tow; No. 799 pulled seventeen including the four heavy flats bearing the Jeffrey quads.

Cassie calculated the day's coaling stops. According to his figures, they would reach Hiawatha, the first town in Kansas, at 7:30 A.M. or thereabouts. This seemed as good a place as any to detrain the animals and give the men breakfast, assuming Van Impe approved. Cassie put his estimates in a note and sent it forward to Headquarters Car in the hands of the porter Tobias. "If there's no light showing, slip it under the lieutenant's door."

"Jes as you say, Cap'n!"

Tobias, as fat and sassy as any Pullman porter was permitted to be, returned promptly.

"Was he awake?" Cassie asked.

"Sho was, Cap'n!"

"Well, what did he say?"

Tobias gave a big smile, showing lots of gold in his mouth and reminding Cassie that a crafty porter could grow rich on tips. "Dint say nothin', Cap'n! Too busy rakin' in dem greenbacks!"

Cassie savored the knowledge that Van Impe was merely playing cards: Miss Candace would be safe asleep in her berth. The drawing room in Headquarters Car was perfectly suited to poker and other games of chance; the officers had started play immediately upon departure from Fort Meade. Only the colonel remained aloof. The troopers back in the day cars enjoyed similar pursuits. Sound sleep was not possible, so the soldiers filled up the long hours between meals by telling stories and playing cards for money. They had greenbacks enough from their last payday, some of them, to build some pretty fair pots. It reminded Cassie of serious locker room games in Columbus, Ohio, and Kokomo, Indiana, among other places. There had already been one nasty fight over a poker hand in the second section. Doc Rose had been sent for; he did some expert stitching. The officers were not told about it. It was the custom for troopers to settle their differences privately, without involving the brass collars. Differences of opinion among the enlisted men never went higher than Jacko Mudd. He would let two fellows go at it until one was cut; that ended it. These jungle fighters had a liking for the blade. They were anxious to start cutting up the Mex, so any cutting they did aboard the *Pancho Villa Express* was no more than practice for what lay ahead.

Cassie expected clear running into Hiawatha but was soon disappointed. At the next coaling stop, Auburn, still in Nebraska, a brakeman from the second section came to get him: "You'd best see the hogger in Seven-nine-nine, Cap'n! He's about as hot as his box!"

Cassie dropped back the short distance and climbed into the cab. J. L. Edwards was waiting for him. On another occasion, the hogger might have been taken for sweet-dispositioned and amiable. Now he had blood in his eye.

"Either you get me a proper crum-boss, sonny boy, or me and Ollie here is walkin'!"

The angry hogger shot a great wad of tobacco-laced spittle against the firebox door, producing a loud hiss and a puff of white smoke. His fireman went right on stuffing the box, his stubby arms working like levers on a machine. He was squat and muscle-bound and black as a Negro from coal dust and sweat. He wore his coveralls over nothing but skin; the remainder of his clothing he kept safe and clean in a nearby satchel.

Crum-boss was yet another name for conductor. "It's Nelson, the top porter, who's doing that job just now," Cassie said.

J. L. Edwards gave a contemptuous snort. "Ain't no nigger bossin' yers truly."

"Now look here—"

The hogger gathered up his greatcoat and dinner pail and made a pretense of shutting down. "There'll be a grievance filed over to the brotherhood, you can count on it!"

"We're a bit short up for crew, is all," said Cassie.

"Ain't *that* the truth!"

Cassie did not mind the hogger's threats so much as his manner. "On second thought," Cassie said, "we're not so shorthanded as all that. Stay put and mind your boiler. You'll have yourself a proper boss in two minutes flat."

Cassie ran back to the van and woke Rocks. "Get your boots on. You're going to work."

"Hey, Cass, what's got into ya? Yo're lookin' awful ornery and that's the truth!"

"Don't talk, *move*. Get your coat and follow me."

Rocks trailed along, keeping quiet for once. They marched back to the guardhouse at the tail end of the second section. The sentry on duty saw them coming and brought his Springfield to the ready.

"Hold it, misters! This here caboose is off limits to all but troopers."

"It's the sergeant major we've come to see," said Cassie.

"So it's *you*," said the trooper, recognizing Rocks. "Come back for more, have ya?"

Cassie remembered the trooper. He was one of those who had taken a hand in breaking Rocks's teeth. "Tell the sergeant major it's Conductor McGill who's come to see him."

"He ain't to be bothered," replied the trooper.

"It's orders from the colonel, tell him," said Cassie.

The trooper hesitated, then went inside. Rocks had a good laugh. "You just made yerself a friend fer life, Professor!"

The trooper returned at once, making way for Jacko Mudd. The sergeant major was still buttoning his jacket as he hit the trackbed.

"By God, it's young Cassius himself! And t'other fine lad, li'l Rocks! How's thet mouth o' yers, young fella? So it's to be orders from the colonel, is it?"

The sergeant major appeared to be nine parts drunk to one part sober. Cassie stated his proposition in slow, clear words. Either Rocks returned to duty as helper conductor in that caboose or else Cassie would report to the colonel in the matter of the hookers.

"*Hookers* is it!" Jacko Mudd roared like a great moose. "Damn it to hell, young Cassius, if you ain't the brainiest lad I come upon in a dog's age! Why, we'd be most honored to have li'l Rocks come back to our dear bosom! All grudges is forgot—fair 'nough? Only there's this one wee catch in it."

"What is it then?" Cassie asked.

"Simple as pie! Yer pal's to stick to his business, see? He's to keep his friggin' nose out o' what don't concern him. Fair 'nough?"

Cassie took Rocks aside. "You heard him. Can you swallow it?"

"Swallow it easy," Rocks whispered back. "The fellas are *fond* o' me, Cass—sure they are!"

"So fond they busted out your teeth?"

"That's just rough housin', Cass. Go on—say it's a bargain."

Cassie turned back to the sergeant major. "Anybody lays a finger on him and I'm back with the colonel."

"You're a hard one, young Cassius!" replied Jacko Mudd. "Why, hurtin' li'l Rocks here would be like hurtin' me own dear son. . . . Climb aboard, boy—there's whiskey inside to warm yer limbs."

"Come see me at every stop," Cassie warned Rocks.

"Bet on it, Professor!"

"And watch your gauge. Less than fifty pounds, you yank that cord, hear?"

But Rocks was already inside. Cassie stopped by No. 799 and told J. L. Edwards who his new crum-boss was to be. The hogger grunted in assent. Cassie did not take to Mr. J. L. Edwards and was sorry to see a good Negro like Nelson suffer on account of an ignorant hogger. He met Nelson trackside. The Negro had already put on the white serving jacket and black trousers of a porter. His career as a helper conductor had been brief, but he did not cry over it.

"Mistah Edwards, he's surely correc', Cap'n. I got no biness doin' white man's work."

"Anyhow," Cassie said, "I want you riding the first section with me. That private party takes more watching than I can give it."

"Thank you kindly, Cap'n. Only you'd best take this ol' timepiece o' mine—seems yours is on the blink."

Cassie borrowed the watch with gratitude. He liked Nelson a good deal, but naturally could not say it. "We'll board up, then," Cassie said. He called for steam. They began to roll.

They made Hiawatha in time for breakfast, as Cassie had predicted. Van Impe obtained the colonel's permission to detrain the animals. As soon as the last of the animals hit the ground—four more never to rise again—the troopers lined up trackside for hot coffee and porridge. Kansas was balmy after Nebraska—the temperature was something above freezing.

Cassie's job was to calculate arrival time at Fort Leavenworth and get that on the telegraph. Using Nelson's watch and the maps in *Busby's*, he decided on noon straight up. He wrote out his message and carried it over to the Hiawatha station.

"You off o' that rig out there?" the station boss said to him. He seemed a nosy, self-important kind of fellow.

"I sure am," said Cassie.

"What would you call a rig like that?"

"Why, sir, that's a war train. Maybe you heard of us—the *Pancho Villa Express?*"

"Oh, we heard o' you, all right," said the fellow. "Who ain't? Only we heard your business is horse meat. Ain't that so?"

Cassie made no reply. He pretended to be busy with his message, which was already honed to perfection.

"There's nary a stationmaster 'tween here and the border who ain't heard of you boys! I'd be much obliged, young'un, if you'd pick up and clear my station *muy pronto*, like the Mex say."

"We've got to run our horses," Cassie said primly. "It's the law."

"The law? Ain't the law got something to say 'bout litterin' the country-side with all them carcasses?"

"We're moving as quick as we can," Cassie said. He deposited his message and cleared out. Horses was one subject he preferred to skip.

Rocks was waiting for him in the van. The shortstop's face was twisted in pain. "I *seen* 'em, Cass. I *talked* to 'em. It ain't *Christian*, Cass. They'll die out there, sure 'nough!"

Rocks told his story. The Army carpenters had been at work in the rear van. They had erected partitions, making a pair of private apartments where two of the girls could work at a time. The third girl, being allowed to rest, was given the privacy of the curtained-off super's bunk. Sitting outside the two apartments was Jacko Mudd or Trooper Snivey or another of Mudd's private army of enlisted men, who collected the cash. Being generous fellows, they shared the loot fifty-fifty with the girls. A single visit of five minutes was two dollars cash, paid in advance, no IOUs accepted. There was no shortage of customers. The stowaways were plied with liquor to make them give in. Jacko Mudd had even offered Rocks a place in line. Rocks no longer had the two dollars that Cassie gave him at Sturgis, so the sergeant major let him go free. It seemed that once these troopers had punched out a fellow, they took him straight to their bosoms.

"That's the way it is, Cass, so help me God!"

Cassie pretended not to be bothered by the girls' fate. "What did you expect?" he said. "They're only hookers. They're not your steady girls."

"So what's that supposed to mean?"

Cassie related Doc Rose's story about hookers.

"You're *lyin'!*" cried Rocks.

"Ask Doc. Go ask him yourself, you don't believe me."

"So what if they are? No, Jolene *ain't!* Jolene's just a *babe,* Cass. She don't want no part of it. They stole her away, Cass—don't that count for *somethin'?*"

Cassie wriggled in discomfort. Rocks had a way of putting him in a corner. But they *had* to be chippies, Cassie figured; no respectable girl would ever leave home on her own.

"You'll sure like her, Cass, once you git to know her. She's a friendly little thing. Know what she was, Cass? Back there in Rapid City?"

"I couldn't guess."

"Manicurist in the barber shop of the Golden Prairie Hotel. Made a real good livin' at it, too. But you ain't heard the best part!"

"What's that?"

"She *knows* ya, Cass!"

"The devil she does."

"It's true! She lived down Hastings way when she was a wee kid and she 'members ya from when ya was pitchin' fer Blessed Sacrament. She'll be pleased to meet ya agin, Cass."

"There's little chance of it now."

"I'm talkin' 'bout when she gits loose."

"Gets loose, huh?"

"That's it, Cass! We *got* to do it—git Jolene and them others out o' there. I *promised* her, Cass. Me and Jolene, we hit it off real good. Maybe when this job's done, me and her can get back up Dakota way. Maybe I won't be goin' off to Mich'gan after all."

"How long did you have with her? Three minutes? Five? And now you're sweethearts."

Cassie shut up. Rocks, too, remained silent. Cassie was sorry for what he had said. After thinking a spell, he began again. "It's not something we could do by ourselves."

"How's that, Cass?"

"Set them free."

The shortstop's pained expression relaxed into a smile. "I *know'd* you'd be in on it!"

"We're no match for Mudd or Snivey or the rest."

"Ain't it the truth! So who's to help us then, Cass?"

"I'm thinking."

"How 'bout the Dutchman? He's all fer orders and reg'lations, ain't he? Sure he can't tolerate such goin's-on out back."

Cassie shook his head. He remembered his talk with Doc Rose. "The officers are most likely in on it—except the colonel."

"So how 'bout yer pal the colonel, then?"

Cassie rejected the notion. He could not picture himself talking to the colonel about hookers. Cassie had been chewing on Pa's advice: Read your Bible, be respectful of your elders, remember the teachings of the Brothers.

"Watcha thinkin', Cass?"

"I'm thinking there's a Father aboard."

Rocks's discolored jaw slacked open, took its time closing. The short-stop scratched his head, squinted, stuck a finger in one ear. "Gee—I *dunno*, Cass. I'm thinkin' that maybe this priest o' yers, considerin' his duties is mostly with them fancy ladies—"

"He's got *God* on his side, doesn't he?" said Cassie irritably. "Do you suppose Jacko Mudd's got God on his side? Or Snivey? Or the rest of that bunch?"

Rocks hung his head. "Maybe I'm thinkin'—maybe I'm thinkin' God ain't up to it neither, Cass. That's right—not even *God'd* have a chance against all them bastards!"

Cassie's own jaw dropped. "You know what that is, don't you? That's *blasphemy!*"

Rocks thought some more on what Cassie had said. Gradually his smile returned and his big sad eyes turned doglike in their admiration for Cassie's scheme. "Sure'n yo're seein' it right, Professor! It's the Father or nobody. That's 'cause you got more faith'n me, Cass. Things ain't so clear back here on the grass where I'm playin' compared to up there on the mound where yo're at. You spent yer whole life riflin' the pill straight down the pipe, while me—I'm jus' prayin' I can git the ball to second base in time to start the double play. . . . *Sure* you got more faith'n me. Yo're battin' a thousand or close to it. Me? I'm sweatin' out ever' day jus' hopin' not to get sent down afore the Fourth o' July!"

As soon as they cleared the Hiawatha town line, Cassie worked his way forward to *The Mother Lode*. Entering through the Pullman's front vestibule, he suddenly found himself cornered by a raging beast. "Easy, boy! That's a good fella!"

The dog was smaller than some, but it growled ferociously and showed a jawful of strong yellow fangs. It was cinnamon in color with thick fur, large paws, a broad snout, and a blue-black tongue. It wore a heavy leather shoulder harness studded in brass and dragged a thick steel chain after it.

"Ho, now, Mushy!" came a welcome voice. "You sit!"

It was Mr. Webster's manservant, Christian. Six feet tall and stately of manner, the Negro wore striped trousers and a black coat with tails. He took hold of the chain and pulled the dog away. "Don't you be scared, Cap'n. Mushy here's friendly enough once he knows a body."

"It seems a fine dog," Cassie said. Nothing like Cassie's dog Flag, it appeared mean-tempered and sly. The dog lowered its hindquarters and sat panting, eyes still fixed on Cassie, black mouth dripping saliva.

Christian explained that it was Chinese and called a chow chow. Mr.

Webster had brought it back with him from a voyage to the Orient. The millionaire was a close friend to the Manchus; Mushy had been a gift of the dowager empress of China herself. The animal had come aboard *The Mother Lode* in a special crate. The porter who carried it thought Mushy to be a baby lion. It might just as well have been, Cassie figured, for all he cared to know of it.

"It's the Father I've come to see," said Cassie. "Would he be up and around, do you suppose?"

"If you'll come with me, Cap'n."

Cassie followed along. Nose-twitching smells drifted from the kitchen: fresh baked bread and the tang of bacon frying.

Christian chained the dog inside the pantry, then led Cassie down the long corridor toward the parlor. "If you'll wait here, sir."

Cassie was uncomfortable. What if Miss Candace should appear? Not likely, he decided; it was hardly nine o'clock. Young ladies fresh from finishing school didn't show themselves till noon, he imagined. He removed his cap and slicked down his cowlick anyway.

The Negro returned. "You may go in, sir."

Cassie entered—and instantly wished he could retreat. The three men at table looked up from their plates: Mr. Webster, Colonel Antrobus, Father Tibbett.

The priest was slow to speak; his mouth had been full of food when Cassie entered. Without bothering to stand, he extended a plump hand, which Cassie reluctantly shook. "And how may I be of service, my son?"

The priest went on eating from a saucer of boiled eggs. Cassie put his age at thirty or thereabouts. It was hard to tell about Fathers, so little of them showed beyond their cassocks. This Father was nothing at all like Father Terwiliger. This one had the soft cheeks of a fellow still in his teens, but he looked weary. He slouched forward with his elbows on the table and his round pink chin barely an inch off his saucer. This settled it: the Father was no Jesuit.

"*Well*, my son? You may speak freely."

Cassie opened his mouth but the words would not come out.

The colonel showed concern. "Perhaps it is a private matter?"

"A matter of religion?" asked Mr. Webster.

Finally Cassie spoke. "Not exactly, sir. But close enough." He blushed at his own ignorance and lack of manners.

"Well then," said Father Tibbett, his voice showing some annoyance, "after breakfast, have Christian show you to my compartment."

"Thank you, Father."

The millionaire, stout as a walrus, bent his great head toward the colonel and spoke privately. Cassie took alarm. He had the uncomfortable feeling they were talking about him. "I'll just be going then," he said, backing away.

"One moment," said the colonel. "You have joined us at an opportune moment."

"Sir?"

"Christian, a chair for the young man," said Mr. Webster. "And fix him a proper plate. . . . You can do with some flesh on those long bones of yours, young man. Sit down."

Cassie sat. He had observed the spread when he entered. There was sausage and ham and beefsteak, eggs both fried and boiled, creamed potatoes, small grilled fishes, bread and butter, various cheeses, tinned fruits, and a silver samovar of coffee. In any other company, Cassie might have eaten himself sick on such a spread.

"Young Cassius," remarked the colonel to the others, "has attained the rank of conductor at the still tender age of—eighteen, nineteen, is it, Cassius?"

"Eighteen, sir. Thank you, sir."

"A lad of ambition and spunk," said the millionaire.

The Negro came forward in easy gliding steps and presented Cassie's plate. It must have weighed two pounds.

"Ah, to have this young man's figure," said Father Tibbett.

The priest came close to spoiling Cassie's appetite. While Mr. Webster was a true giant—two hundred and fifty pounds or more, with the height to carry it—the Father was merely fat, with the delicate light bones of a bird. The Father could not run to first base, in Cassie's opinion.

"Proper diet, exercise, fresh air," said the colonel. "These are essentials for good health and vigor. One need not be eighteen to maintain one's physique, Padre."

Padre. Cassie stopped chewing at the sound of the word.

"I'm afraid you're right, Colonel," replied Father Tibbett. "The sedentary life—well, you are fortunate that your profession enables you to apply yourself with such diligence to matters of physical well-being. On the other hand, for those of us whose province is the world of the spirit, appetites of the flesh are not so easily resisted!" So saying, the priest gave himself another portion of ham, which he smothered in creamed potatoes.

A look of evident distaste rippled across the colonel's taut features. He pushed away his own plate, dabbed impatiently at his steel-gray mustache with one of Pullman's linen napkins, then drew his chair closer to Cassie's, half turning his back on the priest. The millionaire, too, crowded closer. Father Tibbett did not seem offended by his exclusion but went contentedly ahead with his meal. Between bites, he gulped coffee and puffed on a fat cigar.

The colonel's serious demeanor commanded Cassie's full attention. "Consider this, Cassius, to be a council of war. Reports from the border are increasingly alarming. At this very instant the Mexican president,

Carranza, is assembling strong forces with the aim of opposing our pursuit of the bandit Villa. The Mexicans mean business. Otis, if I may trouble you to read aloud that passage—"

"Of course," said the millionaire. He produced a copy of the previous day's *Chicago Herald.* "Yes, here it is: '. . . President Carranza has gone so far as to suggest that "America is slabbering for the daughters of Mexico and thirsting for the blood of her men." ' Imagine it—such slander from a bloody Mexican dictator!"

Cassie wondered what "slabbering" meant. He thought of the three stowaways back in the second-section van.

"Further," Colonel Antrobus continued, "we are informed that General Pershing is now organizing elements of the Seventh, Tenth, and Thirteenth Cavalry into a pair of flying columns that will be thrown against Villa as soon as the necessary supply trains can be arranged. Do you know what this means, Cassius?"

"I'm not sure I do, sir."

"It means that those who are at the front when the order is given to attack—*they* shall share in the honor of noble victory. Whereas those who are not—those who find themselves bogged down at some obscure railroad siding, for example—*those* poor unfortunates shall enjoy only the bitter ignominy of lost opportunity, of failed promise, of mundane duty behind the lines."

The millionaire joined in. "The colonel is quite right, Cassius. I, too, have a stake in this venture. Webster's Machine Lubricant is, I am pleased to say, a prime supplier of war matériel to our government. You yourself have observed samples of the motorized transport which our company is now providing on lease to the punitive expedition. But all our efforts—the colonel's and my own—shall be for naught unless we reach the war zone in time to participate in the Army's initial thrust into Mexico. We have no doubt that war south of the border will be brief and devastating. I would not wager a nickel, sir, on the bandit Villa's chances of escaping the gallows. Thus, you will appreciate our concern for speed—maximum *possible* speed—to the border."

"Yes, sir, I sure do appreciate it. Only—"

The colonel interrupted. "I'm quite sure you do, Cassius. However, Mr. Webster and I have discussed the matter at length, and we believe that we can substantially increase your appreciation of it."

The millionaire reached across the table and tapped the colonel's forearm. "It might be best, Miles, if the padre . . ."

"Quite right," said the colonel. "Padre, perhaps you would excuse us. There are a number of rather boring details which we must now review with Mr. McGill. I'm sure your own duties—"

"Say no more," said Father Tibbett. "While I find this all quite fascinating—especially with reference to my new role as acting chaplain—I have promised to prepare a brief service for our loyal Filipino congregation." The priest rose with difficulty in the narrow space between table and chair. "My son," he said to Cassie, "let us have that chat at your early convenience."

"Thank you, Father."

The other gentlemen seemed relieved by the Father's departure. He was no Jesuit, Cassie told himself again; he would be no help at all to the girls out back. Cassie decided he didn't want that "chat," either.

"Now then," said the colonel.

"Why don't I, Miles?"

"Of course, Otis."

The millionaire drew closer still; Cassie stopped eating.

"We are not unaware, Cassius, that many forces are at play in so complex an undertaking as the running of a train."

"Sir?"

"We have asked ourselves this question: What can be done to *ensure* maximum speed in reaching the war zone? Have you any ideas yourself?"

"I *did* ask the hoggers—the engineers, sir—to keep their throttles in the top notch as much as possible."

"And we appreciate that," said Mr. Webster. "But what we now have in mind, Cassius, is something more *tangible*, shall we say, than mere asking."

"Tangible, sir?"

"In American business, Cassius, we employ various forms of incentive. By that I mean extra wages for extra work, special payments on holidays, bonuses. A Christmas bonus, for example. You're familiar with such devices, I'm sure."

"Yes, sir, I've heard tell of them."

"Well then," said the millionaire, "the colonel and I—keeping the best interests of our nation and government always to the fore—have devised a system of incentives involving this train. For reasons of secrecy—war secrets, you will understand—no word of this must reach beyond the three of us at this table."

"No, sir."

"Nothing can be said to your superiors, much less your subordinates, within the Pullman Company."

"No, sir."

"As a matter of fact—though my good friend Colonel Antrobus here is party to the proposal—no one else in the Army is to know of it, either. For reasons of military secrecy."

"Yes, sir."

"Well, now, what *is* this incentive, you're probably wondering . . . ? It is now Monday morning, and we are approaching Fort Leavenworth,

Kansas. We make the remaining distance to Fort Bliss to be one thousand miles. Would you agree?"

Cassie pulled out his train book and found the proper tables. "After Fort Leavenworth, sir, it'll be another nine hundred seventy miles."

"Quite so," said the millionaire. "And have you estimated our time of arrival at Fort Bliss?"

This was a figure Cassie was half afraid to reveal. "A rough estimate, sir," he admitted.

"And what would that be?"

"Well, sir, as near as I can figure—taking into account the horse stops and stops for coal and water—I figure sometime after supper Wednesday."

The two gentlemen exchanged knowing glances. Mr. Webster smiled. "You've a sharp pencil, Cassius. You have confirmed our very worst suspicions."

"Sir?"

"Frankly, Cassius, we can *not* arrive at Fort Bliss after supper Wednesday and still expect to cross over with the lead columns."

"No, sir?"

"No. As a matter of fact, we have it on good authority that General Pershing's forces will cross the border at first light Thursday morning—meaning that Colonel Antrobus's squadron *must* arrive in El Paso no later than *midday* Wednesday—eight hours, shall we say, ahead of your present schedule."

Cassie shook his head. "Eight hours, sir—that's an awful lot to make up, even on a run as long as this."

"We understand," said Mr. Webster. "Nothing worthwhile is achieved without effort. Let us try to put the task into different perspective, shall we? In my experience, Cassius, the achievement of difficult objectives is largely a function of how clearly—how dramatically—those objectives are presented to the employees involved. So let us try to break down our objective into its component parts. How many changes of crew do you contemplate between here and El Paso?"

Cassie went back to his book. "There'll be a change at Lawrence, sir. And Hutchinson. And then Dalhart, Texas. And then Vaughn, New Mexico."

"Four more changes?"

"Yes, sir."

"Which means, if we are to pick up eight hours' improvement in your present schedule, each of the new crews will be responsible for picking up only two hours—one quarter of the total."

"Yes, sir, I guess that'd be right. Only—"

"Let me carry on without interruption. Each crew works for, what, twelve hours?"

"Never more than twelve, sir—that's the law. Usually it works out to about ten—if everything goes right."

"Fine. Ten hours, then. So we're asking each crew to improve by a matter of two hours in ten. Twenty percent. Does a twenty-percent improvement seem impossible to you, Cassius?"

"Twenty percent? Not to me, sir. But then I've never tooled a locomotive even a mile."

"Well said! No, of course, you haven't. And experience means a great deal in such matters. But let's say for sake of argument that a twenty-percent improvement *is* possible. How do we inspire your engineers to achieve this goal?"

"I guess I don't know, sir."

"Well, now, maintaining our rational approach—"

The colonel stifled a yawn. He seemed weary of the millionaire's "rational approach." For some time the officer had been fussing with his napkin, playing with his fork, gazing to the landscape outside—anything, it seemed, to avoid paying strict attention to Mr. Webster's complicated strategies.

"—what would happen, do you suppose, if you went to each engineer and you said to him: 'Improve your running time by twenty percent—two hours—and you will earn yourself, as war bonus, a twenty-dollar gold piece'?"

Twenty dollars gold! Close to a week's wages for picking up two hours on a run!

"Well, son?" urged the colonel.

Cassie did not have to think long. "I expect most hoggers would about fly, sir, for the chance at a double eagle."

"Splendid!" remarked the millionaire.

"Excellent!" concurred Colonel Antrobus.

"And just to be equitable," continued Mr. Webster, "assuming that all eight hours are made up and we arrive at Fort Bliss no later than noon Wednesday . . ."

"Sir?"

". . . then naturally there would be an additional bonus paid to our conductor—*fifty* dollars, shall we say?"

Fifty dollars! Even if he broke some off to give to Nelson—and maybe a piece to Rocks—that would leave Cassie about double the clear cash profit he could hope to save up from a full year's running for Pullman's.

Christian returned with a fresh pot of coffee. Everyone remained silent until he had gone. A fifty-dollar bonus was not something to be discussed in front of a Negro, who would be lucky to earn that much in two months.

"Well, Cassius," said the millionaire, "what do you think of our proposition?"

"It sounds a good plan to me, sir!"

The two gentlemen seemed well satisfied with Cassie's answer; each one shook his hand. Mr. Webster brought forth his purse, soft black leather trimmed in gold. "Four changes of crew—eight engineers in all?"

"Yes, sir, eight in all."

The millionaire counted out eight twenty-dollar gold pieces and slid them across the tablecloth. Cassie gathered them up with care and placed them in the back pocket of his train book, which had a snap catch to it.

"Not to be paid out," cautioned the millionaire, "until each crew has performed up to expectations."

"Oh, no, sir. They'll not see a dime, sir, till we've made up the time."

"Splendid. Ah—but we mustn't forget our conductor."

From his trouser pocket, the millionaire produced a wad of crisply folded fifty- and hundred-dollar certificates. He manipulated the bills the way a sharp dealer handled cards, causing one of the fifties to pop up from the rest. He invited Cassie to pluck it free.

"I'd as soon wait, sir, till El Paso—in case we don't make up the time."

"Nonsense," said the millionaire. "Call it 'earnest money,' if you like— evidence of determination to succeed at all costs. In the unlikely event that you fail, you will return all unearned moneys. For now, think only of success."

"And of *victory*," said the colonel.

Cassie reached for the bill. It seemed to grow in size in his hand. He folded it over and slipped it down into his watch pocket.

"One more thing, Cassius," said the colonel.

"Sir?"

"We shall dismount at Fort Leavenworth to parade the colors. The commanding officer has kindly offered to mess the troops, so we have no alternative but to accept his hospitality. However, I have instructed Lieutenant Van Impe that in future such extended stops shall occur no more frequently than once each ten hours."

"Ten hours, yes, sir. Not counting horse stops, that would be."

"*Including* horse stops. Such a regimen will save considerable time. Similarly, I would urge you to minimize time lost during the water and coaling stops—especially if you intend to maintain custody of that fifty-dollar war bonus."

"Yes, sir, I sure will, sir. Only about the horses—"

"Do not concern yourself. The wranglers will see to the horses."

"Yes, sir."

"One cannot wage war without casualties."

"No, sir."

"Very well. You are dismissed."

"Yes, sir. Thank you, sir."
Thus ended the council of war.

Cassie locked himself in the crew's toilet room and counted his money. He had started with $16.50 of his own. Meanwhile, he had spent a dollar on telegraph charges, advanced Rocks two dollars from his pay at Sturgis, and spent fifty-five cents in the Omaha station. This left $12.95. The double eagles for the hoggers came to $160. Cassie almost forgot the fifty-dollar certificate in his watch pocket. Grand total, train book and pockets: $222.95!

He took out the fifty-dollar certificate again, unfolded it, stretched it flat. What had old Nelson told Rocks was Mr. Liberty's real reason for not shining?—no tips on government runs? What was this "war bonus" but a tip? And the biggest tip any Pullman captain was ever likely to see! The old master had outfoxed himself this time.

But there was a bad side to it, too, Cassie understood. Remembering the savage quarrels he had witnessed in the day cars—over pots that seldom topped ten dollars—he knew one thing for certain:

He was as good as dead, should Jacko Mudd's boys learn of the great fortune he now carried on his person.

He paused long enough to peek into the kitchen. Chef Kolb was busy stirring a variety of pots on the stove while the Negro, John, cut luncheon chops from a side of lamb. The little German beamed at Cassie and declared, "*You heet dis!*" He stuck a large spoon in Cassie's mouth. The substance was piping hot. It was about the best thing Cassie had ever tasted. He figured it for fish chowder.

"*Is gut?*"

"Yes, sir, it sure is."

"*Ja, wunderbar!*"

Cassie accepted a slice of fresh-baked rye bread and departed. As good as the soup had been, his mind was not yet on lunch. He was more concerned with earning the fifty-dollar bill in his pocket. But he moved too slowly. As he reached the vestibule, he heard his name called:

"Cassius, come ahead, son. No time like the present."

It was Father Tibbett who beckoned to him. Even at a distance, Cassie could smell the Father's shaving lotion, heavily scented with violets.

Cassie stepped into the priest's compartment.

"Don't be shy, Cassius. Please sit down."

The Father settled his bulk into an overstuffed chair by the window, leaving Cassie the hard-backed chair by the bed. There was an even stronger scent of violets in the compartment; Cassie was afraid to take a deep breath.

"Now, how can I be of help, my son?"

It annoyed Cassie to hear Father Tibbett address him as "my son." "Well, Father—"

"Call me Padre. This is the military custom. We are Soldiers of the Cross. Speak up, lad—I shan't *bite* you."

He was not Cassie's idea of a priest. "A question, sir?" Cassie said.

"A question? Yes, of course. You seem a bright young man. What is your question? Would it be a matter of faith, perhaps?"

"No, sir, not faith."

"You are Catholic, I presume. McGill—a good Irish name?"

"Yes, sir, Catholic. Irish, too."

"Well, boy?"

"To tell the truth, sir—"

"*Padre.*"

"Yes, sir—Padre. It's—it's about girls."

"On your knees, son."

"Sir?"

"On your *knees.*"

Cassie knelt down and made the sign of the cross.

"Begin."

"Forgive me, Father, for I have sinned."

No sooner had Cassie got the words out than the compartment door slid open.

"Oh, *pardon!*"

It was Mademoiselle Foix, companion to Miss Candace.

"Five minutes," said the padre. "Perhaps less."

The door closed. Perhaps Mademoiselle Foix, too, had come for confession, Cassie thought.

Father Tibbett leaned back in his chair, closed his eyes. "Begin again, my son."

"Forgive me, Father, for I have sinned. It has been"—Cassie paused to count up the time—"three weeks since my last confession."

"A serious lapse, my son."

"I was on a run, Father."

"Padre."

"Yes, sir. Padre."

"Continue."

"Since my last confession, I have committed no mortal sins. Since my last confession, I have committed many venial sins. Among my venial sins were . . ."

He tried to think of some. There were bound to be some, but he could not think of any. He remembered the girls out back. Just *knowing* about hookers was sure to be a sin. ". . . Unclean thoughts," he said.

"Unclean thoughts? Describe them."

"About girls, sir."

"Sexual thoughts?"

"Yes, sir."

The Father opened his eyes and consulted his watch. "Go on. What other sins?"

Cassie could feel drops of sweat beading on his brow. Pullman's steam heat was sometimes excessive.

"*Other* sins, my son?"

Cassie thought hard. He tried to remember what he had confessed the last time. "Forgetting to say my prayers."

"Yes, yes, *other* sins?" The priest looked to his watch again. He seemed in a hurry.

"I can't remember, Father."

"Sins of the flesh?"

"No, sir."

"Sins of self-indulgence?"

"No, sir."

"Impure acts?"

"No, sir."

"Very well, then. Say ten Pater Nosters and ten Ave Marias."

"Thank you, Father."

"*Padre.* Now say an Act of Contrition, and then you may go."

"Yes, sir."

Cassie did as he was told. As for the girls out back, he had confessed to unclean thoughts and maybe that covered it. He hoped so.

At Pierce Junction, the next coaling stop, Rocks came forward to report.

"Take a good look, Cass, 'cause you won't see it fer long." The shortstop lifted his upper lip to show the gap in his teeth. "Doc promised to make me some teeth soon as we get to 'Paso and he can beg some tools off o' the painless parkers down there. Says I'll be good as new—eat corn off the cob if I want ta! Won't be nothin' I can't sink me choppers into."

"What's that on your belt?" Cassie could see what it was: the short-stop's mitt.

"Tools o' me trade, a-course! There's to be a pick-up game next time we stop fer the horses. A couple o' the fellas played in the Southern League afore joinin' up. Ain't no real pitcher, though. How 'bout it, Mister Side-winder?"

"There's no time for baseball," Cassie declared. "I talked to the Father."

"Did ya! He'll help us, I bet."

"He won't."

"Damn him all to hell! Ain't that a sweet Christian fer ya!"

"We're on our own."

"I knowed it all along. It's me and you, Cass, like always."

"I've got an idea."

"Tell me the scheme, Professor, an' I'm with ya! Only do it quick, while them poor damn babes is still worth savin'!"

"Fort Leavenworth," Cassie said.

"What's that, Cass?"

"I'll tell you when the time comes."

"There's somethin' you gotta know, Cass."

"Is there, now?"

"That damn bastard Snivey? Well—he's wearin' your ma's cross."

Cassie felt the blood drain from his face. "What are you saying?"

"He's got it 'round his neck fer all to see. Oh, it's yers all right, Cass. Ain't two sets o' beads like that in the whole world!"

When Cassie spoke again, it was only to repeat the two words: *"Fort Leavenworth."*

They reached the siding at high noon. It was Fort Meade all over again, only bigger. Troopers by the hundreds were paraded out on the platform. There was an honor guard and a band that played the cavalry tune "Garry Owen." Red-white-and-blue bunting had been tacked up to cover every inch of the train shed. As soon as Colonel Antrobus and his staff emerged from Headquarters Car, the band struck up the government anthem, "Hail, Columbia."

After the horses were led out, the 4th Squadron formed up on the platform and offered themselves for inspection to the commanding officer of the fort. Meanwhile, a detail of cadremen laid out a hot mess on tables made from planks and barrels alongside the trackbed. The stay might last two hours, Cassie estimated. He so informed the engineers, who backed off pressure and stood down themselves with the aim of filling their dinner pails with Army chow.

Rocks came forward. "Poor li'l Jolene! By God, Cass, if ya could *see* her! It ain't human!"

"Let's go, then," Cassie said.

"I figured we could use help," Rocks said. "Looky here."

Cassie flinched at the sight of it. The shortstop carried in his belt a trooper's Colt .45. "How'd you ever come by that?"

"Waited till one o' them bastards had his pants down!"

It was an evil-looking devil, clip fed, holding one cartridge in the chamber and six more in the handle. "Pull the trigger," said Cassie, "and we're both done for."

"Ain't fer *shootin'*, Cass," said Rocks innocently. "It's fer *scarin'!*"

They went down the line toward the second-section van. Along the way, Cassie studied the ranks of troopers formed up on the platform. Behind Colonel Antrobus and squarely in the middle of the ceremonies was Headquarters Platoon, which included the sergeant major, Trooper Snivey, Corporal Romero, and the rest of Jacko Mudd's boys. Mr. Otis Webster's party was nowhere to be seen. Apparently the civilians had remained at home in *The Mother Lode*. This fitted Cassie's scheme to a T.

"Let's do it," he said to Rocks.

The caboose was deserted except for the sentry on guard, Private Rademacher, who sat on the railing of the front vestibule, his Springfield leaning up against the door. "Greetings, gents," he said as Cassie and Rocks approached.

"Seeing as most of the fellows are busy," Cassie said in a friendly way, "we were wondering if we could do a little business inside?" He pulled a pair of two-dollar bills from his train book and held them up for the trooper to see.

"Can't seem to get your fill, huh?" the trooper said to Rocks.

"Got me a *terrible* appetite!" said Rocks. He could be a fine actor when he wanted to.

"Can't see no reason why not," Trooper Rademacher said. "Only the toll's gone up, on account o' Pancho Villa. It'll cost you five dollars a head."

"That's a bit steep for the likes of us," Cassie said.

"That's the toll," Trooper Rademacher repeated. He was a brawny fellow with handlebar mustache and coal-black hair and sideburns.

"Ten dollars then," Cassie said. He reached into his train book and pulled out three more deuces. This left him with a pair of singles and ninety-five cents, not counting Mr. Webster's bonus money.

"Nice doin' business with you," said the trooper. He accepted the bills and stepped aside to let the trainmen pass. "Hobson's choice. Take whichever pair is up and about."

Inside the door, Rocks drew the .45 and held it at the ready. "We done it, Professor! We *done* it!"

"Shush! You want the whole Squadron to hear? Stand guard while I get the girls."

Cassie's scheme was simple as pie: march the stowaways straight down the platform in broad daylight to *The Mother Lode*. The millionaire's party was sure to offer the girls protection and see to it they were returned to Rapid City. Cassie longed to see the sergeant major's face when they made their escape.

He whipped back the curtains to the super's bunk and found Naomi, the part-Indian one. She was off duty and enjoying a nap.

"Cassie McGill, ma'am—conductor of this train. Get on your clothes and wait for my orders!"

He closed the curtains again so that she might cover herself in private. The two jury-rigged partitions had proper doors with peg-in-hole latches. He pulled open the one on the left and discovered the dark-haired Rita. Dressed only in her shift, she was reading a tattered copy of *Liberty* magazine.

"Good day, ma'am—you'll soon be free! Get dressed quick—there's no time to waste!"

He yanked open the other door and introduced himself to Jolene Potts.

"It's me, ma'am—Rocks's pal? Quick, ma'am, before the troopers catch onto us!"

"Where's Rocks, then?" Jolene asked.

"Just outside, ma'am—see there."

Rocks ran forward and embraced his sweetheart with one arm while holding the pistol high with the other. "We're off, babe! And don't you worry none—this cannon's meant for business!"

Cassie checked on the other two. Neither girl had moved. "No time to lose!" he yelled at them. "We're going to make a run for it!"

Still they did not move. They showed no intentions of moving, either. Cassie studied his predicament, then shouted to Rocks: "Let's get the hell out of here!"

"Ain't goin' without Jolene!" cried the shortstop. He was now sweating as hard as Cassie. "I'll pick her up and carry her if I haf ta!"

Rocks made to turn the .45 over to Cassie so as to free himself to carry his ladylove, but the weapon was slippery with sweat. In passing it across, the shortstop caught his finger in the trigger guard and grabbed for the handle with his other hand.

Kerblam!

The pistol seemed to explode in the shortstop's grasp. There was a ton of noise and a clean hole through the Franklin stove.

"The fucker *burned* me!" Rocks screamed.

The three girls emerged from their beds and set up a terrible wailing. Five seconds later, the front door burst open and Trooper Rademacher entered, leveling his Springfield as he came.

"*Don't shoot!*" Rocks cried.

The .45 had kicked away and now lay smoking on the floor. The shortstop's trembling hands shot skyward, followed immediately by Cassie's. In less than a minute, Jacko Mudd and Trooper Snivey showed their faces. "What have we got here?" asked Jacko Mudd.

"Got ourselves a pair o' heroes," said Trooper Snivey. He bent down and recovered Rocks's pistol. "Stolen government property," he noted.

Cassie figured to work the best bluff he could. "We're Pullman Company employees," he asserted. "We have every right to inspect this van. This van is Pullman property."

Trooper Snivey responded with an ugly laugh. The three girls hastily retreated into the super's bunk and closed the curtains. Meanwhile Jacko Mudd instructed Trooper Rademacher to inform Lieutenant Van Impe that a firearm had discharged accidentally, with no damage or injury resulting. The sergeant major then shut and bolted the front door.

"We demand to see the lieutenant," Cassie said. He lowered his hands now that Trooper Rademacher and the Springfield were no longer present.

Moving ever so deliberately, Mudd and Snivey removed their belts and wrapped them around their knuckles. They seemed to have gone through the ritual before.

"Lay a hand on us," cried Cassie, "and you'll wind up in a court of law!" He hardly recognized the strange high voice as his own.

"Mister," said Jacko Mudd, "the only court o' law you're gonna see is right here and now."

The two troopers advanced. Cassie and Rocks backed toward the stalls where Rita and Jolene had recently conducted their business. In a frantic rush, they jumped inside, grabbing hold of the latches. Unhappily for them, the girls' stalls were no better built that the horses'. The green lumber was soon reduced to kindling and splinters.

"Who's first?" taunted Snivey.

"That's me!" cried Rocks. The shortstop rammed his head into the trooper's midsection.

Cassie stayed back and waited, playing the role of the counterpuncher. Being a head taller than the sergeant major, with greater reach, he got in several good blows. But in confined quarters, his height proved a disadvantage.

When it came to fighting, Jacko Mudd reminded Cassie of a catcher called Miggs Noonan with Salina, Kansas, in the Tri-State League. After a close play at home, Miggs had tattooed Cassie's jaw in sharp objection to Nebraska City's 5–4 lead. Like Miggs Noonan, Jacko Mudd appeared to land three punches to Cassie's one. Or that was Cassie's impression before Jacko Mudd's heavy brass belt buckle caught him flush on the button and sent him down.

6

HE AWOKE IN Doc Rose's compartment in Headquarters Car. He could tell from the shadows on the ceiling that the train was under way and making good time. He supposed that Nelson had given the orders and was now acting as master. Doc was leaning over him, sponging off the blood and pressing a towel filled with cracked ice over one eye. Cassie's jaw ached but his tongue told him he had kept all his teeth. He rose up on his elbows.

"I'd not try to get up yet, son," said Doc. "Got yourself a concussion, is my guess."

Cassie saw himself in the mirror on the back of the compartment door. His ghost grinned back at him.

"Drink this," Doc said.

It made Cassie choke. It was whiskey. "How's Rocks, sir? Did he make it?"

"Him? Why, son, you couldn't kill that hardheaded Irishman with a shovel. Meaning no disrespect to your people."

"No, sir. I believe you're right about his head."

"I told him if he's going to get any more teeth knocked out, do so before I waste time fixing him bridgework!" The vet chuckled over his own joke, then gave himself a shot of the whiskey.

"How'd I get here, sir? Can't seem to remember it."

"Why, you was drug in by your pal and that big Negro from the private car. 'Case you're concerned for your bankroll, don't be. I took it off you for safekeeping." The vet handed over Cassie's train book.

Cassie couldn't help himself. He popped open the snap catch and counted the gold coins.

"Ain't they pretty," said Doc.

"Yes, sir, they sure are."

"Don't suppose they'd be poker winnings—not in this outfit!"

"No, sir. Nothing like that." Cassie sat upright—almost swooned.

"Here, keep this pressed to the back of your neck for a spell. You'll feel better." Doc gave him a towel filled with ice. "Your partner says you boys had a little argument with the sergeant major."

"Yes, sir."

"Over the girls, was it?"

"Yes, sir, that's it."

"How you carry your money is your business. But if I was you—"

"Sir? I'd like to explain about the money."

Doc Rose poured them both more whiskey. "If you want to, son—but you've no cause to."

Cassie told the story in full. When he finished, the vet fairly erupted: "If that ain't the *damnedest* thing I ever heard of! Can't get to war quick enough, so they take to bribing the train crew!"

"Oh, no, sir," said Cassie, "not a bribe. It's called a 'war bonus,' sir—it's more like a tip."

Doc Rose laughed. "Call it what you like, son, but them double eagles are bribes, pure and simple."

Cassie slowly withdrew the fifty-dollar bill from his watch pocket. "Then—then I'd best give it back, sir."

"Not a bit of it! It's found money, boy, and nothing for you to be 'shamed of. It's the high-and-mighties who should take shame! This sure follows, after what I heard at Leavenworth. Good friend of mine's vet with the Tenth—there's little gossip that escapes his notice. Seems the whole U.S. Cavalry is watching Miles Antrobus make his mad dash to glory—him and his profiteering partner, Otis Webster. There's hardly a calamity in this world so bad that some fella isn't getting rich on it!"

"Sir?"

"Motor trucks. boy. Them newfangled carts we're carrying. There's a profit to be made from them and Otis Webster aims to be the one making it. And don't you worry about the colonel neither. There's a 'bonus' coming his way, too—you can bet on that. The Army's so short of these gasoline monsters, they've taken to advertising for them in the newspapers. Pay top dollar and take all you got to sell or lease! Prime market for a trader like Otis Webster. See what I mean?"

"Yes, sir, I guess I do."

"Anyhow, you're sitting pretty, son. Our millionaire's taken a fancy to you, I do believe—sent that uppity daughter of his to inquire as to your health."

"He did *that*, sir?" Cassie was astonished to hear it.

"He did. 'Course, in a way you and him are business partners now, so it's only natural. He *needs* you, boy! Watch how you play your cards and you'll collect a lot more than fifty dollars. At the very least, you'll get yourself an education in private enterprise—neither Rockefeller nor Morgan can teach it better. Hell, boy, you've become a Tool of the Interests —there's no path to riches quicker than that!"

They woke him at Lawrence because Dandy Bob Biddle and J. L. Edwards were looking to sign off in his book. He had slept on Doc's bunk straight through the coaling stop at Kansas City and now felt better for it.

Or did he? Pulling on his boots, he pondered the matter of the "war bonus." On the one hand—since Doc Rose had explained it to him—Cassie felt guilty about his part in the scheme. That fifty-dollar certificate sure *smelled* like a bribe. On the other hand, if the millionaire's double eagles got the Squadron to war that much quicker, what was the harm in it? And hadn't General Superintendent for the West Mr. Laurence Cosgrove himself told Cassie that Mr. Webster's "every wish is to be taken by you as a command?" Cassie fingered the fifty-dollar certificate again. A person could feel wise and foolish, noble and base, at the same time, he decided. Either way, being a Tool of the Interests was a harder proposition than Doc Rose had made out.

Whether they were bribes or bonuses or tips, the time had come to put Mr. Webster's double eagles to work. Cassie appeared trackside and bade farewell to the old hoggers, set his mind on the new. It was then nearing three o'clock in the afternoon. According to Cassie's calculations, the *Pancho Villa Express* was to be at White City for supper and exercising of the ponies about eight o'clock that night. But after the colonel's latest demand for speed and his rule that horse stops were to be kept ten hours apart instead of six, Cassie figured they would go straight on to Hutchinson, another two hundred miles. At normal speeds they would make Hutchinson at one thirty in the morning, Tuesday. But by traveling full throttle and hurrying up the watering stops, they could beat the old schedule by two hours, even three. Cassie resolved to tell the new engineers the Hutchinson deadline was eleven that evening and see what happened.

"Well, boy, got yourself kicked by a mule, I'd guess. So where's my orders?" This from Cyrus Mucklestone, engineer in No. 506. He was a tall man with the weather-beaten skin of a field hand, plain as to features, but sporting the longest red beard on the road.

Cassie made no comment as to his black eye and puffed-up cheek. "Got your papers right here, Mr. Mucklestone." He handed over the flimsies he had just finished scrawling out.

It did not take the hogger long to sniff out trouble. "You got any idea of the track, son, 'tween here and Hutchinson?"

"No, sir, sure haven't."

"Hah!" the engineer snorted. " 'Course you don't, or you'd know better 'n to run up an order like this'n. Ain't a quarter mile o' track 'tween here and Hutchinson that's fit to carry a load like this 'n. Ground frost's tore up half the ties, wind's blowed away half the ballast."

According to the map in *Busby's*, this stretch of track, which belonged to the Rock Island, was rated "CC," halfway between "passable" and "good." Hoggers liked to look on the dark side whenever possible. "I'm sorry to hear it," Cassie said. "Going to cost you money."

"And how is that?" replied the engineer.

Cassie laid out Mr. Webster's "incentive" scheme for Mr. Mucklestone to inspect. Cassie did so out of the fireman's hearing so as to keep peace in the cab. If the hogger wished to share his bounty with his stoker—which was not likely—that was his business.

"Twenty dollars *gold*," repeated the engineer. "Paid on the spot when we finish the run?"

"Yes, sir, cash on the spot. It's a war bonus on account of Pancho Villa."

The hogger puzzled over the map, counting water stops on his fingers. "Well, sir, can you make it?"

"Give us five minutes, boy, so the stoker and me can oil 'round. Then call in your flag!"

Cassie hiked back to No. 799 and had the same conversation with the hogger there, Francis Jay Jury off the Santa Fe. He was a smooth-cheeked lad hardly out of his twenties. He possessed long, flowing straw-colored hair, which he combed back every sixty seconds or so, using a tortoise-shell instrument with a sterling-silver spine. He did not take to the Baldwin he had just inherited:

"Flues need reamin', pallie—that's an hour's work right there. Besides which, a good yard mechanic could spend the month of March on her linkage without fixin' all that ails her."

In the end, Mr. Webster's gold overcame all such shortcomings. Mr. Jury's attitude toward his fireman came as a surprise to Cassie: "Hear that, Wiley? A double eagle! An' ten o' that's yours for the takin'! Fire that boiler, you sinnin' jackass, and let's be off!" Whereupon Mr. Jury's sleepy-eyed partner began to shovel like a Saint.

Spirits thus bolstered, Cassie called in his flagmen and headed the *Pancho Villa Express* out across the flat belly of Kansas, throttles in the top notch, stacks spewing black clouds of thunder.

Rocks had set up shop again in Cassie's van. "How be ya, Professor! Damn, ain't that a shiner!"

"How's yourself?" replied Cassie.

"At the top o' me form!"

"So there's nobody bossing the second section?"

"Is so! The Rabbit's got the duty. Troopers love him like a brother, too —he ain't got no pecker, so they say! He's the equal to them A-rabian fellas—*oo-niks* is the word for it!"

"Eunuch," Cassie corrected. Rocks was talking about Mr. Coffin, the second-section brakeman. The trainmen took pleasure in calling him the Rabbit for his odd coloring. He was a peculiar fellow, albino in his markings, pink around the eyes, with pure white hair and skin.

"Then the girls are still out back?" asked Cassie. "They never got loose?"

Rocks told what had happened at the Fort Leavenworth siding. Just when it looked like curtains for him and Cassie, along came Otis Webster and party. The ladies and gentlemen, out to stretch their legs while the Army boys went through their ceremonies, were attracted by the firing of Rocks's borrowed pistol, to the point of making inquiries at the second-section van. Hearing their voices, Rocks broke out and secured Cassie's rescue. But under threats of quick death, the shortstop omitted any mention of the stowaways, who remained in the van.

"The girls are goners then," Cassie concluded.

"Not a bit of it!" cried Rocks. "I been back there already and they're none the worse for what we done—that's the truth!"

"The troopers let you back in?"

"An' why not? I said we wasn't helpin' 'em to 'scape—we was just wantin' their services! The soldier boy with the rifle backed us up—he's got your ten bucks!"

"And they *believed* you?"

"The girls wasn't about to say different! An' who's gonna spin a prettier yarn than me? The soldier boys covered up their sins as usual and your millionaire went about his business—him and the Father, too. Some damn Father!"

Cassie could only marvel at the shortstop's brazen manner. Still, he was unprepared for Rocks's next speech:

"Rita and Naomi—maybe they're yer hookers, Cass. But Jolene sure ain't. Me and her, we talked it out. Next time she's comin' with us an' no argument."

"*Next* time? You must be joking. You *saw* what she did. She preferred them to us—that's the truth of the matter. And who suffered for it?"

Cassie's lip was puffed out; every bone ached. He hoped never to hear the word "hooker" again.

"We took her by surprise is all, Cass! She'd 'a' come, only we scared her half to death, showin' up like we did right there in the middle of the Army! Next time'll be different, I swear!"

"It'll be different for sure," Cassie said. "'Cause it'll be done without Cassius McGill."

Rocks put on his hurt look. "Never thought I'd see the day when Lefty McGill turned quitter."

"Well, you've seen it now."

❖   ❖   ❖

Cassie put more ice on his cheek to bring down the swelling, then cleaned himself up and went forward again, heading this time for *The Mother Lode.* He proposed to tell his "business partner," Mr. Otis Webster, how the hoggers Cyrus Mucklestone and Francis Jay Jury were sure to make Hutchinson by the deadline Cassie had given them and thus earn their double eagles. Also, Cassie meant to ask the millionaire, in so many words, whether a "war bonus" was anything like a bribe.

He climbed up top over Headquarters Car so as not to meet Van Impe. The lieutenant was down there in the "War Room," Cassie supposed, where Colonel Antrobus gathered his officers for much of each day to plan their battles against the Mex; still, Cassie was taking no chances.

He continued across the roof of *The Mother Lode,* then climbed down and let himself into the private car through the front vestibule. Pausing at the pantry door, he put his head inside. The chow chow Mushy was there, well chained and snoring in his sleep. Cassie backed out and instantly came a cropper.

"I should like a cup of tea, Mr. Conductor."

Miss Candace Webster!

"Oh, yes, ma'am!"

The porter Milo was then following along behind Cassie. "One cup o' tea—comin' right up, ma'am!" said the Negro.

"Thank you, porter. I shall be in the parlor." She wore her pretty blue traveling gown. Cassie stood aside to let her pass. "I find Kansas frightfully boring, don't you?" she said to him.

Cassie looked out the window. Kansas was flat farming country; it seemed to him not much different from Nebraska. "I suppose it is, ma'am," he said.

"Can you play chess, boy?"

"My name is Cassius, ma'am—if you'd like to use it."

"My, that punch in the eye has made you insolent, hasn't it! Can you play chess? is what I asked you."

"I don't think I can, ma'am."

"It's not a question of *thinking,* boy. Cassius, then. Either you know how or you don't. Which is it?"

"I guess I don't, ma'am. But I could learn."

"Could you now?"

"Yes, ma'am, I believe I could."

"We shall soon see. Come with me."

The parlor was empty. Cassie guessed the millionaire and his friends were napping—resting up for Chef Kolb's next banquet. Miss Candace motioned for him to sit opposite her at the inlaid Moroccan gaming table that held the chess set.

"You have *seen* a chess set before, haven't you, Cassius?"

"I believe so, ma'am."

The pieces were finely carved, ivory for her, ebony for him. She told him the name of each piece and how it could proceed on the board. Some pieces seemed a bit hard to track, but he figured he would get the hang of it in time.

"We shall play a game," she said.

"Yes, ma'am."

"White moves first."

"Yes, ma'am."

She began by moving a soldier. He did the same. Every time she moved a piece, he did the same on his side of the board. He became confused soon enough.

"How slow you are!" she exclaimed.

"Ma'am?"

She removed one of his pieces. He kept his eyes down to the board except when he thought he could sneak a look at her. She was some beauty! They sat no more than a yard apart. When he dared take a breath, he could smell her fragrance, like roses. He was dizzy from the closeness.

"My, aren't you the *clever* one," she said when he moved one of his horsemen in a certain way.

He could see that she was annoyed with him. "If you'd like me to move differently, ma'am—"

"Certainly not!" she replied. "That would be cheating."

Milo interrupted with her tea. She mixed it half with cream and added three teaspoons of sugar. Cassie watched her soft lips meet the rim of the cup. "It's your move," she snapped.

He could hardly remember how the pieces moved. They played on, and soon she had him in a corner.

"Checkmate!"

"Ma'am?"

"That means the game is over."

"Yes, ma'am. Thank you, ma'am."

"You're no fun at all," she said.

She had a way of pouting that made him think of his sister Cleo; perhaps all ladies indulged in it. "I'd best be going, ma'am."

"How old are you?" she asked him.

"Eighteen, ma'am. Soon to be nineteen, though."

"My, how *mature*. And have you many lady friends? I suppose you must."

Cassie's skin crawled at the idea of it.

"Papá believes you are made of 'fine stuff,' but Mamá dissents. Ha! If she could see you now!"

"Ma'am?"

"In Europe, a boy and girl are never, but *never* permitted to be by themselves. It is considered quite scandalous."

"Yes, ma'am."

"Is that all you can say? 'Yes, ma'am.' 'No, ma'am'?"

"No, ma'am. I mean, ma'am—"

"Why, he is *blushing*. Have I embarrassed you, Cassius?"

"Not exactly, ma'am."

"Do you think me pretty?"

"Pretty, ma'am? Yes, ma'am, I guess I do."

"You *guess?*"

"I'd best be going, ma'am."

"Indeed, Camille is tardy—you would not wish her to find you here. She is not nearly so liberal in her views as I."

Camille was Mademoiselle Foix. Cassie had once before overheard the French lady giving lessons in her language to Miss Candace. Cassie rose. "Thank you, ma'am, for teaching me chess. It seems a clever game, ma'am."

"Please go now."

"Yes, ma'am. Thank you, ma'am."

He went away without ever seeing his "partner."

O Lord, what a perfect woman!

He stuck his head in the pantry again and shouted *"Ho!"* at the sleeping chow chow. The dog sprang forward as far as his chain would allow, trying to get at Cassie.

If only he might have met her under different circumstances, when he was more than a hired hand. If only she'd seen him mow down the side inning after inning against Bloomington!

He wished he had a chess board and pieces so that he could practice up. Who would he play with? Rear-shack Legrand? Rabbit, the albino? Poor black Nelson?

He climbed up top and made his way back to the van. There, suddenly disgusted with himself, he took up his well-traveled *Riders of the Purple Sage* and applied himself where it fell open, Chapter XVII, "Wrangle's Race Run":

> The plan eventually decided upon by the lovers was for Venters to go to the village, secure a horse and some kind of disguise for Bess, or at least less striking apparel than her present garb, and to return post-haste to the valley. Meanwhile, she would add to their store of gold. Then they would strike the long and perilous trail to ride out of Utah. In the event of his inability to fetch back a horse for her, they intended to make the giant sorrel carry double . . .

But Zane Grey's romantic notions failed to work their usual magic and Cassie gave it up, preferring to sulk like a schoolboy and think himself the lowliest of fellows on or off the road.

✿ ✿ ✿

They made White City shortly after sundown. This put them right on schedule to make Hutchinson by the deadline. It looked such a sure bet that Cassie telegraphed ahead to the stationmaster, asking him to warn the next crews to be ready for their early arrival.

Back in the van, Cassie found the colonel's boy, Francisco, waiting for him:

"*Now, sah! De col-o-nel, he say chop-chop! He put ass in fire, you not come pronto!*"

Cassie went forward at once. The colonel was alone in his compartment.

"Fighting and carousing, mister?"

"No, sir."

"Don't deny it! The condition of your eye attests to your misdeeds."

It was a different colonel from the one Cassie had known at breakfast. This one was black-spirited and wrathful.

"What is the name of this train, mister?"

"*Pancho Villa Express*, sir."

"Have those signs removed, damn you! They mock us—*mock* the Fourth!"

"Sir?"

"Use your *eyes,* boy. What would you judge our speed to be? *Look,* boy!"

Cassie bent at the waist, peered out the window, watched as the telegraph poles flashed by in the moonlight.

"Well, boy? What *speed?*"

"Twenty, sir? Maybe more? It's hard to tell—"

"*Silence!* We're scarcely *moving.* Is this what our incentives have gotten us?"

"Sir—"

"What has become of it—the gold that Webster provided for the crews? Gambled it away, have you?"

"*No,* sir!"

"What then?"

"It's *here,* sir." Cassie held out his train book with the snap pocket open.

The colonel brushed aside Cassie's offering. "*Time* is every soldier's greatest weapon. Without time on his side, *no* soldier can hope to embrace victory."

"No, sir."

"There is something I want you to read."

"Sir?"

It was a copy of a Western Union message. Cassie squinted hard to make out the scrawl. The telegrapher was not blessed with a steady hand:

REPLY TO YOUR MESSAGE 031116 CANNOT GUARANTEE PLACE IN
SLOCUM'S COLUMN UNLESS FOURTH SQUADRON ARRIVES BLISS BY
EIGHT A.M. WEDNESDAY. REGARDS & REGRETS.

2D LT GEORGE S PATTON JR

AIDE TO GENERAL PERSHING

"Well, boy?"

Cassie checked the trip log he kept in his train book. "Eight o'clock,
sir—but that's four hours earlier than we bargained for."

"*Exactly!* Four hours that can make or break the reputation of the
Fourth Squadron. . . . I intend that we shall *achieve* our objective—do
you understand me?"

Cassie started to object, but the colonel's grim countenance stopped
him. "Eight o'clock Wednesday morning, yes, sir. I expect we'll make
it, sir. . . ."

Rocks was waiting in the van. "Up top, Cass! Got somethin' to
show ya!"

They climbed into the angel's nest. Rocks wanted privacy; there were
too many trainmen down below. "Feast yer eyes on these!"

The shortstop tossed down a long bedroll, which he proceeded to
spread out on the deck.

"What the—!"

There was a pair of glistening steel blades—cavalry sabers—carefully
wiped over with oil to keep off rust, each with a fancy engraved scabbard and a handle of polished mahogany carved to fit the fingers.

"Must be a *thousan'* of 'em, Cass! There's crate on crate carried special
in one o' the horse cars! An' that ain't all!"

Buried deep in the blanket were three green-painted balls of iron. A
pot-metal lever at the top of each was tied down with cord. Cassie knew
them from photographs of the European war: explosive grenades. He
took one in his hand; it must have weighed several pounds.

"Hold it kinda easy, Cass, on account—"

"I *know!*" Cassie set it down on the blanket. He picked up one of the
sabers, eased the blade from its scabbard. "What do you expect to do
with this? March down the track holding it over your head? Bust your
way into the van and start cutting up the sentry?"

"We can carry 'em down our pant legs," Rocks replied in steady tones,
"an' only use 'em if we hafta. Won't need 'em a-tall, Cass, accordin' to
this new idea I got."

Rocks told his plan. At the next stop, Hutchinson, most of the troopers
would be occupied with running the horses. There would only be the
sentry in the guardhouse to worry about. Rocks would take the grenades

and move to a suitable spot halfway between the two sections and set them off. *BANG! BANG! BANG!* This would draw away the sentry and any other troopers who might be seeking to do business with the girls. At that moment, Cassie would enter through the back door of the van and carry Jolene off to safety. Jolene would be wearing a trooper's long coat, cavalry hat, and boots so as not to be recognized at trackside. Rocks had already stolen a uniform and hidden it away.

"And where do I take her, then? Maybe to the colonel's War Room for safekeeping?"

"Some place even better!" Rocks replied.

"Here, I suppose—right in my own van. Where they're sure to look first thing."

Rocks cracked a big smile. "You pretty near got it, Professor! Not inside —but *under!*"

"You don't mean—"

"Sure as hell do! She'll ride safe as can be till we can make our 'scape ta some pleasant town. I was thinkin' maybe 'Paso!"

What Rocks had in mind for his ladylove was the possum belly under their feet. This was the big chest that usually carried tools for the road gangs or baggage not needed inside the caboose. The last time Cassie had looked, the possum belly was empty except for some burlap sacks. The best thing about it was a large Yale lock, the key for which Cassie had in his pocket. There would be no chance that some trooper might come across Miss Jolene without Cassie's knowing it—assuming he could hide her away without being caught in the act.

"And how's she supposed to breathe then?" Cassie asked.

"Easy! There's plenty of cracks—I checked. We kin poke out some knot holes ta make sure."

Cassie thought some more on Rocks's scheme and didn't like it any better than he had at first hearing. "So what if you kill somebody with those fool grenades?"

"Won't *kill* nobody, Cass. Just make some noise, is all. I'll pretend I saw outlaws or somethin' runnin' away. I'll start yellin' and screamin' and make the tropers go runnin' off to catch the bad men. And while I'm doin' it, you and Jolene kin get free!"

Cassie shook his head. "No. I told you before—I'll not be party to it. I helped out at Leavenworth, didn't I? You saw what that got us. No— you want to save her, you do it yourself."

"*Please,* Cass. I'm *beggin'* ya. See to me gal for me, an' I'll do the rest!"

"No."

" 'Member that time. Cass—at Toledo, I think it was—when those fellas in the pool hall had ya in the corner an' was gonna beat the piss out o' ya on account o' ya wiped their asses wit' yer cue, an' I come in on yer side?"

"It was Cincinnati," Cassie replied wearily, "and I already thanked you for it, didn't I, about a million times?"

"No thanks needed, Professor!" Rocks beamed. "Always glad ta help ya out of a tight spot!"

Cassie continued to shake his head. He had never been able to resist the shortstop's damn Irish grin. "And if it doesn't work this time? If you *still* can't get her free?"

"It's gotta work, Cass! There's nothin' left fer me or her neither if it don't!"

"But no swords, you hear?" said Cassie in a quiet voice.

"If you say so, Cass. Don't need no swords anyhow—grenades'll do the job, bet on it!"

"I guess I'm betting, then," said Cassie.

"I *knowed* it!" cried Rocks. "What else is friends for!"

They rolled on under the bright Kansas moon. At McPherson they encountered cold rain, then hail. But five miles down the track they were out of it, and in the cool night air they seemed to fly, wheels hardly touching the rails.

Three sharp blasts from Mucklestone in No. 506 told Cassie the Hutchinson station lay dead ahead. The idea of mixing again with the troopers set his head to throbbing, but there was no relief to be had short of hightailing it back to Lincoln. Pulling on his mackinaw, he swung off the rear steps and prepared for the worst.

The tight-lipped yardmaster made himself known to Cassie and directed them onto a remote spur. He was well acquainted with the *Pancho Villa Express:* the spur he picked for them was lined with cattle pens, as though he expected the troopers to keep the animals locked up till it was time to move on. Jacko Mudd's boys soon saw to that, dragging down the fences and permitting the ponies to run at will. When the yardmaster protested, Mudd's gang dropped off another half-dozen dead animals right there under the railroader's nose. The fellow ran for his life after that.

By Nelson's timepiece, it was then ten minutes to eleven o'clock. Cyrus Mucklestone and Francis Jay Jury had stolen back their two hours with plenty to spare. The two hoggers climbed down from their cabs with the happiest of smiles on their grimy faces.

"The Army thanks you," Cassie told them. "Me, too." He handed each man his double eagle.

"If ever you're wantin' a fella for another o' these 'bonus' runs," said Cyrus Mucklestone, "you jes call!"

"Same goes fer me," said Francis Jay Jury. He bit hard on his reward to ensure its value.

Another "bonus" run. Cassie flinched at the idea. He said his good-byes and moved off.

The locals were quick to hear about the great war train down at the yards. Two hundred and ninety roughriding troopers and what was left of their mounts: this made quite a show. Citizens soon poured onto the siding. It made Cassie think of opening day at the Nebraska State Fair in Omaha. A line of buggies and wagons, each one packed with farmers and kids and old folk, choked the dirt roads. Cassie wished he could join in the fun—some of the wagons offered victuals for sale, including pies. But he had business to attend to, business that would not wait.

Sticking to the back side of the cars, out of torch light, Cassie worked his way down the line, keeping an eye out for Rocks. Cassie had expected to see the main body of troopers queued up for their grog, but nothing was offered at the cook car except coffee. All the rum had been drunk up, was the rumor. This complicated matters. The troopers began to roam, intent on finding whiskey or worse. Together with the town's men and boys, a good quantity of Hutchinson's females were on foot thereabouts: the troopers smelled them out in no time at all. This would be the liveliest Monday night a Kansas town had seen in many a year.

Cassie came abreast of the second-section van. A pair of dark figures inhabited the front porch. It took Cassie a while to make them out. Rocks himself sat atop the brake wheel, jawing with the sentry. Cassie let out a soft whistle. Neither figure responded. Cassie moved closer and tried again.

At length Rocks noticed him and came down. "That fella's scared o' the dark! Wait'll me bombs go off! He'll be gone quick as any rabbit!"

Cassie shook his head vehemently. "Look around—the place is crawling with townspeople. We'd best wait till Texas."

"There's no more waitin' fer Jolene, Cass. It's now or never!"

Cassie shivered up and down. "If we're going to do it then, let's *do* it."

"Stay put till you hear the bangs—then grab hold o' Jolene and move like lightnin'!"

The shortstop ran off. Cassie climbed under the van and crouched between the rails to wait. He could see nothing but troopers' boots and the legs of a million horses. A stream of phantom figures danced around him in the shadows. His knee joints quickly began to ache. He squatted in several different positions—finally sat right down on an oily tie. The sounds of troopers whooping it up close by set his teeth to chattering. Over his head, inside the van, all was silence. Maybe the ladies were sleeping—or else practicing their business quiet as mice. Cassie prayed that Jolene Potts was off her back and dressed when he came calling.

His nerves began to get the better of him. What if Rocks had been found out—caught with a saber down his pants, his pockets filled with bombs? Cassie started to count. When he reached a hundred, he would make a run for it. . . . Twenty-two, twenty-three, twenty-four, twenty—

The first explosion was no more than a distant *pfuht*. Also the second. Cassie waited for the third. *Felt* it before he heard it.

The caboose over his head kicked backward, nearly slicing off his feet. *The damn fool's blown up No. 799!*

Cassie crab-walked out from under the van and peered up the track. No. 799 seemed all in one piece, but a great metal tank opposite the locomotive burned brightly, lighting up the yards like a giant torch and setting fire to nearby sheds. The night sky began raining down hot embers, threatening the horse cars.

"*Collect those mounts! . . . Lower the spout on that damn water tank! . . . Break out the buckets! . . . Fire detail, form up on the double!*"

Troopers and horses went flying in all directions. Cassie staggered forward, thinking to save No. 799.

"Well, ain't ya gonna *help* me?"

He turned back. It was Jolene Potts, scaring him half to death in her trooper's coat and cavalry hat.

"Grab hold of my arm!"

He helped her down the vestibule steps. There was no sentry to stop them: like everybody else in Hutchinson, the trooper was running toward the flaming beacon.

They hugged the back side of the cars until they reached No. 799. "Hold up!" Cassie ordered. "I got business in the cab. Keep your face down—anybody talks to you, play dumb!"

He bounded up the ladder. "I'm McGill, captain of this rig!"

The relief crew had just come aboard. "Packy LaBelle," said the hogger. "On the wrong end o' that shovel is Dewitt Coffey—ain't so dumb as he looks. What in blazes—"

"Take her back a thousand yards and hold her till I tell you different!"

"Yes, sir, Cap'n! Pleased to obey!"

The roof to one horse car had begun to smolder; Troop C's wranglers were busy dousing it from their buckets.

"Come on, then!" Cassie told Jolene. "We'll run for it!"

The front-end hogger had some brains, too, it appeared. Cassie saw his own van lurch forward, move slowly away from the burning sheds.

"Run! That's where we're headed—that caboose!"

Jolene's overcoat dragged on the ground, slowing her progress. Luckily for them, the new fellow at the throttle of No. 506 was satisfied with a walking pace. Slowly they gained on him. Cassie had little trouble unlatching the possum belly and raising the lid. "Head first! I'll get your legs!"

"I'll never make it!" Jolene cried.

"You will! Here, grab hold of my coat!"

The grinding sound of the van's wheels against the rails scared her. She was close to exhaustion; she began to fall back. "I can't!"

"You *can!* Just dive for it!"

The floor of the possum belly was no more than a foot off the rails. Cassie could see Jolene was afraid of the iron wheels.

"Don't worry—I'll see to your feet!"

He wedged the lid open with his shoulder and used both hands to drag her along. He was exhausted himself and in terrible pain from the lid, which rattled against his jaw.

"In you go!"

He lifted her off the ground and threw her inside. The lid came down, smashing his fingers against the box. "*Sweet Jesus!*"

But she was safely inside. He breathed a great sigh of relief when he heard the Yale snap shut.

"Great little bonfire, ain't it!"

Rocks—a queer grin spread across his blunt features—stood at the edge of the crowd and enjoyed the results of his handiwork. Two sheds, a tank, and a mile's length of fencing had been consumed by the flames. The ponies were scattered to the four winds but none was burned.

"*You damn fool!*" Cassie said.

"Easy, Professor—no harm done!"

"No harm—"

"She's free, ain't she?"

"Oh, she's free, all right. If you count being locked in a box *free*. Here, take the key—I don't want any part of it."

"You already got yerself a part in it, Cass—a big part! For which I'm thankin' ya most sincerely!"

"That third grenade. What the devil—"

"Petroleum spirits, Professor! Whole tank of 'em! Farmers hereabouts put the stuff in their tractors. Ever hear o' such a thing? Stuff sure does burn!"

JACKO MUDD'S WORK GANGS rounded up the ponies, and the *Pancho Villa Express* got under way. They had lost precious time: it was close to two o'clock in the morning before they cleared the yards. Like so many other towns, Hutchinson was pleased to see them go. An inquiry into the source of the fire was begun, but nobody connected it to Army grenades, nor to Rocks McAuliffe. The townspeople already had their suspicions as to the villain at large: he went by the name Spontaneous Combustion.

At Turon, the first watering stop, Cassie visited both cabs and signed up the new crews in his book. The hoggers—Tim Tyler in No. 506 and Packy LaBelle in No. 799—would carry the load as far as Dalhart, Texas, three hundred miles down the track from Hutchinson. Both men belonged to the Santa Fe; neither one had volunteered for the present job of work.

"Ain't drove a Baldie old as this in ten years," said LaBelle, laughing about it, "and don't hope to agin! This fella firin' for me is the best in the business, and look at him. He's about busted and we ain't gone fifty miles!"

His fireman, Mr. Bunny, wore a crooked grin stuck to his face like a mask. He had taken a bath in his own sweat and knew two occupations: grinning and shoveling.

"The government sure appreciates you laboring so hard," Cassie said to LaBelle. Then, in guarded tones, he sprang Mr. Webster's bonus for fast running.

"Don't waste time, boy!" exclaimed LaBelle. "State your deadline!"

Twenty dollars was good money along the Santa Fe, it appeared. Cassie had already set the next horse stop with Van Impe; it was to be Comanche Junction, just over the Oklahoma line. Not knowing how long they would be red-lighted there made it hard for Cassie to figure the running time to Dalhart, but one way or another he settled on ten o'clock in the morning. This would take some doing, but from what Cassie had seen of the hoggers at Hutchinson, he judged them spirited and resourceful. He was not to be disappointed by their reactions now:

"Then you're as good as standin' in the Dalhart station!" said Packy LaBelle. " 'Cept you'd best order Tim Tyler in that sorry hog up front to get the lead out o' his britches. Else we're sure to chew on his 'boose fer breakfast!"

Tim Tyler turned it around: "I'll be sayin' 'bye to ol' LaBelle now 'cause this rig o' mine'll see Texas long afore his!"

This was all Cassie had to hear. He went straight over to the switchman's shed and left a telegraph message for the Rock Island division super at Dalhart:

PULLMAN'S NO. 3 UPDATING ARRIVAL TEN O'CLOCK. REQUESTING EARLY NOTICE TO RELIEFERS. MCGILL, CONDUCTOR.

Cassie reached inside his watch pocket and fingered the millionaire's fifty-dollar bill. With hoggers as good as these, that gold certificate would soon be his for keeps.

Four short blasts on the whistle: CALL FOR SIGNALS. Leaning off the rear vestibule steps, Cassie raised and lowered Captain Gump's lantern several times in the signal for MOVE AHEAD. *Pullman's No. 3* picked up speed.

Inside the van, Cassie found he had visitors. "Caboose's off limits to all but employees," he said. All he could think of was the sixteen-year-old stowaway straight down below the floorboards.

"Well now, 'tis the lad himself," said Jacko Mudd in a friendly voice. He was talking to his steady pal Ward Snivey.

Cassie looked around for help. Rocks and the off-duty porters had apparently cleared out; the caboose was empty except for old Legrand, the brakeman. Being a gentleman, Legrand would go some distance to avoid a fight. He promptly headed up the ladder to the angel's nest.

"Know what I'm thinkin', Jacko?" said Trooper Snivey. "I'm thinkin' o' breakin' this shithead in two!"

Cassie set down Captain Gump's lamp and grabbed the fire ax off the wall.

"*Easy* now, boy—he's only jokin'," said Jacko Mudd. He turned to Snivey. "Ward? Now you go on forward and settle your business with the lieutenant. The boy and me, we're gonna have ourselves a friendly talk."

Snivey did not move at first. Finally he grunted and went out. Cassie lowered the ax.

"How 'bout sittin' for a spell?" said Jacko Mudd. He acted like the nicest fellow in the world.

"It's okay by me," Cassie said. He hung the ax back on the wall.

The sergeant major occupied one of the wicker chairs by the bay window. Cassie sat opposite on one of the bunks.

"Smoke?" The sergeant major offered Cassie the makings, but Cassie shook his head. "Mind if I do?"

"Go ahead," Cassie said.

The sergeant major rolled himself a neat cigarette from golden leaf and brown paper. He was a handsome man in his way. Though balding and with rolls of fat around his middle—too much paperwork, Cassie thought, and too little horse riding—he possessed intelligent eyes, a ready smile, and the smooth manners of a fellow who had known a good home. The stripes on each arm covered the whole bicep—three bars up top joined to three in a curve below, with a diamond in the middle. His uniform was as wrinkled and dirty as any trooper's except for his boots, which were polished to a high gloss. Cassie had the idea that the same privates who cared for the Squadron's harness saw to the sergeant major's boots.

"You and your pal—you boys got spunk, I'll say that for you, Cassius. Or maybe you like 'McGill' better?"

"Cassius is fine."

"Cassius, then. You boys are top cavalry material, I can tell you that. Ever give any thought to the Army for your livelihood?"

"No, sir, I sure haven't."

"There's worse professions for a bright lad like yourself."

"Railroad suits me fine."

"Sure it does. You're a fortunate lad. Got yourself a good job. Lots o' fellas aren't so lucky."

"That's what you wanted to see me about? Joining the Army?"

Jacko Mudd's easy smile faded somewhat. "That and other matters."

"I've got my duties," Cassie said. He looked at Nelson's watch, pretending to be short on time.

"I'll say my piece then," said the sergeant major. "Me and Ward Snivey —we're real sorry 'bout that little dustup we got into with you boys yesterday. From here on out we want to be friends—you, me, Ward, and that great pal o' yours, Rocks. Why, Cassius, we've taken a shine to young Rocks, we sure have. He's tops with us, same as you."

"Which is how come you did your best to *murder* him? And me, too?"

The sergeant major smiled. "Little fight 'tween friends—that ain't murder, Cassius. 'Course, the ways of the military are new to you. How old are you, son? What—maybe twenty?"

"Close enough," Cassie said.

"Hell, boy, I got a son o' my own older than you! Don't you think I know about *boys?* About being friends to 'em?"

Cassie put the sergeant major's age at something near Pa's, maybe fifty or a little more. It was hard to imagine a trooper like Jacko Mudd—a professional fighter on his way to war—having a life outside the Army. Cassie wondered what Jacko Mudd's boy would be like.

"Look, son, let's get down to brass tacks. You and your pal stole something that belongs to us. Give us back what's ours and that's it—we're friends to the end."

"What did we ever steal of yours?" Cassie asked innocently.

"You know the answer to that, boy."

"I don't."

The sergeant major shifted his rump, making the wicker groan and sigh under his weight. "I'm only going to say it the one time, boy. I'm talking about pretty little Jolene."

"Even if we had her, how can you say she's yours? She's a *person*, isn't she? There's no such things as slaves anymore."

"We're gonna find her, you know," said the sergeant major. He continued to smile when he talked, but it seemed hard for him.

Cassie kept an eye on the fire ax—measured the distance to it, figured out in his mind about how long he would take to reach it. Abruptly he said: "I'm thinking she left the train at Hutchinson."

"Oh, no, boy, she's still aboard," said Jacko Mudd. "You can be sure of that."

"Probably up front, then," Cassie replied. "In *The Mother Lode*, I'll bet."

The sergeant major stopped smiling. "That would be bad for you and your pal. For your sake, I hope you're lyin'. I'm gonna level with you, Cassius. You boys took the wrong one, is all. Make off with Rita or Naomi and maybe there's no trouble. But Jolene—she's the favorite. You know how many enlisted men we got in this outfit? Two hundred eighty. I can promise you every one of 'em is on the lookout for Miss Jolene. And when she's found, she's sure to point out the culprits who stole her away. Won't be any way, when the culprits' names is known, that I can save 'em. Their bodies won't never be found—that's a fact."

Cassie's eyes fell to the floor directly under Jacko Mudd's seat. Cassie wondered if Jolene could hear their words.

The sergeant major lifted his weight from the chair with obvious effort. His khaki pants and shirt were stained through with sweat. "I'm going to make it easy for you, Cassius. I'm going to offer you a swap."

"Swap?"

"Something o' yours for something of ours."

"For instance?"

"Them pretty beads o' yours."

The sergeant major smiled again. Cassie did not. "You're talking about my rosary?" Cassie said evenly.

"Rosary, then," said Jacko Mudd. "Seems it's Ward Snivey's property now. But you can have it back. All you got to do is give us the girl. An even trade, Cassius. What do you say?"

A human being for a rosary. Cassie could imagine what Ma would say. "I expect I'll be getting my rosary back on my own," Cassie told the trooper.

"My, my—won't Ward Snivey be surprised to hear it!"

"Go and tell him," Cassie said. "I'd appreciate it if you would."

"Don't worry—he'll know it soon enough!"

"You'd best be going, then. I'll signal for slow running. You drop off when I say so, and you'll get picked up by the second section. . . ."

Rocks jumped with glee when he heard. ". . . Ya *told* him that? Right to his face? An' then tossed him off the train?"

"Didn't toss him off," Cassie said. "Just showed him how to get back where he belongs."

"Wisht I coulda seen it!"

"I'll get back my rosary," Cassie said quietly. "Bet on it."

"*Sure* you will, Cass! It's the same fer me and Jolene. By God, her and me's gonna 'scape from 'em, Cass—bet on that, too!"

"Then what?"

"I don't getcha."

"Say you get away—you and Jolene. Then what? Where can you go?"

"But we got all that *figured!* Jeez, I thought I *told* ya—guess I dint! It's Californie, Cass! Jolene's got family out there, ain't that grand? They'll take us in till we can find somethin' of our own—get me a job, settle down for good."

"Settle down?"

"That's it, Cass. No more road for me. That's okay for you—you're educated, you got a good job. But the road's no place for the likes o' me."

Cassie chewed on this awhile. "So how you going to get there—to California?"

"Easy, Professor. You let us off at 'Paso and we head west. Couldn't be easier!"

"Using what for money? You think the railroads are going to let you and Jolene ride free all the way to the Pacific Ocean?"

"I'll have me pay, won't I?"

"What's that? How many dollars is that?"

"Dint you tell me a dollar a day and grub?"

"Pretend it's two dollars a day and grub. What's that? Ten dollars? How far do you think you'll get on ten dollars?"

"Well then, I'll get me some more in 'Paso. I hear it's a fine town with lots o' people 'n' hotels 'n' all the comforts o' home. Maybe they got a league, Cass. Maybe I'll play me some ball fer a while, then head on out to the blue Pacific. You'd do well to think on it yerself, Cass."

"Baseball?"

"Why, Californie, o' course! San Francisco! Great Goddess o' the Pacific! They got carriages, Cass, drawn up and down the hills by steam power on account o' no horse could climb 'em! Oh, it'll be somethin' to see, Professor!"

It was Rocks's regular line of goods: going down to work as pilots on the Isthmian canal or signing up for an expedition to Timbuktu. Nobody talked malarky better than Rocks McAuliffe. "It sounds a fine plan," Cassie said without enthusiasm.

This remark turned Rocks serious. "But you ain't gonna live to see Californie or even the city limits of 'Paso 'less you do as I say, Cass—which is to stick next to me like I'm your second skin."

"Meaning what?"

"Meanin' Snivey and Mudd—they'd as soon kill ya as look atcha. Take my word on it!"

"But sticking to you I'm safe, is that it?"

"You sure are—long as I got this!"

The shortstop drew back his jacket to show his belt. Hanging inside was another of the troopers' Colt .45 automatics.

"Tell me that thing isn't loaded," said Cassie.

"Bet yer skinny ass it's loaded! It'll bring back your beads any time you say, too—that's gospel!"

"Sure—shoot the bugger and then peel Ma's rosary off his bleeding corpse."

"Tell me a quicker way! Snivey'd do it to *you*, wouldn't he, if it was t'other way round?"

"There's other ways than killing a man."

"Mebbe there is, mebbe there ain't. Tell me one."

"Poker."

"Poker?"

"Poker."

It took a few seconds for the idea to sink into the shortstop's brain. When it did, he leapt in the air and came down with a hoot and a holler. "Then you *got* 'im, Cass! Snivey's a gonner fer sure! 'Cause who's the champeen poker player of all time?"

"I can play some."

"*Some?*" The shortstop's eyes glowed like hot coals. "Can Cobb swipe bases? If you ain't the best five-card player on earth, who would he be!"

Privately, Cassie might have agreed. The true legacy of his baseball days was more than a sore arm; it was the deep knowledge of five-card draw that he had acquired during those traveling days when every rooming house was the University of Poker. Maybe such skill was no Christian virtue, but it was surely his best hope of getting back Ma's rosary and squaring himself with Mudd and Snivey.

"Only, how can ya make them skunks fall into yer trap, Cass? What if they won't play?"

"They'll play," Cassie said. "Is there a trooper on this whole damn train who won't play cards if you ask him?"

"If you ain't the smartest left-hander in Mr. Pullman's bullpen!"

They would soon know about that, Cassie figured. It wouldn't take nine innings to find out, either.

Preston, Pratt, Wellsford, Haviland, Brenham, Greensberg. There was no end to the train towns in Kansas. In the dark, from Cassie's vantage point on top, one looked much like another. The countryside was flat as a billiard table but lacked its greenness. Even by acetylene torch the fields showed up sandy brown. The ground had been plowed shallow and spring planting was on. For the least part of a minute, Cassie entertained pleasant thoughts of planting time on the farm down at Hastings. But he had taught himself to think *now* over *yesterday*, and *now* was the rattle of the rails and the stink of animals, dead or alive, and gloomy forebodings for the sixteen-year-old stowaway down below in the locked tool chest. On such thoughts, Cassie dozed, head bobbing to the rhythms of the road.

They coaled up at Bucklin, a crossroads for the Rock Island and Santa Fe lines down toward the bottom of Kansas. It was four thirty in the morning and they were twenty-seven miles southeast of Dodge City. That was a town Cassie wanted to see some day; he had read a half-dozen books on the place. But that was on a line heading west. The *Pancho Villa Express* was now southbound and would stay that way till she reached the border.

"I'm gonna have a look down under," Rocks told him.

"There's morning light," Cassie warned. "Watch yourself."

Jacko Mudd's boys were moving like a plague of locusts through the train, crawling over every inch of every car. According to Nelson, they had even rousted Chef Kolb and his helper John, looking for Jolene in the pantry of *The Mother Lode*. Would it be long, Cassie wondered, before they started looking *under* the cars?

Rocks soon returned. "She's sick as a dog, Cass! The pore li'l thing's freezin' ta death under there, top o' which she's about shook to pieces!"

Jolene Potts was in dire straits, by the shortstop's estimation. He had climbed down under the van, put his lips to a knothole in the possum belly, and obtained a bill of particulars, coughed out through a torrent of tears. Jolene was sick to her stomach from the action of the car. Also the burlap sacks she had for a pillow made her skin go dry and itchy.

But mainly she needed to find the toilet. She wanted to get down and do her business then and there over the ties, but Rocks refused to unlock the box, knowing that Trooper Snivey was close by. For the time being, Rocks had poked out some more knotholes fore and aft so she could breathe easier and—if worse came to worst—handle her other bodily functions too.

"Know what she wants more 'n anythin' in this world, Cass?"

"What?"

"Ta get forward to *The Mother Lode*."

"Hah!"

"Know what they got up there, Cass? Nelson says they got real porcelain toilets like in a fine hotel. Could that be right? You seen 'em, Cass?"

"Better than any hotel. She's Pullman's best, I told you."

"Jolene—she needs to *go*, Cass. She's gonna get herself sick if she don't."

"Tell her to hold on till Comanche Junction," Cassie said. "It'll be broad daylight by then, but if we're careful maybe we can get her down while the troopers are running the horses."

"I'll tell her, Cass. She'll be ever so grateful to ya! There's jes the one other thing, then."

"What's that?" said Cassie with some exasperation. He couldn't imagine how the girl could have any more troubles than she already had.

"Her ciggies, Cass. If she don't get one soon, she's gonna die sure 'nough. I promised her I'd see to it."

The shortstop was full of promises where Jolene Potts was concerned. But this was one promise he would find hard to keep. Jolene had left her prized possession, a box of Pinchon's Fatima Pure Turkish Cigarettes, back in Jacko Mudd's guardhouse. She might have been sixteen by the calendar but she was grown-up in her pleasures and a fiend for tobacco. She would have smoked a stogie if Rocks had brought her one.

"So what's that to do with me?" Cassie said.

"Two bucks, Cass! You gotta loan it to me!"

"Not on your life."

"It's *Jolene's* life that's dependin' on it!"

"It's out of your pay, then."

"All the better!"

Cassie parted with his last two singles. It seemed too small a sum for a Tool of the Interests to argue over.

Comanche Junction, Oklahoma: railroad station, one sun-baked street, three saloons, and the Office of Agent for Indian Affairs, United States of America.

The *Pancho Villa Express* rolled to a stop at the geographic center of the place, the first section's locomotive touching the town limits on one end, the second section's caboose doing the same at the other. The inhabitants were mostly connected to either the Santa Fe or the Rock Island or the local line, the Beaver, Meade & Englewood. Looking in any direction, there was not a tree to be seen from Main Street to the horizon. The government office was bleached wood siding with a tent for a roof.

Eight o'clock in the morning but already starting to warm up. The ponies were off-loaded in record time by troopers eager to line up at the cook car for breakfast. All but two of the ramps built at Fort Meade had come apart, so some of the more impatient troopers took to jumping their mounts straight off the cars onto the ground. To Cassie's astonishment, not a single animal was injured by this procedure. Loading up would be a different proposition, since the soldiers would have no choice but to wait their turns using the ramps.

The horses quickly wandered off looking for grass, which they never would find in such barren country, while the wranglers unloaded feed and arranged with the townspeople for water. The 4th Squadron outnumbered the locals at this stop three to one. Cassie set out his flagmen, then headed for *The Mother Lode,* hoping to bum some edibles off Chef Kolb. He had gone only a few steps when he found himself sent sprawling by a galloping horse.

"Look out, damn you!" he shouted, trying to catch his breath.

Whereupon the rider wheeled and shouted back at him: "Watch out yourself, Mr. Conductor!"

Miss Candace Webster.

"Oh, good morning, ma'am! Excuse me, ma'am!"

He had hardly picked himself up when another rider tried to run him down.

"Stand clear, McGill! Be alert, man! You nearly spooked the lady's horse!"

Van Impe, the bastard! Cassie flattened himself against one of the day cars and watched as the riders wheeled again and strutted their mounts. Miss Candace rode a spirited gray gelding, Van Impe a small brown mare. The lady wore proper riding breeches and boots, a velvet jacket and a fancy derby. A long pink scarf danced in the wind behind her. She looked fresh out of *Scribner's Weekly.* The lieutenant was done up in a spotless parade uniform complete with silver spurs. The couple might have been promenading in New York's Central Park instead of Main Street, Comanche Junction. They cantered as far as the second-section caboose, then turned and galloped back to *The Mother Lode.* Troopers by the cook car let out a cheer as the riders passed. Otis and Lydia Webster, the padre and Mademoiselle Foix were among the early risers: they observed the riders' merry dash and applauded at race's end. Gallantly, the lieutenant permitted Miss Candace to win, though his mount seemed quicker by far.

Cassie wanted to move closer to *The Mother Lode* but dared not. His Pullman Company uniform was no better than prisoner's stripes: so long as he wore it, he was a slave to countless masters. He watched the happy goings-on with greedy eyes. He *knew* he could ride a horse better than the lieutenant, if only he had the chance. He cursed his luck; cursed the lieutenant too. In the distance he could hear Mademoiselle Foix's amused, throaty greeting to Captain Lonnie Bowles: ". . . *Ah, bon jour, mon Capitaine* . . ."

Cassie wished such a greeting could be meant for him. The private party was a strange new world. He longed to make its acquaintance, study its inhabitants. But now it was all spoiled for him. *Van Impe, the bastard!*

Bastard. The word seemed to float in the air. Without warning, the lieutenant spurred his pony on a line straight for Cassie, pulling up at the last possible moment and splattering Cassie with saliva and dust. The frightened animal was blowing hard and foaming at the bit.

"Ho, McGill! Understand you are a master chess player. Be so kind as to give me a game at your convenience!"

Cassie stumbled back in humiliation. The van was his world; he meant to flee there and hide out. But Otis Webster stopped him.

"Cassius! Good morning to you, son. Here, give us a hand, won't you? Show Mushy a tight rein while I apply myself to this Kodak. . . ."

The millionaire was intent upon making photographs of his daughter and her beau. Cassie accepted the leash as though it were a length of molten lead. How he hated that dog! He was not alone; all the porters had learned to despise it, too. The animal was treacherous and deceitful. It would lie in wait in the pantry, or under a table in the parlor, then leap forward to nip at an unsuspecting passerby. Where was Christian, Cassie wondered. Whenever the train stopped, Christian's first job was to walk the beast. Even so, it thought nothing of fouling the carpets in *The Mother Lode*.

The animal now dragged Cassie along the platform, puffing and growling as it went. "Hold now, Cassius!" called the millionaire after him. "Let us have a smile, won't you?" Cassie did his best but found it hard: the dog was just then fouling his boot. One thing Cassie knew: Otis Webster got value for money.

Later, when the troopers had scattered as far as the farthest pony, Cassie and Nelson and the porters Tobias and Milo formed a line in front of the possum belly while Rocks ducked under and pulled Jolene Potts out and escorted her inside the van. She had been trainsick again and could barely walk. The rank smell of her vomit turned Rocks's stomach, too. Cassie knew of a medicine for it, but the van's Red Cross kit contained none.

Jolene's spirits improved after she cleaned herself up. The van's toilet was galvanized tin, not porcelain, but it served her needs. Afterwards, Rocks produced a dinner pail especially prepared by Chef Kolb together with a bottle of cool drinking water and the thing Jolene wanted most, her box of Pinchon's Fatima Pure Turkish Cigarettes. The shortstop had used Cassie's two dollars to bribe rear-shack Coffin—the Rabbit—to retrieve Jolene's ciggies from the guardhouse. The poor girl broke into tears when she saw them again. She had been crying when she came out of her prison and was crying when she went back in. Rocks's pug face turned as ghostly as Jolene's; his suffering matched hers tear for tear.

They were not out of trouble; far from it. Moving on down the track-bed, Cassie looked back and saw smoke pouring from the knotholes. A person who did not know better might have cried fire.

"Cass?" said Rocks.

"Hush! I see it." Cassie immediately ordered Tobias to stand by the van and smoke cigarettes one after another. Any smoke seen thereabouts would be his. The Negro puffed and grinned like a Chinaman.

Cassie was busy congratulating himself on his great cleverness when the Websters came along, enjoying their constitutional. Cassie hid himself behind the van, but he could still hear Lydia Webster's bitter complaint:

". . . Have you ever! Look there, Otis, a *porter* smoking on duty! What has become of Pullman standards? Upon our return to Chicago, I urge you to pen a strongly worded letter to Robert Lincoln, voicing our extreme displeasure. . . ."

They got rolling again. When he had finished his chores, Cassie sought out Doc Rose, thinking the vet might provide medicine to ease Jolene's discomfort.

"Good morning, sir. Would I be bothering you if I sat a spell?"

"Good morning to you, Cassius. Not bothering me one iota. Won't you join an old vet at his breakfast?"

The vet had made quarters for himself in one of the horse cars by cornering off the box with bales of hay and spreading out his suit coat to make a bed. He preferred to sleep among the sick animals rather than stay up front in the officers' Pullman. The breakfast he was giving himself was a stick of Chef Kolb's German sausage washed down by Mr. Webster's brandy.

"Thank you, sir," said Cassie, "but I already had some bread and cheese in the van."

The vet sat with his back against a hay bale; Cassie now did the same. Doc's vest and shirt were flecked with blood. His eyes never stopped watering, which made him look as though he were crying all the time.

"Matter of fact," said Doc, "you're the second visitor I've had already today. First was Captain Bowles. Real fine fellow, Lonnie Bowles."

"Yes, sir, so I believe."

"Shows the delightful manners of your true southerner. Native of Anniston, Alabama, and grandson of another Captain Bowles, who served as aide-de-camp to Robert E. Lee. Came straight from the colonel this morning, did Lonnie, to inform me that a court-martial will be convened at Bliss, and guess who's on the spot? It's 'cause of my drinking, which, to be honest, is now excessive." To prove his point, Doc went at his brandy again.

"I'm sure sorry to hear it, sir."

"Well, it's not entirely unfair, now is it? These soldiers, you must understand, Cassius, are high on discipline. Discipline is the main stuff of their lives and I've not taken well to it. I say this though I've been a government horse doctor going on twelve years now, adding up the various hitches. I've got no cause for complaint. I made my bed and I'm content to lie in it. This isn't to say—had I to do it over again—that I wouldn't do things different. I would. Fact is, vets aren't the same as real soldiers."

"No, sir?"

The red-faced vet chuckled at the thought. "There's a document, Cassius, known as the 'Monthly Return of the Regiment.' Colonel Antrobus sends it on to the War Department in Washington at the close of each month. This piece of paper is supposed to set out every pertinent fact of the outfit's life—duties for the month, strength, condition of the animals, et cetera. Well, sir, there's an instruction printed on that form that says, 'Veterinarians will be reported by name at the bottom of the list of officers, but will not be included in strength of the regiment.' *Not* included in strength of the regiment! I guess that should have told me, when I first signed on, just where I'd be after all these years—still at the bottom of the list!"

"I'm sorry, sir."

"Don't be. I wouldn't have missed such a career for anything in this world."

"No, sir?"

"Why, look at all the fine people I've come to meet!" Doc laughed good-naturedly. Cassie found it hard to do likewise. "You doubt it, boy?"

"No, sir—not exactly. Only—well, sir, I was thinking of Lieutenant Van Impe."

"Hah! 'Ter-ble Tommy,' the boys like to call him. Stuck-up little runt, ain't he? But he's got excuse for it. Comes from a Dutch family up Albany way. Built the Erie Canal, they did, back in the '20s. He's a terror all right, that boy. Top athlete in his class at the Point—best sprinter at fifty paces, best man with the blade, best horseman. His father is never out of the newspapers—physician to all the great politicians including his cousins, those other damn Dutch, the Roosevelts. Who do you suppose it was saw to McKinley after the President took the Pole's bullet at Buffalo? Why o' course, it was Ter-ble Tommy's pa. His ma's just as bad—society lady from Poughkeepsie—daughter to a Vanderbilt or one o' those. Their sweet Tommy's sure to receive his first star about as early as Pershing did. That's how come poor Antrobus is breaking his ass to hang on to the lad—calling him 'adjutant,' don'tcha know—making him the high-and-mighty 'train commander.' Same goes for Otis Webster. Otis could do a lot worse by way of a son-in-law than young General Van Impe. . . ."

Cassie sucked air at the idea of it: *the bastard Van Impe having his way with Miss Candace.*

" 'Course, being a handsome young fellow, the lieutenant's got himself an itchy cock. Wants the Webster girl for her fine breeding and sweet disposition, but hankers after the French lady, too. Can't say I blame him —she looks an armful! Ambitious little vixen, that one. As humble in her origins as you or me, but aiming for royalty. Rose above her station by catching on as 'tutor' and 'companion' on the *Olympic*—that's one o' them great triple-screw steamers on the Atlantic service, older sister to the *Titanic*. So it was that 'Mademoiselle' Foix hitched herself to the Websters—gave the daughter lessons *en français* aboard ship and never let go . . ."

(Cassie was momentarily confused: Doc Rose pronounced "Fwah" what Cassie had called to himself "Foyx.")

". . . Looking to find herself a rich American husband, is my guess. Meanwhile she's satisfied to hang on the arm o' the 'padre'—ain't *he* the spittin' image of a saint! Fancies himself a 'brother of Damien.' Seeing to Lydia Webster's conversion to the True Faith. Me, I wouldn't be surprised if he turned out to be a girl under that smock! . . ."

Cassie reeled under the torrent of juicy gossip. He had never before known great people to be spoken of with such disrespect. Even a Father!

Doc soon fell silent. The vet helped himself to more of the brandy, then sat staring at the bottle it came from. Only then did Cassie remember what he had come to see Doc about in the first place.

"Sir? Could I ask you kind of a medical question?"

"Speak up, son—though I should perhaps warn you that my recent attempts at healing have not exactly inspired confidence in my superiors!"

Choosing his words with care, Cassie told of Jolene's stomach sickness in the possum belly. Before Doc could comment, a wrangler passed through on his way to another car. Doc waited till the stranger was gone, then sent forth an explosion of coughs and curses:

". . . If that don't beat all! A tiny band of young people in defiance of the age-old corruption of the military! I have the greatest admiration for your courage, my boy!"

"To be truthful, sir, it's my pal Rocks who's got the courage—and Miss Jolene, too. If you had some kind of tonic, sir—she's not used to going by train and—"

"*Mal de mer,* boy. That's the young lady's trouble."

"Sir?"

"Seasickness, lad. Got just the thing for it." Doc rummaged through his bag and brought forth a small bottle. "See that she gets a spoonful four times a day—guaranteed to cure nausea, vomiting, dizzy spells, hot flashes, and whatever else may ail her. Only not to overdo—works like a sleeping potion when taken in excess."

"She'll be wanting to thank you herself, sir, when she's free again. Meanwhile, I'll be happy to pay you for it myself."

"Wouldn't accept a penny! I'm proud to assist, however remotely, in so worthwhile an undertaking. May this tonic serve your partner as the true Elixir of Love!"

"Thank you, sir. I'm sure it'll be just that."

Though, as a matter of fact, the shortstop had never needed help in the loving department.

They soon crossed Oklahoma's narrow panhandle and steamed into Texas. *Pullman's No. 3* slowed its pace. They had been climbing steadily since Hutchinson, which stood at a thousand feet of elevation, and were now over three. Looking ahead on *Busby's* topographical maps, Cassie saw that New Mexico was higher yet, with Tucumcari at four thousand and Carrizozo over five. This meant plenty of steep grades, which would not suit the Baldwins one bit. Already it was all Packy LaBelle could do to stay in sight of the first section; his hog turned out to have shorter legs than her sister up front. Even so, both hoggers were running nicely ahead of Cassie's timetable. He had no doubts he would be paying out Mr. Webster's gold on arrival at Dalhart.

The slowed pace did not sit well with the troopers. After the excitement of seeing their first real desert they became quickly bored again and sought relief in singing their old war songs:

> *I'm only a common soldierman*
>   *in the blasted Philippines.*
> *They say I've got brown brothers here,*
>   *but I dunno what it means.*
> *I like the word Fraternity,*
>   *but still I draw the line.*
> *He may be a brother to William H. Taft,*
>   *but he ain't no friend o' mine.*

Their favorite was sung to the tune of "Tramp, tramp, tramp, the boys are marching":

> In that land o' dopy dreams,
> happy peaceful Philippines.
> Where the bolo-man is hiking
> night and day;
> Where Tagalos steal and lie,
> where Americanos die,
> There you hear the soldiers sing
> this evening lay:
> Damn, damn, damn the Filipinos,
> Cross-eyed khakiac ladrones!*
> Underneath our starry flag,
> Civilize 'em with a Krag,
> And return us to our beloved homes.

The Squadron's own Filipinos—some fifty or more—took no part in these Yankee sentiments. They had songs of their own, which they sang in a tongue peculiar to them called Tagalog.

"White men cannot learn it," said Doc Rose. "The Filipinos are born with it—it is in their blood."

A dozen or more of them in one car would get on the same song, accompanying themselves on their strange little guitars, which they called *ukuleles,* and they made a pretty thing of it. The Filipinos also spoke Spanish and were thus expected to serve a useful purpose in the war on Villa.

"They must show themselves harder in war than any o' their white comrades," said Doc Rose, "or else there is a question as to their loyalty —they bein' kin to the Mex, don'tcha know."

For now, the singing dried up. Some rowdies in Troop A found a more popular diversion: shooting their pistols off the day-car platforms. Pistols were supposed to have been collected back at Fort Meade, along with the other weapons, and deposited in the Squadron Armory, but certain smart-pants had held onto theirs. What the troops were shooting at were long-legged Texas jackrabbits. They were no ordinary rabbits. Some were as big as collie dogs. All of them moved quicker than the *Pancho Villa Express.* Though the troopers sprayed the landscape with government lead, the rabbits traveled in perfect safety.

Soon after the first volleys, two of the Squadron's junior officers, Lieutenant Wallace Armstrong of Troop A and Lieutenant Harley Withers of Troop D, were sent back from Headquarters Car to establish order. Firing in the first section ceased but that in the second grew hotter, the second now running a mile or more to the rear. Cassie offered to give the

---

* Editor's note: Dark-skinned thieves.

signal for SLOW RUNNING so the officers could drop off and catch on to LaBelle's rig, but Armstrong and Withers decided against it. Cassie had the idea that the officers stood in greater fear of the renegades out back than they did of the colonel. Three full days of sitting up in the day cars had turned the best of the troopers mean and ornery. A person was safe enough in the horse cars, which the troopers avoided except when ordered there on clean-up duty; but walking down the aisles of the day cars was a sure invitation to robbery and mayhem. Once, when they had nothing better to do, a nasty bunch from Troop C—after ripping apart their car in search of souvenirs of their journey—grabbed hold of Brakeman Small, stripped off his uniform, and ran him at bayonet point naked to *The Mother Lode.*

After a while, the firing out back stopped of its own accord. These boys soon tired of everything but their quick visits to the guardhouse. The only discipline meted out there came in five-minute doses, one dollar to the minute. According to rear-shack Coffin, even Doc Rose had "dipped his quill in company ink." The Rabbit had a tender way with words, having served as dispatcher with the Baltimore & Ohio in palmier days.

At Deep Wells, they made their last stop before Dalhart. When Cassie returned to the van from his duties, he found Rocks whistling and drinking beer that he had begged off the troopers. The shortstop seemed in fine spirits.

"It's on, Cass! I got it all 'ranged!"

"What's that?"

"The *game,* Cass! Twixt us and them. What else would I be talkin' about?"

"Well?"

"They went fer it, Cass! Jackpots, which you al'ays play and never lose at!"

Jackpots was the proper name for five-card draw, jacks or better. This was the game Cassie and Rocks had played hundreds of times in clubhouses and hotels from Hastings to Niagara Falls and back.

"How many at table?" asked Cassie.

"Five. You, me, Mudd, Snivey o' course, and 'nother o' their gang— don't know his name."

"What stakes?"

"Each player to show with fifty bucks. We play till somebody takes it all. This is you, o' course."

"Rules?"

"Dollar ante, five-dollar limit on bets and raises, table stakes on a fella's last hand so he can't get froze out with winnin' cards. No bug, nothin' wild. Sweet rules, Cass!"

"So where's Ma's rosary in all this?"

"Almost forgot the best thing, dint I!" The shortstop was so excited he could hardly stay in one place—kept crossing his legs as though he wanted to pee. "Damn Snivey says whoever takes the last hand gits yer beads, too—that's you, o' course!"

"And what if I *don't* take the last hand?"

"Fat chance! Why, them beads is good as hangin' 'round yer neck, Professor! Who's gonna beat Lefty McGill at five-card? Not them bastards!"

"There's two things we *got* to have," said Cassie after some thought.

"What's that, Cass?"

"One's a fresh deck. We won't play with those pasteboards they've been using in the day cars. Those cards have so many markings on them they might as well be face up to their owners."

"Where we gonna find fresh cards, Cass?"

"Next stop. Dalhart, Texas."

"I'll tell 'em!"

"And tell them we're playing right here in this van, not out back."

"Oh, they won't go fer that, Cass. I know them soldier boys better 'n you. They like their own turf."

"Tell them."

"I'll tell 'em, Cass."

"There's one other thing, isn't there?"

"What's that, Cass?"

"As if you didn't know. Bankroll. Fifty for me, fifty for you."

"Guess I forgot."

"Guess you did."

The shortstop's lips parted in a big grin. "I seen what yo're totin' about in that great purse o' yers, Professor!"

This took Cassie by surprise. He kicked himself for his carelessness. "That money's not mine," he said. "Matter of fact, it's Pullman's. It's—it's operating capital."

Rocks kept his smile. "What ol' Mr. Pullman don't know ain't gonna hurt him an' us neither! It ain't no *gamble,* Cass, if that's what yo're thinkin'. Damn, it's yer beads back an' a great pile o' the troopers' cash to boot!"

"And if we lose?"

"Ain't gonna *lose,* Cass!"

Cassie could feel his celluloid collar grow tighter at the thought of it: betting cards on another fellow's bankroll. It was nothing he could ever tell Ma or Pa about. But if he got back to Lincoln with Ma's rosary around his neck, who was to say he had done wrong?

"Go see Mudd and tell him what I said. Fresh cards and the game's here. Railroad ground is neutral, tell him."

"I'll do it, Cass!" The shortstop turned to go, but then came back a step or two. His habitual grin had turned sheepish. "Cass? It ain't important, only—"

"Only what?"

"Only—'bout the stakes."

"What about the stakes?"

"There was one li'l thing I had to promise 'em, Cass—if they was to put up yer beads."

"Out with it."

"It's nothin' *bad,* Cass. It's only—if we was to lose, we'd go ahead and tell 'em where Jolene's at. But we ain't gonna *lose,* Cass—so what's the harm in it, tell me that . . . ?"

8

THE CONSTANT GRADE had taken its toll. *Pullman's No.* 3 did not see the town limits of Dalhart until 10:20 A.M., twenty minutes past Cassie's deadline. Even so, Cassie figured the 4th Squadron would reach El Paso in plenty of time to join up with Pershing. The *Pancho Villa Express* had put 1,290 miles under its wheels since Fort Meade and had only 425 more to go.

Under Tim Tyler's heavy hand, No. 506 bore down on the Dalhart platform with all the fury of a Nebraska twister, whistle hooting, bell clanging, stack pouring out black smoke filled with sticky coal tar and ash. Even an ignorant stranger could see that Tim Tyler was running late. The hogger's frantic whistle put half the horses in town onto two legs.

After towns like Comanche Junction and Deep Wells, Dalhart seemed a true metropolis. Cassie had read up on it in *Busby's:*

Dalhart, "Queen of the Panhandle Plains"; elevation 3895 ft.; population 2750; dwellings 598; families 640; Dallam County Seat.

The nearest city was Amarillo, eighty-two miles southeast along the Colorado & Southern. Besides "Panhandle Plains," the country thereabouts was known by the Spanish name *Llano Estacado,* meaning "staked plains." Coronado's party in the 1500s had become frightened upon entering an endless sea of tall grass and so planted stakes in the prairie to help them find their way out again when they finished searching for Indian gold and the fabled Seven Cities of Cíbola. No gold was ever found, but the land proved rich in its own right. Now the prairie was sectioned off into 640-acre deeds and planted in grain. Blades of winter wheat already stood six inches high, making a bright green blanket that reached to the horizon in all directions. Such wheat was called Turkey Red or Crimea back in Hastings; Cassie's nostrils quivered at the scent of it. Clapboard houses fronted onto hand-dug ponds fed by wells a hundred feet deep. Peach, plum, and cherry orchards abounded. Farther out from town, clusters of fat cows and heifers dotted the plains. Cassie liked the look of this country, liked its smell. It was good farmland. Cassie wondered what Pa might have thought of it. But then Pa was a merchant now, not a farmer.

Cassie climbed down from the van and stretched his legs. Up front he could see the officers from Headquarters Car doing the same. Troopers and horses stayed on board: no more stops for them till New Mexico.

Cassie went forward, expecting to meet his reliefers along the way. None showed. Tim Tyler and Packy LaBelle would soon be outlawed, but for now—feeling guilty, Cassie supposed, over their tardiness into Dalhart—the hoggers remained in their cabs and let off steam. They would be itching to talk over their bonuses for fast running, late or not, but first they would run their tenders by the water tower and coaling wharf. They were sure to stay put till their replacements showed. The *Rules of Railroading* demanded nothing less.

The town's two train stations sat catercornered one from the other, Rock Island on the northeast, Santa Fe southwest. Cassie squared up his cap and headed for the Rock Island.

"One moment, Cassius, if you please." It was Colonel Antrobus, trailed by Van Impe.

"Sir?"

"What is your current estimate of our time of arrival at Fort Bliss?"

Cassie drew out his train book and flipped back and forth in the pages to give the idea that he was still doing hard numbers. In truth, he had already made the calculations. But Pa had taught him the trick of saving up pleasant surprises to the last moment, when they would have greatest effect.

"Well, sir, if the grades ahead aren't any worse than those we been seeing . . . give or take an hour . . . I'd say seven o'clock in the morning."

Cassie figured it was more like six o'clock, or even *five*, assuming the rails stayed as empty of traffic as they had been since Hutchinson.

The colonel seemed well pleased. "Splendid news! Even earlier than we had hoped, eh, Thomas?"

Van Impe kept his usual severe attitude. "If indeed, sir, McGill's estimate may be relied upon."

"The lad knows his business—he has proved himself," replied the colonel. "Prepare a wire message at once informing Lieutenant Patton of our early arrival."

"Yes, sir!" The stiff-backed lieutenant saluted smartly and went off at a brisk pace.

"Cassius, you have performed your duties well. Upon our arrival at Fort Bliss, I shall count it a pleasure to recommend to General Pershing that you and the Pullman Company be officially cited for contributions to the success of our mission. . . ."

Cassie only regretted that Mr. Laurence Cosgrove back in Omaha was not present to hear such words!

Cassie entered the Rock Island office with a light step.

"Make yourself to home, Cap'n," called out the agent, taking note of Cassie's cap. "I seen your rig, all right, but I'm tied to this damn wire—still on the receivin' end o' today's orders from Wich'ta."

He was a bright-eyed young fellow, plain-faced and skinny like Cassie, wearing the agent's badge of office, green eyeshade and black sleeve protectors, and pounding the telegraph key as though he had done it his whole life.

Cassie looked over the station. It was small but comfortable. A half-dozen passengers took advantage of the shade, reading newspapers until their trains came.

The agent soon finished his work and shut down the key. "Tinker Dawkins's the name—pleased to meet ya. So where you from and where you bound to?"

Cassie introduced himself. "Out of Lincoln, Nebraska, bound for El Paso. I'd be much obliged if you could point me in the direction of our reliefers. Our colonel's mighty anxious to reach the border."

"Damn the Mex! Had ourselves a pack o' them greasers right here in town, but they was run off last fall when all the trouble started down 'Paso way. Ain't got one left in Dallam County, I don't believe. Just as well, too, 'cause we've got some good ol' boys that'd like nothin' better than a good lynchin'! So how long you been steamin' then?"

"Since Friday," Cassie said. "It sure seems longer."

"Bet it does! Army's put on quite a show for us—got a pair o' specials comin' through yet tonight."

Cassie tried not to show his impatience. "About those reliefers of ours . . ."

Tinker Dawkins scratched his head and stifled a yawn. "Well now, that's just the peculiarist thing, Cap'n. Ain't no reliefers in town, that I know of."

"That can't be right," Cassie said. He felt his stomach knotting up at the idea.

The agent swiveled his chair around and made close inspection of the traffic board behind the desk. "See for yourself—got nothin' on the board 'cept locals. You sure you're expected on this line? It ain't the Santa Fe you're wantin', by chance?"

Cassie gave a nervous laugh. "It's the Rock Island for sure, straight on to Tucumcari. That's where we pick up the Southern Pacific. Oh, we're expected all right—been expected every step of the way since Lincoln, and that's a fact!"

Tinker Dawkins shuffled through a stack of dispatch slips on the desk but came up empty-handed. "That's my boss for ya—don't tell me nothin' he don't have to. Thinks I'm goin' for his job, which I am! He's off to Amarilly to have some boils cut out. He don't trust the local docs—can't say as I blame him. Not comin' back till the seven forty. . . . Tell you what. Your fellas is most likely over to Maude's Place or one o' the roomin' houses on Constitution. Ask your brakies to run 'em down, why don't ya? Meanwhile, I'll get back on the wire to Wich'ta. That way, we'll know for sure. . . ."

Cassie didn't like the sound of it. But having no better idea of his own, he went along with Tinker Dawkins's suggestion. Waiting for him outside on the platform were the hoggers Tyler and LaBelle. They both looked stretched to their limits. Cassie handed each man one of Mr. Webster's twenty-dollar gold pieces, and their soot-smudged faces immediately brightened.

"This is mighty good of you, Cap'n," said Packy LaBelle. "You don't have to give it us if you're thinkin' we dogged it."

"No question of that," Cassie said.

"We ran that hog as hard as we knew how," said Tim Tyler. "Only she didn't have the stomach for it."

"You did your jobs," Cassie told them, "and only missed the target by a gnat's eyelash. The government thanks you—and me, too. Still no signs of the reliefers?"

"Not hide nor hair," said LaBelle. "But don't you worry none, Cap'n— we'll keep up steam till they come, if it means stayin' through Christmas."

The hoggers returned to their cabs. Cassie went down the line until he found Nelson. He instructed the Negro to send porters along to the various rooming houses and hotels in search of the missing crews. Cassie told Rocks to do the same, but the shortstop begged off. He was planning another visit to his sweetheart.

"Make it quick," Cassie said. "We'll be pulling out any time now."

Cassie left the platform and stepped into Dalhart proper, aiming to search out the missing men himself. He was already sweating like a pig; his anger over the errant reliefers only added to his discomfort. A conductor's blue serge was the wrong outfit for Texas. The sun operated here like a blast furnace.

Moving down the street, Cassie met nothing but smiles and polite how-de-do's. Most of the townsfolk looked like farmers, though the men all wore sharp-pointed Texas-style riding boots. There was a plenty of horses to be seen, but most of them were hitched to a wagon or buggy or delivery cart. The town boasted a pair of main thoroughfares, each wide enough to accommodate good-sized wagons in two directions at once. Judging from the ruts, the Texas High Plains sometimes saw rain, but not this month or last. One of the streets was more important than the other; this was Constitution Avenue, running east and west. The other bore an imposing name itself, Independence Avenue. Both avenues were lined by wood-planked sidewalks. The planking was weathered out of true, but the constant blowing sand had filled in the cracks and made for a finish as smooth as any carpenter might want.

It was surely a God-fearing town. Cassie could see four churches from where he now stood: Presbyterian, Methodist Episcopal, St. James Episcopal, and Christian. He could also see three fine-looking saloons, the Prairie Schooner, the Oriental, and the Llano Estacado; these lay on the south side of Constitution. Across from them stood the Panhandle Deluxe Hotel and Emporium and the sheriff's office. Next to the hotel was the Dalhart Cattlemen's Association and Palafox's Eating House—"Meals 5¢ & Up." There was a newspaper, the *Panhandle Gazette,* two banks, a half-dozen real estate offices, a lumber yard, and—at the far end of Constitution—an imposing white house with a sign over the doorway reading *Maude's Place—Rooms & Such.* It reminded Cassie of a similar structure on 6th Street in Lincoln. The place in Lincoln was called "Miss Fanny Bloom's" and was run by a red-haired Jewess from Chicago. Cassie had never been inside, but he supposed all fancy houses were the same: champagne, pink women, and sin abounding if you had the price of it in your pockets.

The town would be too big to search, Cassie realized, if he had had a hundred porters to do it. He hurried back to the Panhandle Deluxe, thinking that well-to-do hoggers might go for such a place.

"Only trainmen expected," said the desk clerk, "are LaBelle and Tyler."

Cassie suffered an awful dryness in his mouth. He broke for the Rock Island office at a fast trot, his heart pounding, sweat dripping over his collar and wetting his shirt and tunic.

At first sight of Cassie, Tinker Dawkins gave up his pleasant smile and turned sour. "Didn't find nobody, ain't that right?"

"That's it," Cassie replied. "Not a reliefer in sight."

"None expected neither. I been on to Wich'ta."

"But this is some kind of mistake," Cassie declared.

"Seems so. No fresh crews expected till the five twenty P.M. from Oklahoma City, and they's already spoke for. Belong to 'nother special— *Pullman's No. 3* out of Omaha."

Cassie's toes curled up inside his boots. "But that's *us!* You're *looking* at *Pullman's No. 3!*"

Tinker Dawkins's squinty eyes turned suspicious. "You said you was out of Lincoln."

"Yes, Lincoln, and then Sturgis, South Dakota, and then Omaha. I swear that's us—*Pullman's No. 3!* See here in my book!"

The agent checked Cassie's orders. "That bein' the case, Cap'n McGill, your reliefers is on the way. Expect 'em ten minutes this way or that from five twenty."

"Five twenty!" Cassie gasped. "Might as well be never!"

" 'Nother six and a half hours, I make it," said Tinker Dawkins. The dispatcher's clock on the wall said 10:54.

Cassie thought of the remaining gold pieces in his train book, and the fifty-dollar bill that had seemed so close to being his. "Your message traffic from midnight on—could I see it, do you suppose?" His voice had gone gritty.

Tinker Dawkins reached in a drawer and pulled out a batch of telegraph forms bound with a rubber band. "Help yourself, Cap'n. I sure hope you find what you're lookin' for—only I don't suppose it'll hurry those fellas from Oklahoma City none."

Cassie flipped the pages back until he found the message he had left to be telegraphed at Turon, Kansas:

PULLMAN'S NO. 3 UPDATING ARRIVAL TEN O'CLOCK. REQUESTING EARLY NOTICE TO RELIEFERS. MCGILL, CONDUCTOR.

"Know what I'm thinkin'?" said Tinker Dawkins, who had been reading over Cassie's shoulder. "I'm thinkin' your message was meant to have an A.M. on it. It don't."

Cassie pulled out his train book and found his own copy of the same message. It had been sent just as he wrote it. Without the A.M.

". . . So some sucker along the way figured you for night when what you meant was mornin'. Ain't that the case, Cap'n? That sucker being my boss, more'n likely!"

Cassie staggered out the door, mortified and speechless. In all his days he had never known such shame. In the street, he ran head on into Jacko Mudd's messenger from Headquarters Platoon, the gruff Private Rademacher.

"Out o' my way, boy. Carryin' a wire for Pershing hisself."

Cassie came to his senses just in time. He reached for the sheet of paper the trooper was holding. "Here, let me have that."

The trooper brushed Cassie aside with a sweep of his arm. Rademacher was strong as a bull. "Army business, mister! Official from the adjutant. Back off, I tell ya!"

"Listen. You don't understand. I *know* about that message. You don't want to send it."

Rademacher had his .45 out of the holster. "Interfere with me in the carryin' out o' my duties and so help me God I'll blast ya ta smithereens!"

The trooper disappeared inside the Rock Island office, backing all the way so that his pistol was the last thing Cassie saw of him.

Cassie broke into a run. The watering and coaling-up were finished, and the Squadron's officers had already boarded. Cassie made straight for Headquarters Car. "I've got to see the colonel," he told the sentry.

"Says you."

"It's your neck if I don't."

"He's not to be bothered 'cept in emergencies."

"This is one, I swear it!"

"It's your ass if it ain't."

Cassie climbed the steps and moved down the corridor to Stateroom A. The stink of stale cigar smoke erased Cassie's worries over his own sweaty smell. He knocked on the colonel's door.

"Come."

Cassie let himself in. The colonel was around the corner from the parlor, in the bathroom. He was sitting in the tub.

"Excuse me, sir—"

"What is it, Cassius? This heat—I find a cold bath to be the only effective remedy."

Cassie could not take his eyes off the colonel's pale body. Only his face and the backs of his hands were brown; the rest of him was chalky white. The colonel was a small man with little meat on his bones. Naked, he seemed weak, almost girlish.

"Well, son? I assume your visit has some purpose."

"Yes, sir. You see, sir . . ."

The colonel listened in silence. Cassie told of his mistake in leaving off the A.M. from his message and of the resulting delay, six and one-half hours. He did not admit, in so many words, that the *Pancho Villa Express* would miss the deadline into Fort Bliss, but he knew from the colonel's blank stare that the officer understood. At times during his account, Cassie paused, hoping the colonel would yell at him or curse him or maybe even rise up and strike him. But the colonel only sat there in the tub of cold water, his thin white body hardly moving.

At last, the colonel spoke:

"You may go now, Cassius."

Cassie found himself holding one of Mr. Webster's double eagles in his hand. He held it out for the colonel to see. "Sir—"

"*Go*, I say!"

Cassie went. Outside, he cursed himself on the colonel's behalf—then realized that he had forgotten to tell the colonel about that obstinate donkey Rademacher, who had gone ahead and sent the wrong message to General Pershing.

Word of the war train's delay spread from car to car, bringing cries of joy from the weary troopers. Any excuse to touch ground was good enough for them. The Rock Island yardmaster, a ructious redhead named Monk Shivers, backed both sections a half mile east, then brought them into town along a holding spur, where the *Pancho Villa Express* would be out of the way of through traffic. Townsfolk were drawn trackside like flies to a dung heap.

Sergeant Major Jacko Mudd gave the order most favored by officers and men alike: "*Squadron! . . . Dismount!*"

Off came the animals, first the live ones, then the carcasses. The dying of the ponies had slowed since the warming up of the weather after Kansas City. With so many animals dead and gone, there was now more comfort in the horse cars. Horses still died, but they did so one at a time. "As for feedin' 'em," said Monk Shivers, "the last outfit passin' through dumped their hay there in the street. Can't see why you shouldn't do the same . . ."

Dalhart was soon awash in horse manure and khaki. Water and oats would keep the animals close; Jacko Mudd decided against hobbles. The local liveries pitched in, setting up troughs and running pumps from nearby wells. Meanwhile, the outlawed hoggers, Tyler and LaBelle, saw to the banking of their fires. Then they dragged the yards till they found the Rock Island's chief mechanic and arranged to have the flues bored out on both locomotives and new fires set at 5:00 P.M. This way, the re-liefers from Oklahoma City would have nothing to do but set their butts in the cabs and open the throttles. As anxious as Tyler and LaBelle were to find clean beds in the Panhandle Deluxe, they saw to their personal wants only when they were sure Nos. 506 and 799 would be fit to finish the run into El Paso. Cassie was as pleased with the hoggers as he was disgusted with himself.

The colonel remained in his compartment while the other officers knotted along the spur, preening themselves in the hot morning sun and wondering how the Squadron would pass its time till they loaded up again. About half the men were lined up beside the cook car, wanting lunch. The other half edged away, hoping to explore the town before the officers put it off limits.

A pair of fancy four-in-hands soon came clop-clopping down Constitution at a sprightly pace. This proved to be a welcoming committee from Town Hall. The coaches pulled up before Captain Lonnie Bowles, who was acting commander of the Squadron in the absence of the colonel. A big-smiling Texan named Ed Spangles made the introductions:

". . . This here's Sheriff J. D. Hicks . . . the Reverend Sam Turcott . . . Mr. Darrel Corn, president of the Patrons of Husbandry . . . Major Josiah Spinks, president of the Dallam County Cattlemen's Association . . . Mr. Porter Hackett, president of the Dalhart Volunteer Fire Department . . ."

Spangles passed out cards to Captain Bowles and the other officers showing that he was attorney-at-law and mayor of Dalhart. He displayed himself in black frock coat, white vest, morning trousers, starched collar, and a splendid black Stetson. Raising his voice so that all the troopers and onlookers could hear his words, he announced:

"We welcome each and every member of this great regiment and hereby proclaim you all to be honorary citizens of our fair city! We invite you to partake of true Texas hospitality for so long as you may care to stay! And I'm sure my colleagues on the Town Council join me in saying that special prices shall prevail in all shops and establishments in Dalhart this day. Naturally, there'll be free eats in all saloons, and beer's a nickel!"

The troopers and citizens together sent up a full-throated cheer. Other members of the welcoming committee added their own compliments, and then Captain Bowles replied on behalf of Colonel Antrobus, who, the captain said, was "suddenly indisposed":

". . . The courtesy shown by y'all does honor to the Twelfth Regiment of Cavalry and makes us proud, every man, to be defendin' the soil of Texas and seekin' retribution 'gainst the cowardly bandit Villa. . . ."

Captain Bowles and Mayor Spangles thereupon shook hands, and a photographer for the *Panhandle Gazette* preserved the moment for history. Afterwards, Captain Bowles dispatched a messenger to Colonel Antrobus in Headquarters Car. The trooper soon returned, nodding agreement. Jacko Mudd called the Squadron to attention and Captain Bowles spoke again:

"With our colonel's blessin', the Fightin' Fourth shall enjoy liberty till five o'clock. Y'all be on your best behavior, hear?"

"*Squadron! . . .*" cried Jacko Mudd. ". . . *Dismissed!*"

The men sent up another great cheer, then bolted in all directions. Cassie backed away from the troopers' celebrations. He could take no pleasure in their newfound freedom. All he could think about was the blank stare the colonel had shown at the news of the *Pancho Villa Express*'s delay. Cassie wished he could find a hole and crawl into it and die.

He started back toward the van but was cut off by Christian, who was out doing his duty with the chow chow Mushy. Then Mr. Webster and his whole party came along. Cassie ducked between cars before they could spot him. Miss Candace was as beautiful as any belle in her bright yellow sun dress and parasol, but even her great beauty had little effect on Cassie this morning. He watched from afar as Mayor Spangles and other prominent citizens gathered up the Websters and Mademoiselle Foix and the padre and escorted them on over to the Panhandle Deluxe. There they were soon joined by Captain Bowles and Van Impe and the other officers for a grand luncheon Texas-style, which meant ribs of beef cooked over an open fire. The smell of it had already reached as far as Cassie's stomach.

Cassie resumed his march toward the van, only to be run to ground by a smiling Rocks.

"What's the matter with ya, Cass? You sick or what? Your sure look awful hangdog for a fella who's about to pick the teeth o' them damn sons-o'-bitches!"

"What are you saying?"

"Poker, Cass! I got the game all set up wit' Mudd and his boys. I told 'em we'd be ready fer 'em by the time they downed their grub. That'll be soon, too."

Cassie shook his head. "I can't do it."

Rocks pretended not to hear Cassie's reply. Instead he changed the subject, which was his usual trick when Cassie confounded him. "Some town, huh, Cass! It's the real West, sure 'nough! Git a look o' that pie-bald—that's an Injun pony, bet on it! Speakin' o' which, what'd ya think o' Hicks?"

"Who's Hicks?"

"Why, the sheriff, who else? That's J. D. Hicks hisself."

"Don't say."

"Do!"

"So who's he supposed to be, then?"

"You're *joshin'* me!"

"Suit yourself."

"By golly, you ain't! Only Wyatt Earp's *deputy*, is all! Only the last o' the top lawmen o' the West! Ya know, I don't think that Zane Grey o' yours teaches ya nothin'."

"Zane Grey is made up, you dunce. It's not real life."

"Then how come ya waste yer time on it?"

" 'Cause it beats real life, what else?"

"Well, J. D. Hicks is real life, Cass, that's the truth. Did ya see it, that great revolver o' his?"

Cassie had seen it. It was hard to miss—a beautiful ebony-handled Colt .44 hanging from a broad leather cartridge belt. Despite what Rocks had said, Cassie was thinking that Sheriff Hicks—smart in a gray suit and waistcoat topped off by a black slouch hat—might have stepped straight out of Zane Grey, or maybe Owen Wister.

"I can see ya got things on yer mind," said Rocks.

"Doesn't matter."

"Can ya jus' tell me the one thing?"

"What?"

"Ya comin', Cass, or ain't ya?"

"To the poker?"

"That's it."

"What about the fresh deck?"

"Got ol' Nelson over there ta that emporium buyin' us *two* fresh decks!"

"I got business over to the Rock Island first."

"Then you'll come? 'Cause we're sure ruint if you don't!"

"Then I guess I'm coming."

"I knowed it all along! An' can ya pay ol' Nelson fer the fresh decks? It'll be 'bout a dime."

Cassie was already thinking ahead. When he had won all of Mudd's and Snivey's greenbacks, he would add his own war bonus to the millionaire's and would drive the crews so hard they would *still* reach El Paso by the colonel's deadline.

He knew what he had to do. He would do it.

Citizens now passing through the streets of Dalhart suffered considerable peril to life and limb in the jam of buckboards, hacks, broughams, surreys, democrats, phaetons, and plain wagons. Farmers and homesteaders from miles around, made curious by the repeated bold blasts from the whistles of No. 506 and No. 799 during Monk Shivers's switching, figured there was fun to be had and perhaps money to be made at trackside; so they dropped their chores and hurried to town.

The Dallam County seat had seldom before seen such a population, which included a fair proportion of females. The troopers wasted no time in obtaining full rations of whiskey and introductions to what unescorted women they could find. Jacko Mudd's guardhouse had been shut down for the afternoon. This meant that Rita and the Indian girl Naomi got liberty, too. Jolene Potts, still locked away in the possum belly, might gladly have swapped places with the other girls, as they at least had the opportunity to drink vanilla ice-cream sodas and smoke their cigarettes in public.

The saloons had struck gold. Troopers who could afford it bought full bottles of whiskey and took an armload of sandwiches and retired to Joe Eddy's Nickelodeon & Vitagraph Palace, which was tenting put up over a wood foundation. There they found Miss Pearl White's latest *Perils of Pauline* for a nickel; also Little Mary Pickford in *Two Romances* and *New York Hat* and Lillian Russell giving her temperance lecture, "Drink & Be Ugly," on the Kinetoscope. During intermissions, George M. Cohan's patriotic song "It's a Grand Old Flag" was performed on the pianola. Down the street, the Opera House offered *A New and Novel Musical Comedy Featuring Impersonations of Charlie Chaplin & Billie Ritchie*, while all over town show bills proclaimed:

WHAT WAS "LADY AUDLEY'S SECRET"?

Theda Bara, that Famous Vampire Woman,
tells you in the most thrilling of all Photoplays!

---

at the
TEXAS GRAND
Prices 10 & 20 cents

Cassie had no time for Dalhart's various entertainments. He reported back to the Rock Island office. "It's me again," he said to Tinker Dawkins.

The agent seemed glad to see him. "They didn't give ya the firin' squad, no how!"

"They might better have," Cassie said.

"Well now, your customers don't seem to mind the layover none."

Cassie saw that Tinker Dawkins had a sense of humor. "They don't," Cassie agreed, "but I can't say as much for their colonel."

Tinker Dawkins's smile widened out. "Would his name be Antrobus by chance?"

"That's the one."

Tinker Dawkins produced a sheet of paper with Lieutenant Van Impe's scrawl on it. It was the message delivered by Private Rademacher.

Cassie adopted a glum expression. "That's one message that was better off lost in the sending."

"That's what I figured," said Tinker Dawkins. He rolled Van Impe's message slip into a ball and pitched it expertly into a wood barrel across the room. "It musta been lost, Cap'n, 'cause we sure dint send it from here."

What a fine fellow, Tinker Dawkins! At least the colonel would not be made to appear a total fool, bragging that his outfit would make Fort Bliss by 7:00 A.M. when 12:00 noon was now closer to the truth. "Seeing as you've done me such a great favor already today, Mr. Dawkins, I'm wondering how you'd feel about doing another?"

"What good is it bein' railroaders," said Tinker Dawkins, " 'less we kin stick together?"

"I couldn't help but notice your safe."

"Not plannin' to blow it, are ya? Be easier if I jus' give ya the combination."

"Matter of fact," Cassie said, "it's only some banking I'm after."

He pulled out his train book, unbuttoned the flap pocket, and removed three of the remaining four double eagles. From his watch pocket he took out the fifty-dollar bill.

Tinker Dawkins whistled at the sight of Cassie's bankroll. "You sure found yourself the best part o' railroadin', I'd say!"

"I could give you an argument on that," Cassie replied. "I'd appreciate it if you could break this for me into tens, fives, and singles—mostly singles, if you please. More than that, I'd be asking you to hold on to the double eagles and allow me to buy them back from you in three or four hours' time."

Tinker Dawkins scooped up the coins and bill with a practiced hand. "It'd be the Rock Island's great pleasure to handle your transaction, Cap'n. Only I'm bound to advise you—speakin' frankly, one railroader to another—that I don't know a single pleasure this town's got to offer that'd cost you anything near to this sum. Heck, you could have Mayor Spangles's daughter Bess for this amount, and she's a true beauty and innocent to boot!"

"Nothing of the kind." Cassie answered. "To be honest, it's for poker."

"Ah—business instead o' pleasure. Well, luck o' the Irish to you then."

"And never needed more!"

9

Rocks was waiting for him outside the van.

"It's tough, Cass! They search ya when ya go in!"

"Looking for what?"

"Yer *gun,* o' course!"

"I've got no gun."

"Me neither. I give it ta Jolene for safekeepin'!" The shortstop nodded in the direction of the possum belly.

"She's surviving in there, is she?"

"Happy as a rabbit in a hole! That med'cine o' Doc's done the trick—that an' her ciggies. It's a hot box, though, Cass. She's stripped clear naked and is still burnin' up. She's nappin' now—the med'cine knocks her out fer hours at a time. Before she dropped off agin, I told her she'd be free as the birdies soon as you and me clean out the Army. She sure liked the sound o' that, Cass!"

For a moment, Cassie worried that Doc's elixir might cause the girl harm. But at least she had stopped throwing up.

They entered the van. The troopers had lowered the shades. What light there was formed a dusty shaft from the angel's nest up above.

"Well now, boys—come in, come in!" called out Jacko Mudd. "Ever see a finer day for a gentlemanly game!"

Mudd's pal Private Rademacher patted them down with bony fingers. When satisfied, he nodded to the sergeant major. "They're clean."

" 'Course they are. Come, boys, sit yourselves down."

"Yeah, suckers," said Trooper Snivey, "hit your asses. Sooner ya sit, sooner we fuck ya!"

Private Rademacher went outside, slamming the door behind him. Mudd had detailed the trooper to stand guard on the front porch and keep nosy parkers away. The porters and brakemen, who might ordinarily have sacked out in the van, had already been run off.

Players in this game had to sit on the floor. A pair of Army footlockers had been dragged in and covered with a soiled green baize to make a table. Cassie had known more comfortable gaming rooms in many a flea-bag hotel.

"You boys met Corporal Binyon?" Jacko Mudd asked politely.

Binyon was nothing much to look at: short, dark, weasel-faced. He returned their nods, said nothing. His long thin digits were wrapped around a deck of cards.

"Gonna level with ya," Mudd said. "Thad here's none but the champeen poker player of the whole Twelfth Regiment. Prefers cards to women, truth be told!"

Mudd and Snivey had a good laugh at this remark, but Binyon never cracked a smile. The way they sat down, Cassie looked across the table at Mudd and Snivey with Binyon on his right and Rocks on his left. Clockwise, it ran Cassie, Rocks, Mudd, Snivey, Binyon. Cassie liked the arrangement. Whenever possible, he preferred to sit downwind of trouble. If Mudd or Snivey opened or made a bet, Cassie would have a chance to see what Binyon was up to before making his own play.

Snivey pulled out a black cheroot and lighted up.

"I'd sure enjoy me one o' them stogies, Mr. Snivey," said Rocks. The shortstop smiled as though Snivey were his best friend.

"That'd cost you a dollar," Snivey said back.

Rocks lacked the dollar. His smile slipped a bit.

"Stakes on the table, gents," said Jacko Mudd.

The three troopers showed fifty dollars apiece as their stakes. Cassie counted out a hundred from the bills Tinker Dawkins had supplied. He kept fifty for himself and passed the rest over to Rocks. The crisp green bills made Cassie think of Mr. Webster down the street, having his lunch at the Panhandle Deluxe. This was the first time in Cassie's life he had played cards with another man's money. He did not care for the sensation.

"That's a lot o' swag for a pair o' shit-face railroaders, ain't it?" questioned Snivey.

"Why, this'd be the pay of a lifetime for any trooper!" crowed Rocks.

Snivey glared at the shortstop, then let go a stream of brown-stained spittle that passed close by Rocks's nose.

"Ain't no chewin' nor spittin' allowed!" Rocks protested. "Them's Pullman rules, you donkey!"

Rocks's knowledge of Rules & Regs came as a surprise to Cassie. Snivey laughed and spit again.

Jacko Mudd called for order: "You know the rules of play."

"Aye," said all.

The sergeant major insisted on repeating the rules anyway. Game was five-card draw, jacks or better, nothing wild. Ante was one dollar; limit on bets and raises, five dollars. Three raise maximum. Table stakes would apply to a fellow's last hand. They would play until one player cleaned out the rest.

"Two matters," said Cassie in a quiet voice.

"What's that, boy?" said Jacko Mudd.

"My rosary."

Snivey came instantly to life. "So it's *yers*, is it?"

Smiling all the while, the trooper pulled off his jersey and undershirt. There, dangling from his neck, was Ma's rosary. Cassie held himself back, resolving to take his revenge through the pasteboards.

"The boy's right," said Jacko Mudd. "It's already agreed. You take the final pot, Cassius, and Ward here will make you a present o' them beads."

Snivey did not look happy about it, but Cassie knew that Jacko Mudd's word was law among troopers.

"So let's play cards," said the sergeant major.

"That's not all," said Cassie.

"What is it *now*, boy?" The sergeant major's irritation was beginning to show through his polite manners.

"The girl—Jolene Potts."

Jacko Mudd's frown grew as deep as Snivey's. "What about her, boy?"

"If we win," Cassie said, "she's free and clear. You and your men will leave her be."

"*Yer fuckin' ass we will!*" roared Snivey.

"That ain't agreed," said Jacko Mudd.

"That's it!" cried Rocks. "Fair's fair!"

Corporal Binyon, meanwhile, held himself back from the conversation. He seldom looked up, concentrating instead on manipulation of the dog-eared cards in front of him.

"And if we don't go by your rules?" said Jacko Mudd.

"Then we don't play," said Cassie.

This put Snivey onto his feet. "They been askin' fer it, Jacko!"

Jacko Mudd's angry command "*Sit*" brought Snivey back down. The sergeant major put on a different voice for Cassie. "Okay, boy. Seein' as how you're bound to give her up if you lose, then maybe it's fair you should take her if you win. That's the bargain, then. *Now let's play cards.*"

Cassie reached inside his tunic and brought out the fresh decks that Nelson had bought at the emporium. He handed the cards to Jacko Mudd.

Mudd set one deck aside and broke the seal on the other. He removed the jokers, shuffled three or four times, and placed the cards in the middle of the baize. "High card deals." He took the first cut himself: three of diamonds.

They went around the table. Binyon, with a jack, was high.

"Ante up," said Jacko Mudd.

Everybody anted. Corporal Binyon riffled the cards like a fellow Cassie had once seen in a poker club in Chicago. The cards seemed to float out of his hands onto the baize. He would probably win a pot or two on the strength of his fingers, which were beautiful to watch.

Cassie found he had been dealt a bust. He checked to Rocks. Rocks opened and bet a dollar. The troopers all stayed, checking to Rocks. Cassie folded.

"Cards?" said Binyon.

This was the first word Binyon had spoken since Cassie and Rocks sat down. His voice was strangely soft, like a woman's. It made Cassie think again of that cardsharper at the poker club in Chicago.

Rocks took three cards, Mudd three, Snivey three.

"Dealer takes two," said Binyon.

Rocks had his mind all made up. "Bet ten dollars!"

"Limit's *five* dollars," Cassie told him sternly. Rocks could be mighty generous on another man's money.

"Maybe you boys want to play open," said Jacko Mudd. "Is it table stakes you're wantin'?"

"Limit's five dollars," Cassie repeated.

"Five dollars then," Rocks said.

Mudd and Snivey got out. Binyon stayed. "Your five and five more."

Twenty-four dollars on the table. Rocks looked as happy-go-lucky as a fellow could. "Okay," he said, "your five—and five more on top o' that!"

Corporal Binyon's expression never changed. He picked up his stack of bills and slid out a ten spot. "Your five and five more," he repeated.

Forty-four dollars on the table. "That's three raises," Cassie said.

Rocks studied his cards. He no longer looked so happy-go-lucky. He made Binyon wait as long as he could, then tossed in his cards. "Damn! Almost made it, too!" A silly grin crossed his face.

Fool! thought Cassie.

Corporal Binyon pulled in the pot without saying another word.

"Let's see them openers," Snivey demanded.

Rocks showed a pair of queens. "Good enough fer ya?"

Cassie gathered up the cards. Along the way he managed to sneak a quick look at Binyon's discards—a pair of tens to which the corporal had drawn only two cards. This horse soldier was a true poker player and master of the bluff. A fellow like this could make for a long afternoon.

The next hour's play confirmed it: Binyon was the one to watch. He knew how to set up his victim with a bluff, then blow him down with a true winning hand. Thanks to Binyon, it was the roughest game Cassie had been in since baseball days. Cassie was just able to hold his own, winning several small pots and dropping out most hands, using the rules Uncle Leo had taught him. He was thankful for his schooling under Leo. Rule 1 was that most players were morons or worse and begging you to take their money. Rule 2 was never stay on less than a pair of queens since the fellow who opened had jacks or better. This rule would keep you out of trouble for your whole lifetime, Leo said. Rule 3 was never stay on a four-card straight or flush; the odds were against you. Rule 4 was bluffing. The only place to bluff was in drawing cards. If the opener drew one card, you drew one card with him; if he checked, you raised him no matter what you had in your hand. Rule 5—last rule—was don't stay just to be playing. Cassie had seen boys in the clubhouse get an ace in the deal and then draw four cards. With fellows like that in the game, even a fool could make his fortune.

But these horse soldiers were not fools—at least not Binyon. These fellows played poker about twenty hours in the day, and many of them knew more about games of chance than Hoyle. Only good strong poker, along with a liberal dose of luck, was going to beat these fellows.

". . . Check," said Cassie.

It was Binyon's deal. Cassie, sitting to Binyon's left, held a pair of aces; still he did not open. He was playing possum now, hoping to change his luck. Even with strong cards, he had lost good pots on the last three hands he had played out. Something was wrong.

Rocks and Mudd both checked. "Fuckin' right I'll open," said Snivey. "Bet two dollars."

Everybody stayed. Fifteen dollars on the table. "Cards?" said Binyon.

Cassie knew that a pair of aces should win in such a game. He meant to sandbag the table. "One card," he said.

"Flushin' are ya?" said Snivey with an ugly grin. "Or maybe it's a wee straight. Yo're sure to be screwed either way, sonny boy!"

The others took three cards apiece. Cassie figured Snivey and Binyon for a pair of face cards, Rocks and Mudd for low pairs. Chances were poor that any two players of five would draw all four aces between them.

Snivey, with openers, bet the limit, five dollars. Binyon called.

Cassie studied his hand. As expected, he had not helped the aces. "Your five and five more," Cassie said.

Rocks and Mudd dropped out. It was back to Snivey again. "Yo're sayin' ya filled yer hand? Shit no, ya dint! I'm callin' yer bluff."

The trooper called but did not raise, meaning he had not helped his openers, either. Cassie knew he had Snivey beat.

Binyon's turn. "Your five," said the corporal to Cassie, "and five again."

This was the second raise on Snivey's original bet. Binyon was saying that he had found that third face card in the draw. Cassie doubted it. He looked again to his aces, then to his dwindling stack of greenbacks, then to the pot. There was already fifty dollars on the table, thirteen of it Cassie's. He was sorely tempted to make the third raise, but something in Binyon's expressionless gaze stopped him.

"Call," said Cassie, adding five more to cover Binyon's bet.

Binyon showed winners: three eights.

"Bastard!" hissed Snivey. He tossed in openers: a pair of jacks.

"It's all yours," said Cassie. He buried his aces in the discards before the others could see what he had been up to.

"Damn bad luck, Cass!" exclaimed Rocks.

Cassie figured it was more than that. A strong player like Binyon would never stay on a pair of eights in the deal unless he *knew* the third eight was coming his way. Three eights took a lot of luck in five-card draw with five players at table and everybody taking cards. Cassie's aces *should* have been enough to win.

Something was wrong, and Cassie knew what it was. Binyon seldom played out a hand except when he was dealer. And when he was dealer, he seldom lost.

Dealing seconds.

There was no other way, and Binyon had the fingers for it. When it was his turn to deal, he would spot a winning hand—three of a kind, say— while gathering in the discards before shuffling. He would then squirrel them away under the top card in the deck and give them to himself in the deal and, later on, in the draw. Cassie had been watching the corporal's hands the way a spider watches a fly. He had not seen a thing. But Binyon could still be doing it—*must* have been doing it. A mere club player like Cassie has no chance in the world against a true expert. In Cassie's opinion, this Binyon belonged in New Orleans or Chicago or on the Mississippi even, knocking off stiffs for his living. He was wasting his time in the cavalry.

Cassie looked across the baize at Ma's rosary hanging on Snivey's neck. He would have a better chance of tackling Snivey on the ground and tearing off the beads with his bare hands than trying to win them back at poker. There was no way he could win, no way at all.

Not unless—like them—he cheated.

To do it right, he would have to take it slow, move in easy steps. It took as much patience to cheat as to win honest.

First, he had to set himself up with the necessary tools. "Time for a fresh deck," Cassie said. "Maybe it'll change our luck, huh, Rocks?"

"Praise the Lord!" said Rocks.

"Your funeral," said Jacko Mudd.

The sergeant major tossed Cassie the second of Nelson's decks from the emporium. Cassie unwrapped it slowly and carefully, for all to see. He removed the two jokers, showed them around, and stuck them in his breast pocket. In the same motion, he palmed the ace of hearts and slipped it to the bottom of the deck. He shuffled hard three times, keeping the ace to the bottom. Then he offered the deck to Mudd for the cut.

Mudd, who was counting his stack, knocked instead of cutting. Cassie dealt. Nobody could open till they got around to Binyon.

"Bet two dollars," Binyon said in his soft voice.

Cassie studied his hand. Pair of tens. "I'm out," he said.

Rocks dropped out, too. Mudd and Snivey kept Binyon company.

"Cards?" said Cassie.

He gave each man what he asked for—and gave himself the ace off the bottom of the deck, slipping it unnoticed into his boot. Binyon won the hand on his openers, a pair of queens.

After that, Cassie bided his time. They played four more hands. The troopers won all four, with Cassie sitting out three. He had about half his stake left. Rocks was down to eight or ten dollars. The deal came around to Cassie again.

"Fer a pair o' damn Irish weepers, you sure clammed up on us!" said Snivey. He had won a few dollars and was feeling good about it.

"Now, Ward, that ain't polite," said Jacko Mudd. "These boys is our honored guests."

Binyon made no comment. He was far and away the big winner. While pulling in the scattered cards after Binyon's deal, Cassie eyed the pair of aces from the corporal's last winning hand and tucked them away under the top card of the assembled deck. They would make fine partners for the ace in his boot.

Cassie shuffled twice, and Rocks cut. Rocks cut easy, the way Cassie liked, and the pair of aces stayed where they started. Cassie dealt the hand around.

Rocks looked at his cards and checked.

"Seein' as how it's me birthday," said Jacko Mudd, "I'm openin'." He tossed down five dollars.

Snivey was itching to bet. "I'm callin' ya, Jacko," he said in a hoarse, excited voice, "an' I'm *raisin'!*" He dropped a ten spot on the pile of bills.

Binyon's turn. The corporal thought a bit, then added ten to the pot.

Cassie studied his hand, frowned, stroked his chin. He made a great show of it, hemming and hawing and shaking his head as though he could not decide whether to stay or get out.

Snivey's itch was getting the better of him. "Come on, piss-ant! You in or out?"

"Sumbitch!" said Rocks. "You take yer time, Cass. There's no rules says ya gotta hurry yerself."

Cassie kept on a while, folding his hand, opening it again, pretending to be about out. "Guess I'm in," he said finally. He subtracted ten singles from his stack; this left him seventeen dollars. "It's up to you," Cassie said to Rocks.

"Me, I'm out," Rocks said, throwing down.

This brought it back to Jacko Mudd. "Gonna see ya, Ward," he said to Snivey. He kicked in another five. The pot was up to forty-five dollars.

"Cards?" Cassie said.

"Three," said Jacko Mudd.

Cassie counted out three cards.

"Two cards!" cried Snivey.

Meaning he had obtained three of a kind in the deal and was praying for a fourth—odds against which were higher than heaven.

"And you, Corporal?" Cassie asked.

"Three cards."

Again, Cassie figured Binyon for queens or better. The corporal would not stay on less with Cassie dealing.

"Dealer takes two," said Cassie. In one sweeping motion, he tossed in his discards, gave himself two cards from the deck, and straightened up the discard pile. All eyes were on the deck he was dealing from, and nobody noticed that he discarded three cards, not two. This left him with only four cards in his hand. "Who was it opened?" Cassie asked, as though he had forgotten.

"Me, o' course," said Jacko Mudd.

"Your bet!" Snivey shouted. The trooper had ants in his pants; he could not sit still. "Come on, Jacko—what's it to be?"

Meanwhile, with the others looking to Mudd, Cassie palmed the ace from his boot and filled out his hand, which now reflected the correct mixture of skill and luck, including three aces.

Snivey was dying. "Come *on*, Jacko! You gonna bet or what?"

"Seems ol' Sarge Snivey's got some cards, don't it?" said Jacko Mudd. "Well, now, Ward, if you'll not be taking offense, I bet five dollars."

"Your five and five more!" Snivey countered immediately.

This made it too rich for Binyon. Without saying a word, he tossed in his cards and eased back, lighting up a cheroot. Cassie had the idea that Thaddeus Binyon preferred a politer kind of game—one without Ward Snivey in it.

"It's to you, then, McGill," said Jacko Mudd.

It was ten dollars to Cassie. "Call and raise five dollars," he said. This was the second raise. It left him with two dollars from his fifty-dollar stake.

Jacko Mudd had had enough; Cassie's bet drove him out. This left it between Snivey and Cassie.

"*Got ya!*" Snivey roared. His ugly grin was so wide it threatened to split his lips. "I'm seein' yer five and bettin' everythin' I got!" At this, the trooper yanked off Ma's rosary and threw it atop the pile of silver certificates.

Snivey's act brought Rocks to his feet. "Damn blasphemer!" the shortstop cried out. "Tossin' them blessed beads onto filthy lucre! Ya damn skunk! Dint yer pa never teach ya nothin'! Or maybe ya dint have one ya could name!"

Snivey came up swinging, but Jacko Mudd wrestled him down again.

"*Ease up, Ward!* You're near to collectin' the last pot, ain't you?" The sergeant major whirled and took a wild poke at Rocks, missing by inches. "You stinkin' runt! Close your yap or I'll close it for ya!"

Rocks crabbed away till he met the Franklin stove.

"*Play cards!*" ordered Jacko Mudd. "Your bet, McGill. Bet or fold."

Cassie pushed his last two dollars into the pot. "Call," he said. Playing table stakes, he was entitled to play on that amount, no matter how much Snivey bet. He would make the most of his free ride. He had Snivey beaten, and he would claim Ma's rosary in the bargain.

Snivey meant to enjoy his triumph and so made his showdown one card at a time. "Read 'em and weep, *civilian!*" He made "civilian" sound worse than "bastard," which was his favorite word of all.

Four of diamonds.

Four of spades.

Four of clubs.

Ace of diamonds.

Ace of hearts.

"Full house, pantywaist!" laughed Snivey. "Got yer loot an' got yer beads both!"

Cassie blinked in disbelief. The triumph he planned for himself had turned sour.

"Picked clean as a chicken!" said Jacko Mudd. "Yo're out o' the game, boy! Now where's that li'l girl o' yours? Bargain's a bargain, ain't it?"

"Hold on now," Cassie squeezed out.

Snivey's dark eyes were blood-streaked and teary. "How's that, boy?" The trooper left his massive fists right where they were, atop the money and Ma's rosary.

"What are you sayin', boy?" demanded Jacko Mudd. "Bet's a bet."

Cassie kept his eyes down—talked straight to the table:

"What I'm saying is—that's a mighty strange hand, considering the hand I got myself."

They all leaned in as Cassie showed his cards:

Nine of hearts.

King of hearts.

Ace of spades.

Ace of clubs.

Ace of diamonds.

Snivey was momentarily stunned. But he soon recovered himself. "*Shit!* Full house still beats three of a kind, don't it?"

Nobody breathed for five seconds more. Then Jacko Mudd saw it.

"*Five aces!* Hell, boy, now why'd you want to go and do a stupid thing like that? Know what you done? You just signed your death warrant. . . ."

* * *

Everybody scrambled to his feet at the same time, kicking the foot-lockers askew and knocking cards and greenbacks every which way. Rocks's move was toward the door, but Mudd got there first and blocked his path. Snivey flew straight across the lockers, wrapping his meaty fingers around Cassie's neck. Binyon took no part in the brawl. Instead, he dropped down, made a sack of the green baize, and pulled up cards, bills, and rosary.

Cassie could not get his breath: Snivey's thumbs were shutting off his windpipe. Even as he slid toward the floor, he could see in his mind's eye how they had tricked him. While he was palming the pair of aces for himself, Snivey was recovering an extra ace from the first deck, which Jacko Mudd had conveniently set aside. *Five aces.* What a simpleton's trick.

"That's it, Cass!" shouted Rocks. *"Use the .45 on 'im!"*

The shortstop's desperate outburst saved them for the moment. Jacko Mudd spun around to see how Snivey was faring. At the same time Snivey let go of Cassie's neck in order to check his pistol. This gave Rocks the chance he needed. The shortstop dove straight out the bay window, taking shade, curtains, glass, and mullions with him.

The sunset's red glow slanted in, blinding them. Cassie was shocked by the lateness of the day; he had lost all track of time during the game.

Jacko Mudd threw open the front door and hollered to the sentry, Private Rademacher:

"After him! A week's furlough if you catch the bastard!"

Rademacher went off in hot pursuit of the fleeing shortstop, followed by the wily Corporal Binyon, who still clutched the baize and its valuable contents.

Cassie retreated back in the van. *Damn,* he wished the shortstop had gone out the window facing toward town! Instead, Rocks went out the back, where there was nothing but grain fields and a scattering of Army wranglers watching over the ponies. Either way, Rademacher and Binyon would never catch up to Rocks, Cassie knew. The shortstop would soon bring help.

Meanwhile, Cassie had to stay alive on his own. The two troopers came after him together, pinning him back in the corner. Cassie feinted Mudd right and went left at Snivey, catching the trooper alongside the jaw. It was a good blow: Snivey dropped like a side of beef.

But the trooper got up again, madder than before. Cassie drew back his fist to deliver another blow. Before he could do so, Snivey came at him head down and butted him to the floor.

The two troopers dragged him out to the middle of the room, where they could manage him easier. Snivey sat on his chest while Mudd held his flailing legs.

"So where's she at, boy?" Snivey spit down at him. "Where's that li'l cunt o' yers? Tell us, boy! 'Cause if ya don't, ya ain't never gonna have no use fer a woman agin!"

Cassie squirmed from side to side, trying desperately to roll over and protect his groin, but the troopers held him tight.

"Best tell, boy," advised the sergeant major, "or Ward here'll ruin ya for sure. I seen him do it afore."

Cassie wrenched one wrist loose from Snivey's grip and jammed a thumb in the trooper's eye. Snivey screamed in pain but stayed on top.

"Yo're *dead,* boy! Yo're in yer grave!"

The trooper kept one hand over his injured eye and made a fist with the other, raking it backwards and forwards in a great arc, battering at Cassie's defenses.

Cassie fought back as best he could, clawing and scratching like a girl, sinking his fingernails into Snivey's cheeks, tearing at the ugly scar that ran across Snivey's jaw.

"*Ow!* Git his goddam hands, can't ya, Jacko?"

But Mudd suddenly had other ideas. "*Hold up, Ward!*"

"What the hell fer? I'm gonna *kill* this bastard!"

"*Easy!* You smell somethin'?"

"I smell this goddam skunk," Snivey growled. "Gonna smell his puke, too!"

"Listen to what I'm tellin' ya! *Look there!*"

The sergeant major pointed to the floor beside Cassie's head. Cassie craned his neck around to look for himself.

It was smoke. Thin, wispy curls of smoke coming up through the floorboards. Now Cassie could smell it too. It smelled of Pinchon's Fatima Pure Turkish Cigarettes.

Cassie understood at once. Poor Jolene—awakened from her drugged sleep by the ruckus overhead—had sought relief in her ciggies. And now she would pay for it—and so would he.

The scowl on Jacko Mudd's fleshy face eased into an evil smile. "*Well* now, Ward—I don't believe we're gonna be needin' this young fella's help in findin' pretty Miss Jolene after all!"

"Under our asses the whole game!" Snivey cried. "Lemme go git her!"

Snivey jumped to his feet, leaving Cassie to crawl off into a corner again.

"Let's not rush it," Jacko Mudd said, thinking a bit. "She ain't *goin'* no place, now is she? First we gotta take care o' this young fella. We can see to Miss Jolene in our own sweet time."

Snivey laughed himself into a coughing fit, then spit on the cracks the smoke was coming through. "Enjoy yer fags, li'l girl, while ya still kin!"

Cassie shuddered at the idea of it: Rocks's sweetheart, trussed up like a porker on the way to market and no escape possible, thanks to that stout Yale lock. If he knew anything about troopers, they would blast the Yale to kingdom come with their .45's and make Jolene sweat plenty before they ravished her again.

Cassie's fearful thoughts were interrupted by a shout from outside the van:

"Hallo in there! Ho! Cap'n McGill?"

Tinker Dawkins from the Rock Island!

Before Cassie could answer, Snivey was on him again, slamming the cold blue steel of a Colt .45 against his brow and clamping Cassie's mouth shut with a black sweaty palm.

"He ain't here!" answered the sergeant major. "He's forward to the locomotive, I do believe!"

"Seems you fellas had yerself a little accident," replied Tinker Dawkins. He was calling in through the broken window. "Would ya be needin' a doc or anythin'?"

"Naw," said Mudd, "suffered nary a splinter! You'd best be seekin' Cap'n McGill up front!"

"Thank you, sir, most kindly."

The sound of Tinker Dawkins's footsteps receded in the distance.

"That busted window's sure to bring snoopers," said Jacko Mudd. "I'm goin' forward to smell out the Dutchman and see what's up in HQ. We'll be off inside the hour—ain't that right, boy? Meantime, we'd best move Mr. Conductor here into one o' the horse cars fer safekeepin'. Besides, I was thinkin', Ward—maybe you'll be wantin' to teach this young fella a lesson 'bout cheatin' on the cavalry."

Snivey drooled at the prospect of it. The bad eye Cassie had given him was swollen and watery. The trooper had no trouble working Cassie's arm around back and nearly lifting him off the ground with it.

"Make a sound, boy, an' I'll snap her like a twig!"

He lifted up on it sharply to make his point. Cassie howled.

"Sound off agin an' I'll splatter yer brains on the ceilin'!"

Cassie took his pain in silence after that.

Whatever had become of the shortstop? Cassie saw his chances of escape running out on him minute by minute. Mudd and Snivey tossed him up into the first horse car, which was empty. Snivey then climbed up, and Mudd shut the two of them in, bolting the doors from outside.

The horse car was dark but for the odd rays of sunlight that filtered in through cracks in the boarding. Cassie backed to the far end of the car and crouched down behind the hay bales. The flooring under his feet was wet and slippery from straw and horse droppings. The stink was awful, the heat oppressive. Cassie could hardly breathe.

"So it's jes the two of us, eh, boy?" Snivey called out to him. "Come here, boy. Take yer beatin' like a man."

The trooper advanced on him, taking slow, easy steps. He moved like a man about to enjoy himself, swaggering and boastful.

"Ya shouldn'ta thumbed me, boy. That ain't fightin' fair. Nor scratched me neither—look there, ya got me ta bleedin'! Strip down, boy—it's too damn hot fer uniforms. Besides, I wanna see yer skin after I git done with it!"

Cassie skipped away, clinging to one wall.

"Oh, such a quick one, ain't he! Thank ya, boy—yo're only addin' ta the fun!" The trooper had fat about his middle but muscle elsewhere. He kept a moronic grin on his face all the while, like the Mongolian idiot in a sideshow. He moved forward, arms outstretched, making big fists. "*Now*, boy! Ain't no use ta run!"

Cassie tried a head feint. The trooper went for it.

"Oh, my, laddie, ain't you gonna *pay* when yo're caught!"

Cassie wished he were a top fighter like Frank Moran, the heavyweight champion, but Moran got beat, too, in '14, by Jack Johnson. Cassie knew from clubhouse brawls that he lacked the skills of a Moran, much less those of the crafty Negro. Another defeat for the Irish! When it came to fisticuffs, he was pure amateur whereas Snivey might have gone many a round in the prizefight ring, given the queer shape of his nose.

Cassie slithered back the way he had come, aiming for the other end of the car.

The trooper moved on him again, puffing from the heat and from anger at Cassie's quick dodges. "*Gotcha now, me lad!*"

Cassie retreated through the remains of the rope stalls that had come apart after Fort Meade and the lumber framing put up at Rapid City. Slipping and sliding on the straw and dung, he stepped on something hard.

He saw it: the glint of five steel fingers in the straw. Reaching down, he soon had his hands on it. A pitchfork.

"*Come on, boy—time's up. I'm gonna bust yer balls!*"

A different look came into the trooper's eye when he saw the fork. He backed off without Cassie's having to say a word.

"So it's to be that kind o' game, is it? So yo're wantin' to play fer keeps. Ward Snivey ain't gonna disappoint ya!"

Hanging off the hardware above the side doors were a dozen baling hooks that the troopers used in hauling hay to the animals. Snivey grabbed one down and held it out for Cassie to see in the murk.

"Fair and square now, ain't she, boy! You with that great long fork—me with this tiny little hook!"

The handle on Cassie's fork was so long he kept banging it into the wall behind him as he moved. "Stay off me!" Cassie shouted.

"Sure, boy. Why, I'd be crazy to get close to them long needles ya got pointed in my direction!"

The trooper came closer. Cassie kept his back to the wall and edged along, heading for the door on the town side. If he could get it open even a crack, he could get help from passersby—trainmen or even townsfolk.

But Snivey cut him off. "Now, you ain't meanin' to stick me, are ya, boy? Me who ain't never done ya no harm?"

Cassie tried another feint, pretending to break to the trooper's left, then cutting back sharply toward the door. He might have made it except for the droppings underfoot. He went down. Just as fast, Snivey kicked away his fork.

"*Now, boy! Yo're 'bout done, ain't ya!*"

The trooper stepped over Cassie and brought a boot down hard on one wrist. The trooper could do anything he wanted now. He chose to take back his hook and aim it at Cassie's face.

"*Please!*" Cassie begged.

He rolled aside at the last possible moment. The flooring squealed and splintered as Snivey yanked back the hook to strike again.

Cassie rolled the opposite way, fighting to regain his feet. Snivey doubled him up with a kick to the stomach. Cassie lay pinned between wall and flooring, unable to move. He watched Snivey draw back the hook again, aim it, start it down—

A flash of light from above blinded him. It was followed by a deafening roar. Cassie felt himself splattered with hot blood, pieces of flesh, bone.

He knew he was dead. He said a last prayer: "The Lord is my shepherd, I shall not want. . . ."

"*Die, you damn bastard! Die, die, die!*"

Fearfully, Cassie opened his eyes. Trooper Snivey was even then obeying the shortstop's command.

10

ROCKS CLIMBED DOWN the ladder from the hatch in the roof. He kept the smoking .45 pointed straight at Snivey's head, but he had no need to. There was a neat hole in the back of the trooper's head and nothing but gore in front.

Cassie squirmed and kicked frantically, trying to get out from under the trooper's leaden corpse. He had never seen a corpse before. He vomited over a hay bale, then cleaned himself off with straw.

Rocks had the tremors. "It was you or him, Cass!"

"*You saved me!*" Cassie cried out.

"What'll we do? Make a run for it, s'pose!"

The stench of gunpowder burned their nostrils.

"Where'll we go?" Cassie asked stupidly.

They stood in the darkness, panting like dogs, listening for the sounds of alarm. Nobody came. They heard nothing except the general commotion of the town outside.

"Ain't *poss'ble* nobody heard!" gasped Rocks.

"Oh, they heard all right," said Cassie.

But now he wondered. Inside the car it had sounded like a crack of thunder. But maybe the thunder had been swallowed up by the hay bales. Maybe what was deafening to them was little more than a dull *thump* to outsiders.

"Out the back, then!" Rocks said. "We can be 'cross the plains an' far as the h'rizon 'fore anybody misses us!"

"Where are we running to?" Cassie asked, directing the question more to himself than to Rocks. "What do we do when we get there?"

They got down on their haunches and spoke in whispers.

"No," said Cassie, "there's no answer in running."

"Then what'll we *do*, Cass? I'm scared, tell the truth!"

"Give ourselves up, maybe. Tell what happened. We didn't do *murder*."

Rocks moved closer so Cassie could see his face. "Yo're expectin' 'em to believe the likes of *us*, Cass? Yo're expectin' Jacko Mudd, maybe, to take our side? When he *knows* what this sumbitch here"—the shortstop gave the corpse a kick—"was aimin' ta do ta ya?"

"We won't be talking to plain troopers," Cassie said. "We'll go to the colonel himself. He's sure to believe us."

Rocks shook his head. "Ask Doc. When it comes ta Army 'gainst civilians, it's Army every time, Cass. They got no use fer us, ain't that plain? They'll string us up to the nearest telegraph pole an' who's to say against it? They're their own law, Cass! Ya think we're gonna get a fair trial out o' *them* boys?"

"We've got to do *something*," Cassie said. "We can't just sit here and cry for ourselves."

"I say run!"

"Just set out across the prairie?"

"Run till we drop! Get as far away from this hell train as it's possible to be!"

"And Jolene? What about her?"

"She can meet up with us later."

"What about when Mudd's boys break her out of the possum belly, if they haven't already got their hands on her?"

"They ain't. I seen to it."

"How's that?"

"Ol' Nelson come along when I dropped down to get me gun. He's put her in a steamer trunk and carried her forward."

"Where to?"

"*The Mother Lode,* o' course!"

"You're lying."

"Tell me someplace better! She's gonna hide out in Kolb's wine cellar—ain't nobody allowed in there 'cept Kolb hisself, and he's got no more use fer troopers 'n you or me!"

Cassie's brain was drowned in contrary thoughts. The image of Jolene Potts hiding out amidst the millionaire's wines and victuals only served to confuse him further. "There's no more time for talk," Cassie said. "Here's what we'll do. . . ."

Since nobody had come running after the gunshot, they could assume they were free and clear for the time being. There would be no trouble, probably, until Snivey's body was discovered. So the thing now was to hide the body away and play for time.

They went to work. They dragged Snivey's body into a corner of the car and covered it with straw. Then they stacked hay bales over it. Depending on how fast the remaining ponies went through their feed, nobody would come upon the corpse for some hours yet—maybe not till they reached El Paso.

"I really did it this time, dint I, Cass?" Rocks shook his head sorrowfully. The shortstop was either up or he was down: one minute full of fight, the next ready to cry.

"Saved my life in the bargain," Cassie said.

"If ever a fella had it comin' to him, that fella did. He'd a cut out yer gizzard with that hook, if he coulda."

"He was a mean one."

"I don't feel nothin' over it, Cass."

"You did right."

"Try tellin' that to the soldier boys! They'll sure skin me alive, given half a chance."

"They won't have the chance."

The shortstop kept on shaking his head. "Sure wish we'd got free o' that fella some other way!"

"What's done is done."

Rocks put on his best smile. "Guess yo're glad ya let me talk ya into comin' along, huh?"

Cassie couldn't help smiling himself. "My friend—that I am!"

The Squadron bugler stood in the middle of Constitution Avenue and blew "Recall." The clock on the Bank of Dalhart said 5:05. Another quarter hour and the reliefers were due in from Oklahoma City. Cassie changed clothes in the van. His best uniform was beyond salvation, being stiff with blood and manure. He went through the pockets, then knotted it up and pushed it down behind the sawed logs in the woodbox.

That was when he noticed it: his train book was gone. No telling where he had lost it—but most likely in the horse car with Snivey. He thought of going back to look for it, but the train was now crawling with troopers, and the wranglers were preparing to board the ponies. All his train orders were gone, and his money, too. He had lost $100 when Corporal Binyon grabbed up the baize, and he had now lost the rest of it—$30.95—which was tucked into the snap pocket. Of course, $130 of it properly belonged to Mr. Webster; this was Cassie's debt to repay. He laughed out loud. His luck had turned so bad he could only laugh at it. Luck of the Irish!

Cassie went outside and crossed over to the Rock Island office.

"Well, now, Cap'n," said Tinker Dawkins, "been lookin' all over tarnation fer ya! Figured you'd be wantin' to buy back yer gold, which I don't mind tellin' ya is about to burn a hole in my britches!" The agent tossed the coins down on the counter to hear their pretty ring.

Cassie blushed. "That's sure kind of you, Mr. Dawkins. Only there's been a hitch in my plans, so to speak. That gold's now the Rock Island's to keep."

"Ah. Sorry to hear it, Cap'n. Well, I hope you got yer money's worth."

"Can't say I did. I'd sure be in your debt for yet another favor, though."

"You only got to ask."

"I'd like to get a message off to my folks in Lincoln. Could you send it collect, do you suppose? I'm a bit short just now."

"Wouldn't think of it," Tinker Dawkins said. "Here, write it on the pad, and it'll be in Lincoln, all paid up and proper, afore you give yer 'All aboard.' "

Cassie sat down at the desk and wrote it out:

MR. BEN MCGILL

NO. 9, 16TH STREET

LINCOLN, NEBRASKA

REQUIRE GRUBSTAKE SOON AS POSSIBLE CARE OF LINTON P. MAC-
ADOO PULLMAN COMPANY EL PASO TEXAS. DON'T WORRY. LOVE,
YOUR SON, CASSIUS.

Tinker Dawkins gave the message a once-over-lightly. "If you'll pardon me sayin' so, Cap'n, you seem to be carryin' an extra heavy load on yer shoulders this trip."

"That's so," Cassie replied. He tried to smile, but he made a poor job of it. "I'll not be forgetting your kindnesses on this stop, Mr. Dawkins, that's for sure."

"Think nothin' of it, Cap'n. Believe me, Dalhart ain't gonna fergit the Fourth Squadron neither! *Whoooopeeeee!* These customers o' yers sure know how to enjoy theirselves!"

"Is that so?" said Cassie. "I guess I failed to notice it, having private business of my own to attend to."

"Dint *notice* it? Then you're deaf and dumb both, Cap'n!"

Tinker Dawkins was pleased to give Cassie the particulars:

While Cassie was playing cards, a boastful gang of the Squadron's crack horsemen—discontent with life in the saloons after drinking their fill—took to wagering against the townsfolk on quarter-mile races. The finish line was stretched between the Prairie Schooner Saloon on the north side of Constitution and the Llano Estacado on the south. The Army ponies were put up against the best the Texans had to offer. The betting was hot and heavy. This brought out the town's multitudinous land speculators. The drunker the horse soldier, the wilder his wagering. Plots of useless prairie were put up against anything a soldier might have on his person or in close proximity thereto, including his horse, which was government property. The colonel's boy, Francisco, turned out to be fastest jockey in the West this day and thus in demand for every race. Usually he was good-humored. But when asked to ride a particular mount in about his tenth straight heat, he refused and the mount's regular rider knocked him flat. This led to a catch-as-catch-can championship of boxing. The Filipino boys were well schooled in the art of fisticuffs. Almost every night in bivouac they would test their skills, with much wagering on the side. Five good bouts were now staged, each ending in knockout. One of the combatants, a saddler from D Troop named Marcos, had once stayed five rounds with the flyweight champion of the world, also a Filipino. There were no cowboys of his weight willing to mix with him; so, to get a bout, he gave away forty pounds and took on a tough ranch hand. The local fellow was counted out in less than a minute, and a thousand dollars—more, some said—changed hands.

At four o'clock the front windows of the Panhandle Deluxe were blown out by a horse and rider then exiting the lobby. The rider about severed head from body; his horse had to be shot. The faro players in the downstairs lounge never looked up from the tables.

Another such incident led to a rousing good fire, which allowed Dalhart's volunteers to career down Constitution Avenue in their fine new fire engine drawn by three superb mounts which trampled a pair of innocent citizens and broke a good many bones before they could be reined to a stop. The building in question, a rooming house, burned to the ground. The town's brand-new automobile ambulance, freshly arrived by freight train from St. Louis, got its first use, picking up a half-dozen heart attacks and collapses of other kinds and generally serving the community well.

Drink was most probably at the root of all this evil. Eventually, a group of the town's best ladies, attired in their Sunday sunbonnets and other finery, came marching down the street: a mighty parade of the Dalhart Temperance Union. The ladies did their best to restore order, but it was too late in the day. Various of the looser women of the town had already traded their virtue for prime souvenirs, including half the 4th Squadron's rich blue horse blankets, all marked with the splendid gold "U.S." in the four corners.

One final incident broke the town's back. A pair of privates from C Troop, short on manners but long on desire, affronted a pretty young music teacher out behind the Cattlemen's Association. They more than affronted her: they left her tearful and largely ruined. If this were not sufficient, she turned out to be Mayor Spangles's only daughter, Bess. The man on the spot was Sheriff J. D. Hicks. The mayor demanded justice. Sheriff Hicks was calm by nature and well experienced in reasoning with ranch hands and dirt farmers who had taken an excess of drink. But he was out of practice in handling boisterous fellows with modern Colts hanging heavy from their belts. In the end, the sheriff was obliged to call out the militia. He assembled one hundred able-bodied men down by the livery stable and swore them in as special deputies. As soon as a good proportion of them could get home and find their pistols, the sheriff marched them to the western outskirts of town and began a sweep eastward, beginning with the redlight district—so-called for the trainmen's lanterns that graced the front stoops of the fancy houses, trainmen being prime customers of such places. Whenever a dozen or more troopers were collected, the deputies would escort them over to the day cars and put them aboard, with or without their uniforms, sidearms, and wallets. In this way, the *Pancho Villa Express* was gradually loaded. By the time "Recall" was blown, half the troopers were already asleep in their chairs.

"And what of the officers during all this?" Cassie inquired. "Most of the time, they keep these boys on short rein."

They might have been officers, but they were also mighty drunk. According to Tinker Dawkins, the shortest and most belligerent of the military men, a red-headed viper of the name Van Impe, had found it necessary to regurgitate his luncheon into the middle of Constitution Avenue. He and Mr. Webster's daughter had found the Panhandle's French champagne entirely to their taste.

The local from Oklahoma City did not show till 6:00 P.M. Cassie went out on the platform and greeted the reliefers. "Sure glad to see you!" Cassie said, pumping their hands in turn.

"What's going on here?" asked the first engineer with alarm.

"The Mex ain't got up *this* far, has they?" said the second.

They and their firemen, taking note of conditions in the town, looked surprised, then scared. The hoggers bore the names Merle Dickie and Ambrose "Grits" Delong. The former was tall and bearded, the latter short and clean-shaven. They were both off the St. Louis & Southwestern. Merle Dickie volunteered that they had done lots of charters for Pullman, but none with soldiers. Cassie started to tell them about Mr. Webster's bonus for fast running, but remembered that there was no sense to it with the millionaire's deadline far beyond their reach and the bonus money gone, too.

"You already got fires in your boilers," said Cassie. "I'd be much obliged if you'd sound your whistles as soon as you make sufficient steam. We're running sinful late, no fault of yours."

"Recall" was sounded again for the benefit of stragglers. Few responded. Captain Bowles, who had taken command of the Squadron in the continued absence of Colonel Antrobus, dispatched teams of officers to inspect each car and take the roll of men and horses. Cassie stood out on the siding and held his breath while the horses were counted. But he need not have worried. Nobody knew for sure how many horses there were supposed to be anymore, so inspection of the horse cars was casual at best.

"McGill! Get your ass over here!"

The shout came from Sergeant Major Jacko Mudd.

"What do you want?" Cassie said.

Cassie made sure to stand out under one of the gas lights that lined the platform. He wanted to be in plain sight of the officers at all times.

"You *know* what I want!" roared Mudd.

" 'Fraid I don't."

"I want to know what's become of Ward Snivey, that's what."

"Him?"

"*Him.*"

"How should I know?"

" 'Cause you're the last one to see him, that's how."

"Can't help you."

"Ward wouldn't be missin' less there was foul play."

"That's your opinion," Cassie said.

"There ain't no other explanation!"

"Wouldn't say that."

"What do you mean?"

"I heard another one," said Cassie.

"Meanin' what?"

"I heard he went off with Miss Jolene."

The soldier's eyes blazed like a mad dog's. "You're a damn *liar!* Where'd you hear such a damn lie?"

"I heard it," Cassie said.

"You're a damn liar!"

Cassie put on his most innocent face and manner. "Sorry, but I got work to do. We're heading out any time now."

"This trip ain't over yet, boy!" The sergeant major seemed as desperate as a man could be.

"Sure wish it were," Cassie replied truthfully.

When the officers finished calling roll, they were still short eight men and maybe five horses. Captain Lonnie Bowles came out on the platform and called for Cassie.

"Sir?"

"We appear to have eight AWOLs, Mistah McGill," said the Alabaman. "I shall delay departure till another search can be made."

"Yes, sir."

"Get up steam and be watchin' for my signal."

"Doing just that, sir."

The Squadron bugler was made to stand in the middle of Constitution Avenue and blow "Recall" over and over until his lips went dead. Captain Bowles's search parties made one more sweep. Up a short spur belonging to the Fort Worth & Denver City, they found six troopers and Dr. Olan Rose. The delinquents were sitting on the track with their heads in their hands; they were sick from bad alcohol. Dr. Rose had the D.T.'s: he was shivering, cursing, and vomiting all at once. Captain Bowles ordered a pair of Filipinos to carry the vet back to his compartment in Head-quarters Car and tie him to his berth. Corporal Romero was detailed to go each half hour to loosen the ropes and be sure that Doc didn't swallow his tongue or drown in his own vomit or otherwise ruin the car.

All members of the 4th Squadron were now accounted for except Ward Snivey of Headquarters Platoon. All civilians were accounted for except Helper Conductor Riley McAuliffe.

Captain Bowles summoned Cassie to Headquarters Car. "Don't this *bother* you none, Cassius? That your best friend, Mistah McAuliffe, is missin' without leave?"

"Yes, sir."

"You sure don't seem worried 'bout it. P'raps the Pullman Company cares less for its employees than the U.S. Army does for its enlistees."

"No, sir. Only—" Cassie tried to think up a lie the captain might swallow. He could imagine Rocks up front in *The Mother Lode,* carrying on in private with Miss Jolene. "Only he has trouble holding his liquor, sir."

"An' you think he's merely sleepin' somewheres? From drinkin' too much? Is that it?"

"I suppose he is, sir."

"Well, we can't affo'd to waste another moment on the likes o' him. Kindly signal yo' engineers to make speed."

"Right away, sir."

"An' Mistah McGill?"

"Sir?"

"In 'bout an hour's time, you come see me, hear?"

"Yes, sir. Thank you, sir."

The renewed clatter of the rails brought Cassie brief respite from his woes. Bone weary though he was, he could neither disconnect his brain nor silence his noisy conscience. No matter which way he looked, he saw Snivey's carcass growing cold and stiff in the horse car just ahead.

When he could bear the torment no longer, Cassie came down from the angel's nest and woke the brakeman. "Mr. Legrand?"

"Cap'n?"

"Take the lookout, would you please."

"My pleasure, Cap'n."

Cassie went outside and danced across the roofs of the swaying cars. Passing by the very hatch cover that had admitted Rocks and ensured Snivey's demise, Cassie made the sign of the cross and said an Our Father for the dead trooper. He kept up his prayers until he reached *The Mother Lode* and presented himself at the door to Father Tibbett's compartment.

He stood there five minutes or more, trying to get up his nerve. The pounding of his heart was so loud he feared the Father would hear it through the teak door. Finally he knocked. There was no answer. He said an Our Father and then a Hail, Mary and knocked again, harder. This time he thought he heard something. He could not be sure. He hesitated, then knocked yet again.

There was a muffled reply.

Cassie thought the voice said, "Come in." He prepared himself. Under his breath he said, "Forgive me, Father, for I have sinned." He opened the door.

"Gracious!" said Father Tibbett.

"*Forgive me, Father!*" Cassie cried out.

He turned and ran as fast as he could. He did not know whether he was running forward toward the locomotive or back toward the van: his tears blinded him. He had never run so fast or hard in his life. Still, he could not escape the specter that now pursued him:

Not Snivey's cold corpse—but the padre, naked in the lower berth, belly to belly with Mademoiselle Foix.

III

EATING DIRT

New Mexico and the Border
March 14–20, 1916

"We'll use a signal I have tried and found far-reaching and easy to yell. Waa-hoo!"

ZANE GREY, *The Last of the Plainsmen* (1911)

1

CASSIE HID OUT in the van. "Anybody comes looking for me, Mr. Legrand, you say you can't find me, hear?"

He kicked off his boots and settled down in the super's bunk, pulling the curtains around him.

"Feelin' a mite sickly, are we, Cap'n?"

"That's it."

It did not work. A good-natured trooper named Kinloe was sent to fetch him.

"I'm ailing just now," Cassie told him. "Got the grippe, like as not."

"I heard it called lots o' things," said Kinloe. " 'Magine you got yerself a dose back there at Maude's. Jus' the same, get yer boots on and follow me on the double. Captain's waitin'."

Like most troopers, Kinloe was short in height but scrappy by nature. Cassie did not argue. He got into his boots and followed along, pasting down his cowlick with spit as he went.

Captain Bowles had set up a special court-martial in Headquarters Car. About half the Squadron was up on charges of one kind or another growing out of the "Dalhart Massacre," as it was now called. A long line of sorry-faced troopers snaked back through the cook car and beyond into the day cars. The captain dispensed justice with great dispatch and little mercy. He docked their pay and gave them extra duties as punishment. Most of them were broke anyway from all the wagering and from visits to the fancy houses. A few of the lucky ones now owned deeds to lots on the outskirts of Dalhart, which they would probably never see again. Others had met proper ladies and were aiming to stop back through Dalhart after the war to claim their brides. Still others suffered from beatings they had taken at the hands of the farmers and cattlemen who had served as Sheriff J. D. Hicks's deputies.

Trooper Kinloe took Cassie to the head of the line and presented him to the captain. Jacko Mudd sat on one side of the captain, stating charges; Corporal Romero sat on the other, writing down punishments.

"Step forward, McGill," said the captain. "Sergeant Major Mudd has made a serious allegation concernin' you and your partner, Mistah Mc-Auliffe. He says y'all caused the disappearance of Ward Snivey, indisposin' him and mebbe even doin' him great bodily harm. What say ya to the charges?"

Cassie lowered his eyes and maintained silence.

"There it is, Captain!" cried Jacko Mudd. "See it for yourself! He's the guilty one, all right. It's written on his face!"

The captain remained peaceful. "That so, Cassius? Am I to 'cept the sergeant major's allegation to be fact?"

Cassie did not answer.

"Very well," said the captain. "The sergeant major believes Trooper Snivey to be aboard this train, injured or incapacitated in some way. I'm orderin' that each car be searched from top to bottom, front to back— every cupboard, every nook an' cranny. Iffen what the sergeant major says is correct, then you an' your pal is in for a great measure o' grief. . . ."

On leaving Headquarters Car, Cassie was accosted by the colonel's boy, Francisco:

"*Ola! Meester!*"

"What is it, Francisco. I'm busy just now."

The Filipino grabbed at Cassie's sleeve. "What you say to Col-o-nel? Why he no eat? Why he no speak?" The boy's eyes were tearful. He looked frightened, and determined, too. "If you do heem bad—I *keel* you, Capitan. Swear to Jesus!"

"You don't know what you're saying," Cassie replied. "It's not my *fault*. It's—"

He broke loose and headed back to the van. Whose fault was it then? he asked himself. His deceptions fooled nobody—not Captain Bowles, not Jacko Mudd, not even a poor native boy like Francisco.

He paid a short visit to the last horse car. Jacko Mudd's search parties were still a long way off, but the hay in the car was going down fast. It would not be long before the troopers found something besides hay.

"You want somethin', sonny?" one of the wranglers called out to him.

"Lost something of mine," Cassie replied.

"An' what would that be, exactly?"

"Book."

"Got any value to it?"

"It's just train orders and the like."

"Hardly worth lookin' for then, ain't that so?"

Without seeming too interested, Cassie let his eyes go on searching in case the book might expose itself. It did not. If he had dropped it there in the open, it would have been found by now anyway, he figured, or shoveled off with the horse droppings along the right of way.

"If it's found," Cassie said, "there might be a reward in it for the fellow who turns it in."

The wrangler stopped swinging his fork. "And how much would that amount to, then?"

"Oh, could be five dollars," Cassie said.

Not having five dollars or even a penny to his name, Cassie was immediately sorry he had not offered more. In the event somebody did find it, Cassie supposed he could get the Company to advance him some pay at El Paso and thus redeem his property, without which he could not be paid anyway. A conductor's pay account occupied the last page of his train book.

"If I come on it," said the wrangler, going back to his labors, "you'll be first to know after me."

"Much obliged," said Cassie.

He went on his way, worried now that he had started the fellow to making a proper search of the car. Where had his common sense got to?

The first town into New Mexico was called Nara Visa. The countryside thereabouts formed a plateau some four thousand feet above sea level. It was nine o'clock at night but might as well have been noon, the moon was so bright.

From Nara Visa an easy grade took them southwest to Logan and then across the Canadian River, which surprised everybody by having water in it. The night turned balmy; as many men as could manage to do so rode up top on the roofs of the horse cars. The temper of the soldiers seemed to improve with each passing mile: the men seemed buoyed up by the promise of war. Only the horses remained fearful; many were still passing blood, but the wranglers had no remedy for it in the absence of Doc Rose. Doc was still tied to his berth.

They eased into Tucumcari before eleven o'clock. A pair of extra locomotives were jockeyed into position to join up with the regular hogs. The tracks from Tucumcari south belonged to the Southern Pacific, and it was their practice to run doubleheaded into El Paso because of the grades. The yardmen also had orders to give each of the Baldwins an extra water tender. The great altitude was going to make the last part of their journey a real pull.

While the switching went on, Sergeant Major Jacko Mudd and his boys prowled about like coon hounds on the scent, sniffing the air and poking into every corner in their search for Ward Snivey. Skirting one party after another, Cassie made his way forward to *The Mother Lode*, intending to warn Rocks. He entered by way of the kitchen. As usual, Chef Kolb was busy fixing a fancy spread for Mr. Webster's guests—even then, close to midnight.

"Can I bring you anything, Mr. Kolb—from the wine cellar?"

The German understood Cassie's meaning at once. "*Yah, yah—ist safe now!*"

Cassie went out through the pantry into the passageway and knocked softly at the door to the first of the private rooms. "Pssssst—it's me," he whispered.

Rocks opened up at once. He cracked a great smile. "Have yerself a taste, Cass! You'll not find better!"

Rocks was deep into the millionaire's red wine. The shortstop's normally pale complexion was now considerably brightened.

Cassie entered and bolted the door behind him. "Kolb'll tan your hide, he finds you into Webster's private stocks."

There was hardly room to stand. Cases of wine and other provisions were stacked from floor to ceiling. Rocks squeezed between the boxes and settled on the lower berth; Cassie followed. There was a musky smell to the place, which Cassie traced to Miss Jolene. She was asleep in the upper berth. Her confinement in the possum belly had done little to improve her natural odor. She had often bathed in cigarette smoke, but not recently in soap and water.

Rocks leaned across and offered Cassie the bottle. "Here now, have yerself a wee taste—it'll cure yer aches and pains. Ya sure deserve it, Professor!"

Cassie declined. He had no stomach for strong drink then, though he might have welcomed its medicinal effects. "I've got to get a move on," Cassie said. "We'll be heading out soon."

"Ever seen a better hidin' place, Cass?"

"Safe enough now," Cassie agreed. "But maybe not for long."

"Safe till 'Paso is all we care. After that, me an' Jolene'll be gone fer good!"

Cassie told of the search parties that were taking the train apart inch by inch looking for Snivey.

Rocks was full of fight at the news. "Well, one place they *ain't* searchin' is the millionaire's own private railroad car! Ain't that so?"

Cassie turned palms up. These troopers seemed to live by their own rules. Who was to stop them?

Rocks finished off the bottle he had been nursing and applied himself to opening another. He had no corkscrew, so went at the job with a borrowed table knife. After his first mouthful, he spit out unwanted bits of lead and cork. He kept his usual silly smile, but now his voice sounded tearful: "You're right, o' course. Them troopers is sure to get the best o' me in the end. But what's the sense o' cryin' over't? I'd sure feel better if you'd share some o' this drink with me, Cass."

Cassie agreed to a sip. It was a fine wine, he had to admit. There was no telling what such a bottle might have brought at Kunzler's House of Wines & Spirits back in Lincoln. At Rocks's second passing of the bottle, Cassie had himself a long draft. He nodded toward the upper berth. "It's best she gets her sleep while she can."

"Jolene? Hell, Cass, she's tougher than you or me by a great stretch. My God, she's tougher than any *trooper,* comes to that. She's a fine gal, Cass. She'll come out of all this a lot better off 'n you or me, bet on it!"

Cassie nodded absentmindedly. He had another swallow of the wine. "I got to go," he said.

"Sure do thank ya fer comin', Cass!"

"Keep off the drink for a bit, can't you? When time comes, you're going to have to run for it—you and Jolene both."

Rocks lifted the window curtain an inch or so and peeked out. "So what's this place, Cass? Why, it's the border sure 'nough!"

"It's a place called Tucumcari."

"Look there—I can see true cactus! It's the West, all right, Cass. I'd swap me mitt jus' ta set foot out there an' git me a fine souvenir!"

"You stay put," Cassie ordered. "Jacko Mudd's all you'd find out there."

"Then you'll do it fer me, won't ya, Cass? Bring me a cactus leaf maybe? Or a pocketful o' true desert sand?" Rocks's eyes seemed to glow in the darkness. "Or maybe even a lizard, huh, Cass? If you kin catch me one?"

Cassie drank more of the wine. "Cactus and sand and a lizard. Happy to fill your order, sir. Satisfaction bein' our aim."

That was the way Pa talked back in the shop on Market Street. If a customer came in for coffee or tea or roasted peanuts, Pa would say: "Happy to fill your order, ma'am. Satisfaction bein' the aim o' McGill's Coffee & Spices!" Lincoln seemed a million miles away.

"I got to go," Cassie repeated. "Bolt the door, hear me?"

Rocks offered the bottle one more time. Cassie took another swig. The bottle was nearing empty. Cassie's tongue felt swollen and slow. He had two more good gulps and felt better for it. Rocks followed his example. The shortstop's face had gone from rosy to plain red. The bottle was empty.

"I'm off, then," Cassie said.

"Gonna be a swell feed when we git started up," Rocks said. "Feast fer yer colonel an' all—John's promised us the leftovers. Fact is, Cass, there's lots better eatin' up here with the coons than back in yer caboose! Ain't me an' Jolene the lucky ones? Jus' when ever'thin's turnin' ta shit, we set our asses in a tub o' butter! . . ."

Pullman's No. 3 rolled on. Cassie retired to the van and read the extras printed by the *El Paso Morning Times* and *El Paso Herald* and delivered by motor truck to Tucumcari. Almost every line in both papers concerned Villa and Pershing's "punitive expedition" against the Mex:

TROOPS READY TO CROSS LINE AT COLUMBUS

Orders from Commanding Officer Limit Equipment of Soliders to Such as May be Carried on Back or in Saddle.

By Associated Press.
San Antonio, Tex., March 14.—General Funston said tonight he had not been advised of General Pershing's intention to enter Mexico tomorrow morning, but added that General Pershing's orders were such that he might begin the campaign whenever he was ready.

MEXICAN HOTEL WAITER
SEIZED AS VILLISTA SPY

Columbus, N.M., March 14.—Alfredo Aregon, who for several weeks had been a waiter in the Columbus Hotel, was arrested today under charges of having in his possession goods looted from stores during the Villa raid and being one of the men who guided the horde of Mexican bandits into town before dawn last Thursday.

CARRANZA PLACES ORDER FOR FIVE BIG WARPLANES

Chicago, Ill.—Gen. Carranza, through Capt. Don Smith of Carranza's flying squadron, telegraphed an American here to rush construction of five big aeroplanes of 50 to 90 horse power, designed to carry 50 pounds of nitro-glycerin.

Two of the stories struck Cassie close to home:

. . . The strong undercurrent of excitement which is throbbing along the border was intensified by the report that a Southern Pacific train had been fired upon at Balen, seventeen miles east of here. Conductor Rogers, in charge of the train, said that several shots had been fired from the under-brush near the station. . . .

. . . Several hundred horses and mules are being sought by the United States Army for the expedition into Mexico. Specifications for government cavalry service are that the animals be between 15 and 16 hands high, 5 to 8 years old, weighing about 1,000 pounds, broken to ride, and abso-lutely sound in wind, eye, and limb. Only solid colors will be bought, all gray horses or mules not being desired. . . .

Cassie read until his eyes blurred. News of the war came as welcome relief. Thinking on other people's problems helped a person to forget his own. Even so, his mind soon returned to Snivey's corpse and Mr. Web-ster's money and Ma's rosary—and the padre in bed with the French lady.

The wine he had drunk with Rocks made him drowsy. He longed to sleep and did.

". . . Cap'n, sir? Sorry to be botherin' you—"

"What the devil!" Cassie awoke in a terrible fright. The rattle of the rails told him they were running hard.

"Pardon, Cap'n. No cause for alarm."

Cassie raised himself on his elbows. The dark figure bending over him was Christian, Mr. Webster's manservant. "What is it then?"

"Mr. and Mrs. Webster send you best wishes, sir. They respectfully invite you to join them and their guests for a light repast in celebration of journey's end."

Christian never spoke but in a high-toned way. He was a Negro of some education, according to Doc Rose. Cassie fumbled for Nelson's watch. It was 12:25 A.M. He could not have slept for more than five minutes.

"Oh, gosh, Christian," was all Cassie could think to say. In his mind's eye he could see Miss Candace in her pretty party dress and himself in his rumpled uniform. He had kept one good celluloid collar in reserve for El Paso so his neck would look clean. But the rest of him . . .

"Could you beg off for me, Christian? I've got duties that need tending to. Besides . . ."

The Negro's glistening brown face took on a sorrowful expression. "Mr. Webster—he's accustomed, Cap'n, to having his personal invitations accepted by folk fortunate enough to receive 'em."

The millionaire would want an accounting of his funds and an explanation for the long delay at Dalhart. Sweat dripped from Cassie's brow. "I guess you'd best say I'm coming then, Christian."

"Mr. Webster will be most pleased to hear it, Cap'n. Party's already begun, sir, if you'd like to come directly." The Negro departed.

Cassie shook his head. Midnight had come and gone: it was Wednesday, March 15. The Ides of March, thought Cassie, remembering *Julius Caesar* and the speeches he had learned from it at the Christian Brothers:

"Yond Cassius has a lean and hungry look; he thinks too much: such men are dangerous."

"Forever, and forever, farewell, Cassius! If we do meet agai·., why, we shall smile; if not, why then, this parting was well made."

Cassie also remembered the words of the Soothsayer: "Beware the Ides of March."

This day, too, was beginning in the same foreboding way.

He stood in the doorway for several minutes, afraid to go in. The parlor was dimly lighted by candles alone; the gas lamps had been turned off.

Still, Cassie was sure that his uniform's many shortcomings would be shamefully illuminated.

Mrs. Webster and Father Tibbett chatted amiably on a plush settee. Miss Candace and her companion, Mademoiselle Foix, sat together in front of the pump organ. Four gentlemen stood at the far end of the car, in the observation room, smoking their cigars; these were Mr. Webster, Captain Bowles, Lieutenant Van Impe, and—the devil's own surprise!— Doc Rose. The colonel was absent.

"I now share Mr. Hearst's opinion," the millionaire was saying heatedly. "Eventually—as much in their interests as our own—we shall be obliged to annex all the territory south of the border to the far side of the Isthmus Canal. You and your brave comrades, gentlemen, shall have more work than you can handle, with or without the European war. These wicked upstarts must be punished, if only as a lesson to others. We must teach them: *Do Not Affront Your Betters!* Imagine, primitive Mexicans shooting down American citizens on American soil! Who would have *conceived* of such an outrage?"

"Don't worry, sir," said Van Impe. "We shall teach them a sharp lesson, all right." He patted the .45 hanging from his Sam Browne belt— producing, Cassie noted, a look of mild disgust on Doc Rose's weathered face.

The conversation proceeded on to a discussion of the various Mexican leaders—Madero, Carranza, Obregón, Zapata, Villa—who had overthrown the dictator Diaz in '10.

"We should have supported Diaz when we had the chance," said the millionaire.

Doc disagreed. He was drinking whiskey again, and the veins in his temples appeared ready to pop. "Not a bit of it, Otis. Damn Diaz got his power from an army coup—he was not fit to serve. Thank God we do not suffer such doings in the United States of America. Here the Army only serves, it does not rule. . . ."

Van Impe glared at the vet but did not argue. Silence reigned for the moment. Seeing his chance, Cassie started forward again—hesitated again. If he was not keen on joining the assembled guests, could he be blamed for his reluctance? How was he to face the padre or Mademoiselle Foix when he had seen them so shockingly exposed? (Or was it a dream? Or was *this* a dream?) He thought of his chess game with Miss Candace, played in this very room. He blushed again. His legs went weak. He grabbed the back of a chair to keep from falling.

They noticed him. "Ah, splendid," said Otis Webster, "it's our young trainman, at last." The millionaire broke off from the other gentlemen and came out to shake Cassie's hand. "With our journey so near its end, Cassius, Mrs. Webster and I thought it seemly to give this small party in honor of our brave commander, Colonel Antrobus, and his staff. Unfortunately, the colonel has not been entirely well of late."

Cassie gave a shudder. Was the colonel's illness not due to Cassie's own "dereliction of duty"?

"Yet," continued the millionaire, "we have hopes that the colonel will soon join us, if only briefly. He has a great deal on his mind, as you can imagine, preparing the Squadron for war on the morrow."

Mr. Webster turned to the other guests and announced in his big fruity voice: "I thought it only right that we invite this young lad as representative of George Pullman's company, which has provided such fine service."

Not a word about the lateness of the run—or where his double eagles had gone to! Cassie was of the opinion that gentlemen of wealth and position were far better at minding their manners—even when they had good excuse not to—than ordinary folk.

"Meanwhile, Cassius, help yourself to food and drink. I believe you know everyone present. Please feel perfectly at home."

"Yes, sir. Thank you most sincerely, sir."

Cassie wished fervently that he really *were* at home, in Ma's plain kitchen.

A "light repast," Christian had called it. The mahogany dining table was set out with tiny sandwiches and cheese pies and pickles and liver paste and fish eggs. This latter item was to be spread on thin fingers of toast, sprinkled with chopped onion and hard-boiled egg, wet with lemon juice—then slid down the gullet on a wave of ice-cold champagne!

Cassie resisted the fish eggs, accepted the champagne. Christian poured the wine into a glistening silver goblet, which perspired from the cold. Cassie took a sip, then a gulp. He enjoyed it more with each swallow. It sure put Rocks's red in the shade. If only the shortstop could see him now! This was traveling first class, make no mistake.

Doc Rose, looking remarkably fit after his bout with the D.T.'s, joined Cassie by the buffet. His pewter teeth reflected the glitter of *The Mother Lode*'s candlelight.

"Then you're well again, sir?" said Cassie.

"Indeed, I am, lad. Appears we got our hands on some bad whiskey back at Dalhart. Brought a band of us low and very close to giving up the ghost, I can tell you! For a while there, quick dispatch by one of Van Impe's bullets would have been most welcome! But time mends most such ailments, thank the Lord. Best stick to the lighter spirits, I'd advise, such as this fine champagne." Doc had switched from his regular whiskey to the wine.

"To your health, sir," Cassie said. He lifted his goblet high.

"And yours, sir!" cried Doc. "And to good men, wherever they be!"

They drank.

"Ever see such great bottles, sir!" exclaimed Cassie.

"Magnums, boy—that's their name."

"Latin, sir," said Cassie. He was feeling pleased with himself. The wine seemed to agree with him. "Means big, I do believe."

"A scholar for sure!" replied Doc Rose. "I'll teach you a lesson not to be found in books. Remember this, boy: a man who buys his wine by the magnum expects to have a good time in life and generally does so!"

"I'll remember, sir!"

"Christian! This boy has developed a thirst!"

The Negro poured promptly.

"Awful kind of you, Christian," said Cassie. "And please not to skip Doc Rose!"

They were having themselves a fine time. Their merriment attracted Father Tibbett.

"Well now, young Cassius," said the padre, "a blessed morning to you."

Cassie choked on his wine.

"Easy there, lad—no cause to drown yourself," said Doc Rose.

Mademoiselle Foix joined them. The French lady giggled and sent a sly wink in Cassie's direction. Cassie was of the opinion that Mademoiselle Foix's appearance was considerably improved by her clothes. Naked, she had nearly no bosom at all, whereas now she appeared to have a quite remarkable one.

Mrs. Webster soon added to the gathering. "Do please *gorge* yourselves on the caviar," said the lady. "Otherwise, it shall go to waste in this abysmal desert climate."

"Lydia, my dear," said the padre, "an absolutely *Lucullan* feast. Come, Cassius," he went on, "you've a good appetite, I'll wager. Let us jointly attack these splendid delicacies before us."

Following Father Tibbett's example, Cassie made himself a generous sandwich of the fish eggs and took a large bite.

"Ah, such innocence, such *youth*," Mrs. Webster was saying to Mademoiselle Foix. "Isn't it *lovely* to find someone so—so *unspoiled* by life."

"There is much for a young man to *learn*," said the padre. The priest had eaten his first sandwich and was preparing a second. "But I expect you are a fine student, Cassius. Perhaps before we reach our destination, you and I shall have the opportunity to discuss a variety of appetites—fleshly as well as spiritual." There was a special twinkle to the padre's eye, like bubbles in the wine. "What would you say to that, my son?"

Cassie might have replied but for the fishy substance in his mouth. He could not swallow it down and was frantically searching for some way to spit it out without disgracing himself. He began to gag. He turned sharply away from the others, intending to run out to the kitchen, but Lieutenant Van Impe now blocked his way.

"Well now, McGill. Don't suppose you've seen much of *The Mother Lode* before, have you? Except to play chess, of course!"

Cassie stared back through bulging eyes.

"Well, man, speak up. Cat got your tongue?"

He had no choice but to swallow. About half the sticky business lodged in his throat, producing a fit of hoarse coughing and gagging.

Lydia Webster saw his distress and rushed to his side. "Hands over head, young man! Do as I say!"

Cassie tried to smile but could not. Through teary eyes he saw his benefactress as an image like that in a kaleidoscope. She was a proper lady from New York, who always wore a great hat crowned with flowers. The flowers now seemed to be running down her head like watercolors on wet drawing paper.

Doc Rose saved the day. He pounded Cassie on the back, then poured champagne down his throat. Cassie thanked the Lord that nothing came up! Puking on *The Mother Lode*'s fine carpet would surely have cost him his job then and there.

Supper was done; Mr. Webster held forth in the observation room while the ladies remained in the parlor. Cassie stood to the rear of the men and enjoyed a stogie that Doc Rose had given him.

". . . It's to be a mobile world," the millionaire was saying. He pointed to Cassie. "This young man shall reap the multitudinous rewards of technological advance." Mr. Webster was a graduate of the Rensselaer Polytechnic Institute of Troy, New York, a fact he never kept secret from any listener. He was a firm believer in the World of Science. "This shall be a nation on wheels, mark my words. Mr. Ford's Model T is but the start. The day will come when even the common workingman—an ambitious and enterprising young lad like our Mr. McGill here—shall own and operate his own mode of mechanized transportation. . . ."

Cassie liked the sound of it. Any motorcar would surely be easier to clean up after than any horse. But Doc Rose objected to this line of thinking:

". . . You can talk all you want o' these newfangled wagons-cum-motors and what have you. But there ain't never going to be a substitute for a good horse. A horse can *think*, which no damned machine can do or will ever be able to do. That's the difference, ain't it? So a man and his horse is *two* thinking animals, ain't that right? Which is better than one. None o' these friggin' Jeffrey wagons o' yours, Mr. Webster, is ever going to *think*."

"My dear doctor—"

"Hold on, sir! Let this old vet finish his piece. You there, Cap'n Bowles —see if you don't agree. A man on a horse with a fine weapon like these

Springfield repeating rifles of ours—he is the last word in modern warfare and not likely to be displaced by any man riding on a *wagon*. Am I correct, sir? Or am I wrong?"

Captain Bowles kept a friendly smile on his moon face. "I do believe I share your high opinion o' good horseflesh, Doctah Rose. However, in fairness to Mistah Webster, I must admit to hankerin' for the Jeffreys too."

Doc Rose would not accept the compromise. "*No, sir!* Why, the boys in this outfit—them and their mounts—is as fine a fighting machine as you'd ever hope to find on this earth! Yes, sir, there's no better—even if, just now, some o' the ponies ain't feelin' at their best. . . ."

Doc began to weep. They helped him to a chair and gave him water. The mood turned gloomy. The millionaire, however, was not undone by it. "I cannot quarrel with the good doctor," he said to the others, "when he invokes such noble thoughts of our gallant comrades in arms. I am particularly saddened by the absence of my dear friend, Colonel Antrobus. The colonel is—as I'm sure I need tell no man aboard this train—a most brilliant officer who has sacrificed personal ambition on the altar of public service.

"For myself, I can only attest that I would be the happiest man on this earth to emulate the patriotism of our colonel—and I shall attempt to do so in another field, namely politics, where I shall shortly offer myself as candidate for public office in our dear adopted state of Colorado. I hope it is not immodest of me to suggest that Webster's Mineral & Mining of Denver today offers substantial employment in our state, and I believe that our good citizens will not be ungrateful. . . ."

Miss Candace played the organ and sang:
"*. . . Believe me, if all those endearing young charms . . .*"

If ever a thing was to be called beautiful, Cassie reflected, it would be the girl across from him. She was done up in a pink silk dress, with rose-colored ribbons in her hair.

"Come now, Cassius," she called to him gaily. "Thomas refuses to sing with me. It's quite a simple song—do you know it?"

Van Impe thereupon changed his mind, sharing the bench with her and working the pedals and singing along in a badly tuned voice. He had on his full-dress uniform and looked quite the dandy. What galled Cassie most was the idea that it was an Irish song they were singing, one he knew about as well as his own name and one he might have sung himself under different circumstances. He drank his wine and stayed back, pretending to have no interest in music.

Father Tibbett was then persuaded to sit down and perform, which he did most ably. Under the seat of the organ bench, the Pullman Company provided its customers with sheet music to the best popular songs. The padre made his way in spirited fashion through "Yankee Doodle Boy" and "Alexander's Ragtime Band" and "Meet Me in St. Louis, Louis" and "In My Merry Oldsmobile."

When the priest tired, the cover to the keyboard was closed and Miss Candace took charge of the Victrola, setting a record of "On the Banks of the Wabash" on the machine and proceeding to dance a two-step to it with Van Impe. The other side of the shiny black platter was "My Gal Sal," and they danced to that, too, doing the turkey trot. Afterwards, they performed a tango. Cassie was about as impressed with the officer's dancing as with his singing, but the other guests seemed to approve.

"A most graceful couple," Lydia Webster declared.

When Miss Candace and the lieutenant finished their dancing, Mr. Webster came forward and took command of the Victrola.

"Cassius, come closer, why don't you, son? We're about to be entertained by the finest singer who's yet set foot on this earth."

Cassie edged closer. "Would you be speaking then, sir," he asked, "of Mr. McCormack?"

"Ah, you refer to the Irish lad," said the millionaire. "No, I am speaking of the great Neapolitan tenor, Enrico Caruso. Mrs. Webster and I first heard his glorious voice at the San Francisco Grand Opera on the evening of April 17 in the year 1906. Next morning, very early, the Great Earthquake destroyed the city!"

"Do tell, sir!" Cassie marveled at the millionaire's good fortune in witnessing such a spectacle.

Mr. Webster placed a disk on the machine and gave a strong wind to the crank. He also changed the needle to a special "loud" model. It was made of steel and was nothing like the cactus needles that Uncle Leo employed on his machine down at Hastings.

"Now, boy," said the millionaire, *"listen!"*

Cassie bent his ears to the task. It sounded like the roar of a lion. How lifelike it was! Even over the clack of the rails, the foreigner made himself heard. He seemed far stronger than Harry Lauder or Mr. McCormack, the voices Cassie knew best from listening to Leo's "phono-graph."

When the first disk was done, Mr. Webster immediately put a second on the machine, then a third.

"Well, boy? What say you?" asked the millionaire when the singing ended.

It seemed to Cassie that the "Neapolitan"—whatever that was—possessed a manly voice but was a bit of a bellower and not at all so sweet as Mr. McCormack.

Cassie chose his words with care. "I like him fine sir. Maybe if I could understand the words, I'd like him even better."

The others found this comment humorous; they had a good laugh over it. Cassie laughed, too.

"McGill here is not long off the farm," said Van Impe in his superior way. "That's *opera*, man. Opera is always sung in a foreign tongue."

"Now, now, Thomas," said Lydia Webster, "a young man who has never been exposed to the musical arts must be excused his natural ignorance of them. I don't suppose you've been to the theater, Mr. McGill?"

"The theater, ma'am? Yes, ma'am. We went once to Omaha to see Ethel Barrymore. It was *Captain Jinks of the Horse Marines*, ma'am. And I been to Chautauqua shows lots o' times." The wine had loosened his tongue to an unnatural degree.

"How fascinating," said Lydia Webster. "But you've not been to the opera?"

"Well, ma'am, I'm not sure about that."

"Not *sure?*" said Van Impe. "Speak up, man—either you have or you haven't."

Cassie kept his eyes on Lydia Webster. "What I mean is, ma'am, I had the privilege to see Mr. McCormack himself. In a tent show."

"And he sang opera, did he, Cassius?" inquired Mr. Webster.

"Mostly he sang songs, sir. But he did some bits in the foreign languages, too. I do believe it was opera."

"Well now," said the millionaire, "that must have been a memorable experience. Why don't you tell us about it?"

Cassie had another gulp of his wine and told how all the McGills had bundled up in Pa's new wagon with their two best teams pulling and joined up with a great wagon train composed of most every other Irish family in Lincoln and spent three whole days to cover the seventy miles west to Holdrege, where Mr. McCormack was appearing. That was in the spring of '14. There must have been ten thousand men, women, and children in the tent when the great man appeared. He sang all the best songs, "Ah, Moon of My Delight" and "Bonny Wee Thing" and "By the Short Cut to the Rosses" and "I Hear You Calling Me" and "The Meeting of the Waters" and too many others to recount, including many that Pa liked to sing of a Sunday evening with good Irish whiskey in him.

"It was a *grand* time," Cassie concluded, "especially for us McGills, as, in a manner of speaking, we're close cousins, the McCormacks and the McGills."

"Are there any two Irishmen who are *not* cousins?" asked Van Impe scornfully.

"*Hush* now, Thomas!" scolded Lydia Webster playfully. "Pay no attention, Cassius. You were saying?"

"Yes, ma'am. It's only, ma'am, that Mr. McCormack is from Athlone in County Roscommon, whereas the McGills are from County Sligo nearby."

The millionaire seemed surprised. "You were *born* in Ireland, then, Cassius?"

"No, sir—in Hastings. That's in Nebraska. But Grandma and Grandpa McGill were born in Ireland. Ma's people were born there too."

"You are of large family, Mr. McGill?" asked Lydia Webster.

"No, ma'am. About regular size."

"How large would that be?"

"Besides Ma and Pa, there'd be two boys, ma'am—Dwight and Dewey, they're twins, age nine—and two girls, Cleo, she's sixteen, and Ada, she's fourteen. That's all, ma'am."

"Five children," the millionaire said to Father Tibbett. "We would count that a large family nowadays, wouldn't we, Father?"

The padre removed his glass from ruby lips. "Among the poor, sir, large families are the rule, not the exception."

It had not occurred to Cassie that the McGills were poor. Compared to lots of families in Hastings, the McGills were rich, in Cassie's opinion.

"A great many of the Irish," said Lydia Webster, "prefer employment in the railroads, I do believe."

Doc Rose now came forward. He had kept still for as long as Cassie had known him to be.

" 'Tis the Irish who have *built* the railroads of this country, madam," proclaimed the vet.

"This is true," Van Impe said. "Not as investors or managers, of course, but in the construction—pick-and-shovel work, to be exact. Isn't this so, McGill?"

"In fact, it is often said," the padre remarked, "that the Irish constitute the *back*-bone of our country."

Such a clever joke! Again Cassie laughed with the others.

"I have never been one to despise a man for his physical prowess," said Doc Rose.

This remark served to pique Van Impe. "Rose. Is that an *Irish* name, Doctor?" He said *Irish* as though all men born of that soil were low vulgar fellows from the meanest walks of life and hardly fit to carry the hod.

"No, it is not," said Doc Rose, "though I would be the last to rue it if it were. I believe Rose to be English back many centuries, but I would feel no shame at all if it were Irish before that."

Lydia Webster took alarm from the brouhaha that had begun. "Enough of politics, gentlemen," she said sternly. "Otis, let us have one final selection from the Victrola, then to bed."

"Entirely agree," said the millionaire. "Perhaps we can go the Victrola one better. Cassius? Being of family so recently settled in this country, would you favor us with a song in the authentic Irish style?"

To sing before such an audience! Even with an excess of wine in him, Cassie was suddenly terrified.

"I lack a great deal, sir, from being Mr. McCormack!"

"Come now, lad," said the millionaire, "you're among friends here. You needn't be bashful."

"Perhaps Mr. McGill doesn't *know* any Irish songs, Papá," said Miss Candace.

"But he *must*," said Van Impe. "These immigrants bring nothing to America save the clothes on their backs and the songs their mothers taught them. Isn't this so, McGill?"

The officer's taunt stung him. Cassie could feel his ears going as red as the velvet that covered the chaise longues. He supposed that with so much wine now coursing through his veins, he could sing before the Pope himself as well as to this tiny gathering of "friends"! He spoke up, addressing himself to the millionaire:

"There's a song I do know, sir, from County Tyrone in the North. It tells of a singer in the old days—back to the Troubles even. We call it 'The Song of Phelim Brady, the Bard of Armagh.' "*

"Splendid," said Mr. Webster. "Perhaps the padre here will accompany you at the organ. Padre, if you don't mind?"

Singing to the accompaniment of Father Tibbett! Cassie's cheeks turned as red as his ears. In a flash he saw the padre's fat buttocks—and Mademoiselle Foix's creamy thighs, the soft red hair between.

"Delighted to serve," said Father Tibbett. He squeezed himself down again between bench and keyboard. "Not being acquainted with your Mr. Brady, Cassius, let me add a chord here and there, when I think one fits."

The guests all crowded around.

"Proceed at your pleasure, gentlemen," said Mr. Webster.

Cassie cleared his throat of the wine he had been drinking, took a deep breath and began:

> *"O list to the strains of a poor Irish harper*
> *And scorn not the strings from his poor wither'd hand.*
> *Remember, his fingers could once move more sharper*
> *To raise up the mem'ry of his dear native land."*

To Cassie's own ears, his voice seemed weak and uncertain: the noise of the rails threatened to drown him out. He sang the words as nicely as he could but knew that he lacked Pa's fine shadings and sweet tenor:

> *"At fair or at wake I could twist my shillelagh*
> *Or trip thro' the jig with my brogues bound with straw.*
> *And all the pretty maids in the village and valley*
> *Lov'd their bold Phelim Brady, the Bard of Armagh."*

---

* Editor's note: "The Bard of Armagh" is today best known in the United States, with new lyrics, as "The Streets of Laredo."

Cassie felt his voice growing stronger, sweeter. The padre, too—now that he knew the tune—seemed to enjoy himself more with each fleeting measure:

> *"And when Sergeant Death in his cold arms shall embrace me,*
> *Lo' lull me to sleep with sweet 'Eringobragh.'*
> *By the side of my Kathleen, my young wife, O place me,*
> *Then forget Phelim Brady, the Bard of Armagh."*

Cassie took a step backward, bowed his head, touched a sleeve to his sweaty brow.

At first, there was only the clatter of wheels on steel and the distant mournful sound of No. 506's whistle. Then Doc Rose uttered a sigh. "Well now. *Well* now!" Cassie was most embarrassed, for tears again poured down Doc's ruddy face.

"Bravo! *Bravo!*" cried Otis Webster. "What a *splendid* performance!"

"Such a fine *voice*," said Father Tibbett.

They applauded him as an audience in a theater might have done; Cassie was dumbfounded.

"Truly *beautiful*, Cassius," said Lydia Webster. "You have a lovely gift and must not abuse your voice by loud shouting on the train platform. Oh, but I find Irish songs entirely too sad."

Captain Bowles and Mademoiselle Foix complimented him, too. Then Candace Webster came to his side and took his arm. He was aware of his own smell and wished he had some Paris water to disguise it.

"A gentleman of hidden talents and charm," she cooed to him, smiling in her mischievous way. "And to think you wouldn't sing with me. I'm truly offended, Cassius. Yes, I am."

"Sing for your supper, eh, McGill?" said Van Impe. "Martial airs are what's called for, man, not these sentimental Irish tunes."

Cassie continued to worry about Doc Rose. He bent down and whispered to the older man: "I didn't mean to embarrass myself, sir."

"Didn't embarrass nobody but maybe some o' your listeners!" said Doc. "Be proud, boy. You done nothing to be 'shamed of!"

"Did I not tell you, Otis," said Father Tibbett, "that our Cassius is a boy of considerable wit?"

"You did, Padre, and I have since learned his qualities for myself. Unless one's ears tell lies, I must conclude that this boy has genuine musical talent and should give serious consideration to the development of his natural ability. . . . Cassius, you are a modest young man, as befits your age and experience. But you must not hide your gifts under a bushel basket. When time permits, we must sit down, you and I, and have a serious discussion as to your future ambitions and opportunities—indeed, as to your present employment. For now, we would be most pleased to hear another of your excellent ballads. Say you won't disappoint us."

"I sure don't want to disappoint anybody, sir. Only just now my throat's kind of dry."

"Christian? Champagne for the young man. . . . Ladies and gentlemen, Cassius has generously consented to give us another Irish ballad."

The padre again took his place at the organ.

"If you don't mind," Cassie said to them all, "I'll be singing another song from the County Tyrone. It goes by the name, 'The Maid with the Bonny Brown Hair' . . ."

But he never got even the first word out of his mouth. Two intruders suddenly appeared from the direction of Headquarters Car: Colonel Antrobus followed closely by Sergeant Major Jacko Mudd. Captain Bowles and Lieutenant Van Impe immediately snapped to attention. Mr. Webster, looking as surprised as Cassie, rose to his feet and welcomed the newcomers:

"How splendid! Our guest of honor himself—and just in time to be entertained by our brilliant young Irish balladeer. Greetings, Miles—a hearty welcome to you and your aide."

The colonel marched to the middle of the room. Jacko Mudd stationed himself between Cassie and the doorway, as though to cut off Cassie's retreat.

The colonel seemed unnaturally pale. His eyes shone big and bright like a wild animal's. "Thank you, Otis," said the officer. He bowed from the waist and brought his heels together sharply so that the spurs jingled. "But I regret that there can be no thought of entertainment so long as duty remains to be done."

"Duty, Miles?" said Mr. Webster in a puzzled tone of voice. "But surely tonight—"

"Cassius McGill!" barked the colonel.

"Sir?"

"By the authority granted me under the Articles of War, I place you under arrest!"

The ladies gasped in one voice at the shock of it. Lydia Webster appeared ready to swoon.

Cassie looked to the sergeant major. The soldier glared back, then held forth an object. It was Cassie's train book.

The colonel finished his speech:

"Cassius McGill, you are hereby charged with the foul murder of Trooper Ward Snivey. . . ."

2

"THE GOOD LORD sometimes lets us get up on high," Cassie could hear Uncle Leo say, "just so He can bring us low again at His pleasure."

Now the colonel spoke in searing, hateful tones. "Do you *deny* the charge?"

"Yes, sir, I do!" replied Cassie.

Mr. Webster leaned over and whispered into the colonel's ear. The colonel seemed to have shrunk a bit, or the millionaire to have grown taller. The colonel listened to what the millionaire had to say and nodded in agreement. The millionaire turned to his guests.

"The charge against Cassius is most grave. Ladies, Padre, Dr. Rose—I think it best that you excuse us now so that we may conduct the necessary proceedings in private. Christian, if you will leave us the brandy, please . . ."

Father Tibbett and the ladies and the servant departed at once. Doc Rose, no stranger to trouble himself, insisted on staying. "Fair play dictates there be at least one witness for the defense," said Doc, "and I guess I'm it." He gave a series of small belches and burps from all the food and wine and whiskey he had consumed.

The colonel ignored the vet and stepped closer to Cassie. "Do you deny this is your book?"

"No, sir. It's surely my book. See, it's got my name in it."

"Have you any idea where it was found?"

"No, sir."

The Colonel ordered Jacko Mudd to explain. The sergeant major was pleased to do so. The search parties had finally reached the last of the horse cars in the first section. There, a trooper jammed his pitchfork into something soft: Trooper Snivey's belly. Snivey was long dead and never felt this final insult to his humanity. His discoverers moved his corpse to examine both ends of the bullet hole that had done him in and thereby came upon Cassie's train book, which lay under the corpse and which, according to Jacko Mudd, told the true story of Ward Snivey's undoing. The story it told was that the good and loyal trooper had been provoked into a fight by Conductor McGill, and McGill had gunned Snivey down with the trooper's own Colt .45.

There was more. Another search party, making its way through the second section, had opened the rear van and discovered a pair of stowaways, Miss Naomi and Miss Rita.

"Astonishing!" cried Otis Webster.

"Ain't it the truth!" said Doc Rose, giving Cassie a wink of his blood-shot eye.

"As the unauthorized ladies are civilian," said the colonel, "I would take the liberty of proposing, Otis, that they be sheltered here in *The Mother Lode* for the few remaining hours of our journey. To safeguard the ladies' honor, you will understand."

"By all means, sir!" said the millionaire. "There is a spare compartment available for such a purpose. I am certain that Mrs. Webster will wish to take the ladies under her personal supervision."

"As for the prisoner," said the colonel, "he shall be escorted to the guardhouse and there confined until placed in custody of the Judge Advocate's Office at Fort Bliss. Sergeant Major, take charge of the prisoner."

"Yes, sir!"

Doc Rose spoke up. "Now hold on, Colonel. Cassie's a good lad and not about to run off at the first sign of heavy weather. You let him go about his duties, and I'll vouch for his stayin' on board."

"May I remind you, sir," said the colonel, "that you yourself are under house arrest and face serious charges upon our arrival at Fort Bliss?"

"True enough, Colonel. And I'm askin' the same for Cassius—house arrest. With his partner gone, Cassius here is the only conductor we've got."

Jacko Mudd objected, but in the end Doc Rose prevailed. Cassie was free to go about his business until they reached Fort Bliss, where a proper investigation would be conducted.

The colonel returned Cassie's train book to him. Cassie checked the snap pocket. Empty. Whoever had found it was thirty dollars richer for his trouble. But money was not on Cassie's mind. What concerned him now was the prospect of Lydia Webster and her wards, Miss Naomi and Miss Rita, busting in on Rocks and Miss Jolene in the wine cellar. There was no telling what the roughneck might do in a pinch.

Jacko Mudd saw Cassie out of *The Mother Lode*.

"Tell me one thing, boy. How'd you get his pistol off him? Ward Snivey wasn't one to give up his sidearm lest he had to. There was the two of you, ain't that so?—you and your pal Rocks? That's how you got the drop on him, ain't that right?"

Cassie made no comment.

"So where's your pal now, huh? Got him hid away with Miss Jolene, ain't that so?"

"They got off at Dalhart," Cassie said suddenly.

The sergeant major smiled. "Ain't gonna work, boy-o. Naw—my fellas would'a seen 'em. I figure 'em for El Paso, meanin' we still got plenty of time to find 'em. And when we do . . ."

Except for coal chutes and waterspouts, there was nothing to stop them for the next three hours. The desert grade made itself known, but the extra hogs taken on at Tucumcari served to flatten out the roadbed, while throwing back a volcano in cinders and smoke. The extra locomotives were Atlantic ten-wheelers built by the American Locomotive Company and used for nothing but doubleheading over these desert runs; the Pullman Company hired them from the Santa Fe. Their engineers went by the names Oates and Noble. They took their orders from Milo Dickie and Grits Delong, regular hoggers always being senior to "spot" men, according to the *Rules of Railroading*.

Wherever Cassie went now, he was followed by Private Rademacher. Jacko Mudd had ordered the trooper to dog Cassie's trail, expecting Cassie to lead them to Rocks and Miss Jolene. Cassie let himself into *The Mother Lode*, where common soldiers could not go; only the colonel and Captain Bowles and Lieutenant Van Impe were welcome there. With Rademacher standing outside in the vestibule, Cassie knocked softly on the door to Chef Kolb's *Weinkabinett*.

The door was opened by the Indian girl, Miss Naomi. "So it's you," she said sullenly.

"Morning, ma'am," said Cassie. He doffed his cap. "Sorry to bother you, ma'am, but I'm wondering if you've seen my pal Rocks?"

The girl motioned for him to come in. "Look what we got here, sis."

"Sis" was the other girl, Miss Rita. Cassie was surprised to find them awake; it was not yet 5:00 A.M. Miss Rita lay atop the upper berth while Miss Naomi sat on the lower. They were dressed in clean nightgowns— gifts from Lydia Webster, Cassie supposed—and showed no concern for their modesty. Cassie blushed on noticing the sharp peaks made in the flannel by Miss Naomi's nipples.

"Now why'd you s'pose he'd be hidin' in here?" asked Rita.

Cassie let his eyes roam. There was no sign of Rocks or Miss Jolene either, and no sign of the wines and spirits and other provisions that once occupied the compartment. "I just thought—"

The two girls were set to giggling by his hesitation. He did not fancy their coyness. How different they were from Candace Webster!

"I'll be going then," he told them. He tried to back out but Naomi rose up and blocked his way.

"Sit down, honey," Rita said, "and help yourself to breakfast—there's far more'n we can eat 'tween us."

Chef Kolb had provided them with fresh-baked bread, strawberry preserves, and English tea to celebrate their release from bondage. Cassie was still feeling the effects of Mr. Webster's champagne and fish eggs.

"Already had my breakfast, ma'am," he said. "Thank you just the same." Naomi passed him a cup of tea anyway. "Yes, ma'am. Thank you, ma'am."

Rita slipped down from the upper berth. The two girls whispered between themselves. Naomi found robe and slippers. "Got business to tend to," she said with a wink to her "sis."

Cassie stood back and let the girl pass. He couldn't imagine where she might go in such a state of dress. He put down his cup.

"I'd best be going, too, ma'am," he said to Rita.

She handed him a slice of bread which she had spread with preserves. He took a bite. She stood very close to him while he ate. He found himself staring down at her bare feet.

"I do hope you're feeling better, ma'am," he said. "The ride'll be a lot smoother up here than in back. It's on account of slack action."

She lighted herself a cigarette and offered it to him.

"Oh, no thank you, ma'am."

She put it between her own lips and had a puff. She was a modern girl.

"Guess you'll be glad to see El Paso, eh, ma'am?"

She laughed. "Glad ain't the word!"

"It's liable to be a rough town, though, ma'am, after Rapid City."

"Rapid City? You think Rapid City's heaven on earth? You ever *been* there?"

Cassie backed off. "No, ma'am, can't say I have. Except on this ride, that is."

"It ain't heaven, let me tell you!"

"No, ma'am, suppose not."

She sat on the lower berth. "Come sit beside me, Cassius."

"Ma'am?"

"Don't be scared. I ain't gonna bite you—less you want me to!"

She smiled at him in a curious way. He backed toward the door, licking jam from his fingers. "I *got* to go, ma'am."

She leapt up and rushed at him, placing her powdered face no more than a hair's breadth from his chest. She whispered up to him: "Honey, you are the *prettiest* thing!"

He had difficulty keeping her arms from around his neck. "Really, ma'am—"

"Won't cost you nothin', honey. Not a penny for the likes o' you!"

"Wish I could ma'am," he gasped, dragging open the door. "Only I'm Catholic, ma'am—God's own truth!"

Cassie ducked into the kitchen. The crew was apparently still asleep: he could hear snores from the pantry, where the bunks were situated.

But someone had been up not long ago: there were several loaves of hot bread on the counter and a pot of chicken bones boiling away on the stove.

"*Vel, boy! Vot you vant now?*"

Cassie jumped. He had not heard the pantry door open. There stood Chef Kolb, struggling to pull on his red velvet robe. He was naked otherwise.

"Sorry, sir! Didn't mean to wake you."

"*You should giff vorning, boy!*"

Cassie looked past the chef into the pantry. It was dark there; the only light came from the oil lamps in the kitchen. Cassie squinted to help his eyes. The snoring was louder now. It came mostly from the chow chow Mushy, bedded down in his special crate. Old Ling Hee and the Negro John lay asleep in their swing-down berths high up over the serving counters. The one lower berth belonged to Chef Kolb. It was now occupied by Miss Naomi.

Chef Kolb shut the pantry door. He pointed to the loaves of bread. "*Bredt is gut—you heet!*" He sliced off a thick piece and handed it to Cassie. He jerked his head in the direction of the pantry. "*Dese yonk girls—zumtimes zey vant oldt men too!*"

Cassie made no reply; his mouth was filled with bread.

"*Ach! You vunder, no? Vut has happen to zehm? Komm—I show you!*"

Chef Kolb opened the door to the walk-in food locker. As far as Cassie could tell, the room was empty except for sacks of peas and beans and potatoes and the other comestibles that went along on every Pullman charter.

"*Down dere.*" The chef pointed to a pair of large chests along the floor.

"You mean, sir—?"

"*Sssssh! Be zilent, boy—dey zleep now.*"

Cassie wanted to laugh and cry at the same time. Poor Rocks, poor Miss Jolene—trapped like rats, unable to stand or move a muscle without fear of being caught. Still, they were probably safer there than anyplace else on the train.

"I'll be going now, Mr. Kolb. Thanks for the bread—and for taking care of them, too."

"*De pleshur is mine!*"

Cassie went off, glad that the kindly German had Miss Naomi to see to his needs.

They pounded on toward the next stop, Carrizozo, where fresh crews would be taken on. Already there were signs of light in the east. Sunup came early to the desert.

Cassie had just closed his eyes for a catnap when Doc Rose appeared in the van. Doc looked grayer than usual; older, too.

"Got anything to drink back here?" Doc asked.

"No, sir, sure don't. If you'd like, I can send Nelson forward to get some wine from Chef Kolb, though."

"Don't bother on my account. May I sit?"

"Yes, sir—of course."

Doc plopped down on the super's bunk. Cassie sat opposite on the seat covering the coal stores. Nelson and the rear-shack Mr. Legrand were smoking tobacco by the back door; they paid Cassie and Doc little attention.

"Thank you, sir," Cassie said, "for all you done for me with the colonel."

"Save your thanks," Doc said.

"I guess I'm still in bad trouble, sir?"

"That you are, son."

"Yes, sir. So I supposed."

"Self-respect, young fella," Doc said. He cradled his head in his hands. The skin across the knuckles was parched and cracked from the powerful horse liniments he used. "Self-respect is the most important thing a man can have in this life. It's something you can't buy in the general store, can't learn in school, can't get any other way than by *earning* it. That's the hardest way possible."

"I expect it is, sir."

"No matter how far down you get, you *got* to have belief in yourself."

"Yes, sir."

"Otherwise you're no better off than a mule."

Doc made Cassie think of Pa. Neither man was at his best with words. Each preferred to show by doing.

"Next stop," said the vet abruptly. "What's it to be?"

"That's Carrizozo, sir."

"How far?"

"Well, sir, it was eighty-six from Vaughn."

"It'll do, then. When we get there, I'll be making use of the wire to Fort Bliss. The colonel—the colonel's not seeing things straight. He's got an illness which is mental and for which I've got no remedy in my bag."

"Sir?"

"Delusions of grandeur, boy. I fear poor Antrobus's succumbed to the grandiose schemes of his pal, Otis Webster."

"Mr. Webster, sir?"

"This war we're goin' to. For Webster it's business and social both. Why, it's like attendin' the opera! He's invited a half-dozen of his society friends to meet him down at the border and enjoy the skirmishes and killin' from the comfort of his private railroad car. Ain't it the life! Besides which, he figures to make himself a million or more sellin' them

damn motor carts. He can't lose, boy! The more wars, the better for ol'
Otis Webster.

"Then there's our colonel. For him, it's all Duty and Honor. Poor bastard. He figured Webster has friends in Washington—could maybe get
his name moved up the rolls for promotion, don'tcha know? Only our
millionaire friend is fickle. He don't need the colonel, the colonel needs
him! There's been a falling-out, is my guess. Since Dalhart, they ain't so
close as they was.

"Antrobus, he never was the politician—never learned to kiss ass.
While Pershing made first captain of the Corps of Cadets, Antrobus had
to settle for lieutenant. Been that way ever since. Always fancied himself
another Custer, Antrobus has. Custer was brevetted brigadier general at
the age of twenty-three—youngest in the Army since Lafayette. Pro-
moted to major general by the time the Civil War ended, but afterwards
had to go back to his true rank in the line, which was captain. He was
lucky to make lieutenant colonel before losing his scalp—same rank as
Antrobus today. Looks to me like our colonel's bound for the same fate.
It's a curious life, the Army. Don't suppose you've a taste for it, eh, boy?"

"No, sir, I sure don't."

"I expect you didn't murder that damn trooper, Snivey, neither."

"No, sir, I did not."

"Wish I could hold the same generous sentiments toward your partner,
Mr. McAuliffe. But I can't. Still, there'll be justice at Bliss."

"That's good to hear, sir!"

"For now, you'd best stay clear of Mudd and that lot."

"I mean to, sir."

Doc's eyes were suddenly brimming with tears. "My own time in this
Army is drawing to a close."

"I'm sorry to hear it, sir."

"But it's nothin' to cry over. You *sure* there's no whiskey back here?
What kind o' caboose is it that carries no whiskey?"

There was a water tower and a windmill and a shack for the switchman. A weathered signboard nailed to the windmill said:

CARRIZOZO, N.M.—Elev. 5429

A spur ran off east to a place called Capitan, which, according to
Busby's, was less populous than Carrizozo. Both sets of track belonged
to the Southern Pacific; so did the switchman.

The time was 6:00 A.M. but the sun was already peeking over the horizon, and the mountains to the east had a ghostly purple glow to them. The air was the thinnest Cassie had ever breathed: it gave him a headache.

The horses noticed it, too, and gave loud complaint. Like the men, the animals wanted to get down and stretch their legs; neither man nor beast had exercised since Dalhart. Jacko Mudd put the matter to Captain Bowles, who asked the colonel for permission to run the ponies. With Fort Bliss less than 140 miles down the track, the colonel refused. He stepped down from Headquarters Car and spoke to all within earshot:

"War is in the air, gentlemen! Can't you smell it? On to the border!"

The colonel would have to wait some. There was water and coal to take on, and fresh crews for the Baldwins. The spot men in the Atlantics, Oates and Noble, would be staying on to El Paso; this was their regular run, Tucumcari to El Paso and back again.

Cassie said good-bye to the hoggers then finishing.

"We heard o' yer troubles," said Milo Dickie, "an' sure wish ya well in gettin' out o' them!"

"Screw the bastards!" said Grits Delong.

Cassie thanked them for their votes of confidence, then turned his attention to the new hoggers. They went by the names Laird O'Dundee and Harold "Indian" Toombs. Both could write enough to sign their names in Cassie's book, but not much more than that. Toombs appeared to be forty or so, with sleepy eyes and cheeks puffed out on both sides from chaws of tobacco. He settled down in No. 799. Laird O'Dundee in No. 506 was both a Scot and a real western character, or so he pretended. He was got up in a parfleche jacket with deerskin pantaloons and Indian-style leggings and moccasins. He had more hair on his face than Buffalo Bill. Cassie knew this for a fact because he had once seen the real Buffalo Bill at a performance of the Sells-Floto Circus in Grand Island. This new fellow was well suited to the circus himself; he had the mouth of a sideshow barker:

"What's this I hear, boy? Your troopers tore up Dalhart so bad she'll never go t'gether again?

"Is it true, boy, there's whiskey for crew an' customers both on this run? An' what about them *ladies*, eh, boy? Share an' share alike—ain't them the rules? When now would it be me own good turn, eh, boy? Well, *come on*, boy—speak your piece, can't you? An' don't be sassin' your elders neither!"

Cassie reckoned O'Dundee's age at twenty-five or thereabouts. As was well known in railroading, companies in the West often had to make do with undesirables. Cassie guessed such was the case with the Santa Fe and Mr. O'Dundee.

"Someone's been filling your ears with the worst kind of poison," Cassie told him. "Mr. Dickie's left you a good head of steam. We'll roll as soon as you're watered up. War won't keep."

They cleared the yards in fifteen minutes. Cassie waited till the troopers settled down to the ride again, then went forward in hopes of getting a word with Rocks. Before he could reach *The Mother Lode,* Captain Bowles buttonholed him:

"I been talkin' to Doctah Rose."

"Sir?"

"He tells me that as far back as Rapid City you expressed yourself as to the unsuitability of our boxcars for the carryin' o' horses."

"I guess I did, sir."

"That you even got on the telegraph to advise your boss o' the situation."

"Yes, sir."

"Got a copy o' that message, son?"

Cassie produced his train book and turned to the pages dealing with Rapid City. "This is it, sir—if you can make out my hand."

BOXCARS UNSUITED TO HORSES. HORSES DYING. REQUEST PROPER LIVESTOCK CARS OMAHA. THIS IS SERIOUS SITUATION. YOURS, CAS-SIUS MCGILL.

"And what reply did you receive?"

"Sir?"

"Surely your message was answered?"

"Not exactly, sir."

"Don't talk riddles, boy!"

"The superintendent in Omaha, sir—Mr. Cosgrove?—he spoke to the matter, sir."

"Sayin' what?"

"Saying the makeup of *No. 3* was none of my business, sir."

"Not your *business?* You got any idea, boy, how many horses been *destroyed?*"

"A lot, sir."

"Fifty-four at last count."

"I'm real sorry, sir."

"You're aware, I 'spect, that Doctah Rose will be subject to court-martial at Fort Bliss."

"He told me, sir."

"Your testimony will most likely be required."

"Sir?"

"You'll be notified in good time. Meanwhile, keepin' your nose clean, boy?"

"Yes, sir."

"Not thinkin' 'bout runnin' off, are ya?"

"No, sir."

"Didn't suppose you were. Go 'bout your duties, boy, an' keep your chin up."

"Yes, sir. Thank you, sir!"

He had not taken two steps before one of Jacko Mudd's boys grabbed him and said he was wanted by the colonel.

"Best keep yer asshole covered, boy!" said the messenger. " 'Cause a good many o' these swell troopers ya see 'round ya got their minds on reamin' ya out fer what ya done to Ward Snivey!"

Cassie quickened his step and reported to Headquarters Car. The trooper called Ax Larsen was doing sentry duty outside the colonel's compartment.

"Well, if it ain't the mordering son o' de bitch hisself!"

"The colonel wants me."

"Don't he ever! Pass on, morderer!"

The colonel was alone, sitting on the lower berth. He had taken off his uniform and was wearing a silk bathrobe over his undergarments. The robe was cavalry blue with a gold A on the left breast. By the washbasin stood a bottle of Kentucky bourbon whiskey. The colonel was taking his breakfast straight from a double-shot glass without benefit of seltzer. On the coverlet in front of him lay a Colt .45. The colonel was getting it ready for war, Cassie supposed.

"Stand at ease, Cassius. Thank you for your promptness. To be prompt when called is a fine habit for a young man."

"Yes, sir. My ma says the same, sir."

"I am informed, Cassius, that you possess a most refined and cultivated singing voice. So Otis Webster tells me."

"It's just the voice I was born with, sir. It's not for fancy singing or anything grand."

The colonel took a sip of his whiskey. "Modesty becomes a young man. Later in life, however, you may find the benefits of modesty to be largely exaggerated." The colonel showed a gentle smile on these words but seemed weighed down by a great sadness. "You are apprehensive, no doubt, as to the purpose of my summons."

"I know the tight spot I'm in, sir."

"Of course you do. But you need not be unduly alarmed. Captain Bowles believes you to be innocent of any crime—and I share his opinion."

"Thank you, sir!"

"This is not to say that you are relieved of all responsibility in the matter of Trooper Snivey's death."

"No, sir."

"Lieutenant Van Impe and Sergeant Major Mudd, among others, be-lieve you to be guilty, if not of murder, then of acting as accessory to murder. In a purely legal sense, they may be correct."

"Yes, sir."

"But for now, let us dispense with technicalities and go to the heart of the matter. Your colleague Mr. McAuliffe murdered Trooper Snivey, did he not?"

"No, sir! It's not in him to do murder."

The colonel had another sip of whiskey. "The point is, Cassius, Mr. McAuliffe must come forward to answer charges. Until he does, he will be considered a fugitive from justice. Should you meet him, kindly tell him so."

"Yes, sir, I will. And thank you, sir, for believing Captain Bowles—and not believing the others."

"In the end, Cassius, a commander must rely upon his knowledge of men."

"Yes, sir."

"I have instructed Sergeant Major Mudd to draw up formal charges against Mr. McAuliffe. When we reach Fort Bliss, you will be required to give evidence before the judge advocate there and to answer any ques-tions he may put to you. You will be provided legal counsel, should you desire it. This will be done according to Army regulations. If you will now give me your solemn word that you will appear at the time and place designated, then I shall release you from house arrest. Have I your word?"

"Yes, sir."

"You may go now."

"Thank you, sir."

The colonel reached for the whiskey bottle, and Cassie turned to go.

"Cassius?"

"Sir?"

"I do wish I'd heard your song. The ladies were most touched by it. Some men are born with a special gift—most are not. You are a fortunate young man. Bear that in mind. . . ."

Formal charges to be drawn against Rocks!

Cassie hurried forward to the kitchen of *The Mother Lode*. Chef Kolb and John were busy fixing breakfast. Despite the lateness of the cham-pagne supper, Mr. Webster's party was up early in anticipation of arrival at Fort Bliss.

On the counters were ham, sausage, bread, tinned fruits, butter, preserves, cheese, and pitchers of cream taken aboard during the coaling stop at Alamogordo.

"*Take vot you vant, boy!*" said Chef Kolb. "*Heet! Heet!*"

The chef whistled a merry tune as he fried eggs and flapjacks on the griddle. Cassie figured Miss Naomi was the cause of the German's good humor.

"Thank you, sir," said Cassie, "only I've got business to see to. In the larder, sir."

"*I lock the door after you. Ve keep udder peoples out, don't vurry!*"

Rocks was sitting on one of the potato bins, making a meal of German sausage and red wine. The larder had no windows to it; Rocks was eating by candlelight. His smile seemed as broad as ever.

"Been achin' to see yer ugly face!" Rocks cried out.

"What about *her?*" Cassie asked. He pointed down to the food chests.

"Jolene? Oh, she ain't *there*, Cass. She's ridin' first class with Naomi and Rita. That compartment is sure more comfortable than any potato bin, I can tell ya!"

"You let her—"

"What's the worry, Professor? They'll not give her up to the troopers— bet on it! An' the ol' lady don't never come in without she knocks oh-so-polite first."

"What old lady is that?"

"Why yer millionaire's wife, o' course! Here now, have yerself a taste o' this fine sausage—take the bottle, too!"

Cassie refused. "There's no time to waste. There's things you've got to know."

But the shortstop was apparently in no hurry to hear Cassie's news. "Sit, why don'tcha, Cass? You're pacin' like a chained bear! . . . Ya know, I been thinkin'. How is it that a man like this millionaire o' yers ever come by so much money as to live the way he does? His own damn train, all the grub and spirits a fella could ask fer, all the riches o' the 'and. How is it you and me can't never hope fer the hundredth part o' such a thing?"

Cassie stopped his nervous pacing and sat down on a sack of potatoes. He had seldom seen Rocks so calm and thoughtful. The shortstop spoke in a wistful, dreamy fashion, which thoroughly puzzled—and annoyed— Cassie.

"It's not a matter of hoping," said Cassie. "It's how you're born. If you're born to money, you can live anyway you please. If you're not, then you can't."

"But fellas like us—"

"Fellows like us work for a living. What could be simpler than that?"

"I was meanin' *Irish* fellas, Cass. I guess if yo're born Irish, then there's no way ta 'scape yer troubles—isn't that so?"

"There's worse things than being Irish," said Cassie, though he said so without much conviction.

"S'pose yo're right, Professor. You most always are. From what ol' Christian says, I guess yo're about ta climb aboard the gravy train yerself."

"How's that?"

"There's sure no *disgrace* to it, Cass. I'm *happy* fer ya—gettin' yerself a fine uppity girl like her. 'Candace'—now what sort o' name do ya s'pose that'd be?"

"You don't know what you're talking about."

"Do, too! Besides, yo're sure to get yerself one o' them swell office jobs —Chicagy, now there's some town! Yer millionaire's gonna pay off fer ya, Cass—an' who deserves it more?"

Cassie feigned ignorance of such thoughts. "I'm not here to talk foolishness. Now *listen* to me. They're on to us. They figured out how Snivey met his end. The colonel as much as told me so."

"*Bugger me!*" Half-chewed sausage flew from the shortstop's mouth. "But hold on, Professor! If they figured it out, then we're free and clear!"

"Nothing like it," Cassie said. "There's to be a trial at Fort Bliss. They mean to charge you with killing Snivey."

"An' so I did!"

"They mean to call it *murder*."

"But that ain't fair!"

"The colonel says I'm to give evidence."

"Only ain't nobody gonna *believe* ya, Cass! Me, neither."

"Doc Rose says there'll be justice."

"A lot Doc knows of Army justice!"

"The Army has to give us a lawyer. That's according to regulations."

"Yo're expectin' an *Army* lawyer to turn on his own?"

"Then we'll get our *own* lawyer," Cassie said.

Rocks gave a weak laugh. "Hell, Cass—Clarence Darrow hisself couldn't get us off!"

Rocks was speaking of the crack lawyer for the Chicago & North Western, who was never known to lose a case. Cassie had another idea. "I'm thinking of a fellow better than Darrow."

"Who'd that be?"

"Bryan," said Cassie.

"Bryan?" said Rocks.

"*Bryan.* William Jennings *Bryan.* He's from Lincoln, o' course."

"Is that so?" said Rocks. "Well, how's some fella from Lincoln s'posed ta go up against the whole damn U.S. Army?"

"He's not 'some fellow' from Lincoln," said Cassie impatiently. "He's only run three times for President, is all."

A puzzled look crossed the shortstop's impudent face. "Never won, did he?"

"Of *course* he never won—you'd have heard of him if he'd *won*, wouldn't you? The thing is, he's a top lawyer, and he's bound to help us when he knows we're from Lincoln. I'll get on the wire soon as we reach El Paso. What do you say?"

The shortstop thought hard on the matter for several minutes, then announced his decision:

"Call him if ya want, Professor, but the odds are a bit long for the likes o' me and Jolene. We're Irish, Cass. Is this lawyer o' yers—Bryan—is he Irish?"

"I don't suppose he is," Cassie said.

"Dint think so," said Rocks. "Naw—me and Jolene, we kin drop off this rig anytime we see fit. That's it fer us, Cass—an' no horseback-Johnnie better try 'n' stop us, neither!" The shortstop opened his shirt to show the pistol jammed down inside his waistband.

Cassie sighed in resignation. "Then you're meaning to run?"

"That's it! Me an' Jolene'll be in Californie long afore you're back to Lincoln, Professor!"

"Without a penny to your names?"

"We'll git there, Cass—bet on it!"

Cassie pulled out his train book and tore off a blank sheet from the back. "Pay attention to what I tell you." He wrote out a message as he talked. "Fort Bliss comes before El Paso. It's not more than two hours from now. You'll hear five short blasts on the whistle when we're a quarter mile short of the platform. Wait till we're down to walking speed, then jump. That's your best chance.

"By the map, it's four or five miles to town. When you get there, ask for the Pullman office—it's close by the Southern Pacific depot. Present yourself to the superintendent. His name is Linton P. MacAdoo. Hand him this note and he'll give you back money. It'll be forty dollars cash. That should see you and Jolene to San Francisco with something to spare. Remember—five short whistles and get set to jump."

They rose together. Cassie stuck out his hand and Rocks took it.

"Cass—yo're the best there ever was!"

"And you're the worst, too," Cassie replied with a smile.

They grabbed each other in a hug, then parted, neither one dry-eyed, neither one knowing when or if he would ever see the other again.

EL PASO MORNING TIMES, *Wednesday, March 15, 1916*

3

THE *Pancho Villa Express* CAME IN SIGHT OF Fort Bliss at
9:55 A.M. This was two hours late, according to the colonel's schedule,
but it did not seem too far off the mark to Cassie. Villa and his boys
already had six days' head start on the U.S. Army.

Cassie kept a sharp lookout from the angel's nest but saw nothing of
Rocks and Jolene. This pleased him, for if he had not spotted the fugi-
tives, then neither had Jacko Mudd's boys. Across the Rio Grande was
Old Mexico. Cassie could see the Mex's big town over the river, Ciudad
Juárez, and beyond that the very mountains of Chihuahua where Villa
was supposed to be hiding. It seemed to Cassie that the cavalry would
not have to ride far to corner their man.

Off in the distance to the west was Comanche Peak, still capped with
snow. The big Texas sun was already high and hot. The thin clean air,
which had been cold during the early morning hours, was now more
than pleasant. This hospitable Texas climate sure beat Lincoln in winter,
Cassie reflected. His good feelings toward the new landscape were
further bolstered by the thought that he would soon be rid of his customers. They had come 1,715 miles together since Fort Meade—one
hundred straight hours!

There was a soldier acting as switchman by the Fort Bliss order board
a hundred yards short of the platform. Cassie gave him a wave. The fellow cried back:

"Ho, boy! So this here's the great heroes o' Dalhart! Such ferocious
lads! If I was Villa, I'd sure take to my sick bed on account of not wantin'
to meet up with you fellas!"

Before Cassie could fashion a proper sarcastic reply, the fellow ran off
toward the fort's front gates. Engineer Laird O'Dundee shut off the air
brakes and brought the first section to a noisy stop. The Squadron's
wranglers immediately ramped down four ponies, saddled them, and
brushed them up for show. These mounts belonged to Colonel Antrobus
and his personal staff, Captain Bowles, Lieutenant Van Impe, and
Sergeant Major Mudd. The remaining troopers and mounts stayed
aboard, awaiting orders.

The colonel had abandoned his garrison dress and now appeared in
fighting khakis like a common trooper, a .45 on his belt. The strap to his

broad-brimmed cavalry hat was pulled tight under his chin; he looked ready for business. The colonel's party cantered down the line, to the cheers of the troopers hanging out the windows, then came back to where they had started and set up in formation opposite Headquarters Car. There they waited.

Not a soul appeared on the platform to greet them. This seemed strange to Cassie. In the distance the Army's campground looked almost deserted: Fort Bliss was a ghost town, from what Cassie could see of it. Nearby was a great field of grass, mowed close and well tended, on which several horsemen dressed all in white raced to and fro hitting at a ball with long wooden mallets. These gentlemen paid no attention to the *Pancho Villa Express* but kept on with their game; if there was war in the offing, they showed no interest in it.

The colonel and his staff continued to hold themselves smartly at attention. Cassie's curiosity soon got the better of him; he went forward.

"Colonel, sir? I'd best be giving our hoggers their orders, sir. Will you be wanting to off-load the horses here, sir? Or would that be up the spur?"

"Stand easy, Mr. McGill. We await orders ourselves. Kindly instruct your engineers to keep steam up, should we be dispatched forthwith to the border."

"Yes, sir. Thank you, sir."

Cassie passed the word to Laird O'Dundee and Indian Toombs, then returned to the platform and waited within earshot of the colonel. Presently, a whirlwind of desert sand could be seen approaching from the far reaches of the camp. As it moved closer, Cassie saw that it was a motorcar.

"*Staff! At-ten-shun!*" barked the colonel.

The vehicle braked to a stop. It was an open Dodge touring model, dull green in color, with a small flag, red with a gold star in the center, attached to the running board. A legend in muted gold across the doors proclaimed:

AMERICAN EXPEDITIONARY FORCE

The driver kept his eyes straight ahead. Out of the back seat climbed a young lieutenant in battle dress. From the peak of his cavalry hat through his wiry body to the toes of his gleaming boots, he combined discipline and swagger. Marching directly to the colonel, he gave a brisk salute and declared:

"Welcome to Fort Bliss, sir! I am George Patton, Eighth Cavalry, aide to General Pershing. The general sends you personal greetings. He would be here himself but for the imminent commencement of operations against Villa. I bear orders for your unit, sir. If we may speak in private . . ."

Colonel Antrobus dismounted, and the two officers retired to Headquarters Car. They did not stay long. Without warning, the colonel burst onto the platform, trailed closely by the younger officer, and spoke briefly to Captain Bowles. The colonel then settled himself in the rear seat of the waiting Dodge while Lieutenant Patton occupied the front. The lieutenant immediately slapped the side of the motorcar with his riding crop, and the Dodge roared away in a great cloud of sand.

"Staff . . . at . . . ease!" cried Captain Bowles. "Mistah McGill!"

"Sir?"

"The Squadron will stand down for the next hour. The horses will be exercised there"—the captain pointed out to the field where the mallet-and-ball game was still being played—"and given water and oats. You are to maintain steam, however, and be prepared to move at a moment's notice."

"Move, sir?"

"Are you deaf, boy?"

"No, sir. Only—"

"Obey orders, then!"

So the run was not done yet! Cassie relayed Captain Bowles's instructions to his hoggers.

"Not me!" bellowed Laird O'Dundee. "Ain't movin' this rig 'nother mile. Check your book, sonny boy—I'm signed on ta Bliss, and this is Bliss!"

The same held for Indian Toombs. It seemed that both gentlemen had been promised an easy ride to the fort and nothing more. They were Santa Fe employees and owed precious little to the Pullman Company.

"Well, stay put," Cassie told the rebels, "till I scare up your relief."

Meanwhile, the 4th Squadron's buglers sounded "Boots and Saddles," which the troopers had not heard in a spell: it pleased them greatly. What animals were left after so many trackside funerals were quickly coaxed down the few serviceable ramps and sent off at a gallop.

There was a telephone in the Santa Fe shack by the platform. Cassie persuaded the yardman there to let him use the instrument to ring the Pullman Company offices ahead in El Paso.

"This is Cassius McGill speaking, master of No. 3."

"Is it you then?" said the fellow on the other end. His voice sounded high-pitched and shrill over the wire. "Where in damnation you been?"

"We've had our troubles," Cassie said. "Can you send us fresh hoggers? The fellows I've got now are about to quit me."

"Hold your breeches, can't you? They'll be out to you by handcar when

I say so. Till then, you'd best keep up steam, else it's a bad end for you, ain't it?"

Cassie ignored the fellow's lack of manners. "Have you got orders for me? This platform finishes our run out of Lincoln. I'm without paper from here on."

"Your orders is to stay put till you get orders. Hanging up now—this line's wanted for business more important than yours. There's to be war this morning, didn't you hear?"

The line went dead before Cassie could ask for Mr. Linton P. Mac-Adoo. Cassie was concerned for his grubstake, which by now was surely in the hands of the Pullman agent. The more Cassie thought on the matter, the itchier he got. What if Mr. Linton P. MacAdoo failed to honor Cassie's note saying to give Rocks forty dollars cash? The agent might suppose it was a great sum for the likes of Rocks McAuliffe. He would be right about that.

Cassie hurried back to trainside and waited with the other crewmen.

"I think I see 'em, Cap'n," said Nelson finally.

It was a handcar all right, making good speed and bearing four dark figures in Santa Fe coveralls.

"Comin' like the wind, ain't they!" judged Laird O'Dundee. The Scot was as anxious to clear out as Cassie was to have him gone.

It was a while before the reliefers got their breath and could talk. The hoggers were John "Buster" Rattle and Thomas C. Greedy, the firemen Ickes and Culpepper. Buster Rattle was dark and stocky with an oft-broken nose that appeared to conflict with his amiable disposition. His seersucker coveralls were smeared with grease, showing that he spent considerable time under his hog. Tom Greedy might have been Buster Rattle's younger brother. At the corner of his mouth he kept a fat cigar, which he chewed more than he smoked. As for Ickes and Culpepper, the two firemen were indistinguishable from their brethren on roads the world over: gray, put-upon fellows who could find no other line of work.

"Keep a hundred and twenty pounds and watch for my signal," Cassie told the new men. "The colonel doesn't take to delay or excuses."

"Best do as the boy says!" warned Laird O'Dundee. "He looks a babe but don't take excuses neither!"

O'Dundee and Toombs climbed down from their cabs. They meant to board the handcar and follow the reliefers' trail back into town. "Hold up," Cassie told them. "Might have an extra passenger for you."

Cassie ran off down the line and found Captain Bowles. "Problem with the reliefers, sir! Asking your permission to go with those fellows by that handcar there and clear my orders in the Pullman office. Don't expect it'll take an hour, sir. I'd be much obliged!"

The captain bought Cassie's lie. "Don't dawdle, boy. Be off with you!"

Cassie joined the hoggers in the cart and applied himself to the pump lever, sitting beside Toombs and opposite to O'Dundee. The Scot boasted biceps of iron and had no difficulty keeping up his end of the bargain. They got to the Santa Fe yards in no time at all. Cassie bid the hoggers farewell and watched them head for the nearest saloon. It was only then that he discovered he was nowhere near to the Southern Pacific, where Pullman kept its offices.

Pumping the car all by his lonesome took some doing, even with the weight of two bodies removed. Cassie took off his tunic and used it for a seat, but still he found himself drowning in sweat after a quarter mile or less. In the distance on both sides of the track he could see dwellings, business establishments, maybe fifty livery stables, and all the other signs of a lively town. He had often heard that El Paso was awash in hospitality of every kind for men who followed the rails for their living, and he intended to find out for himself as soon as his duty was done. According to *Busby's*, El Paso had 50,000 residents—more than Lincoln—with telephones in most every house, good gravel roads, streetcars, automobiles galore. She boasted a half-dozen railroads, of which the Southern Pacific was the top line, having opened up the whole territory in 1881 by connecting St. Louis to California. The town was now reputed to offer a hundred saloons and half that number of fancy houses. But the greatest pleasure Cassie could think of at that moment was a hot bath in a proper tub with no shortage of soap or time in which to enjoy it.

"*Ho, boy!* And where do ya think you're going with that car? She's railroad property and not to be tinkered with!"

A yardman came along at a slow trot. Cassie's pace was such that the fellow kept abreast without breathing hard.

"It's railroad business I'm on!" Cassie shouted back. He was glad to stop pumping. "Look here." Cassie flashed this brotherhood card.

The fellow's face turned from scowl to smile. "Pleased to know ya, McGill! State your business and iffen I can help, I shall!"

Cassie explained.

"Right church, wrong pew!" the fellow told him. Cassie had found the right part of the yard but the wrong spur. The yardman jumped aboard and they pumped back a hundred strokes or so, then got out and hauled the car across to a different set of tracks. After that, it was less than two minutes to where Cassie wanted to go.

". . . That there's the San Jacinto Plaza. That there's San Francisco Avenue. And that buildin' there, that's your Pullman Company. . . ."

"Much obliged!" Cassie said.

The yardman helped drag the car off the track again and promised to safeguard it till Cassie returned. Finding such an amiable fellow improved Cassie's spirits. He knocked the dirt from his boots and climbed the stairs to the second floor. The building was pink adobe with the timbers sticking through. However, the insides looked much like the Pullman office back in Lincoln.

"Closed on account of war!" the clerk yelled at him first thing.

Cassie recognized the fellow's voice at once. It had the same tinny sound to it in person that it did over the wire.

"I'm McGill off *No. 3*," Cassie said. "Much obliged to you for sending out the new crews so quick. Got me out of a tight spot."

"You're welcome, I'm sure. But we're closed today. If it's vouchers you've got, come back tomorrow."

This from a snotty-nosed kid who—according to the hand-carved wood sign on his desk—went by the name Vernon Paisley. *Vernon Paisley,* some name! He had a mustache and sideburns that grew long and curly.

"I've come for my money, is all," Cassie told the fellow. Cassie was not planning to salt his conversation further with "much obliged" or "thank you most sincerely" or any other "grace" words, as Ma called them. This fellow called for different treatment.

"And what money would that be?"

"Money sent to me by my pa in Lincoln, Nebraska."

"Don't have none."

"But you must."

"Good day to you. We're closed."

"I sent for it on the wire back at Dalhart and know it must be here by now."

"Nothing like it here."

"Can't you look in your traffic?"

"Nothing to look for. If there was money, I'd know it."

"I've come off a long ride," Cassie said in a careful voice, "and I'm a bit short on manners. This money is *awful* important to me, and I've got to have a better answer than any you've provided so far."

"Is that right!"

"Let me see Mr. Linton P. MacAdoo then."

"Ain't here."

"Where would he be?"

"Gone across to Juárez. Doin' Company business."

"When do you expect him?"

"Depends on the war."

"How so?"

"If he stays across the bridge till Villa's strung up, who's to say when he'll be back?"

"Till then, you'll do business for him, I suppose?"

"I'm sure capable of it, if it's any concern o' yours. Anyhow, we're closed. I ain't gonna tell you again."

Cassie had been carrying his tunic and cap in his arms. Now he put them on. This left his hands free. He looked around till he found the gate to the railing that separated the outer office where he was standing from the inner part where Vernon Paisley was sitting. Cassie reached over the railing and undid the latch and let himself in.

"Hold up, now! Where do you think—"

Cassie approached to within an arm's length of Vernon Paisley's nose. "It's something over a hundred and seventy-four dollars. It's sent care of Mr. Linton P. MacAdoo. It'll be in your Western Union traffic. Let me see your traffic for today—and yesterday, too."

Vernon Paisley now admitted as to how he could, on this one occasion, bend Company rules sufficiently to permit Cassie to see his traffic. While Cassie went about his search, the Pullman clerk took up a watchful position by the far wall, near to the windows. Cassie went through all the orders back for two days and found nothing from Pa to Mr. Linton P. MacAdoo.

"When is it, then, you're expecting Mr. MacAdoo? I forget your first answer."

"In time for his dinner. I'd sure be pleased to tell him you paid us a visit!"

"You do that. Tell Mr. MacAdoo I was here on behalf of Mr. Otis Webster, the millionaire, who is a top customer of the Company. It's his private varnish *The Mother Lode* that's riding over on the Fort Bliss siding. I'm charged with seeing to all his needs and requirements. This is on orders of Mr. Laurence Cosgrove, General Superintendent for the West. You'll be wanting to write this down, won't you?"

"Oh, yes, sir!"

Vernon Paisley began to scribble at a furious pace. Cassie kept on. "As soon as the money gets here, you'd best notify me by telephone. Or, better, come tell me yourself. I'll be aboard *No. 3*, wherever she sits. There's a part of the money that's to be given to Mr. Riley McAuliffe— he's got a note for Mr. MacAdoo that explains it. It's private business and not to be talked about to another soul but Mr. MacAdoo himself."

"You can trust me, sir!"

"For your sake, I hope I can," said Cassie.

There was a dinky taking some empties east down the line. Cassie stole a ride on it so as not to break his back pumping the handcar out to the Fort Bliss platform.

They had not missed him. The men and animals were finished with their exercises and settled along the trackbed, the horses grazing in the short prairie grass and the men sneaking rations off their belts in the absence of a hot meal from the cook car. Captain Bowles had ordered the Squadron to remain at the ready, which meant no messing or other activities that might keep the troopers from mounting up at the first note from a bugle.

It was noon before the colonel returned. He climbed down from the same green Dodge motorcar that had taken him away. This time the young lieutenant did not accompany him, only the driver.

"Captain Bowles, kindly assemble the officers!"

"Yes, suh!"

The troopers were formed up by their sergeants out in the grassy field and put at "parade rest" while their officers collected on the platform in front of Headquarters Car. Cassie watched from the kitchen window in *The Mother Lode*.

". . . Gentlemen, we have received our orders from General Pershing. . . ."

There was an upward tilt to the colonel's chin, but his raspy voice seemed to flutter in the dry desert wind.

". . . Minutes from now . . . two columns of the American Expeditionary Force shall cross over the border into Mexico. . . ."

A loud cheer went up from the officers. The colonel waited for silence before starting again. ". . . The lead column, under command of Colonel Dodd, shall proceed from Hachita, New Mexico. . . . The column shall consist of the Seventh Cavalry . . . the Tenth less two troops . . . and Battery B of the Sixth Field Artillery. . . .

"The second column, under command of Colonel Slocum, shall proceed directly from Columbus. . . . This column shall consist of the Thirteenth less one troop . . . one battery of horse artillery . . . one company of engineers . . . and the First Aero Squadron, with eight aeroplanes. . . ."

The officers sent up another round of hurrahs. Aeroplanes! It was to be modern warfare with no holds barred. The officers edged forward eagerly. So far there had been no mention of the 4th Squadron. The colonel was saving the best for last: Cassie sensed it.

". . . And now, as to our own areas of responsibility . . ."

A hot gust of wind blew up a cloud of sand and grit, blinding the colonel. His eyes teared over; he had to use his handkerchief before he could speak further.

". . . The Fourth Squadron shall proceed to Hachita, New Mexico, and take up station, replacing the Seventh and the Tenth. . . ."

The officers cupped their ears toward the colonel, striving to hear his words more clearly.

". . . Detachments will be placed along the border at Las Cienegas, Alamo Hueco, Campbell's Well, and Lone Cabin. . . . These units shall perform outpost and border-patrol duties to be specified in future orders. . . . Constant vigilance shall be exercised, lest we, too, be bloodied as were Slocum's forces at Columbus on that fateful night when Villa struck his cowardly blow. . . ."

The officers were looking into each other's faces now, and not liking what they saw.

The colonel continued:

". . . The bandit Villa has shown himself no stranger to treachery and surprise attack. . . . There is now strong rumor that his forces intend to invade the United States in strength. . . . Thus, the Fourth Squadron—bold cutting edge of the illustrious Twelfth—must be prepared to repel the bandit whenever and wherever he dares strike—and to hunt him down as one hunts a vicious animal."

The colonel stopped abruptly. He seemed all talked out. He whispered a few words to Captain Bowles, then strode off toward Headquarters Car. The officers snapped to attention and remained that way until the colonel had disappeared from sight.

"Return to your commands and await further orders!" shouted Captain Bowles.

The tight knot of officers broke apart, each man heading off to his troop. The officers came away long-faced and miserable.

Cassie left *The Mother Lode* and sought out Captain Bowles. "Begging your pardon, sir—"

"*You!* Of all the damn faces to show just now!"

"Sir? I was only wondering if you had orders for the hoggers?"

"*Damn you, McGill!* Take my advice and stay clear o' the officers o' this command, 'less you want a cavalry spur put up your precious ass!"

Cassie settled in the shade of No. 799's tender and puzzled over the captain's angry words. He had never before heard the Alabaman speak so harshly. Army life was hard to figure.

Hachita. Colonel Antrobus had pronounced it in the Mexican fashion, "Ah-cheé-ta." Cassie got out *Busby's* and found the place. It was a tiny dot in the desert 117 miles west along the El Paso & Southwestern, population 100. The town sat astride the Continental Divide a dozen miles or so from the border. Its business was cattle; more than 40,000 head were shipped north from Hachita by rail each year. According to *Busby's* symbols, the town offered a water tower and coaling chute but no telegraph office, just a wire that a rig might patch into. The nearest place to it of any size was Deming, fifty-eight miles northwest on the Southern Pacific. Deming claimed 3,170 residents. All in all, Hachita looked an unlikely place for war. But then so was Columbus, which was seventy-three miles closer to El Paso and which the bandit Villa had attacked at his pleasure.

Cassie's meanderings were interrupted by fresh activity on the siding. Captain Bowles had dispatched a short detail to the fort; it now returned, bearing a pine box. The corpse of Ward Snivey was gathered up and

trooped off. There was no music—not a single drum. In Cassie's imagination, there was a band of the kind that had serenaded them at Fort
Meade and Fort Leavenworth.

"McGill! Halt in your tracks, louse!"

It was Jacko Mudd. He had Private Rademacher and another trooper
in tow.

Cassie put a coupling between himself and the soldiers. "What is it you
want?" he asked them as they approached.

Mudd made no reply but leapt over the coupling and caught Cassie
flush on the mouth with a solid punch, dropping him half under the
tender.

Cassie tasted blood; his teeth had cut through his bottom lip. He was
not about to fight the three of them. He scampered back against the axle
and studied possible routes of escape.

"You'd best stay there, too, scum!" Mudd called to him. "We know
it was you who fucked up at Dalhart, nobody else. Thanks to you, a
fine officer's to lose his career, an' a top outfit's to miss a good fight. . . .
Yer days are numbered now, boy-o. Not a man in this outfit'll sleep sound
agin till you paid yer debts. . . . That includes what you done to Ward
Snivey, too. . . . Wanna make it easy on yerself? Drop a noose over yer
neck and jump off that engine, why don'tcha. . . ?"

The sergeant major and his pals carried on with threats and curses
until Captain Sanderson of D Troop came along and summoned them to
duty. Cassie stayed put till most of the troopers had lined up by the
cook car for their chow. Then he eased himself from between the trucks
and ran forward to Headquarters Car.

Doc Rose was alone in his compartment.

"Begging your pardon, sir?"

"Why, Cassius, good day to you. Ah, but your call would be medical,
would it, rather than social? Come sit, boy, while I take a look at that
lip of yours."

Cassie told what had happened. Doc listened and made his examina-
tion at the same time, breathing so close to Cassie's nose that Cassie
could taste whiskey.

"That's going to require a stitch or two, son. Here—lie back on the
bunk. First, take a good swallow of this."

Cassie took as much of the whiskey as he could stand. Doc went to his
bag and pulled out what he needed: needle, fine thread, alcohol.

"Take more whiskey, boy—there'll be some pain to it."

Cassie took more whiskey and Doc began to sew.

"Aaaaaaaaaaaaaaaaaaaaaaaaaaaaaaaaaaaaaaaaaaaagh!"

Doc cleaned up the blood and made Cassie hold a wad of cotton over
the stitches. "You're still pretty, son—but not so pretty as you was! Lie
quiet till the bleeding stops."

The vet took back the whiskey bottle and helped himself to a deep draft. "You've ruined it for 'em, Cassius—that's how they see it. Soldiers live for war, don'tcha know, and now they're going to miss out. They're blaming you for it, but I've got a notion that Nigger Jack wasn't planning to take Miles Antrobus with him anyway.

"Oh, you should see the expression on that mug o' yours! That's right, Nigger Jack. This is on account of how Colonel Jack—excuse me, *General* Jack—made his name with the Tenth Cavalry, which is all Negroes 'cept for the officers, of course. So they called him Nigger Jack, only I see now by the newspapers that they've refined it a mite.

"Anyhow, Jack and his pals Dodd and Slocum get the glory, and Miles Antrobus eats dirt. Housekeeping duty in the New Mexican desert— that'd be bitter medicine to swallow for *any* trooper, much less Miles Antrobus. And it ain't his only problem, neither. He's to answer for his animals and he knows it. Better'n sixty ponies now dead. This would be a grave loss for a whole regiment, much less a squadron! It smacks of dereliction of duty. The Army will not stand for it, mark my words.

"Poor dumb brutes! Still, maybe they're better off in their way than the colonel is in his. Their Day of Judgment has come and gone, while his lies just down the track. . . ."

As Cassie stepped down from Headquarters Car, a swarm of Snivey's friends appeared trackside. Cassie only saved himself by diving back under the car. In so doing, he drove splinters from the ties into both knees, suffering such pain that he could barely stand after the troopers had passed by.

He moved ahead one car and hid out in the pantry of *The Mother Lode*. Nelson soon found him there. "Fresh orders, Cap'n. Only they ain't the ones we been hopin' foh!"

Cassie leafed through the flimsies. They were signed MACADOO, EL PASO and had come by messenger. *Pullman's No. 3* was to stay put till seven o'clock that evening, when the war traffic cleared, then proceed down the line to Columbus, New Mexico. There *The Mother Lode* and the flat cars bearing Mr. Webster's motor trucks were to be cut out. The remaining cars were to proceed as far as Hachita. When Cassie had thus delivered his customers, he was to return with his rig to El Paso and await further orders. Orders taking him to Lincoln, Nebraska, Cassie dearly hoped!

Meanwhile, the 4th Squadron sat and waited. In the distance could be heard bugle calls and other sounds of war. Countless long freights bearing supplies rattled down the line bent for Columbus and beyond. These rigs had top priority and put outfits like the *Pancho Villa Express* in the hole. Except that the *Pancho Villa Express* was no more. The

Squadron's carpenters went from car to car pulling down the signs. She was just *Pullman's No. 3* again.

Cassie lay on Chef Kolb's berth and tried to sleep. His mouth throbbed where Doc Rose had stitched it; his spit still ran bloody. Outside on the platform an old trooper who had done border duty with the 7th Cavalry in past years was strumming a guitar and singing a dismal song:

> *"I'm learnin' to eat a tortilla,*
> *along of the border patrol.*
> *An' say chili, Carranza an' Villa,*
> *a-dooin' my border patrol.*
> *I'm happy today; tomorrow I may*
> *be hikin' for some other goal.*
> *Whichever the way I'm headin' my bay,*
> *I'll be with the border patrol."*

Finally, Cassie slept. A nightmare soon spoiled it for him. He saw himself lost in the desert, Jolene Potts at his side. They were running to escape Jacko Mudd and the ghost of Trooper Snivey. Pullman's had set the Pinkertons on their trail, too; the railroad dicks were sniffing them out with dogs. The dogs were Chinese chow chows, black-tongued and vicious. *"No! No! Leave me be!"* Strong hands had him by the neck. He drew back against the wall and prepared to fight. *"Leave me be, can't you?"*

"Well now, ain't ya gonna say yo're glad to see yer pal?"

Cassie opened his eyes. In the darkness of the pantry, he made out the pug nose, the flapping ears. *Bastard!* It was Rocks himself, in trooper's garb.

"Damn you all to hell!" Cassie roared.

"Easy now, Professor!" The shortstop had a smile on his face the size of Teddy Roosevelt's. "Save all that fightin' spirit fer fellas meaner 'n me!"

It took a minute or so for Cassie's heart to stop pounding. "So how'd you get back aboard?"

"Never left, Professor! Been prisoner o' the tater bins all along! Jolene dint want no part o' jumpin' off a movin' train. Besides, there was too many troopers likely to see us. Li'l Jolene, she prefers to wait till yer soldier boys git off. Then me an' her'll ride into town with ya and git off in grand style at the best hotel!"

"So how'd you come by that?" Cassie said, pointing to Rocks's uniform. The hat was too big and threatened to fall down over the shortstop's eyes, being held up only by his ears.

"Swapped for it, Cass! Easy as pie."

"What'd you have to swap?"

"Big bottles o' wine, Professor—what else!"

Cassie considered the turn of events. "Maybe it's just as well you stayed aboard—my money's not come yet. We're ordered to a place in the desert called Hachita. There's to be no stop at El Paso, so if you and Jolene mean to get off, you'd best do it right here soon as we start to roll. That'll be seven o'clock. Wait a day or so, and then ask for Mr. MacAdoo at Pullman's, the way I told you. My money will surely be here by then. Watch out for a jackass called Vernon Paisley. Whatever brotherly love he might have had for me is now used up."

Rocks showed little interest in Cassie's instructions. "That wee sum o' yers, Cass? Damn if we need it now!"

"What are you saying?"

"*Money*, Cass! *Real* money! Take a gander at this!"

The shortstop pulled from his pocket a scrap of paper torn out of the *El Paso Herald.* Under the photograph of an Army officer was the legend: SAID TO HAVE OFFERED LARGE REWARD FOR CAPTURE OF VILLA.

Cassie read the story that followed:

> Columbus, N.M., March 15.—Colonel Slocum of the Thirteenth Cavalry is reported to have offered $50,000 reward for General Villa's capture. The offer is made to anyone, Mexican or American. It is declared that for $50,000 or a less sum Villa's own comrades would risk their heads to get his.
>
> Colonel Slocum could afford to pay the $50,000, being a nephew of Margaret Olivia Slocum Sage, the philanthropist. Widow of Russell Sage, her fortune is reckoned in excess of $64,000,000.
>
> Colonel Herbert Jermain Slocum, commanding the Thirteenth Cavalry, was the ranking officer of the garrison at Columbus, N.M., when Villa invaded and attacked that town. A graduate of West Point, he is regarded as one of the most efficient officers in the cavalry branch of the United States Army.

"What am I supposed to make of this?" Cassie asked.

"Don't ya *see*, Cass? *Fifty thousand!* Why, you and me and Jolene, we could live the rest of our days in grand style, specially in Californie!"

"So you'll just swim the river, I suppose, walk up to Villa, hog-tie him, swing him up on your shoulder, tote him back across the line, and get payment on demand for his carcass. Is that your idea?"

"Hell, Cass, it ain't gonna be *easy*. Nothin' good ever comes easy—dint ya tell me that? Sure, we'll need horses, but there's a plenty to choose from, even if that colonel o' yers has tried his best to ruin near ever' head!"

Cassie fell silent. There was no way to talk sense to the shortstop when he put his mind to some scheme or other.

"Fifty thousand, Cass! More money than a man'd need in two lifetimes! Am I *lyin'*?"

"Promise me one thing," Cassie said finally.

"What's that, Cass?"

"That you'll stay put till I tell you to move."

"Ya just said get off, Cass, 'cause this train's goin' straight to the desert."

"Forget what I said. Stay put till I tell you."

"Sure, Cass. If you say so."

The time had come for a good lie, Cassie decided—the bigger the better. "I made us a deal—with the millionaire."

"Ya *did?* What kind o' deal, Cass?"

"He's to help us the minute we reach Columbus. He'll take our side with the civilian authorities. The Army won't be able to lay a hand on us after Columbus."

"Ya *told* him, Cass? 'Bout Snivey?"

"As good as told him, that's right. And he's sworn to help us. So there's no point in you running."

"I'm still goin' after Villa, Cass."

"Fine with me. Only you're to stay put till I tell you. Once we're free and clear, you can chase Villa or go to California or do anything else you want. Meantime, get back in the larder, why don't you, so you won't get caught and spoil everything."

The shortstop's eyes went tearful again. "Gosh, you're sure a pal, Cass! Where's a fella ever to find hisself a better pal 'n ol' Sidewinder McGill, kin ya tell me that . . . ?"

ACROSS THE BORDER

El Paso, Tex., March 16—Incidents of the spectacle yesterday as the American columns went over the international line reached here today by couriers. From a hill overlooking the six square miles where the Army was still encamped at 11 o'clock yesterday forenoon, the military organization appeared to civilian spectators a vast confused swarm of men and horses, grey cannon, wagons, mule teams and ambulances.

But at 11:40 a.m., when the word was given to form for the pursuit of Villa, the apparent confusion disappeared. In a very few minutes, each organization of cavalry, infantry and artillery, ambulances, signal corps and the cook's wagons, grouped and dovetailed into a rapidly lengthening column. At the van, the red and white guidons of the Thirteenth Cavalry snapped in the breeze.

The Dalhart Texan, March 17, 1916

4

SCREWING UP HIS COURAGE once again, Cassie went down the passageway to the parlor and asked to see Mr. Webster.

"Sorry, Cap'n, but Mr. Webster's got business with the colonel," explained Christian. "Maybe you can come back later?"

"Guess I must," Cassie said.

He was not heartbroken over the delay. He would prefer to see Mr. Webster after he had obtained his grubstake and could thus repay the millionaire the $130 owed. Trouble was, with *Pullman's No. 3* set to move out that evening, Cassie reasoned he might not obtain his grubstake from the Pullman office for several days yet—whereas he and Rocks required the millionaire's help at the earliest possible moment.

With sundown came work. The hoggers who had come aboard that morning, Buster Rattle and Tom Greedy, got off. They had spent the day standing still at the Fort Bliss siding but earned their pay all the same. The new engineers were Mr. Robert J. Boilheart and Mr. Burghley Dance. They were younger men, western in their dress, sporting wide-brimmed Stetsons, long handlebar mustaches, and pleasant sun-browned faces. Cassie was pleased to think these were the last hoggers he would put in his book on this run. He had been through a great string of these fellows since Lincoln and found them generally good men, with the exceptions of J. L. Edwards, who had made trouble over Cassie's appointment of Nelson as temporary conductor, and the great Laird O'Dundee, who had a big mouth.

Cassie gave his signal for START TRAIN promptly at 7:00 P.M. The true meaning of the Squadron's orders was now known to every man; the troopers had become a mean and surly lot. No soldier liked "housekeeping duties" when there was war to be had. Cassie stayed in the pantry. He would not chance a return to the van for fear of what Jacko Mudd and his boys had up their sleeves.

Minutes later, the train slowed, then came to rest at the Southern Pacific platform in El Paso. Cassie waited until several of the officers showed themselves before climbing down. The Squadron had no business in El Paso, but Mrs. Lydia Webster had requested the stop for the purpose of letting off Miss Naomi and Miss Rita. The ladies had decided that El Paso was more promising than Rapid City for the practice of their profession, Cassie supposed. The girls wore new dresses, hand-me-downs from Miss Candace. A buckboard with a smart Negro driving came down Sam Houston Street and gathered them up. Cassie stepped forward on the platform and doffed his cap, but the ladies were so grand by now that they pretended not to know him. He figured the two of them would be millionaires in about a week's time.

While waiting for a green board, Cassie ventured fifty paces to the Western Union office. A band of men and boys had gathered out front to hear the latest war news cried out by a spindly clerk through a megaphone so big he could barely lift it. On the sides of the horn was an advertisement:

SPRINGER'S HOTEL & SALOON
Best West of St. Louis

". . . *Pershing crosses to Mexico! Vows capture or death to the bandit Villa within twenty-four hours!* . . . *Funston places embargo on news from Columbus!* . . . *Anti-American sentiment prevails in Chihuahua!* . . . *'Flying Column' of US Cavalry crossed border at midday!* . . . *President Wilson congratulates General Funston on prompt reply to Mexican affront!* . . ."

Down the street Cassie could see the Paso del Norte Hotel. It had its name spelled out in electric lights and must have been five stories high. It was white stucco in the Mexican style with broad tile-roofed verandas opening off every room. Cassie meant to get a room there himself some day and partake of the pleasures of the town, if ever his luck changed.

He returned to trackside in the nick of time: green board. Cassie waved his lantern in a broad arc and No. 506 began to spin its drivers.

"*Dar's de bastar' now! Git 'im!*"

A pair of troopers came at him out of the dark. Cassie leapt aboard *The Mother Lode*, spun around, and kicked out at the figures that pursued him. Both troopers went sprawling on the platform. Cassie looked back and saw them swing aboard the second section. He recognized one of them as the big Swede, Ax Larsen, known for his friendship to Ward Snivey.

They mean to murder me.

Cassie pulled up the steps and slammed shut the outside door. *The Mother Lode* was civilian territory; troopers would not dare enter it. But where would Cassie find sanctuary after Columbus, when the private car was cut off?

✻   ✻   ✻

Despite a big orange moon, Cassie could see little on the horizon, but he could feel rocky outcroppings on both sides of the track. The pass they were now climbing through had given El Paso its name. It was barren land broken frequently by ravines and culverts that had not seen water since the Flood. Cassie knew it well from his Zane Grey.

He settled himself again in Chef Kolb's berth. Whenever he tried to set foot outside *The Mother Lode,* he met Private Rademacher or Ax Larsen or Jacko Mudd himself. If Cassie wanted to give an order to the crew, he had to do it through Nelson or one of the porters. He was no better off than Rocks or Miss Jolene next door in the larder; like them, he was a prisoner of the Army. The stitches in his mouth were pounding now and making him dizzy in spells. His top lip felt the size of a melon. Overcoming the pain, Cassie ate one of Chef Kolb's chickens for his dinner, drank half a bottle of red wine, and then slept again.

"Fire! Fire! Emergency brakes, Cap'n! It's fire sure 'nough!"

It was the porter Toby who gave the first alarm. Cassie yanked the cord twice for STOP AT ONCE, then searched for his boots while *Pullman's No. 3* screeched to a stop. Cassie looked back in the distance and saw it: it was his own van, blazing brightly.

Cassie ran back in the company of Captain Bowles. The caboose burned to its steel frame before the Squadron's fire detail could draw water from No. 799's tender. Cassie searched out the smoldering ruins but found nothing to salvage. He had lost his telegraph key, extra uniform, dinner pail, valise, Bible, *Riders of the Purple Sage,* and *Nigger of the "Narcissus."* He had nothing left but the clothes on his back, his train book, *Busby's,* and—thank the Lord!—Mr. Gump's lantern. He could never have explained the loss of Mr. Gump's lantern to Mr. Hebb back in Lincoln.

Lieutenant Van Impe came out of the darkness and made his report to Captain Bowles: "Carelessness, sir, I do believe. Embers from the cook stove, I suspect. Damn Negroes . . ."

It was Van Impe's job, as train commander, to investigate such happenings. The brakeman Mr. Legrand and the porters Milo and Jesse had been asleep, but they smelled smoke and avoided the flames by jumping off. Mr. Legrand sprained an ankle in the jump, but nobody suffered worse.

Captain Bowles was not pleased. "A sorry mess, eh, Mistah McGill?"

"Yes, sir."

"I suggest y'all pay more attention to your duties and less to your messin'. Say now, boy, what's happened to your mouth?"

"Accident, sir. But Doc's fixed it real well."

"Accident, huh, boy? Seems to me there's a great string of 'accidents' goin' on here'bouts. Ain't that right?"

Cassie remained silent. The captain did not press him further. A detail of troopers was ordered to remove the smoking wreck from the rails. Cassie now placed his crewmen in the last horse car, where Snivey had met his end. With the side doors open so the brakeman could see out, it would serve as makeshift caboose for the few miles remaining on the run. Cassie followed Captain Bowles forward and hid out again in Chef Kolb's berth. *Pullman's No. 3* resumed its journey.

They made Columbus at 10:00 P.M. or thereabouts.

"*Pullman's No. 3!*" Cassie called down to the first switchman he saw. "We're bound to Hachita but first aiming to cut out four flats and a Pullman."

"Wait your turn on that spur yonder!" the fellow yelled back, kicking a switch at the same time. "No tellin' when that'll be, neither!"

They eased down the spur and clanked to a halt. Cassie passed the word to the hoggers to bank their fires but be ready to make steam again on short notice. Then he climbed up to the roof of *The Mother Lode* and surveyed the countryside spread out before him.

Without the Army, Columbus was little more than a watering stop in the desert. The place was all alkali, dirt, scrub brush, yucca, and the giant man-shaped cactus trees the Mexicans called *saguaro*. There was a freight station and a handful of other timber buildings. What permanent dwellings there were were adobe huts built by the Indians. The town had one hotel and one saloon. There was a small stone church with an adjoining lean-to that served as the school. That was the true Columbus, population 308.

But now—Cassie's eyes grew wide at the sight of it. The local residents were nowhere to be seen, having been swallowed up by invaders in khaki. The visitors appeared to number a million or more, all in uniform. For every trooper who had crossed over with Pershing, ten remained behind in Columbus—quartermasters, wranglers, supply sergeants, mechanics, cooks, clerks, mule skinners. A dozen freshly laid spurs ran off in every direction, with more trains littering the rails than a body might expect to see in the Burlington's yards at Chicago. There must have been twenty trains, *fifty* trains. Kerosene torches mounted on fence posts cast ghostly shadows over the prairie. The sidings were covered with forage for the animals, tenting, ammunition, gasoline motors, truck frames, axles, wheels, tires. Tents had sprung up like weeds wherever a gap in the sagebrush and rails permitted. This new Columbus reminded Cassie of the great campground at Lake Ogallala, near North Platte, where he had gone to play ball during a convention of Bryan's "Free Silver" Party back in '12. Only here in New Mexico there was no lake.

Cassie stayed up top and admired the sights and sounds of the camp until he was called down and ordered to report inside to the millionaire's parlor.

"Yes, sir?"

"Good evening, Cassius," said Mr. Webster. "Have you obtained for us a permanent siding? Naturally, we are most anxious to unload the quads."

The colonel sat at a writing table nearby but said nothing.

"We've been told to wait our turn, sir," Cassie said. "This place is running over with trains just now."

"So I see. Even so, we cannot tolerate delay. Our vehicles are sorely needed by General Pershing. Kindly send for the yardmaster."

"Yes, sir, I sure will." Cassie glanced nervously toward the colonel before addressing himself again to the millionaire. "There's a private matter, sir—"

"Presently," said Mr. Webster. "Now kindly fetch the yardmaster."

The trackbed was lighted up like a circus, which it much resembled. Makeshift corrals had been roped off between trains to hold several hundred horses—replacements for animals that had died en route to the border, like the 4th Squadron's, and for those sure to die later in battle. Since *Pullman's No. 3* let off steam, two fresh strings of livestock cars had arrived and were now occupying the next tracks over. These contained ponies belonging to a squadron of the 10th Cavalry, the Negro outfit. The blacks did not wait for orders but began ramping down their animals and tying them to a picket line then and there. They had hardly accomplished this task when another train backed in, this one weighed down with oats and other provisions.

"*Look sharp, donkey!*" a yardman shouted at Cassie.

Cassie jumped to avoid a pair of boxes then being split off. "Thanks for the advice!" Cassie called back. He put all the poison he could into his words. "It's the yardmaster I'm looking for."

"Pardon, Cap'n!" said the fellow. "Dint take notice o' yer cap! But there's a war on, now ain't there!"

"I'm still looking for that yardmaster," Cassie replied.

"He's a big-boned fella in coveralls—ugly hawk nose and temper to match. Saw him crappin' out by yonder windmill. He's called the Judge, 'cept to his face."

Cassie went looking for the Judge. Inside of a dozen paces he had picked up so much sand in his boots that he could hardly walk. He sat on a rock to get the sand out but leapt up at a queer sound and saw that he had been close to squashing a snake that had come from its hole to watch the commotion. Cassie limped off, enjoying the sand in his stockings and keeping to the trackbed whenever it was not occupied by a war train.

"Would that be the Judge?" Cassie asked another fellow, pointing off to a good candidate: hawk nose and mean manner.

"Oh, no, that is Jesus Christ hisself," said the fellow. "Don't believe me? Ask him!"

It was the Judge all right. He was a head taller than any other man around and gave orders out of the side of his mouth while standing atop the rear seat of an open Locomobile motorcar. This vantage point allowed him to see traffic in all directions.

Cassie approached to the running board of the Locomobile. "McGill, sir—master of *Pullman's No. 3.*"

The Judge did not acknowledge him.

"Mr. Otis Webster of Chicago, sir—he's our customer in Pullman's best private varnish, *The Mother Lode.* He's doing business with the Army, sir, and he'd be much obliged if you could spare him a few minutes of your time."

The Judge continued calling out orders to the yardmen circling around.

Finally, when Cassie did not know what else to do, he called up to the Judge: "Mr. Otis Webster, sir, is personal friend to the secretary of war, Mr. Newton D. Baker. He travels, sir, on special orders of Mr. President Wilson himself."

This last invention got the judge's attention. "Oh, is it *me* you're addressin', lad?"

"Yes, sir, it sure is!"

"Well, now, let me provide you with a message for this Mr. Webster o' yours."

"Thank you sir! Mr. Webster will be most grateful."

The Judge removed a black stogie from his lips and gave Cassie a friendly smile. "Tell your Mr. Webster he's to take them orders o' his from Mr. President Wilson and poke 'em up his arse. . . ."

Cassie stayed out front of *The Mother Lode,* not wanting to go in, not knowing where else to go. Through the windows of the parlor, he could see Mr. Webster in earnest conversation with a portly Army officer. Colonel Antrobus was nowhere to be seen. The new officer was not one of the 4th Squadron's, Cassie was sure of that. By now he knew the face of every damned trooper in the outfit from high to low; this was knowledge he longed to forget.

Several troopers came down the trackbed in Cassie's direction. Cassie skipped between cars and hid himself. *Jacko Mudd, Rademacher, Ax Larsen.* What were they up to? They circled around *The Mother Lode,* poking under the car, pointing here and there, talking mysteriously among themselves. When they finished their business—whatever it was—they slowly wandered off, talking and gesturing among themselves.

All at once Cassie knew what they were up to. The idea produced in him a cold sweat. They were thinking they had gone over every inch of the train in their search for Rocks and Miss Jolene—every inch except for *The Mother Lode*. Now they meant to search the private car. They knew the car was about to be dropped off with the Jeffreys onto another siding. The millionaire and his party would no doubt get off to watch the motor trucks being unloaded and driven away. This would give Mudd's boys their chance.

Cassie rushed inside *The Mother Lode* and presented himself again at the door to the parlor.

"Mr. Webster, sir?"

The officer unknown to Cassie was at that moment accepting a wad of banknotes from the millionaire. They looked to Cassie like fifty-dollar silver certificates. The millionaire seemed mightily annoyed by the interruption. "What is it *now*, Cassius? Have you not learned to *knock* before entering?"

"Beg pardon, sir! The yardmaster sends his regards, sir. Only he's occupied just now with trains that got here before us. He'll be along, sir, I expect, when he can."

"You needn't concern yourself further," said Mr. Webster. "Captain Bellamy here, of General Pershing's Quartermaster Corps, has taken full charge. On Captain Bellamy's signal we shall move to the Camp Furlong siding nearby. There you will instruct your engineers to uncouple *The Mother Lode* and the flatcars bearing the quads. We hope to accomplish these maneuvers within the next fifteen minutes—isn't this so, Captain Bellamy?"

"Quite so," said the captain. He might have been an older brother to Father Tibbett, possessing the same soft and plump look about him, the same rosebud mouth.

"You may go now, Cassius," said the millionaire. He seemed anxious to resume his business with the officer.

"Yes, sir. Only—"

"Well, what *is* it, boy?"

"There's a matter, sir—"

"But of course—how thoughtless of me." The millionaire permitted himself a gentle smile. "You're no doubt concerned that we won't have an opportunity to chat about your prospects—indeed, about gainful employment for you in Webster's Machine Lubricant. No, lad, I've not forgotten. Come see me as soon as we've decoupled at Camp Furlong. I have a proposition to put to you—one that I believe you will find most attractive."

"Yes, sir, thank you, sir. I'll be going then, sir."

Cassie backed out and caught his breath in the passageway. Less than fifteen minutes to uncoupling! Time was his great enemy now.

He let himself into the kitchen. Chef Kolb and several of the porters were in the pantry, playing cards. Without disturbing them, Cassie entered the larder and gave Rocks's hiding place a kick.

No reply.

Cassie went back through the kitchen and along the passageway to the *Weinkabinett*. There he banged hard on the door, saying in a strong voice:

"*Next stop, Camp Furlong!*"

The door soon slid open. "So whatcha yellin' fer, Cass?"

Cassie was momentarily speechless. It appeared that he faced a *pair* of troopers: Jolene, too, wore the khaki. With her boyish bobbed hair and slim figure, she suited the cavalry well.

"Now listen to me—"

"Hold on, Cass. Who give ya that lip? It's a doozie!"

"*Listen to me.* Mudd and his boys were sniffing out this car not ten minutes ago. They're bound to make a search while we're uncoupling down the line at a place called Camp Furlong."

Cassie was in a true swivet, but not Rocks. "So let 'em try!" The shortstop reached in his belt and pulled out his most prized possession, the Colt .45.

"It's not a *game* now," Cassie pleaded. "These fellows are out to do *murder*. You've got to run for it—you, too, ma'am. There's no time to lose."

"Rocks, honey," said Jolene, "maybe we oughta do like yer friend says."

Rocks held his ground. "We're waitin' till the damn troopers git shipped off—*then* we're goin', an' not a minute sooner."

"And if they come along and break down the door?"

The shortstop put on his serious squint. "What happened to Snivey can happen to other fellas, too!" He pulled the pistol's clip out and held it up for Cassie to see. One gleaming brass-colored bullet stuck out the business end. Rocks slammed the clip home and pulled back on the hammer, cocking the pistol.

"God is supposed to look after drunks and fools," Cassie replied. "I guess you're safe on both counts."

Camp Furlong was a half mile down the spur to the southeast. They backed all the way, the second section leading. Burghley Dance and Robert J. Boilheart showed they were true experts when it came to fine-tuning their throttles.

Though the hour was late, it might well have been high noon for all the electricity and carbon arcs the Army had brought to bear. Camp

Furlong was, in Army lingo, a "cantonment," which meant the men slept in dog tents instead of wood barracks. It had been the campsite of the 13th Cavalry, which was now in Mexico. Camp Furlong was the very place where Villa had made his attack, murdering eight of Colonel Slocum's troopers in their sleep. It was rumored that Villa had been angry over a bad transaction with a hardware dealer in Columbus. The dealer had sold Villa defective Mauser rifles for his renegade forces, which were doing battle with Villa's rival, the Mexican president, Carranza. Villa intended to teach the merchant a lesson but met up with the 13th Cavalry instead.

Now, Camp Furlong was given over to the new motor trucks. An enormous sign, paint on canvas, declared it to be:

1ST MOTORIZED TRANSPORT MAINTENANCE DEPOT
8th Cavalry Brigade

Everywhere a person looked there were Whites, Packards, Fords, Simplexes, Franklins, Dodges, Hudsons, Locomobiles, and—thanks to Otis Webster—Jeffrey quads. According to reports, the Army hoped to have 250 vehicles in battle by summer, though no one supposed it would take that long to catch Villa. The War Department had advertised for motor trucks in the newspapers and was even hijacking shipments meant for the British and French armies in Europe. As many trucks and "flivvers" as possible were needed to support Pershing's flying columns. The trouble with cavalry—so said Mr. Webster's new friend, Captain Bellamy, who was from the infantry himself—was that the troopers could carry on horseback only enough ammunition and provisions for a few hours of fighting. After that, they were at the mercy of fresh supplies brought up on the backs of mules or else in trucks. Each Jeffrey quad could carry what ten mules could, and ten times as fast, too. But motor trucks were on the delicate side and required steady repairs. There in the cantonment the Army had built concrete ramps that the trucks could run up so mechanics could work underneath.

Pullman's No. 3 again let off steam. Captain Bellamy appeared trackside and ordered decoupling of *The Mother Lode*. Cassie put his four brakemen to work—Coffin, Legrand, Small, and Toomey—then jumped aboard *The Mother Lode* himself. He could not wait a moment longer.

"Mr. Webster, sir?"

He had hoped to find the millionaire alone this time, but there was Colonel Antrobus again, sipping brandy and looking to be in some pain.

"Not *now*, Cassius," said Mr. Webster. His voice had a sharp edge to it. "I shall send for you when I'm ready!"

Cassie withdrew. The devil's own luck!

The car received a jolt—rolled forward several yards. The switching was underway. Cassie knew what he had to do. Candace Webster—she was their last true hope. Underneath her great beauty and polite manners, she was a spunky girl—Cassie was sure of it. If she seemed rude at times, it was on account of her fine upbringing. Besides, she liked him—he knew it from the way she had smiled at him and taken his arm after he sang "The Bard of Armagh."

He removed his cap and knocked softly on the door to her compartment.

"Miss Candace, ma'am?"

"Yes? What is it?"

"It's me, ma'am—Cassius McGill."

She slid the door open part way. "Good evening, Cassius. My, this *is* a surprise. I thought perhaps you'd been avoiding me. But you've hurt yourself again, haven't you? Is that blood I see?"

He licked his fat lip. "It's about healed up, ma'am. Thank you just the same."

"I do wish you would stop calling me 'ma'am.' It's as though you were addressing my mother!"

"Yes, ma'am—sorry—Miss Candace."

He had interrupted her preparations for bed. She wore a pink quilted robe over a white flannel nightgown. She had let her long blond hair down and was brushing it out.

"I suppose you've come to say good-bye. How nice of you. We've enjoyed a most pleasant journey. I'm certain Papá will send a good report to Mr. Lincoln."

"Oh, no, ma'am—Miss Candace—it's nothing like that."

"Not 'Miss Candace.' Simply 'Candace.' Or 'Candy,' if you prefer."

"Candace, then. And I wasn't trying to avoid you, ma'am—Candace. It's just—well, I've had my duties to tend to."

"And now—"

"If I could come in, ma'am—"

"You may *not* come in. I'm hardly dressed to receive visitors. And at such an hour—"

"That's all right, ma'am—Candace—I can tell it from here."

"Tell what?"

He looked both ways in the corridor: no signs yet of Mudd's gang.

"My pal Rocks—Riley McAuliffe—him and his lady friend, Miss Jolene—they're being hunted down by a gang of troopers who mean to take revenge for Trooper Snivey."

"Astonishing!"

"If you could help—"

Her pretty lips tensed. "Help? But I'm only a woman."

"Could they stay *here,* ma'am, do you suppose?"

"*Here?* And what have they done, these friends of yours, to suffer such a predicament?" Her expression betrayed alarm, but her voice remained calm and ladylike.

"You see, ma'am—Candace . . ."

As rapidly as he could—looking over his shoulder from time to time—he gave an account of their difficulties with Jacko Mudd, skipping over the true nature of Trooper Snivey's death.

Miss Candace listened intently. Whenever he faltered or needed an extra breath, she would say, "Yes, yes, go on—what happened next?"

". . . So if Rocks and Miss Jolene could hide out for a spell, why, they'd be free to go on their way as soon as the Army's off to Hachita."

"And you say they're aboard the train even now?"

"They're in this very car!"

"And nobody knows but *you,* Cassius?"

"Me—and now you. If the troopers were to find out—well, it'd be a bad thing."

"Where in the car would they be hiding?"

"Just down the aisle—in the extra compartment where Miss Naomi and Miss Rita stayed. Chef Kolb calls it his *Weinkabinett.*"

Candace chewed her lip for a moment, thinking. "Very well. Ask your friends to remain where they are until I can dress and make arrangements. Then you may bring them along."

"Oh, Candace . . . Candy."

He leaned forward and brushed her cheek with his lips. He half expected her to resist, but she did not. He felt a tingling clear down to his toes.

"You'd best go now," she told him, "before Papá finds us out."

"You'll never, *never* be sorry!" he pledged. He bent to kiss her cheek again, but she directed him to her lips instead. Doc Rose's stitchery produced a sharp stab of pain, which Cassie did not mind in the least.

Cassie dropped down to trackside to check on the progress of the switching.

"Easy as she goes!" cried the foreman.

No. 506 was then pulling free. *The Mother Lode* sat out on the spur by herself, a splendid Queen of the Night. Her gas lanterns gave her the appearance of a mighty ocean liner floating in the desert sea.

The switching crews now turned their attention to the flats bearing Mr. Webster's war machines. This was the signal for Mudd's boys to close in.

Cassie boarded *The Mother Lode* ahead of them and pounded on the *Weinkabinett's* door. *"It's me again—Cass!"*

Rocks opened up and let Cassie in. The shortstop held a bottle of the millionaire's wine in one hand, the Colt .45 in the other. "Is it true we're loose from 'em, Cass? With all that clunkin' about, I'm guessin' we're free!"

"Now listen to me," Cassie said impatiently. "I told Miss Candace the whole story, and she's agreed to help. You're to hide out in her compartment till the Army leaves. Grab your stuff and come with me—*quick!"*

"Dint I tell ya ol' Cass'd save the day!" cried Rocks to his lady.

Cassie slid open the door, stepped out—felt the icy paw of Private Rademacher on his neck. Cassie kicked the door shut before Rademacher could stop him.

"Easy now, boy! Ain't no sense ta squirm!"

They were soon joined by Jacko Mudd and Ax Larsen. "Time to pay your debts, McGill," said the sergeant major. "Back inside with you."

But Judgment Day was put off yet again.

"Tennnnn-shunnnnn!" cried Ax Larsen.

Lieutenant Van Impe appeared from the direction of the parlor. He was followed closely by Candace Webster.

"Well now, Sergeant Major, what have we here?"

"Acting on information, sir!" said Jacko Mudd smartly.

"And what information would that be?"

"The escaped fugitive McAuliffe, sir! He's to be found there, sir—inside that very compartment!"

The lieutenant turned to Cassie. "Is this so, McGill?"

Cassie looked in desperation to Miss Candace. "Military's got no business in *The Mother Lode*, ma'am!"

"Want me to break it down, sir?" asked Jacko Mudd.

"That won't be necessary," said the lieutenant. He seemed to be enjoying himself. "McGill will have a master key. McGill, open the door."

"Don't have any key," Cassie lied. "Lost my keys in the fire." He stared at Miss Candace, silently begging for help. But she avoided his gaze.

"How regrettable," said Van Impe. With great deliberation he drew his pistol. "Stand away!" He took aim at the lock.

At that instant, the door slid open. Miss Candace screamed, Van Impe took a step backward, Troopers Rademacher and Larsen grabbed for their .45s.

"Wanna come in, do ya?" cried Rocks. "Why don'tcha, now!"

The shortstop's beady eyes seemed twice their normal size from fear and all the wine he had drunk. Still, he was sober enough to keep his .45 trained on Van Impe's Adam's apple.

5

I T L O O K E D T O B E a Mexican standoff.

Cassie didn't like Rocks's chances, but he liked Van Impe's even less. There was a look of stark terror on the shortstop's face. Cassie could see that Rocks meant to take Van Impe to hell with him, if it came to that.

"Well now," said the lieutenant in a calm, polished voice, "let's discuss things in a civilized manner, shall we? . . . There's no need for violence or bloodshed, don't you agree? . . . First, why not ask your lady friend to retire in the company of Miss Webster? . . . There's no cause to upset the ladies further, isn't that right? . . ."

Rocks thought the proposition over, then turned to Jolene. "Ya wanna go?"

Jolene looked pathetic in her trooper's uniform. Without saying a word, she accepted the lieutenant's invitation; her eyes did the talking for her. She could hardly walk in her oversized cavalry boots. Rocks lowered his .45 so she could pass by. This was his mistake. Jacko Mudd sprang forward like a hungry cougar—caved in the shortstop's cheekbone with the butt of his pistol.

Both ladies screamed now. Jolene, ashen-faced, fainted beside her fallen lover.

"You *bastard!*" cried Cassie. "You *murdered* him!"

Rocks moaned in pain; he was not dead yet.

Van Impe gathered up Jolene and placed her on the lower berth in the *Weinkabinett*. "See to her, Candy, won't you?" he said, closing the door and leaving the ladies to recover in private.

The lieutenant turned his attention to Rocks. "Sergeant Major!"

"*Sir!*"

"Escort the prisoner to the guardhouse!"

"*Yes, sir!*"

Cassie laughed at the madness of it all. This was naught but a repetition of the shortstop's first encounter with Van Impe and the troopers back in South Dakota!

Rocks would have to be carried. "At least have Doc Rose tend to him!" Cassie demanded. The shortstop's blood was fast staining the Pullman carpet.

Troopers Rademacher and Ax Larsen reached down for Rocks as the shortstop came to life. He lashed out, catching Rademacher flush on the nose. Jacko Mudd raised his pistol again, aiming a blow at the short-stop's skull.

Van Impe intervened. "Sergeant Major! Provide chains for the prisoner!"

Jacko Mudd went outside onto the platform and shouted orders to his men. Soon a squad of troopers appeared bearing manacles and shackles and enough chain for a dozen prisoners. They trussed Rocks up, dragged him outside to the first section, and paraded him through the day cars and the horse wagons and then through the second section until they reached the guardhouse. In this way, all the troopers of the 4th Squadron could see that Trooper Snivey's murderer was caught and getting what he deserved. *"Lynch him!"* became the cry in every car.

For his part, Cassie was marched off to Headquarters Car and presented to Captain Bowles.

"You are a boy who cannot stand prosperity—ain't this so?"

"Sir?"

"What have you to say for yourself?"

"Nothing, sir."

"Nothing? Your best pal is caught for murder, and you say *nothing?"*

"He didn't do murder, sir."

"He is caught and will pay. What are your arguments on his behalf?"

"I believe I'd best save up my arguments, sir, till I see the judge in Fort Bliss. Whenever that'll be, sir."

The captain burst out laughing. "Don't say!"

"Yes, sir. The colonel told me—"

"The colonel has changed his mind!"

"Sir?"

"For now, consider yourself again under house arrest. You're not to leave this train under any circumstances till we reach our destination. After that, we'll see. Is the switchin' done, mistah?"

"I believe it is, sir. Only—"

"Lieutenant Van Impe?"

"Sir!"

"Inform all troop commanders we shall depart this station forthwith. McGill, kindly signal your engineers."

"But, *sir—"*

"What *is* it, McGill?"

"If I could have just five minutes, sir. Tell the truth, I've still got business with Mr. Webster."

"Request denied. Prepare to depart this station."

"But, sir—"

"Silence. For once, you'll do as you're told, boy. Oh, I 'preciate you're a privileged lad with friends in high places. But you'll now *obey orders,* hear me? *Sentry!"*

The sleepy-eyed private called Solly Toothaker appeared in the door-way. "You callin' me, sir?"

"Mr. McGill here is not to leave the train till we reach Hachita. See to it!"

"Yes, sir, Captain."

"And if he disobeys—use your weapon!"

Pullman's No. 3 was soon running flat out again. The hour was close to midnight, the desert air cold and stinging on the brakemen's faces. The veterans of the "Zamboanga Brigade" resumed their singing, rocking the day cars with hard rhythms and proving that their spirits had risen again after the bitter disappointment of Fort Bliss:

> *"Home, boys, Home!*
> *It's Home we ought to be.*
> *Home, boys, Home!*
> *In God's Countree.*
> *Where the ash and the oak*
> *and the weeping-willow tree*
> *And the grass grow green*
> *In North Amerikee!"*

Rifles had been passed out during the stop at Columbus, in case one of Villa's marauding bands should lie in ambush up ahead. Troopers sat in the aisles oiling their weapons and counting out ammunition. Each man was permitted fifty cartridges for his Springfield, twenty for his pistol, and three-days' dry rations for his pack.

Hachita came into view at 1:15 A.M., Thursday, March 16. The name on the signpost had been crossed out and a new legend added:

> LAST TOWN ON EARTH
> So sez Cpl. Dink, 7th Cav

There were several coal bins, a black steel water tower, and a run-down platform. There was no station. The town itself was a half mile south of the tracks toward the border. Not a single light in the town came on when *Pullman's No. 3* let off steam.

"Bank your fires and wait for orders!" Cassie told his hoggers. How many times had he used those words on this run! The 4th Squadron had come 1,822 miles from Fort Meade, doing it in nine hours short of five days. Cassie had expected to entertain thoughts of great joy and satis-faction on finishing the ride, but his feelings took a different turn now.

He was heartsick for Rocks and scared for himself, too. Private Solly Toothaker dogged his every step. Now Cassie understood what it was to be under another man's boot.

The troopers ramped down their mounts and formed up along the right of way. Captain Bowles came out on the platform and gave orders for the Squadron to make bivouac. The horses were set out first. Instead of forming a picket line as they had done during horse stops on the run, the troopers hobbled the animals on the prairie nearby to graze as the beasts saw fit.

"Less'n two hundred head! Hell an' damnation!" swore one of the wranglers.

There had been two hundred seventy at the start, Cassie remembered. This meant that one man in four had no mount. How was the 4th Squadron to resist Villa's attacks with so many troopers on foot?

Led by their sergeants and corporals, the troopers marched north into the desert several hundred yards from the trackbed and put out oil lanterns to form a boundary. Then they tied ropes between stakes and marked off ranks and files for the dog tents, with footpaths between. In the moonlight, the ground appeared littered with objects, but these were merely yucca and mesquite and tumbleweed. Every man took care where he sat down: there were desert snakes and, here and there, a tin can with sharp uplifted lid. The troopers who occupied this land before, and who had now gone over the border with Pershing, left nothing behind but their garbage.

When the tent city was completed and sentries posted, the men were offered an extra ration of hot coffee at the cook car. Only half the troopers lined up for it; the others were already asleep on the ground in their bedrolls. As unyielding as the prairie might have been, it beat sitting up in the day cars.

No longer having a van to repair to, Cassie settled in one of the empty horse cars with the porters and brakemen. The engineers and firemen stayed in their cabs, where it was warm.

Nelson had obtained an El Paso newspaper during the stop at Columbus; Cassie now read it by candlelight:

UNITED STATES TROOPS ENTER MEXICO

U.S. Army Will Recruit 20,000 Men

---

5 Ranchers Executed by Villa

---

by Associated Press
Deming, N.M., Mar. 15—United States troops crossed into Mexico shortly after noon today, according to automobile courier arriving here this afternoon from Columbus.

Juárez is Calm and Quiet

Rumors of the advance of the punitive force did not disturb the usual calm of Juárez today. The garrison soldiers appeared entirely friendly to visiting Americans, as was the native population.

There was an account by an American woman, Mrs. Maud Hawk Wright, who had been kidnapped by a Villista officer and made to accompany the bandits on their march:

". . . I knew that Villa intended to attack Columbus. It was freely discussed by the men and the officers. Some of the latter told me that Villa intended to kill every American he could find, but they pointed to me as an example of their decision not to harm women. An officer said that Villa intended to kill everybody in the U.S. and would be helped by Japan and Germany. At Boca Grande I saw evidence of their determination. I did not see the three American cowboys named McKinney, Corbett and O'Neil slain, but I saw Villa's officers wearing their clothing. . . ."

What a bloody business it was! "Others in this world are worse off than you," Cassie told himself, "or even Rocks."

Hewing to this thought, Cassie slept.

He woke to the smells of bacon and coffee and beans. He was immediately filled with appetite but could not bring himself to stand with troopers in the chow line, even though Nelson and the other trainmen were doing so. Cassie thought maybe he would borrow money from Nelson and look for a meal later on at an eating house in Hachita. Even a town with a hundred people in it would have an eating house.

While the others ate, Cassie let himself into one of the day cars and used the facilities. With the fire banked in No. 506, the hot water from the tap was no more than lukewarm, but he had himself a shave anyhow and felt better for it. Afterward, he went forward to Headquarters Car and sought out Doc Rose.

"They let you see him, Doc?"

"Saw him for sure," Doc said. "Made 'em take off them manacles, too, so I could get a close look. Had him tied up like a porker on the way to slaughter, they did!"

"Yes, sir. I watched them do it."

"He's a boy with a natural fondness for trouble, I do believe."

"It's always been so, sir. Rocks never knew his pa."

"I warned him to see a medical doctor 'bout his cheek—it's busted for sure. He's never gonna smile the same, that much we know."

"I'll see he gets treatment, sir."

"I hope you can arrange it. But I have my doubts."

"Sir?"

"It's now a question, son, of how much time your friend's got left on this earth."

"But you said, sir—"

"Nothing medical's going to kill him. What I'm referring to is the firing squad."

"Sir?"

"The Army punishes murder, boy, by firing squad."

"But Rocks isn't a *soldier,* sir. And he didn't do *murder!* I know it for a fact, sir, because I was there!"

"Well, then, boy, I urge you to have yourself a heart-to-heart talk with the colonel. 'Cause he's bent on exercising his prerogative of command. Know what that is?"

"No, sir."

"Go see the colonel. He'll be pleased to explain it. Now leave me alone, boy. It's past time this ol' vet got himself pie-eyed. . . ."

Cassie presented himself outside Stateroom A. "I'm McGill. I'm here to see the colonel."

The Pole, Tor Przewalski, was doing sentry duty. He was a thin, suspicious fellow with dark circles under his eyes and wispy blond hair. "I know who you be." The Pole spoke slowly, as though he were picking his words from a dictionary.

"I'm here to see the colonel," Cassie repeated.

"Move along. Can't stay here."

"I've got a message for the colonel from General Pershing," Cassie said. "I got it over the railroad wire. But maybe you won't let him have it. The blame's on you."

The Pole's mouth hung open. He looked Cassie up and down, then turned and let himself into the colonel's compartment.

The Pole soon came out. Angrily, he jerked his thumb toward the door. "He see you now!"

Cassie went in. The colonel was sitting in a high-backed chair having himself shaved by his boy, Francisco.

"Well now, Cassius, please reveal this urgent message from Jack Pershing." The colonel showed a gentle smile through Francisco's shaving soap.

"That was only a ruse, sir. Otherwise the sentry wouldn't let me pass."

"Resourceful lad! Ambitious lad! I salute you, sir. Now please state your business."

There was something strange about the colonel. It was as though he had forgotten all about not going along with Pershing into Mexico. He seemed a different person from the one Cassie had known earlier in the ride.

"It's about Riley McAuliffe, sir," Cassie said.

"Well?"

"He didn't do it, sir—murder that trooper. He was keeping *me* from murder—that's the truth."

The colonel nodded gently so as not to disturb Francisco's blade. "Continue."

Cassie gave a correct accounting of the incident.

"Loyalty to one's fellows—this is a quality in short supply," the colonel said. "Yet loyalty must not be permitted to interfere with judgment."

"Sir?"

"While it is noble of you to offer this defense of your friend, I fear that your words will be unavailing. Nonetheless, I shall inform the court that your testimony is to be heard with that of the other witness."

"Other witness, sir?"

Francisco was done with his barbering. The colonel rose and wiped his thin face with a towel. "An eyewitness has come forward."

"Oh, but that's not possible, sir," Cassie replied. "The only witness besides me was Rocks."

The colonel busied himself with his shirt and tie. When he finished, he turned to Cassie and said: "I speak of Private Rademacher."

Cassie took a step back. "Oh, no, sir. Mr. Rademacher sure wasn't present—I swear it!"

"The court will judge."

"It can't *be*, sir. Not Mr. Rademacher."

"So you've said. The matter is now out of my hands. The court will decide."

Cassie was thinking fast. Not knowing exactly where he was going, he blurted out:

"I been on to Mr. MacAdoo, sir—with the Pullman Company there in El Paso? He's most anxious to know about the trial, sir—so he can send out a Company lawyer to stand up for Mr. McAuliffe. I promised to get on the wire, sir, soon as I know what day it is."

"That will be all, Cassius. You are excused."

"If you could tell me the day, sir—"

"*Dismissed!* . . . *Sentry?* Show this man out!"

Tor Przewalski put him out.

Cassie felt something akin to pleasure. He had never known such grim determination in his life. Rocks had been correct all along: troopers only looked out for troopers. But they weren't beaten yet. As long as there was a wire connecting them to El Paso, they had powerful friends within easy reach. Pullman's great Palace Car Company surely wouldn't allow the shooting of any helper conductor, even a spot man like Rocks. This was *fact*. Cassie lengthened his stride, heading back to the van to get his telegraph key—then realized that the van was gone and his kit burned up with it!

This slowed him, but not for long. He explored the adjacent campground until he found a big double tent marked 1ST SIGNAL CORPS DETACHMENT. Already the Army had strung lines out to the railroad's wire along the right of way. Besides the telegraph and telephone, they had several big Marconi sets. They could reach El Paso even if the line was down.

The operator on duty was a light-skinned corporal called Josh Pernell. He had seemed civil enough the time or two that Cassie had come across him during the ride. "Good morning to you," Cassie said on entering.

"It's a good morning if you're partial to lizards and scorpions and the like. Squashed me the largest centipede you'd ever want to see!"

Cassie was relieved to find that Pernell was not one of those who blamed Cassie for the Squadron's failure to cross with Pershing. "Would you be having a line open to El Paso that I could borrow on Pullman business? We're in sore need of a yard mechanic to do work on one of the Baldwins. Else we're likely to remain stuck here till you fellows get done with the Mex!"

The corporal chuckled at this remark and gave a polite smile. "Only too glad to help, Mr. Conductor. 'Cept we're closed down on account o' Mexican spies twixt us and Bliss. No outbound traffic allowed 'cept on written order o' the colonel hisself."

Cassie thought a bit. "Well, he'd surely write me out the order, only he's awful busy right now, what with Villa being just over that hill there. Suppose you could let me send my message first and bring you a slip from the colonel on another occasion? The Pullman Company'd be most indebted. I wouldn't be surprised if they sent you a little token of their gratitude straight from Chicago."

The corporal, too, thought a bit. "What sort o' 'token' might that be, then?"

"Oh, it'd be cash money, I should think."

"Ah."

"I suppose it'd be on the order of a ten-dollar gold piece. But then I'm on the stingy side myself—could be something more."

"What's your message?" asked Josh Pernell.

"I'm a brass-pounder myself," Cassie said, nodding in the direction of the corporal's key. "It'd take me no more than a minute."

"How do I know you're good for it? The gold piece?" The corporal was on his feet now, sweating already in the early-morning heat.

"I'd give you a piece of paper. It'd be good as gold with any Pullman cashier. I'd sign it official. You'd have no worries on that score." Cassie was sweating, too.

"Write out your paper, then."

Cassie tore a sheet from his train book and wrote out the order:

TO ANY PULLMAN COMPANY PAY DESK:

KINDLY PAY THE BEARER OF THIS NOTE TEN DOLLARS GOLD FOR
SERVICES RENDERED.

CASSIUS MCGILL

CONDUCTOR, PULLMAN'S NO. 3

"Take a seat and be quick about it," said Corporal Pernell.

Cassie got on the line and raised El Paso without delay. He had only finished tapping out FOR IMMEDIATE ATTENTION LINTON P. MCADOO when a flash of light exploded over his right ear. His chair toppled and he found himself looking up from the sand.

Jacko Mudd towered over him like a furious bear bent on devouring him even to the bones. "Caught you, dint I! Violatin' Army orders! Offerin' a bribe to a soldier on duty! I heard every word, mister! Ol' Ward Snivey's lookin' down from heaven and laughin' himself silly!"

On entering, Cassie had noticed a flap at the back of the tent. He dove for it now, scampering on all fours like a dog.

He got through. Regaining his feet, he sprinted straight ahead, expecting to feel bullets with each stride he took. None came his way.

When he was a good half mile out in the desert, he fell on his face and lay panting until a lizard passed before his eyes and jerked him upright again. The sun told him he had fled north. Off in the distance he could see sharp sawtooth mountains. He had *Busby's* in his breast pocket to give them their names: Apache Hills, Sierra Rica, Little Hatchet Mountains, Coyote Peak, Pyramid Peak, Gage Mountains, Klondike Hills. It was hard to imagine that any land could be so barren and wasted. Not even a poor dry farmer would have had it for free. One of the old Zamboanga veterans had already said it: "There's farther to look and less to see than in any country I've yet known."

Cassie circled back first east, then south across the tracks, then west, keeping a safe distance from the bivouac and approaching Hachita from the direction of the border. He must have covered five miles or more and was sweat through by the time he reached the town limits.

A dozen adobe huts had been set down in the swirling brown sand, prickly chaparral, green cottonwood, and dried-up mesquite. There were two wood-frame structures, neither one with any paint left on it. The bigger of the two had a sign over the door:

> MISS OPAL'S MANZANITA SALOON & EATING HOUSE
>
> Beds 25¢

Cassie worked his way into the shadows beside the saloon. As he paused to catch his breath, three riders came down the dirt street, dismounted, and tied their ponies to the railing out front. They were true cowboys, lean, dark-skinned from the sun, wearing sweat-stained Stetsons, leather vests, Levi's trousers, and high-heeled boots.

Cassie moved to a side window and watched the cowboys enter. The glass was wavy with a greenish hue and made the men look like they were swimming underwater in some gloomy creek. They went up to the bar and got beer. As far as Cassie could tell, there were no troopers in the place.

He got up his nerve and pushed through the swinging doors. The cowboys, beers in hand, were then disappearing out the back. Cassie couldn't imagine where they might be going.

There was a long mahogany bar and a dozen stools and one large table set between a pair of benches stolen from a railroad station. The one remaining customer sat at the table and nursed his beer. His face was darker than the bar's mahogany, and he wore western dress topped by a *sombrero*.

Behind the bar stood a woman. Cassie took her for Miss Opal, the proprietress. She had a face more square than round, weighed as much as a full-grown cow, and sported bright orange hair. She wore men's wool trousers covered with chaps. When she saw him, she came around the end of the bar and yelled out:

"Oh, what a pretty one! Look, Hay-soos, what the cat done dragged in!"

The woman had a voice like hard coal tumbling down a chute.

"Morning, ma'am," Cassie said. "I'm just off the Pullman and need to use the wire on railroad business. Would there be a sending set hereabouts, do you know?"

She gave a great belly laugh. "Damnation, boy! Railroad's got its own telegraph, don't it!"

"Yes, ma'am. Only—"

Cassie couldn't think how to explain matters.

"Closest telegraph's Lordsburg, boy—or Deming, same distance. You brung my pool table by any chance?"

"Ma'am?"

"Danged table's been on order from St. Louis since summer and no sign of her yet!"

"No, ma'am, sure don't. She's a war train, ma'am, not a freight."

"Well now, never you mind, boy. Come sit down. First *cerveza*'s on the house for railroaders."

Being so fat, she had difficulty walking. She got behind the bar and poured him a beer from a keg with an eagle burned into it. It was brown beer from Mexico. Cassie did not much care for beer, but his thirst was so great he drank the dark brew right down.

"How many boys you brung with you, son?" Miss Opal asked him.

"There'd be nearly three hundred, ma'am."

"So many! But crossin' over yet today, 'spose."

"No, ma'am. Staying right here, I believe."

"Is that so!"

"Yes, ma'am."

"How-de-doo!"

What Cassie truly craved was food. He felt in his pants pockets. He still had ninety-five cents.

"Would you be serving dinner yet, ma'am? Afraid I missed my breakfast."

"No eats, boy, till my cook gets back—iffen he *gets* back. He's up to Deming for grub, only he ain't dependable so as you'd notice it. Hungry, are ya?"

"Yes, ma'am, sure am. For now, I believe I'll have me another of those fine beers."

She drew him one. "Tell you what. Danged Chino's due back afore sundown. You come back tonight and bring some o' them soldier boys with you, and we'll roast up some beef and maybe toss in some taters, too."

"Yes, ma'am. I'll sure try, ma'am."

"Bring *enough* o' them boys and your own meal won't cost you nothin'."

"Yes, ma'am."

"Fact is, you'll git yerself a bonus besides!"

"Ma'am?"

"Sample the goods right now, why don't ya?"

"Ma'am?"

"Now, don't you go wanderin' even one step, boy!"

She went out the same way the cowboys had gone. Cassie scratched his head and worked on his second *cerveza*. It would take him a while, he anticipated, to know the ways of western folk.

The customer called Jesus got up and took the stool next to Cassie's. He seemed a gentle fellow, forty or fifty years of age. He said to Cassie: "Cleanest house around, *amigo*. You are wise to come here. There is nothing so clean in Deming, I promise you."

"Sir?"

Cassie did not wait long to find out the gentleman's meaning. Miss Opal returned, trailing behind her an Indian girl, barefoot with long stringy hair.

"Maria, say hello to the boy. Ain't he beautiful?"

Cassie stood up. "Got to be going, ma'am," he said. "Got to find the telegraph."

"For you, ten dollar," said Miss Opal. "Maria's the best girl I got and much in demand. She'll do anything you want as many times as you want it."

"Five girls here," the Mexican gentleman said, nodding in agreement with Miss Opal. "Maria's the best. I had me all five!"

"Sure do appreciate it, ma'am," said Cassie. "Only—"

"For you, *eight* dollar," said Miss Opal. "It's a fair price, boy. A girl like Maria brings fifteen, maybe twenty dollar in 'Paso."

"Really, ma'am—"

Cassie was busy thinking up a new excuse when one was provided to him ready-made. Through the wavy green window glass he detected the telltale blue-and-gold of the U.S. Cavalry.

It was a scouting party, Cassie figured—or maybe it was Jacko Mudd and his boys hard on Cassie's heels. He didn't wait to find out. "'Bye, ma'am! 'Bye, sir!"

He threw himself out the back door with seconds to spare.

He kept running till he was winded, then lay down in the mesquite and watched and waited. The cavalry boys stayed inside Miss Opal's awhile, then came out the back door, bringing the Indian girl Maria with them and entering the house next door. They showed no interest in where the fugitive Cassius McGill might have gone.

Thirst soon overtook him. Nearby was a cactus bearing a luscious red fruit like a plum. Avoiding the needlelike spines, he plucked off a juicy-looking specimen and bit into it. He spit the pulp right back out. It was bitter as a chokecherry.

He stripped to his BVDs and lay close to a yucca tree but found little shade. The sun bore straight down and cooked him until the sand under him was wet with his drippings. In an hour's time he was as parched as the mesquite around him. Fits of dizziness took him until he tasted the bile in his stomach. Finally, he slept.

Sounds in the distance woke him: girls singing, dogs barking, the slap of harness, the squeal of axles, the cough of combustion engines.

He sat upright and pulled on his boots. Cupping both hands to his eyes, he peered over the low-lying brush and saw them: wagons filled with women and children, men on horseback, a caravan of motorcars. There must have been thirty automobiles or more, crawling like giant black beetles across the hot sand. A pack of dogs circled them, barking noisily and leaping sometimes onto the running boards.

It made Cassie think of a county fair. The motorcars and wagons drew up in a circle with their noses pointed in toward the center, which became a kind of show ring. They were no more than a hundred paces from where Cassie sat. The drivers and their passengers climbed out and put up tents and brightly colored pavilions. The ladies brought forth picnic lunches and iced lemonade, which they served on collapsible tables. A half-dozen buckboards filled with Chinamen arrived last, setting up their wagons like open-air shops at a farmers' market. The children played games; the dogs barked.

They had come from Deming to the north, Cassie figured. It was to be a market all right, and a circus, too. These fresh arrivals were the sellers; the 4th Squadron was to be the customers. Cassie knew he was correct when he spotted guidons off in the distance. The troopers were on foot, marching in close formation, their boots kicking up clouds of dust and sand. Captain Lonnie Bowles marched at the head of the column. Two steps behind Captain Bowles was Lieutenant Van Impe. Cassie flattened to the ground, seeing the Dutchman again. Short of the great circle, the 4th Squadron came to a halt. After a few words from Captain Bowles, the troopers broke ranks and settled in among the civilians.

Cassie pulled on his trousers and shirt and moved forward, keeping low to the ground and aiming for the Chinamen's wagons; they appeared to offer foodstuffs for sale. With his jacket and cap off, Cassie figured he looked as much like a civilian as most, but he needed a cowboy hat to complete his disguise. Hanging from a buckboard was the very hat he required, its crown filthy from wear but the brim still suited to keeping off the sun.

Pretending he was Rocks McAuliffe, Cassie sidled up to the cart and, with a wave of the hand, purloined the desired object. He moved three wagons down the line before putting it on, in case its owner was around to spot him. Now he was just another cowboy and more at his ease. Not wanting to push his luck, he climbed under a wagon and sat in the shade behind a big-spoked wheel. Except for his hunger and thirst, he was about as comfortable as a body could be in the desert.

The show began. It was to be a true Mexican *rodeo*. Some underfed calves were run into the enclosure, and a cowboy on a fancy spotted Indian pony worked among them, cutting out this one and that, until the crowd gave him a round of applause. The next rider came in and ran down one of the calves, roping him on the run, tossing him to the ground and hog-tying him. Some half-broke ponies were next brought in and several cowboys tried to ride them, without success. One of the fellows was tossed up onto the hood of a motorcar, doing damage to it and himself both. The crowd gave a lusty cheer.

Cassie couldn't think past his stomach. The Chinamen had built a good fire by one of the wagons and were roasting beef on it and cooking beans in a great iron pot. Spectators would come by carrying their own tin plates and cups and fill up on this grub. Cassie's nose moved him out from under the wagon where he had taken refuge and straight to the fireside.

"Sir? How much would it be for beans and some of that nice beef to go with them?"

"Won dollah," the Chinaman said to him.

A whole dollar! Cassie checked his pants pockets again: ninety cents. "I believe I'll come back later," he said.

There was beer being passed out at another wagon. This one was mostly surrounded by troopers, so Cassie stayed clear of it. The Chinamen, who were left over from the building of the railroad, Cassie supposed, were better than fair merchants: they were getting a dollar apiece for eggs and three dollars for a hog. Of course, there was war close by and high tariff for bringing provisions to such a place.

Cassie's stomach wouldn't leave him be. He returned to the Chinamen's food wagon. "And how much, sir, just for beans?"

"Beans won dollah," the cook said to him.

Cassie backed off again and told his stomach to be quiet. He sat under a wagon and watched the others eat and drink. The beer soon put the crowd in an excellent mood. Every time a cowboy hit the dirt, a spectator ran up to him and wet his lips with the dark liquid. After a dozen events, the troopers, who had consumed their own share of spirits, demanded to join in. They announced they would sponsor barrel races, matching their own ponies against the best of the locals. Some of Jacko Mudd's quartermaster boys ran back to the supply wagons and returned with a dozen large nail kegs, which were set out to make a proper race course. The riders had to execute a figure eight around the kegs and return to where they started.

A detachment of troopers entered the circle, leading out the best animals the Squadron had left. Compared to the mangy desert breed, these graceful, small-boned mounts were pick of the litter. If Cassie had had any gold of his own, he would surely have bet it then and there. He would have won, too. Of ten such races, the Army won ten. The locals soon demanded to go back to Mexican-style rodeo, which was roping cattle and breaking wild range horses. The troopers agreed to it. One foolhardy corporal bet ten dollars he could ride the wildest of the cowboys' bucking mustangs. He went off in a cloud of dust and landed on his head. The cowboys took his money and gave him beer in return.

The sun dropped low in the west, but there was no slackening in the crowd's appetite for entertainments. A pair of the Squadron's crack riders showed off the cavalryman's best trick, rolling their ponies onto their sides and then falling across the animals' bellies and firing their Krag carbines over the crowd's heads. The ponies remained still and silent on the ground, as though sleeping. Lieutenant Van Impe's pet squad from D Troop then brought out the Benét-Mercié machine guns. Several wagons and motorcars were moved aside, and the troopers opened fire on imaginary targets in the distant sage. One bullet in six was a tracer—its phosphorus tip burned white hot and showed where the stream of lead was going. This drew hearty applause from the civilians. After that, the Squadron's Filipino prizefighters came forward and put on lively boxing matches. These were a novelty to the cowboys and brought more furious wagering between them and their guests. Cassie wished Rocks had been there to see it. The shortstop liked nothing half so much as a display of fisticuffs—the bloodier the better.

Cassie remained in hiding until the sun touched the horizon. Then he went in search of Doc Rose. He had about given up hope of finding him when he spotted the vet's tousled gray hair through the rear window of a Hudson motorcar. Doc was asleep in the back seat. The automobile's owners, who had climbed up on the roof to have a better view of the rodeo, did not seem to mind Doc's presence.

"Doc Rose, sir?"

Cassie had to shake the vet's shoulder repeatedly to wake him. There was a fresh bottle of whiskey cradled in Doc's arms, an empty one at his feet.

"Leave me be, can't you?"

"It's me, sir—Cassius."

The vet pulled away. "I know who you are. There's no use talkin' to me, boy. I done what I could for your pal, an' it weren't sufficient."

"Well, sir? What's to become of him?"

The older man attempted to send Cassie off with a feeble wave of his hand. "He's been court-martialed, boy. Nothin' to be done now. It's God's business now, I 'spect."

"Court-martialed, sir? But that can't be. It's to be at Fort Bliss, sir, with me as witness. The colonel told me so."

"Your pal done murder, son, and must pay."

"No, sir, he did *not!*"

"He's to be shot, boy. That's the truth of it."

"*No, sir!*"

"Command decision, boy. Time o' war."

"He's *civilian,* sir. He's no damn trooper!"

"Done murder on a military reservation, boy—train travelin' on government orders, same thing."

"*No, sir!*"

"Colonel's like a ship captain at sea—it's all proper and legal, boy. Your pal's to be shot at first light, and that's the end of it. Now be off with you! Git! Leave an ol' man alone, can't you? Damn all you boys! Damn all you innocent boys! . . ."

The vet struggled to free himself from the back seat of the motorcar—finally fell forward out the door. Cassie left him where he lay, face in the sand.

Skirting the show ring, Cassie headed north to the tracks. *Pullman's No. 3* had not moved. Cassie stayed in the deep shadows of the second section until he neared the guardhouse.

There was only one sentry on duty, the corporal called McEvoy. He was having his supper from a mess kit. Cassie gave him a wide berth, moving off to where most of the ponies were hobbled.

He looked the animals over with an eye to soundness of limb and quiet disposition. He found a sturdy bay gelding, freed its legs, and made quick friends with it. The animal wanted to keep grazing, but Cassie pulled it away by its halter and led it down to where the dog tents lay in neat rows. A pair of saddles had been set out for inspection in front of each tent. Cassie was quick to find the leather he wanted, worn and comfortable-looking, and a good thick blanket. He tossed blanket and saddle onto the gelding's back and cinched up. The animal's belly seemed well filled with water and oats. It would go many a mile before suffering thirst or hunger.

Cassie led the mount back toward the tracks and tied it to the horse wagon nearest the van. He then climbed up into the wagon and found a fire ax. Sliding the ax head down the handle, he had himself a stout shillelagh. He eased back toward the van, keeping an eye out for troopers who might have returned to camp.

Corporal McEvoy had finished his meal and settled on the van's back steps to have himself a smoke. His Springfield rifle lay across the top step; his .45 was holstered at his side.

Cassie moved forward on cat's feet. He was less than a yard away when the corporal heard him and started to turn around. Cassie brought down the ax handle. The trooper dropped like a sack of beans.

Cassie stooped, found the corporal's keys, and bounded up the steps into the van.

"Rocks, babe!"

"Cass! O sweet Jesus!"

The shortstop was in a bad way. On seeing Cassie, he began to weep. His face was so puffed and bloody he hardly resembled the true Rocks McAuliffe.

"Easy, babe!" said Cassie. "I'll soon have you free."

The troopers had kept Rocks chained to the wood stove. Cassie was able to undo the leg irons, but none of Corporal McEvoy's keys seemed to fit the shackles that bound the shortstop's hands. There was a two-foot length of chain between them.

"*Open, damn you!*" Cassie swore, but none of the keys would turn in the lock. "Stay put!" he told Rocks.

He ran outside and obtained Corporal McEvoy's pistol. The trooper lay still on the ground. Cassie feared that his blow had been too hard against the trooper's bare head. "*Please, God, say he's not done in,*" Cassie prayed.

He rushed back inside the van. "Hold out your hands!" he told Rocks. "Turn your face away!"

The shortstop drew into a tight ball and shook with fright. "Can't do it, Cass. Yer bullet's bound to get me 'stead o' these damn locks."

"You want to get away, don't you?"

"I'm *beggin'* ya, Cass!"

Cassie gave it up. "Come on, then. Can you walk?"

"I kin try, Cass!"

They went outside and down the steps. The shortstop looked sore in all his joints; he walked gimpy-legged; the moxie was drained out of him. He was not the same Rocks McAuliffe who would pitch the Pope for pennies.

"Listen to me," Cassie instructed. "I've got you a good horse. I'll head you north—keep going a mile or so, then turn east. Columbus is forty-four miles. Think you can make it?"

"I'll make it, Cass!"

Corporal McEvoy began to stir. Cassie breathed easier; the trooper was not done in.

Cassie retrieved the gelding and brought it over to Rocks. The short-stop could not mount by himself; Cassie gave him a boost up.

"This sure is a fine li'l pony, Cass!"

"At Columbus you can catch a ride on an east-bound empty, long as the master doesn't see those cuffs. When you get to El Paso, find yourself a smithy and he'll knock them off. Tell him it was a joke some fellows played on you. Then get over to the Pullman office and wait for me there. You still got that note I gave you?"

"I got it, Cass. It's in me boot, so I ain't gonna lose it."

"That's it, then."

"Cass?"

"What is it?"

"You'll tell Jolene where I'm at?"

"If I can. Sure, I'll tell her."

"You'll see she gets to Pullman's?"

"Wait for her there. I'll find her, so help me."

"You're a true pal, Cass—always were!"

"Ride, damn it, before the troopers get wise to us."

"A fella in C Troop's got me mitt, Cass—I give it 'im fer safekeepin'. Name's Billy Joe Hardesty—played some third-base over ta Keokuk once 'pon a time. Git it from 'im, will ya, an' have Jolene bring it along? Never know when I'm gonna find me a game!"

"Damn you, *ride!*"

With a clatter of shackles, the shortstop rode out. Cassie watched him go until man and horse were swallowed up by the purple haze of night-fall.

Then he remembered to look out for himself—and turned back into the muzzle of Corporal McEvoy's Springfield.

PEONS UNTRAINED BUT BRAVE

ARMY FACES SERIOUS TASK

By John Reed

Famous war correspondent whose dispatches from Mexico at the time of the occupation of Vera Cruz were so graphic they resembled Kipling's Indian tales. Mr. Reed has just returned from the Balkan War front.

(By International News Service)

NEW YORK, March 13—We Americans really consider other races than ours as inferior. We call aliens "Bohunks," "Wops," and "Chinks," and "Greaser" in the common name of a Mexican. When we think of a Mexican we usually picture, half-derisively, an under-sized, treacherous little half-breed, fit to kick around on a section gang, but really not worth much.

This is a serious mistake. . . . The American expeditionary force is not up against cowards. It will encounter ignorant peons, untrained in military maneuvers, badly fed, badly equipped, and armed with a dozen different kinds of rifles, dating from a dozen different revolutions. But they are as good natural rifle shots as there are in the world. . . . However the Mexicans fight among themselves, I believe that they will unite against the invader, especially if he is an American.

6

THEY CHAINED HIM to the stove, using the same leg irons Cassie had taken off Rocks. His hands remained free: Rocks wore the manacles.

Cassie had never been chained before in his life; he now felt the shame of it. He had expected that Corporal McEvoy would take revenge on him, but the trooper was more concerned for his own health. He had a lump on his head the size of a pigeon's egg and the scalp bled some. The corporal was sent off to the Red Cross tent while other troopers went looking for Doc Rose. Cassie wondered what sort of treatment Doc might give, in his condition.

The new sentry on duty was Private Dallas Meek, a scrawny redhead from Ohio. "I brung yer supper. Don't git sick eatin' it all!"

A tin cup of water and two pieces of war baby. The water was tepid, the bread moldy. Cassie did not mind for himself, but worried that Rocks had suffered the same diet and would lack strength to ride forty-four miles in the desert. Cassie began to wonder whether he had been right in breaking the shortstop out and giving him that pony.

Around midnight, Private Meek jumped up from his nap to answer a pounding on the door. It was Captain Bowles. "Wait outside, Private."

The sentry gathered up his boots and rifle and quickly departed. Cassie wanted to stand but could not, the way he was chained.

"You done it now, boy!" said the captain.

"Yes, sir."

The Alabaman wandered about the caboose, making an inspection. He paid special attention to the remains of the two "apartments" the Squadron's carpenters had built for the girls after Rapid City.

"S'pose here was where those damn floozies . . ."

The captain came back toward Cassie and paced angrily around the stove. "Any idea o' the charges 'gainst you, boy?"

"Not exactly, sir."

"Let me list 'em for you. . . . Theft o' government property, bein' a horse . . . Assault on a noncommissioned off'cer, bein' Corp'ral McEvoy . . . Aidin' an' abettin' a pris'ner in escape from gov'ment detention, bein' Mistah McAuliffe . . . Access'ry after the fact o' murder, victim bein' Sarge—'scuse me—Private Snivey. There may be more, boy, by the time the judge advocate gets his hands on the Report o' Findin's."

Cassie remained silent.

"You got nothin' to say for yourself?"

"I'm glad Rocks got away, sir."

The captain ceased his pacing. "You are, are you?"

"Yes, sir. It wouldn't be right to shoot a fellow for a murder he didn't do. And with no fair trial either."

The captain reached down and slapped Cassie's face.

The blow caught Cassie on the lip that Doc Rose had stitched; it smarted until tears came to his eyes.

The captain resumed an officer's stance, upright and stiff-legged. "I—I apologize, son. I had no cause to strike you. But I cannot permit a civilian to impugn the integrity o' this command. McAuliffe's trial was strictly accordin' to regulations. There was an eyewitness to the crime."

"*No, sir!* Not Private Rademacher, if that's what you're meaning. I *told* the colonel, sir. There was nobody witness to it but me and Rocks. I swear to *God,* sir!"

"Swearin' comes cheap nowadays, boy. Private Rad'macher, he swore his heart out on the Bible."

"Then he *lied,* sir."

"Maybe he did. Even so, did you *really* s'pose we'da stood by and seen your damn pal put before a firin' squad without appeal to Bliss?"

"Doc Rose said—"

"Useless ol' rummy! He's earned his discharge long 'fore this. Well, by God, he'll have it now!"

"Are you saying, sir, that Rocks—"

"I'm sayin', boy, that your pal is wanderin' off somewheres on a gov'-ment pony when he should be enjoyin' the hospitality o' this damn ca-boose!"

In his mind's eye, Cassie spied the shortstop—wrists raw from the manacles—trying to point his tired horse eastward by starlight. It seemed to Cassie that whichever way he turned of late, he did wrong.

The captain summoned the sentry. "Remove those damn chains! The prisoner's to remain confined to this car, but he's not to be h'rassed."

"Yes, sir!" replied Dallas Meek. "Only Lieutenant Van Impe, sir, he said—"

"If the lieutenant offers objections, you direct him to me, hear?"

"Yes, sir, sure will, Captain!"

At first light they woke him for early breakfast, which was the same as supper. Corporal McEvoy was back on duty. The top of his head had been shaved and he wore a plaster over his injury. Drunk or not, Doc

Rose had made a good job of it. The corporal sat across the super's table from Cassie and ate his own breakfast, which was hardtack, cold beans, and Mexican *tortillas* obtained in Hachita. "What'd you hit me with anyhow?" the soldier asked pleasantly.

"Handle to a fire ax," Cassie replied.

"You hit hard. I'm still seein' double most o' the time."

"I'm sure sorry. If there'd been another way, I'd have taken it—you can believe that."

"So why'd you do it then?"

"They were going to shoot my pal—or so I thought."

"He's a no-account, ain't he?"

"Some say so. But he's a pal all the same."

"Helpin' a pal ain't the worse sin, I s'pose."

"Sure am sorry, though, for your head."

"The vet says it'll heal up good as new. Here, eat some beans. That's poor grub you got there, and I had my fill. . . ."

After breakfast, the corporal let Cassie go up into the angel's nest. The desert was a mighty parade of purples and pinks: there was nothing like it in Nebraska. Looking south, Cassie watched the troopers sneaking back to their tents from the direction of Miss Opal's. Her five girls had enjoyed a busy night, Cassie did believe. Now a bugler on horseback trotted from corner to corner of the bivouac blowing his first call of the day. Every time he put his instrument to his lips, more troopers came crawling out of the mesquite, dodging their sergeants and aiming for the chow line.

Cassie stayed up top until midmorning, enjoying the sun's warmth and then dozing. He found himself awakened by what sounded like the whine of a distant hornet. Looking out, he saw nothing but the troopers. Some were occupied with boiling their soiled uniforms in great galvanized drums, adding borax and poking at the garments with big wooden paddles. Others were seeing to the animals, bringing water from the Hachita tower, and generally tending to their duties.

The high-pitched buzz persisted and grew louder until finally Cassie saw it—not the object itself, but the cloud of dust that encircled it. It was coming on from the northwest like an angry whirlwind.

It drew closer, following the ruts of a narrow trail that ran straight as an arrow for twenty miles or more. A quarter mile out, it turned into a recognizable object: a motorcycle. Cassie watched it come with joy in his heart. It appeared to be civilian, yet carried a measure of authority and promise.

The machine skidded to a halt at the camp perimeter. The rider was covered from head to toe in brown leather; a skull cap and goggles hid his features. He spoke briefly to the surprised sentries, then pitched his machine forward again, making straight for the second-section van.

Cassie climbed down from the angel's nest and watched through the side window as Corporal McEvoy stepped out on the front porch. "State your business afore advancin'," the corporal called out. He held his Springfield at the ready.

The rider dismounted and pulled off his cap and goggles. "Messenger o' the Southern Pacific! It's Cassius McGill, master o' this rig, I'm seekin'!"

This was good enough for Corporal McEvoy. He invited the rider in. "Prisoner's just there," the corporal said, pointing at Cassie.

"Prisoner, is it?" said the rider. "Name's Terence Sweeney—I bring ya greetin's from Mr. Linton P. MacAdoo!"

Cassie shook the fellow's hand. "*Awful* good to meet you, Mr. Sweeney! *Awful* good!"

"MacAdoo's havin' himself a rupture over your long silence, Mr. McGill. Is your telegraph not in workin' order, then?"

Terence Sweeney was a black-haired pixie of a man, not five feet tall, about Cassie's age, with a handlebar mustache that curled back to his ears. He had an abrupt, peppery way of talking and seemed well suited to his profession, being all bone and muscle and rawhide.

". . . Though I've never had the pleasure to meet the gentleman—me bein' in Lordsburg and him in 'Paso—I suspect MacAdoo's not the most congenial o' men! He's been on to ya twelve whole hours by the wire and not had so much as a how-de-doo for his troubles! Fit to be tied, he is! He's been over to the fort there—Bliss! Ain't that a fine name for it!— only there's nobody 'round the place who knows your name. All the generals are off to Chihuahua chasin' after Villa. So finally he's got on to us at Lordsburg by the telephone. On account o' which I've done forty miles or better since midnight, and blinded by insects most o' the way!"

"It seems a fine machine you've got," said Cassie, admiring the sleek black motorcycle through the window.

"That she is! There's no finer bike than the Indian. She's all of fifteen horsepower and goes like the wind. I'll take ya for a ride if you want!"

"Easy now, mister," said Corporal McEvoy, who had been listening suspiciously. "McGill here's a prisoner an' ain't goin' nowhere 'less the captain orders it. You'd best settle your business and be on your way."

"It's like that, is it?" said the rider.

He gave Cassie orders from Mr. MacAdoo. Cassie was to return to El Paso with his rig as soon as possible and take on a load of freight bound for St. Louis.

"I'd like to oblige!" Cassie said. "Only—see for yourself."

Cassie related the circumstances of his imprisonment, and Rocks's escape. ". . . So unless Mr. MacAdoo can change the Army's mind . . ."

"He'll get your message straightaway!" said Terence Sweeney. He had a broad smile closely akin to that of Rocks McAuliffe. "I'd go right on to

'Paso myself, only my boss back at Lordsburg would skin me alive. . . . Naw, I'd best return home and explain matters to MacAdoo by 'phone. He'll get your message that much quicker!"

"I'm sure in your debt," Cassie said.

"Compliments o' the Southern Pacific!" said Terence Sweeney. "I'm off soon as I pay a quick visit to your town there and buy me some breakfast. Thanks to my trusty Indian, it'll be supper in Lordsburg—that's a promise!"

"Would it be stretching rules too far," Cassie asked Corporal McEvoy, "for me to step outside and take a look at the Indian?"

The corporal was as curious as Cassie. "Can't see no harm in it," he said.

The three of them went out. Terence Sweeney was showing them how the kick start worked when a squad of troopers rushed up, headed by Jacko Mudd.

"What's this I see?" asked the sergeant major in a loud voice. He drew his pistol. "Prisoner broke loose again, eh, corporal?"

"No, Sergeant Major!" cried the corporal. "Prisoner asked to take the air, is all! He ain't free to go nowhere!" The corporal brandished his Springfield to make his point.

"And this other turd?" demanded Jacko Mudd. "He takin' the air, too, is he?"

"Railroad messenger!" replied Corporal McEvoy.

"That's me," said Terence Sweeney. There was a pleasant lilt to his voice. "I'll be on my way then, beggin' your pardon."

"*Hold where you are, mister!*" ordered Jacko Mudd. He put on a mean smile and turned to Cassie. "A great one for unauthorized messages, ain't you, McGill? What you been tellin' this boy?"

"Nothing but railroad business," Cassie replied. "Mr. MacAdoo of the Pullman Company at El Paso is anxious for his train. He's sent Mr. Sweeney to find out what's become of her."

"Has he now?"

"That's it," Terence Sweeney agreed. "Now if you fellas don't mind, I'll just mount up and be gone." He pulled on his skull cap and goggles and sat astride the machine.

"I said *hold*, mister!" barked Jacko Mudd. He trained his .45 at Terence Sweeney. "You ain't goin' nowhere. You're under arrest—breakin' the perimeter of a government reservation durin' wartime. Also, criminal trespass."

Terence Sweeney showed no signs of fear. Moving deliberately, he dismounted, pushed his goggles up on his forehead, and looked Jacko Mudd straight in the eye. "I'll be talkin' to your boss, if you don't mind." His voice kept its sweet lilt.

"Rademacher! Larsen!" shouted Jacko Mudd. "Help this little prick find his way to the guardhouse! An' if he gives you any trouble, blow his head off!"

Terence Sweeney did not wait for further orders. Spinning around, he regained his mount and began working the kick start.

"*Git him!*" roared the sergeant major.

The troopers had all the best of it. They knocked Terence Sweeney over and pinned him to the sand under his machine.

"Secure that motorcycle!" Jacko Mudd ordered.

Ax Larsen stepped up and put the butt of his Springfield through the wire spokes of both wheels.

"*You mis'rable bastards!*" wheezed Terence Sweeney. He struggled to his feet and made for Ax Larsen. Cassie jumped between them and wrapped his arms around Terence Sweeney. The motorcyclist could probably fight, but not against a dozen Springfields.

So it was the same old story: swallow Army "justice" and bide your time.

Terence Sweeney made a good cellmate. Cassie gave him the super's bunk and lay down himself on the mattress over the coal bin. The motorcyclist was lively and of a pleasant temperament. He had a quick temper but got over it about as fast. "Danged spokes needed fixin' anyhow!"

He could even laugh about being locked up by the Army: "Wait'll my ma hears! She'll have a word or two for Mr. Mudd out there! My step-pa, too! He's well acquainted to a judge up in Albuquerque, so look out, Army—you're in the soup now!"

They tried to keep their spirits up and largely succeeded. When the sun reached its zenith, fresh sentries came on duty and brought dinner for the two prisoners. As a joke, the troopers had spread the war baby with generous swipes of rancid butter. Cassie and Terence Sweeney made a meal of warm water.

"And I was countin' on a dozen eggs and a mess o' ham in your fine town o' Hachita!" remarked Terence Sweeney. After that, the little rider sulked a bit; Cassie could not blame him.

They slept when they could, and otherwise suffered the boredom of any prisoner. Late in the afternoon, they received a surprise.

"You hear that noise?" Terence Sweeney asked.

Cassie heard it too. "Motorcycles?"

"Not likely!"

They climbed into the angel's nest and peered east. Terence Sweeney was the first to spot it. "There! See it?"

It looked to Cassie like a giant buzzard.

"She's a JN-2, all right!" cried the motorcyclist. "A Jenny! I been up in one! Fourth o' July at Albuquerque! Cost a dollar for five minutes! Ain't she a beaut'! Sixty horsepower! Army's got eight of 'em!"

Terence Sweeney was well acquainted with aviation; he had made a study of it. The aeroplane belonged to the 1st Aero Squadron at Fort Sam Houston near San Antonio and was to be used in searching out the enemy. "They'll chase down Villa long afore any horse can do it, take my word!"

The aeroplane circled low over the 4th Squadron's bivouac as though trying to make up its mind whether to drop down. It was painted black but for a red five-pointed star on the tail. There was a cockpit in front for the observer, one in back for the pilot.

"*She's fixin' to land!*" shouted Terence Sweeney.

They watched the war bird drop out of cloudless skies and set down in the desert to the west of camp. The troopers had to be fast on their feet to keep the ponies from bolting at the noise.

A crowd of townspeople and cowboys soon gathered around. The two fliers made their way through the spectators toward *Pullman's No. 3*. They were dressed in outfits similar to Terence Sweeney's. Instead of leather pants, they wore the cloth riding breeches called jodhpurs. Cassie knew from the single bars on their collars they were lieutenants.

The officers disappeared into Headquarters Car.

"You know what I'm thinkin'?" asked Terence Sweeney.

"What?"

"I'm thinkin' it's *you* they're after!"

"What makes you say that?"

"This is just like MacAdoo. He's famous up and down the road for it. He never gives up. He wants his train and no excuses will do! Why, he's probably been on to Washington, D.C., demanding satisfaction. And so the Army's dispatched its best birdmen! What's more likely?"

Cassie didn't put much stock in Terence Sweeney's theory; the Company didn't hold its conductors so dear as that. More likely, the Army had secret orders for Colonel Antrobus. Maybe the 4th Squadron would yet join the hunt for Villa.

Twenty minutes later the fliers appeared trackside. Cassie and Terence Sweeney pressed their noses to the window but could make little of what they saw. The two aviators, wearing angry scowls, were escorted on both sides and to the rear by a squad of troopers. Their destination was one of the large tents reserved for officers. At the same time, another detail of men marched out to where the aeroplane had come to rest and began walking guard duty around it. This was a wise precaution, Cassie figured—the spectators from Hachita had grown so numerous they threatened the well-being of the war bird's canvas skin and fragile woodwork.

"Hell and damnation!" Terence Sweeney declared. "If those fellas are seeing to your rescue, McGill, they're taking their sweet time about it!"

Sundown came without any further news of the aviators. Their mission remained a mystery until Doc Rose paid a visit to the van.

"My presence here is suffered with some reluctance by Lieutenant Van Impe, wouldn't you know. It's for the purpose of examining your injuries, Cassius—and any you may have suffered, Mr. Sweeney, during your apprehension. Come now, Cassius, let's have a look at that lip o' yours."

Doc was saying this for the benefit of the sentry, Cassie soon discovered. "You may wait outside," Doc told the fellow. "I'll call out when I want the door opened."

The sentry withdrew. Doc's craggy face immediately displayed a ruddy grin. "First off, I prescribe a draft o' this med'cine." From his bag he produced a bottle of corn whiskey.

"You seem a mighty fine sawbones to me, sir!" said Terence Sweeney, taking his "med'cine."

The whiskey was both food and drink to their empty stomachs. One swig fell hard upon the heels of another. Soon their predicament seemed not quite so awful.

When Doc was good and ready, he told them what he had come to say:

"Those fellas from the aeroplane? They're prisoners just like you! Yes, it's so. . . . Our colonel's gone and done it. . . . Crossed over to the Land o' the Loonies, he has. No other explanation fits.

"Those fellas are Lieutenants House and Jeffers. They're straight from Bliss. What I say now, I say without rancor or prejudice. Remember, Cassius, back there at Tucumcari, when I got off and paid a visit to the telegraph? Well, I did my duty—filed a report on the condition of our animals, which is my business and nobody else's. Went out of channels, I did—sent it straight to Eighth Brigade Headquarters, Pershing's own command!

"To wit, these fellas and their aeroplane. The Army don't take to dead ponies any more than yours truly. The colonel's been called on the carpet to explain it. And that ain't all—Dalhart needs explaining, too. The mayor back there filed an official complaint to the War Department in Washington, D.C. This is a great embarrassment, lads, to any line commander. Add to this the matter of Ward Snivey, whose corpse lies in cold storage at Bliss awaiting the coroner's inquest. So you see, boys, the colonel's in a heap o' trouble and not likely to escape it with his oak leaves intact. . . . Say now, let your benefactor have a swig o' that med'cine, won't you? . . .

". . . What was I saying? Ah, the colonel. Well, he's accepting none of his misfortune. Ain't *admitting* to it! Ups and arrests the messengers who brung the bad news! Telegraph's been shut down since we got here, so there's no way for Bliss to know. Digging himself a deep grave, is Miles. And Lonnie Bowles? Fit to be tied! He's been mulling things over since the colonel passed judgment on your pal, Mr. McAuliffe. But it's hard for a West Pointer to forget rank, and the colonel's a colonel, true enough. Only now—now he's crazy as sin, so that even Lonnie Bowles can't ignore it. You boys looked out the window lately? You seen what the colonel's up to?"

Cassie and Terence Sweeney peered out. The Squadron had formed up in front of the bivouac, the troopers mounted and dressed in battle gear. "Sabers! Pistols!" cried Terence Sweeney. "Judas priest, the whole outfit's off to war!"

"Sabers and pistols," said Doc sadly. "Miles fancies himself back to the Indian Wars. He was the greenest of shavetails at Wounded Knee with the Seventh, don'tcha know—that was in '90, and that's where Miles is now. There's seventy-odd boys with no animals to ride. What you see there, boys, is the last dregs o' the Fourth Squadron. Didja ever see anything half so sad . . . ?"

The colonel completed inspection of his men. He wore the same blue-and-gold dress uniform he had worn on the night of Otis Webster's champagne supper. The other officers and men wore khaki. The four troops faced south toward the border, the fluttering red-and-white guidons declaring the units—"A" on the right running to "D" on the left, with the machine-gun platoon and its horse-drawn carriages bringing up the rear. The colonel and his staff now trotted out to the head of the formation, and the colonel delivered a brief address.

"Haranguing 'em, he is," said Doc Rose. "Telling 'em to do their duty for God, country, and the Fighting Fourth!"

Then, with the sun half buried below the horizon, the colonel turned, raised his saber, and signaled his men forward. The other officers immediately took up the cause:

"*Walk! . . . Trot! . . . ho! . . .*"

The Squadron's left flank brushed past *Pullman's No. 3.* Cassie absorbed the sounds of scabbards rattling against spurs, the smell of hot leather and horsehide, the blurred visions of sabers flashing overhead in the last rays of the hard-slanting sun.

"Up top then!" cried Terence Sweeney.

Doc Rose had to be helped. He was too unsteady on his feet to climb a ladder by himself. They settled in the angel's nest and watched the skirmish line take shape below them. Clusters of townspeople gathered on both flanks of the formation. The civilians were in holiday mood and apparently took the Squadron's parade to be more of the maneuvers they had seen at the rodeo. As the troopers passed by, a rough company of cowboys fell in behind. Great billowing clouds of dust soon hid the riders from view.

"*. . . At the gallop . . . ho! . . .*"

Ever so faintly in the distance, the Squadron's bugler could be heard sounding the charge.

"Such madness!" cried Doc Rose.

Terence Sweeney was puzzled. "Do you suppose, sir, that Villa is up here by the border, and not down by Agua Caliente or Santa Ysabel, as Pershing thinks?"

The motorcyclist was a steady reader of the El Paso newspapers, which were delivered to Lordsburg each evening by rail, and fancied himself an expert on American strategy.

"There is nothing in front of that outfit but chaparral and ruination," Doc Rose declared. His scratchy voice broke with sorrow.

When there was nothing more to see, they climbed down and sat by the stove. The thin desert air, with no sun to warm it, stole away a man's comfort before he noticed it was gone. Doc Rose had another bottle of spirits in his bag, which they soon got into.

The Squadron returned by moonlight. "It's over," said Terence Sweeney. "The battle's finished, so it seems."

The sentry outside, Private Kinloe, invited Doc and the prisoners to sit on the stoop and watch the men return. The colonel was no longer at the head of the Squadron; Captain Bowles now had this honor. He walked his horse, as most of the troopers did. Many of the animals were lame, but many had started out that way.

Toward the rear came the colonel. His mount, called Black Knight, was hobbled by injury. The colonel's boy, Francisco, led it along, pausing to rest the animal whenever he could. When the last squad had passed over the tracks, the Squadron broke formation. The weary animals were set loose on the prairie; they would not range far. The men retired to their dog tents, the officers to Headquarters Car, except the colonel. The colonel wandered among the tents, looking after his men. As he came by, each trooper would jump to his feet, salute, and tell his name. The colonel would comment briefly and then move on.

Captain Bowles soon appeared at the colonel's side. The colonel had taken a fall during the charge. One trouser leg was covered with cactus spines; the colonel's blood stained through. The two officers returned to the siding and passed close by the van. Through the window Cassie heard Captain Bowles say to the colonel in a gentle voice:

"It's only proper, suh, that you retire to quarters. You've given of yourself to the utmost, and must now look to your wounds."

"Thank you, Captain," said the colonel. "It's kind of you to accompany me. I must confess to a certain weariness."

Later, Captain Bowles came to the van. "Release the prisoners," he told the sentry. "Dismissed!"

"Yes, sir, Captain!"

The officer turned to Terence Sweeney. "The Army will make good the damage done to your 'cycle. In the mornin', report to the quartermaster, and he'll see what our smiths can do."

"Much obliged, Captain! The Southern Pacific will be most relieved to hear it!"

"As for you, McGill—"

"Sir?"

"If Corp'ral McEvoy wants, he can bring charges. Then it's your neck."

"Yes, sir."

"He's Irish, ain't he?"

"I expect he is, sir."

"Maybe if you're a good talker, he'll let you off."

"I hope he will, sir!"

"The other charges against you will be dropped, most likely."

"Thank you, sir!"

"*Most likely,* I say—meanin' if you stay on your good behavior and conduct yourself in a respons'ble manner."

"Count on it, sir!"

"I shall. Your troubles are still not over."

"No, sir?"

"On the morrow, you are to report to Bliss. You'd best alert your crews now."

"Yes, sir!"

"You'll be required to make a sworn statement, in writin', in the matter of Ward Snivey's death. Report to the Office of the Judge Advocate General without fail."

"Yes, sir."

"One more thing. Tomorrow, you'll be carryin' a special passenger. He'll be escorted by an honor guard appropriate to his rank."

Doc Rose, who had been sleeping on the super's bunk, now edged forward so he could hear what the captain was saying.

"I'm referrin' to the colonel," continued the captain. "He's been taken sickly and needs attention from a doctor. The colonel . . . he's a fine off'cer and true gentleman." The captain seemed for a moment to have trouble finding his words. ". . . He's to be accorded all due respect and courtesies. . . . He has served his country in numerous campaigns . . . goin' back to the capture of Geronimo. . . ."

Doc Rose moved in closer. He made a peculiar noise with his mouth—his oft-repaired teeth sometimes bothered him—and the captain took it amiss:

"Do I hear a sound of *derision,* Doctah? Is that a smirk I see on your damn face?"

"Not a bit of it, sir! I apologize for a nasty habit. And I smile in gratitude to you, sir—not in contempt for our colonel."

"As usual, you are drunk, Doctah," replied the captain. "Be on that train tomorrow—you are detached from duty with the Squadron, 'fective now. Should you make one unkind remark, one unseemly gesture toward the colonel—"

"Rest yourself, Captain! Though I may be inebriated on occasion, I've never been one to make a meal of another man's misfortune."

They stood in silence for several uneasy moments, until the captain spoke again:

"Well, what y'all waitin' for? Cassius, you fellas haven't had supper, have you? Be off to the cook car while you can. Damn ignorant civilians! . . ."

7

SHORTLY AFTER DAYBREAK, the hoggers Burghley Dance and
Robert J. Boilheart sounded their whistles to show they had steam up.
They had been off duty a full day and were legal again.

Cassie went down the line rounding up his boys; they had slept in the
aisles of the empty day cars. Of the brakemen, Mr. Toomey and Mr. Coffin were feeling poorly, while Mr. Legrand and Mr. Small were in good
spirits. All four had paid visits to Miss Opal's during the layover. The
porters, being Negroes, had not been allowed in Miss Opal's. They'd
stayed aboard and bet on cards.

The Army had cleared out the cook car and set up its mess in a big
tent on the desert. Cassie sent Nelson to bring back coffee for the crew.
Nobody wanted another meal of beans and war baby, preferring to wait
for El Paso, where civilian food was available in good quantity and
cheap.

With two cups of sour brew in him, Cassie headed off to the Signal
Corps tent and found Corporal Josh Pernell.

"It's *you* again!"

"Didn't Captain Bowles tell you about me?"

"That he did. You're to have free use o' the wire. There's nothin' I can
do to stop you, so be my guest."

Cassie figured the corporal had had some grief from Jacko Mudd over
Cassie's failed attempt to get a message off to Mr. MacAdoo.

"I'm sorry about yesterday," Cassie said.

"Ain't your fault," the corporal replied. "Mudd's a sure-'nough bastard
the best o' times."

"Would your telephone be connected as far as El Paso?"

"Goes to Bliss and Central, both. Like talkin' next door, so clear it is.
Help yourself."

Cassie sat at the table and worked the instrument:

". . . Hello, Central? . . . It's Mr. Linton P. MacAdoo of the Pullman
Company I'm calling. . . ."

A minute or so later, a gruff bellow echoed down the line:

"This is MacAdoo. Who calls?"

"It's me, sir—Cassius McGill off *No. 3.*"

"*Is* it, now? My assistant, Mr. Paisley, has had some fine words of

praise for you, McGill. I'm surely sorry to have missed your kind visit to
our office. How generous of you to report. . . ."

When Mr. MacAdoo finished scolding Cassie, he issued orders. There
was no spur for switching at Hachita, so Cassie's rig was to back the
forty-four miles to Columbus and turn the locomotives around there in
the Columbus yards.

". . . Make yourself known to the yardmaster and he'll tell you what
to do."

"He's the fellow they call the Judge, I believe."

"Indeed he is. Even so brave a lad as yourself will do well to obey his
orders. You have the green light to Columbus, McGill. I suggest you take
advantage of it."

"Sir, there's something important that needs your quick attention.
That's—"

"Your draft of moneys. Oh yes, it has arrived, McGill. You are no doubt
wondering why I haven't dispatched Mr. Paisley to inform you of it in
person, as ordered. Well, we shall discuss that upon your arrival here.
Good day, McGill."

"No, sir, you don't understand. You see, sir, this helper of mine from
Lincoln—"

"I may as well tell you now, McGill, no funds will pass to you until
we've settled the matter of the van."

"The van, sir?"

"Your caboose, Mr. McGill. Your buggy, hack, crummy, shanty, cage—
use any word you like for it. The fact remains that a caboose under your
charge has been destroyed. Its burnt-out remains are visible out the
window from this very desk. The Pullman Company is not accustomed to
accepting such losses without satisfactory explanation and, if appropriate,
reimbursement. We shall discuss the matter upon your arrival. Good day
again, McGill. Have a profitable run. . . ."

There was activity out by the aeroplane. Cassie went directly there and
found Terence Sweeney and a gaggle of cowboys from Hachita and a
good many troopers, too. The Jenny was preparing to depart.

"Talked my way aboard!" Terence Sweeney called out to Cassie. He
was busy loading the wheel rims from his Indian into a compartment in
the belly of the craft.

"How is that?" Cassie replied. "You're joking, of course."

"Just watch me!"

It was true. The motorcyclist had persuaded Lieutenants House and
Jeffers to take him to Fort Bliss, where the Army was to repair the
broken wheels. The smiths of the 4th Squadron had found the job too
taxing.

"I'm off, McGill! Best o' luck to you—hope you find your pal, an' hope you inherit all the riches o' the earth!" On these words, Terence Sweeney climbed into the same compartment in which he had stored his wheels. He would make the trip to El Paso flat on his stomach, not seeing a thing but the pilot's feet on the pedals.

". . . Well, now, Cassius," said the colonel, "prepared to give of your best, are you, son?"

"Good morning, sir. We'll try as hard as we know how."

"That's all to be asked of any man. . . ."

The whole Squadron was on parade there by the platform. The colonel was decked out in a fresh uniform, but he wore blue bedroom slippers in place of boots.

Captain Bowles called for three cheers for Colonel Antrobus, and the men shouted *"Hip, hip, hooray!"* three times. Then it was time to go. The colonel was the first to board, followed by 2d Lieutenant Harley Withers from Troop D and eight privates. Lieutenant Withers, the junior officer of the Squadron, had been chosen by Captain Bowles to command the Honor Guard. He seemed scared out of his wits at the prospect.

From the top of the steps, the colonel looked down and said to Captain Bowles:

"I would not leave you, Lonnie, were the call from any but Black Jack himself. At time of battle, a commander wants his own men around him . . . and so I must depart this land, which I have so loved since my first posting at Fort Bayard in '87. . . . Godspeed to the Fighting Fourth! . . ."

When the colonel was settled in his compartment, Cassie sought out Captain Bowles.

"Sir? I know it's not the best of times, but there's a matter—"

"What *is* it, McGill?"

"About Riley McAuliffe, sir—"

"Damn scalawag!"

"Yes, sir, only—"

"*Enough!* Your pal will have his day in court *iffen* he gives himself up an' returns the horse he stole an'—"

"*I* stole the horse, sir."

"Don't interrupt, boy!—*iffen* he returns the horse an' makes a truthful statement in writin'. Nex' time you see that fella, you tell him so, hear?"

"Yes, sir. And he'll do it, too. He's no horse thief. Only—do you suppose you could have some of your men go out looking for him, sir? He's probably not gone far. He's got no compass, sir, and no food or water."

"Can he follow a set o' railroad tracks, boy?"

"I suppose he can, sir. Only he was headed away from the tracks, sir, when he rode out."

Burghley Dance in No. 506 sounded his whistle again; *Pullman's No. 3* was loaded and ready to roll.

"You'd best get aboard, boy," said the captain.

"Just going, sir. Only, if you *could* be on the lookout for him . . ."

The Alabaman spoke now in a softer voice:

"I 'spect you make a good friend, boy, an' a bad enemy. . . . War patrols will be goin' out shortly. If damn McAuliffe's not already sittin' in Deming or Lordsburg laughin' at us, then our boys'll find him."

"*Thank you, sir!* That's the best news a fellow could have!"

The captain fished in his pockets and brought out a bright shiny object. "Take this, boy—somethin' to 'member the Fightin' Fourth by."

It was a brass pin in the form of crossed sabers, the sign of the cavalry. Troopers wore them in pairs on their collars.

"You *mean* it, sir?"

"Now be off, boy. An' take my advice—stay clear o' this man's Army!"

"I aim to, sir! Thank you, sir! Good-bye, sir!"

Cassie kept watch along the right of way for a single rider heading east. He saw none. Knowing Rocks as he did, Cassie had to figure that the shortstop was sacked out by a deep pool of water somewhere, having sweet wines poured down his throat by beauteous women. There was no profit to be had from worrying over Riley McAuliffe.

They reached Columbus in less than two hours, stopping once at a place called Hermanas for water. They never saw a cloud the whole time. Columbus in the daytime was little improvement over Columbus at midnight. Supply wagons lined every inch of rail inside the town limits. There were so many horses and mules in the road that no pedestrian could compete with them. Most of the troopers that Cassie had seen on his first visit were gone to war now, but fresh trains could be seen up the spurs toward El Paso, waiting their turns at the platform.

Cassie set out to find the Judge. The hawk-nosed yardmaster was right where Cassie had left him two nights before, crying out switching orders from the back seat of his Locomobile.

"Sir? It's me again—McGill, off *Pullman's No. 3?*"

This time the jam buster was all sweetness and light. "Do you read English, boy?"

"Yes, sir, I sure do."

"Then feast yer eyes on these."

The Judge passed over a stack of flimsies. Cassie looked through them and let out a whistle. They applied to *Pullman's No. 3* and covered Cassie's run to St. Louis, then on to Lincoln.

"Thank you, sir! Thank you much!"

"Thet palace o' yours is waitin' jes down thet spur. Catch her up, boy, and be gone."

"Palace, sir?"

"Be gone, I say! There's other rigs waitin' to dance o'er these rails 'sides yers. . . ."

Cassie backed off and looked again to his orders. The bottom sheet provided all the explanation he needed. *The Mother Lode* was to be added again and hauled back into El Paso. Cassie caught his breath at the idea of it. He had hoped not to see Mr. Webster again until he could make good on the money he owed the millionaire.

And he had hoped not to see Miss Candace ever again.

The yardmen were quick with their switches, moving the locomotives up front on each section and adding *The Mother Lode* to the tail end of the first. Cassie rode beside engineer Burghley Dance in the cab of No. 506 until the train reached running speed. Then he went back to the private car and surprised Chef Kolb in the kitchen.

"You come back! Wunderbar! Zit down, yung boy! Ve talk!"

They all seemed glad to see him again—Christian, Mae, John, Ling Hee. Even the chow chow Mushy gave him a welcoming growl. Breakfast for the private party was over—it was almost 10:30 A.M.—and preparations for the midday meal had begun. Chef Kolb offered Cassie a hunk of cheese and a glass of white wine, which Cassie was happy to accept in place of a real breakfast.

Cassie asked about Miss Jolene, wanting to tell her of Rocks's escape into the desert.

"Nein, nein!" said Chef Kolb. *"A badt girl, dat vun! She run off! Ist O.K. by me!"*

Jolene had already tired of life in *The Mother Lode,* and of Mrs. Webster's "spying" on her. She had gone into El Paso to join Naomi and Rita. This came as a nasty shock to Cassie. He had expected Jolene to stay aboard *The Mother Lode* for as long as they let her. Who wouldn't prefer the life of a millionaire to being always on the run with a hard-luck shortstop like Rocks McAuliffe? Her disappearance put a sour taste in Cassie's mouth, despite the good cheese and spicy wine he was then enjoying. Now he would have to run her down in a city of 50,000 inhabitants. But one way or another, he would find her.

He had another duty to think about first. He finished his meal, excused himself to Chef Kolb, and went down the passageway to the parlor. Mr. Webster was there alone, comfortable in his dressing gown, reading the newspapers that had been brought aboard at Columbus.

"Sir?"

"Cassius, my boy! What a pleasant surprise!"

The millionaire invited him to sit. Lydia Webster looked in and greeted Cassie, but quickly left again. Cassie was glad. What he had to say to the millionaire he preferred to say in private.

First he had to hear Mr. Webster out. They had done their business at Columbus, the millionaire said, and yearned for someplace more civilized, which was El Paso. A number of Mr. Webster's friends from the East were even then en route to El Paso to observe the war preparations firsthand. American businessmen and industrialists felt an obligation to support the government in every way possible. Naturally, the present conflict offered certain business opportunities; Mr. Webster was not ashamed to say so. "I have no reluctance to earn a profit, so long as my country profits in the bargain!"

Mr. Webster would establish his headquarters at the Great Western Hotel and would play host to his friends there, including Mr. Newton D. Baker, the secretary of war. "So I expect we shall be kept abreast of Pershing's progress in ferreting out the rascal Villa. . . ."

The millionaire paused for breath. Cassie spoke up. "Sir? I was wondering—"

"But of course," said Mr. Webster. "The proposition."

"Sir?"

"I hope you are not offended, Cassius, when I suggest that, in some respects, you remind me of myself at your age."

"Yes, sir. No, sir."

"Rough around the edges, perhaps, but full of promise. Native talent that only wants shaping, development, exploitation. What I have in mind for you is this. Firstly, on-the-job training in our shops at Chicago. Secondly, when you have obtained a thorough grounding in practical aspects of the work—proper schooling at my own alma mater, the Rensselaer Polytechnic Institute of Troy, New York. Are you acquainted, Cassius, with the excellent reputation of this college?"

"I believe I've heard the name, sir."

In fact, Cassie had heard the name once in his life, during the millionaire's remarks at the supper after Dalhart.

"Well, what do you say, boy? Does the proposition appeal to you?"

"Well, sir—"

"Take your time. There is no need to rush so important a decision. Perhaps your ambitions lie more in the musical line. If so, I shan't be disappointed—every man must find his own path in this world."

"I surely do appreciate it, sir—what you've said. Only—"

"Speak freely, lad. I shall understand."

"Well, sir—it's the money I've come to see you about."

"The *money?*" The millionaire seemed offended by the word. "At this stage of your career, you are concerned about *money?*"

"The bonus for fast running, sir."

"Ah. *That* money." Mr. Webster, apparently relieved, lighted himself a fresh cigar.

"Yes, sir. You see, sir . . ."

Cassie told what had happened to the last four double eagles and the fifty-dollar certificate, and of Mr. MacAdoo's refusal to give Cassie his draft of moneys from Lincoln until the matter of the burned-out van was settled.

Mr. Webster listened carefully, his fat cheeks growing pinker as Cassie proceeded through his account. The millionaire puffed on his cigar and admired the smoke it gave off. A deep frown creased his spacious forehead. Finally, it was the millionaire's turn to speak again:

"It has taken courage, I realize, Cassius, for you to admit your culpability in this matter. You are to be commended for your intestinal fortitude. This would be a source of pride, no doubt, to your parents. . . ."

Cassie froze at the idea of Ma hearing of it. Or Pa, or the kids.

". . . However, to gamble away another man's capital—to lose such a sum in a *poker game*. This I cannot condone."

"It's an awful crime, I know, sir."

"Worse, it's an example of great folly. It demonstrates a lack of common sense. Surely you know better than to gamble with common soldiers."

Cassie lowered his head in shame. He had no good answer to the millionaire's arguments.

"Very well. A lesson must be learned. Assuming that you remain unsuccessful—for the time being, at least—in collecting your draft at El Paso, how do you intend to repay me the moneys you have misappropriated?"

The millionaire's harsh words cut Cassie to the quick.

"Speak up, boy. How will you repay this debt you have so wrongfully incurred?"

"From my wages, sir?"

"Is that a statement of intentions, or merely a question? If the latter, I find it wholly unacceptable."

"From my wages, sir."

"And what *are* your wages, may I ask?"

"Well, sir—it's $1.87 for each day worked. It comes to almost fifty dollars most months."

"I see. In that case, I shall accept your note. However, I do not indulge in short-term finance—it is bad practice. I shall lend you the money—$130 —for a six-month period. The loan is due and payable September 15. Now then, what interest will you pay?"

"Interest, sir?"

"*Interest*, boy—the cost of money. Surely, you do not expect to have the use of my money *gratis?*"

"Oh, no, sir."

"Four percent per annum would seem to me a fair rate. Do you agree?"

"Yes, sir. Thank you, sir."

"Prepare your note."

Cassie tore a sheet from his train book and wrote out his IOU, signing it Cassius James Patrick McGill. He passed it to the millionaire.

Mr. Webster rose. Cassie did the same.

"I believe you'll find, Cassius, that such an experience straightens the backbone. Make payment by cashier's check to my Chicago office—Webster's Mining and Mineral, Michigan Avenue."

"Yes, sir."

The millionaire escorted him to the parlor door. "A thought occurs."

"Sir?"

"Tomorrow evening Mrs. Webster and I are giving a small dinner party at the Great Western in honor of Secretary Baker. We would be much obliged if you would come by the hotel at, say, ten o'clock and favor us with a selection of your Irish ballads. Naturally, we shall compensate you for your efforts. Shall we agree on one dollar per song? You may simply deduct the total sum from the amount owing under your note. Father Tibbett will be present to accompany you at the piano. Shall we count on it, then . . . ?"

Candace Webster waited for him in the passageway.

"Good day, ma'am." He tipped his cap, as he would to any passenger.

"My, aren't we formal!"

"If you'll excuse me, ma'am—"

"You're angry with me."

"I'd prefer not to say, ma'am."

"I could have you discharged for such rudeness!"

"I believe so, ma'am."

"Your friend was a fugitive from justice. It was wrong of you to expect that I'd keep him hidden."

Cassie said nothing in reply.

"So now, out of spite, you show yourself to be mean and stubborn."

Cassie continued his silence.

"I am *not* without feelings, Cassius—though you obviously think me so. Do you suppose it was pleasant for me to see your friend so harshly treated? I still tremble at the thought of it!"

Cassie reflected for a moment. "Well, ma'am, you're rich, and I'm sure you'll get over it long before Rocks."

Her rosebud mouth assumed a pretty pout. "Being rich, Cassius, does *not* solve one's every problem."

"Maybe not, ma'am. Though I don't expect I'll ever know for sure."

They suffered a considerable silence. He remembered the kiss they had shared. His lips still stung from that kiss!

"I'll be going now, ma'am," he told her.

"If you must."

He went.

Pullman's No. 3 snaked anonymously into the Southern Pacific yards at 11:30 A.M., one of many empties then returning from the war zone. As on most other days in Texas, the sun was blinding in its whiteness, shadows deep black, winds hot and twisting and dust-filled.

A stout gentleman in a white linen suit and straw hat strutted the platform, inquiring as to each train's origin and number. Cassie knew him at once for Linton P. MacAdoo. His self-important manner and weighty appearance exactly matched his telephone voice.

"*You* are McGill?"

"Yes, sir, I sure am."

"I had feared as much. I prefer Mr. Pullman to be in his grave than to have him see this. You call that a uniform, do you, mister?"

Cassie had forgotten he was wearing a pantryman's jacket borrowed from the porter Milo. His own tunic was now hung out to dry from a vent pipe in the roof of *The Mother Lode;* Christian's wife, Mae, had insisted on washing it for him. Cassie preferred not to explain to Mr. MacAdoo how his tunic had been bloodied, or how his spare outfit—also bloodied—burned in the van.

"Sorry, sir—I'll go change."

"Kindly do so. Then return to the platform and await my orders."

The Pullman agent went down the line and saw personally to Mr. Webster's party. From a distance, Cassie watched them climb into buckboards—Otis and Lydia Webster, Miss Candace, Mademoiselle Foix, Father Tibbett. He remembered how they had looked to him that first night at Omaha. They were strangers to him then—"exotic creatures," Ma might have said. He had since carried their bags and sung them a song. He had taken money from one and been offered school and a job for his troubles. He had confessed his sins to another and kissed a third. He had even seen two of them stark naked!

Yet they remained strangers to him. He turned away from them now. They were nothing to do with him.

The Mother Lode was cut off, under Mr. MacAdoo's direction, and sent down to its own spur. It would sit in the yards until called for. Mae and Christian and the kitchen crew remained aboard, having soft duty for so long as the millionaire cared to stay in El Paso. Their toughest chore was to care for the chow chow Mushy, who had been banished, for his bad manners, from polite company.

Cassie donned his clean but damp tunic and met Mr. MacAdoo back on the platform.

"About orders for the hoggers, sir—"

"You've a red board, McGill. The yardmaster will so inform your hoggers. Come with me, boy."

Cassie followed Mr. MacAdoo back to the Pullman Company offices. The agent was barely able to climb the stairs to the second floor; his great bulk seemed a burden to him.

Waiting at the top of the stairs was the clerk, Vernon Paisley. "That's *him* all right! That's the villain hisself!"

Cassie followed Mr. MacAdoo into his private office, leaving Vernon Paisley outside the open door.

"Sit," said Mr. MacAdoo.

Cassie sat.

"You have more nerve, boy, than is warranted either by your age or position."

"Sir?"

"Ordering my clerk around like he's your personal servant. I call that *nerve*, boy!"

"I was in a tight spot, sir. Your clerk didn't seem to want to help me much."

Cassie could hear snickers from Vernon Paisley outside the door.

"So you say." Mr. MacAdoo was sweating from the midday heat. "The fact remains, McGill, you are insubordinate and ripe for discharge."

Cassie did not contest the statement.

"Paisley!" cried the agent.

"Sir?"

"Iced tea. And one for our 'guest,' as well." Mr. MacAdoo was balding, which accounted for the rivulets of perspiration that poured off his dome and sweated up his forehead and eyebrows and cheeks. "There is little comfort to be found in these climes. Your home is at Lincoln, Nebraska, I understand—oh, yes, I have been on the wire to your superior, Mr. Calvin Hebb. He says you are a good boy, but I have my doubts."

Vernon Paisley brought them their tea. Cassie regularly drank tea in Pa's store and had a taste for it.

"A modicum of nerve is no bad thing in a lad," continued Mr. MacAdoo. "But a surfeit of same is vile and the surest road to discharge." The Pullman agent seemed fond of the word "discharge," breaking it off in his mouth with a sharp bang.

"About my moneys, sir," said Cassie. "I guess Riley McAuliffe has not come for his portion."

"Nobody's come for it. Nobody's to *get* it, neither!"

"Sir?"

"There's naught to be done about it, boy, till we've gathered all the facts and sifted them fine, top to bottom."

"But, sir—"

"The *van*, boy. The van that's burned to the very rails! She's just there" —he poked a fat finger out the open window behind the desk—"should you wish to confirm it for yourself. Being an *independent* boy as you are."

Cassie took stock of his position and remained calm. "It's nothing to do with me, sir. She burned on her own, taking my property with her. I'd like to have my money, sir."

"Would you, now!"

"Yes, sir. I've great need of it."

"Have you, now!"

"Yes, sir, I do."

The agent opened the drawer to his desk and pulled out a piece of paper. Cassie could see that it was his draft, written out on Western Union letterhead.

"One hundred and seventy-four dollars and thirty cents," said the agent. "This is a goodly sum, but not near enough to recover a burned-out caboose."

"I require the money now," Cassie repeated.

"I shall not discuss the matter further today," Mr. MacAdoo said. "Return on Monday morning, and I shall hear evidence."

"I've got orders to St. Louis Monday morning, sir."

"So you do. Well then, the matter will be settled in Home Office."

"That won't do, sir."

Outside, Mr. Vernon Paisley was enjoying himself over Cassie's difficulties: his snickers grew in frequency and volume.

"Will not *do?*" exclaimed the agent.

"No, sir. I require my draft today."

"I am no longer amused, boy, by your insolence. Return to your train at once!"

"I must have my draft, sir. That's the law. No one's allowed to interfere with a Western Union draft. I'm a telegraphist myself, sir."

The Pullman agent lifted his great weight to a standing position behind the desk. "*You* have the audacity to lecture *me* on the law!"

"I'd like my draft, sir."

"Mr. Paisley!"

The clerk only had to take one short step to be in the room. "Sir?"

"Mr. McGill is discharged! See to it! Discharged for cause! Inform Mr. Cosgrove by wire! See to a replacement master for *No. 7*, St. Louis-bound!"

"Yes, sir, Mr. MacAdoo!" The clerk was beside himself with joy.

"As for you, McGill, you may collect your wages at Lincoln! Good day, sir!"

Cassie got slowly to his feet. "I sure regret, sir," he said in quiet, measured tones, "that you see things this way."

"Good day, sir!"

"On account of, I can only go now to Mr. Webster himself, who is Pullmans' best customer."

"Oh, yes, so you've said to Mr. Paisley. Be off to see him then—ha, ha!"

"So I must." Cassie made to leave.

"And how would you hope to see this 'best' customer ever again, hey, boy?"

Cassie turned back. "Oh, I'll be seeing him, sir. He's invited me to be his guest at supper tomorrow evening. So I'll surely see him."

"What are you saying, boy?"

"Don't believe me? Ask him yourself, then."

"Hold, boy. Even were it true, what makes you think such a gentleman would interfere in Company business? You're just talking to hear your own wind, boy!"

Mr. MacAdoo sat back down and took more tea. Cassie let him get a swallow down, then said:

"It's 'cause of a favor I did him, sir. It's about moneys paid to some of the hoggers for fast running. It's against the Regs, of course, but to get my draft, sir, I'd be obliged to mention it to the Commission."

Mr. MacAdoo's proud grin sank a bit into his sweaty jowls. "Such presumption! Balderdash!"

"So it may be, sir. But without my draft, that's the only way for me. It's a nasty business and I sure regret it. I'll feel better for confessing my sins, though."

Mr. MacAdoo brought himself up again. "I shall save you a bundle of grief, boy. You can have twenty dollars of your draft, but I keep the rest till the matter of the van is settled."

"I'll have my draft, sir, the full amount." Cassie turned again for the door.

"Hold, you damned upstart! Here I'm taking a Christian attitude, and you such an ingrate! Fifty dollars then—not a penny more!"

"I've nothing against such bribes myself," Cassie said, "but the government may see different. The names and amounts are all in my book, so there's no trouble in finding the hoggers."

"Sixty! That's my limit, boy!"

"Mr. Webster, he's a bosom pal to Mr. Robert T. Lincoln and will no doubt wish to make the most of the troubles. The colonel's in it, too—Colonel Miles Antrobus of the Fourth Squadron. He's witness to the transactions and won't lie to save his skin. I'm sorry to stir up such a hornet's nest of misery, sir, but my back's to the wall. I'd best be going on over to the Great Western Hotel and start the wheels of justice in motion."

This time Cassie did not wait for Mr. MacAdoo's reply. He walked out into the wood-railed pen that held Mr. Vernon Paisley and found the gate and made for the stairs.

"*Stop, boy!*" Mr. MacAdoo cried after him. "Don't you take another step! You are without a doubt the most low-down, insufferable, villainous—"

Cassie kept going. He went out the front door and onto the street as Linton P. MacAdoo appeared on the balcony above.

"McGill! *Stop, I say!* You shall have it! I was merely testing your mettle, boy! Can't you *see* that? Look, here is your draft—it's yours for the asking! Be reasonable, boy! There's no need to cause a fuss!"

"In cash money," Cassie replied.

"What's that?"

"Cash money," Cassie repeated. "Being as I'm not known hereabouts, I'll need you to redeem it for me."

"That will take time, boy. The banks—"

"I'll come back this afternoon, sir. I'd sure appreciate your having my moneys ready for me, sir, as I don't fancy going to Mr. Webster. To tell the truth, he's got a most fearsome temper. . . ."

8

THEY LEFT ALL but Headquarters Car in the yards and rode out to Fort Bliss behind No. 506, with Burghley Dance still at the throttle. This seemed to Cassie a sad end to the *Pancho Villa Express*—locomotive and one sleeper.

They were met on the Bliss platform by a pair of medical doctors and a small detachment of troopers from the 8th Brigade. Cassie went over to pay his respects to the colonel, but the officer seemed not to know him, and Cassie backed off.

"Don't concern yourself, son," said Doc Rose. "The colonel's a bit confused just now. When he's himself again, he'll remember that you did your best and ain't the least to blame for his misfortunes."

"Thank you, sir. I guess it's good-bye, then."

"Farewell, lad! It's been a pleasure to know you! That lip gives you any trouble, you get yourself to a proper sawbones—though God knows what those fellas could do for you that this ol' horse doctor didn't already!"

Cassie went off with a lump in his throat. This was the last he was to see of Doc Rose, and the colonel, too. He signed off Burghley Dance in his book and sent No. 506 back to the yards. The run was officially over now, though nobody thought to celebrate it. Cassie supposed the real end had come earlier—not at Hachita, but when they lay over at Dalhart, or maybe even before that, when they tried roping ponies into plain boxes at Fort Meade.

He still had unpleasant business to attend to at Fort Bliss. He talked his way past the sentries at the front gate and soon found the bleached frame building that housed the Office of the Judge Advocate General, 8th Cavalry Brigade. The place was empty except for a loud-voiced corporal with sad eyes and little patience.

"Return on Monday. There's nobody on duty past noon on Saturdays, can't you see?"

The Army seemed to be run by these corporals. Cassie explained what Captain Bowles had said about making a sworn statement, in writing. This made no difference to the corporal.

"Ain't no justice afore Monday, eight hundred hours. Be off now, 'less you prefer the guardhouse."

Cassie thought to mention that he had train orders to St. Louis on

Monday but talked himself out of it. He would let Monday take care of Monday. He breathed easier outside the gates.

He made his way to the Fort Bliss platform, looking to catch a freight back into town. He had in his pockets ninety cents but expected to have a good bit more within the hour.

He was not alone on the platform. "If this ain't the best danged luck!" the other fellow shouted at him.

"*Same to you!*" Cassie shouted back.

It was the "aviator," Terence Sweeney. They pumped each other's arms like newfound lodge brothers. With Rocks gone and no other friends about, Cassie was glad of the motorcyclist's company.

"Has the Army made repairs to your Indian, then?"

"Their wheelwright's runnin' me up some new spokes this minute. I'm to fly back to Hachita in the Jenny tomorrow afternoon."

"Fall in a pond," said Cassie, "and I bet you come up with fish in your pockets!"

"I ain't complainin'!"

Before long, a string of flats came their way and they climbed aboard. There was a Santa Fe freight king sunning himself on a stack of lumber, and he soon came back to bust their noggins for riding on the cuff. He carried a yard-long oak staff and was nasty-looking even for the master of a freight rig. But he folded at the sight of Cassie's brotherhood card. "Sorry to menace ya wit' me stick, only this line's crawlin' with tramps and bindlestiffs. You're welcome to ride far as Phoenix—that's our turnaround."

The rig took them to within a stone's throw of the Pullman office. Mr. MacAdoo had gone off to eat his dinner, leaving the place in charge of Vernon Paisley.

"I've come for my cash," Cassie told the clerk.

"Right here, sir!" He handed Cassie a manila envelope. "Counted it out myself, sir—but please count it again to be sure!"

Vernon Paisley's manners had improved one hundred percent, in Cassie's estimation, since their first meeting. Cassie opened the envelope. It was all there: $174.30.

"Much obliged to you, Mr. Paisley. Now I'll be wanting to leave a message for you and Mr. MacAdoo."

"Yes, sir, Captain!"

The clerk provided pen and paper. Cassie sat down and wrote out his instructions:

To Whom It May Concern:
A person of the name Riley "Rocks" McAuliffe, about five feet two or three inches, will come to you with a note from the undersigned asking for money. Please send him to the Paso del Norte Hotel, where the undersigned is to be found, the money, too.

He signed it, "Cassius McGill, Master, Pullman's No. 3," then remembered to cross out the latter part. *Pullman's No. 3* was no more.

They walked down San Antonio Avenue until they found the Paso del Norte Hotel. The lobby was crowded with black-suited gentlemen in eastern-style hats. Their cigar smoke and chatter reminded Cassie of Grand Central Station in New York. Cassie soon learned what had attracted them. El Paso suffered a dire shortage of telephones. All these customers were newspapermen waiting their turns to use the long-distance lines to report their war stories back east.

The desk clerk took note of Cassie's uniform, and Terence Sweeney's. "You gentlemen would perhaps be more comfortable at one of the drummer's hotels on Broadway."

"This suits us just fine," Cassie replied.

"Two dollars a night per person," said the clerk. "In advance."

Cassie swallowed hard. He knew a hotel in Boston where the use of a bed, shower bath, clean nightgown, slippers, razor, and toilet articles came to ten cents. But here, with war just over the river and thousands coming south to witness it, Cassie supposed the hotels could charge whatever the traffic would bear.

"Two dollars it is," Cassie agreed. He meant to stay two nights, Terence Sweeney one. Cassie paid for both, Terence Sweeney being "temp'rarily embarrassed." Cassie did not mind. Ma had always told him that charity was high among Christian virtues, and his recent experience with the 4th Squadron had made him see the wisdom of it.

They obtained a large room on the third floor overlooking the plaza. "So we're at our ease!" said Terence Sweeney.

"That we are!"

"And no shortage of funds, neither, I'd say!"

Cassie's whole life savings—all the money he had in the world, not counting what he had coming from Pullman's—now resided in his pockets. He decided on a trick Uncle Leo had taught him. Between the two beds was an armoire containing a Bible placed there by the Christian Commercial Men's Association, the "Gideons." Cassie kept out ten dollars to have in his pocket and tucked the remaining bills into Deuteronomy, Psalms, and Lamentations. Traveling men needed the Good Book, Uncle Leo would say, whereas no thief ever showed interest in it—or else he wouldn't be a thief.

"Now then, please to follow me," said Cassie.

They went down to the basement and had themselves a Turkish bath. Again Cassie was glad to pay. It cost fifty cents and made new men of them.

"Now for some dollies!" Terence Sweeney declared.

But Cassie had another idea. "Before anything," he said to the motorcyclist, "we eat."

"Spoken like a true gentleman," said Terence Sweeney. "Stomachs first, cocks after!"

They went into the street. This was a true boom town, El Paso. Every footpath and byway was choked with horses, mules, dogs, buggies, motorcars, even an electrified trolley. The citizenry was made of cowboys on horseback, Indians squatting on the corners offering their wares, soldiers doing guard duty against the Mex, and countless travelers freshly arrived and bent on seeing the war. Train whistles from every direction played off adobe walls like sweet distant music and gave the place a spirit unknown in Nebraska or anyplace else Cassie had ever been. It would be the best of towns, Cassie was thinking, if only Rocks McAuliffe would show himself to enjoy it.

Terence Sweeney was swept by impatience. "Is it *here*, then, McGill, or elsewhere? Let's not dawdle! There's delights to be savored on every street o' this town, for them that gets going!"

They settled on the Paloma Azul Cafe, a pretty little whitewashed adobe offering the local food. Cassie studied the menu but could not decipher the foreign words. Terence Sweeney, who had lived in New Mexico all his life, ordered for the two of them: *frijoles, tamales, carne asada, chorizo, carnitas.* They sat hunched over their plates and used the Mexican bread, *tortillas,* to mop up the melted cheese and fiery sauces that covered their plates. They did not talk, only ate, washing down the food with icy bottles of *cerveza.*

When they could eat no more, they staggered to their feet and shook hands with the waitress and the cook, too. Cassie settled their bill; it came to thirty cents apiece. Cassie was thankful he was wearing a vest: the top button of his trousers had popped off. He felt like a calf with a cowboy's lariat around his belly.

"Now for the dollies!" cried Terence Sweeney. The motorcyclist looked like a handsome aviator in his shiny high boots. He would have no trouble conquering the female sex, Cassie believed. Terence Sweeney talked of little else.

"I've got another idea," Cassie said. Down the street, in the next block of stores, he had spotted the Western Union. "Can you spare me a minute to do some business?"

Terence Sweeney agreed to it, but Cassie could tell that his friend was not pleased by the delay. They threaded their way through the Saturday crowd. A band of sour-faced Indians appeared suddenly from an alley. Terence Sweeney took Cassie's elbow and directed him across the street. "Yaquis. I've run for my life from 'em more than once in the desert. Every white man's their enemy to the death, the way they see it. Seems they're less fond of us takin' their lands than the Navahos, f'instance!"

Every time Terence Sweeney saw a female who attracted his eye, he would stop and stare at her, even if her male companion noticed Terence's desire and was twice Terence's size. There were loose women in the streets, but these did not seem to offer the same attraction to Terence Sweeney as those with companions. There was lots of Rocks McAuliffe in Terence Sweeney, Cassie decided: never take anything easy if you can take it hard.

They arrived at the Western Union office but couldn't enter immediately because of the crowds out front.

"I'll be just here if you want me," said Terence Sweeney. He preferred to stay in the street and do his business there.

Cassie fought his way inside. The room was no more than twenty feet deep and ten feet wide, but it held more newspapermen than the lobby of the Paso del Norte Hotel. The place was a sea of black suits and celluloid collars. The impatient and angry correspondents formed two great lines which ended in a pair of sweating clerks in shirtsleeves. Cassie had an idea on how to overcome this obstacle. He recovered Captain Bowles's crossed-sabers from his pocket and substituted this emblem for the regular brass SPECIAL SERVICE pin on his Pullman cap. He then stepped boldly into the mob, calling out as he went:

"Easy now, gentlemen! We'll be helping each of you in turn. Be patient, can't you?"

This stratagem worked. They took him for a clerk or something better. As he made his way to the desk, messages were stuffed into his pockets, including fees and tips and bribes of paper money and coin. Newspaper fellows had no regard for cash and spent it like Gypsies, Cassie supposed, figuring there was always more to be had without pain.

"And where do you think *you're* goin'?" one of the real clerks said to him.

Cassie stuck his nose into the other fellow's territory. "Special courier from Colonel Antrobus, Twelfth Cavalry. This is war business. I'll be needing pen and paper."

The weary clerk threw up his hands. "There's no wire open just now, and that's a fact."

"Doesn't matter," Cassie replied. "This message is to be held and delivered only to the persons named on it."

The clerk passed over the counter the items that Cassie had requested. Cassie printed out his note in a large hand and sealed it in the official Western Union envelope. He addressed it:

MR. RILEY MCAULIFFE OR MR. CASSIUS MCGILL

IMPORTANT & CONFIDENTIAL

There was no telling what name Rocks might now be traveling under. The note said:

HOLDING YOUR CASH PASO DEL NORTE HOTEL. COME QUICK. HEAD-
ING TO ST LOUIS MONDAY A.M.

YOURS

CASS

He wrote it in letters so big that even Rocks could read it. In so doing,
Cassie scratched an itch that had bothered him since Hachita—the worry
that Rocks had heard "Western Union" when Cassie said "Pullman's."
Now the bases were covered.

He handed the envelope to the clerk. "You're to give this to none other
but the names you see here."

"It'll be done," said the clerk.

"Oops—almost forgot," said Cassie, laughing at himself. He pulled from
his pockets the messages that had been stuffed there by the reporters.
"These are to go off the first moment your wire's open again."

"Now hold on—"

"Orders from Pershing himself. Argue with 'Nigger Jack,' if you want—
I'm only doing my duty!" Quickly, he piled the bills and coins on the
counter next to the messages. By Cassie's count, it came to something over
fifty dollars. "Take your fees out of this," he said, "and pocket the difference for your trouble."

"Call at any time, sir!" the clerk replied with a smile.

"It's War Department funds," Cassie said as an afterthought, "so spend
it wisely."

He bolted out of the place before he could be found out. His days with
the 4th Squadron had taught him much—most of it on the far side of
proper conduct.

He wished he had been less of a wolf at table. His stomach distressed
him greatly and he burst onto the street with a loud belch—straight into
the faces of Mr. Otis Webster and Father Tibbett.

"Beg pardon, sir! Beg pardon, Father!"

"It's the lad himself!" remarked the millionaire in astonishment. "Padre,
tell young Cassius of our expedition—perhaps he will wish to join us.
Meanwhile, I shall accompany Al on his business."

Mr. Webster was arm-in-arm with another gentleman, smaller and far
younger. The two of them went immediately into the Western Union.

"An expedition, sir?" Cassie said to the padre.

"Quite so." The padre dropped his voice to a whisper. "In truth, Cassius—an *execution.*"

"Sir?"

"But then this will be quite foreign to you. The punishment of criminals
—all very proper and justified. I am certain it will be a Christian cere-

mony—I shall insist on it. There's to be a firing squad. I shall pronounce a Blessing for the Condemned. It's to be just over the bridge at four o'clock sharp."

"It'd sure be something to see, sir. Only I'm in the company of a friend."

"Bring him, too, if you'd like."

Cassie skipped over to where Terence Sweeney was standing and put the proposition.

"I heard of it already," Terence Sweeney said. "It's only a couple o' greasers, and what's the fun o' that? Me, I'll stay and find my fun with the dollies."

"I could join up with you afterwards," Cassie said.

"As you like. Only be sure to pound on the door when you get back, case I'm occupied!"

Cassie returned to the padre. Soon Mr. Webster and his friend emerged from the Western Union. The millionaire's face was bright red with anger, the younger fellow's only a shade less so.

"Inefficiency bordering on chaos!" remarked the millionaire. "Such a damned nuisance! It's a crying shame, to be treated in this manner. Under other circumstances I would have that clerk's position before morning!"

"I must stick it out, Otis," the younger gentleman said. "You fellows go along and have yourselves a time. I'll make the best of it here."

The millionaire finally acknowledged Cassie's presence again. "Al, say hello to Cassius McGill. He's with the Pullman Company and has been our conductor since Omaha. Cassius, this is Al Runyon, a top correspondent from New York City."

Cassie stepped forward, removed his cap, and shook the gentleman's hand. "Pleased to meet you, sir."

"How do, kid. Except my credentials seem downright suspect in this town, where you can only file your stories, so it seems, if you went to kindergarten with the mayor."

The newspaperman looked to be thirty years old or thereabouts, small-ish in build, with clean, neat features, high forehead, and a gentle smile. He had the confident manner and costly clothes of a New Yorker, but the way he pronounced his words showed him to be a westerner.

"Is it a story, then, sir," Cassie asked, "that you're wanting to get on the wire?"

"Two thousand golden words, kid—perishable as ripe tomatoes. But see that great howling mob inside? Each o' those fellows is betting his job on his next story. Any one of 'em would kill to get to the head o' the line and scoop the other fellow. I'm sure to get through sooner or later—only now it appears later, which may not prove altogether pleasing to my editor."

"Maybe there's a way I can help, sir," said Cassie, remembering the grateful clerk he had done business with earlier.

The newspaperman looked dubious. "How's that, kid?"

"He's a resourceful lad," said the millionaire, "and not afraid to bet on himself. What have you to lose, Al?—he cannot do worse than his elders! Speak up, Cassius—what's your idea?"

They gave him his chance. Cassie determined from Mr. Runyon that it was a six-dollar story he wished to file, and so Cassie asked for ten.

"Off you go, boy," said Mr. Runyon, "and there's a nice dinner in it for you, should you succeed!"

Cassie took the money and foolscap and entered the Western Union. His cap still bore Captain Bowles's crossed sabers. Before getting up to the desk, Cassie smoothed out his jacket and adopted a stern air. He made sure to arrive at the same clerk as before.

"Well, good day again, sir!" said the fellow. "Would you be requiring something more?"

It took Cassie less than a minute to accomplish his task. The rambunctious fellows all around him screamed like stuck porkers when he did his business before theirs. But the clerk rebuffed all such complaints, declaring finally: "Keep to your lines and conduct yourselves properly or I shall close down for the day! Can't you see this here's a special messenger o' Pershing hisself?"

They went down Mesa Avenue and crossed over International Bridge. Mr. Webster had hired a carriage; they rode in comfort. Cassie sat next to Mr. Runyon and learned a great deal. Al Runyon's name was really Alfred Damon Runyan. He had changed it to Damon Runyon for the sake of his job. He was now a top writer for the *New York American*. He was thirty-two years of age and came from Kansas. Before New York, he had lived in Denver mostly and worked on a dozen newspapers including the *Rocky Mountain News*. "Before that I was a trooper myself, kid, just like those you dragged down here."

"On the level, sir?"

"Honest Injun. Joined up with the Thirteenth Minnesota Volunteers in '98 and shipped out to the Philippines to fight the Moros, who are a far sight worse than any Mexican. Can't say I'm too proud of my part in it, though. Got my discharge at the Presidio in San Francisco a year later and never looked back. The cavalry's been keeping the peace out there ever since, but you still can't travel in safety twenty miles outside Manila. . . . I much prefer our chances in this new war. There's fourteen million of the Mexicans and a hundred million of us. Still, the Army's a hard place, kid—dirty and dangerous both, unless you're a general. Then I recommend it. . . . Railroading beats the Army all hollow. Of course, *owning* a railroad beats working on one. It's almost as good as working on a newspaper, only without the glory. . . ."

They were in Juárez now, following the swarms of foot travelers past the bullring on the Avenida Ferrocarril—"Railroad Avenue," Mr. Runyon explained—to the main square of the town. Mr. Runyon agreed to be their guide; he knew Spanish about as well as he knew his own tongue. It was by then nearly four o'clock and the sun just tolerable. Soldiers loyal to the Mexican president, Carranza, looked down from the rooftops and ensured against a surprise attack by the Villistas. A military band in red-and-blue uniforms with gold trim performed Mexican tunes for the entertainment of the crowd. It was a marching band but contained guitars and other stringed instruments resembling giant mandolins. The native populace received the music well, applauding each piece at start and finish.

There was sudden commotion at one corner of the square. This marked the arrival of Mr. W. H. Horne of El Paso, who was the official photographer. With the aid of three assistants, Mr. Horne erected his large box camera on a tripod facing one of the adobe buildings that looked onto the square. This would be the place of execution, Mr. Runyon learned from a brief conversation with a Mexican officer.

"He's a general," Mr. Runyon confided to Cassie. "One of every two men in the Mexican Army is a general."

While Mr. Horne saw to the focus of his camera, his assistants went through the crowd offering postcards made from pictures the photographer had taken several days before. They cost one penny apiece plus another penny for postage. All three poses showed piles of Mexican corpses burnt in the desert. Cassie bought one of each, thinking to send them home to Dwight and Dewey and maybe Pa. Ma and the girls would not be pleased to have such a souvenir; Cassie would have to find something else for them.

The crowd was becoming impatient. It was half Mex and half white people, who, like Mr. Webster's party, had come across from El Paso to see the fun. Many correspondents were present besides Mr. Runyon. He was pleased to introduce his friends Floyd Gibbons of the *Chicago Tribune*, Bob Dunn of the *New York Tribune*, Frank Elser of the *New York Times*, and Dan Piggott of *Harper's Weekly*. The reporters were champing at the bit, wanting to get south with Pershing. But Pershing was in no hurry to have these fellows looking over his shoulder, Mr. Runyon said, and so had delayed their means of transport. Automobiles were in short supply. Pershing himself had gone across in a rented Dodge.

When Mr. Horne was ready, he nodded to the Carranzista general in charge. The officer placed two fingers between his yellowed teeth and gave a sharp whistle. A squad of soldiers marched into the plaza from a nearby adobe, bringing with them the three prisoners. The prisoners looked remarkably like their captors, lacking only the rifles and *bandoleras* of the latter. *Bandoleras* were leather belts filled with cartridges and draped over the neck and shoulder. The regular Mexican uniform was plain white cotton trousers and jacket topped by a broad-brimmed *sombrero* or "shade hat." Even at four o'clock in the afternoon, a shade hat was a wise precaution. The three prisoners were allowed to keep theirs.

The prisoners were escorted to where Mr. Horne's camera was set up and placed against the adobe. High up on the whitewashed wall was a weathered poster that the Carranzistas had not troubled to remove. Once intended for visiting Americans, it was written in English:

ATTENTION GRINGO

For gold and glory, come south of the border and ride with Pancho Villa, El Libertador of Mexico.

Weekly payment in gold to dynamiters, machine-gunners, and railroaders. Enlistments taken at Juárez, Jan. 1915.

¡VIVA VILLA, VIVA LA REVOLUCIÓN!

The prisoners were arranged facing the camera. They stood shoulder to shoulder, not more than two or three feet from each other. They were not tied or blindfolded as Cassie had expected them to be. They would be shot from right to left, Mr. Runyon explained.

"What do you suppose they did, sir?" Cassie asked. "To deserve it?"

"They picked the wrong general," replied Mr. Runyon.

Five Carranzistas would be the firing squad. The men doing the killing were sweating like pigs in the sun. Their dark brown skins were caked with dust so they looked like Negroes. They backed off eight paces from the prisoners and stood in a close row, their shoulders touching. The crowd moved as close as the bravest among them dared. Some spectators to the sides were no farther from the muzzles of the German Mauser rifles than were the prisoners.

Another general now came forward. He wore civilian clothes but carried a saber to show his station. The five soldiers of the firing squad loaded their weapons and stood at the ready. The flies were so thick the soldiers could not keep still for more than a second. The military band stopped playing so the musicians, too, could find vantage points in the crowd. Mr. Horne ducked his head under the cloth and took one last look through his lens. The officer in charge raised his saber; the men took aim. When the officer brought his blade down, the men pulled on their triggers.

The shots rang out in ragged cascade. All five reports could be heard, one atop another. The first prisoner fell straight back. His hat sailed off; his bare head touched the wall. Puffs of dust curled from the adobe where the bullets entered. Bullets from a Mauser rifle could go through steel at this range, according to Mr. Runyon.

Seeing it, Cassie felt hot flashes. He had seen a dead body only once before: Trooper Snivey's. He looked around for Father Tibbett. The padre was saying prayers at a good pace. He held his rosary to his lips and kissed it now and again. His expression was solemn, his face white and sweaty under his black priest's hat. Cassie supposed it was the Blessing for the Condemned that the Father was giving.

The crowd murmured its approval, then grew silent. Again the general raised his saber. The five soldiers of the firing squad swung their Mausers over to the second prisoner. This fellow's trembling could be seen by all. He had watched the first volley and now braced himself, eyes shut tight against the picture he remembered. The blade dropped and a second volley echoed across the plaza. The second prisoner took his place beside the first.

Once more the blade was raised and brought down. The third prisoner died as easily as the first two.

Nobody came forward to claim the bodies. "There's no hurry," Mr. Runyon said. "Those fellows will wait." It seemed that there were so many dead in the wars among the generals who ruled the land—Carranza, Villa, Obregón, Zapata—that the Mex had given up putting the bodies underground. The land was so hard and parched and filled with clay that nobody could be found to dig the holes. So the bodies were stacked up with railroad ties and fired by kerosene. When a stack had burned down sufficiently, the remains were scattered over the sand and the wind permitted to do the rest. There were no grave markers; nobody knew the names and particulars of the fellows executed. "It's the modern method," Mr. Runyon explained.

Bandits or not, Cassie figured every man should have his own grave. But then he was new to the business of war and had much to learn.

"You feeling okay, kid? You look peaked."

"Thank you, sir, but I think I'll go off a bit, if you'll excuse me. . . ."

He looked for a private place but the crowd was thick and he had to settle for the nearest gutter. He'd had too much dinner and paid for it now, coughing up the various Mex specialties and putting the bulk of it through his nose, which he hated worse than anything.

He recovered himself in time to see Mr. Webster and the padre having their photographs taken with the corpses. This was a popular attraction and a good bargain: Mr. Horne offered two such poses for fifty cents, including postage to the customer's home. Later, Mr. Horne's assistants went through the crowd taking orders for "Triple Execution in Mexico," three poses, twenty-five cents. They gave a receipt and guaranteed delivery in the form of ready-made postcards within ten days. Mr. Horne had carried on this business for some years in El Paso and was highly respected for it. Cassie felt that he did not require any of the poses offered and so did not spend his money.

The events in Juárez were thus ended. Cassie said his farewells back across the river on Texas Street. The millionaire and Mr. Runyon asked him to come for supper in the Great Western Hotel, but Cassie was not in the mood for it.

"Remember now," said Mr. Runyon, "you get up New York way, you look me up, hear? You've got a head on your shoulders, kid—that's a scarce commodity these days."

Cassie wanted to stay on and listen to more of Mr. Runyon's sayings, but somehow could not. Maybe the millionaire's holding his IOU was behind it, or smelling his own vomit, or seeing that dead men's eyes stayed open—or worrying about Rocks in the desert and having to find Miss Jolene somewhere in El Paso.

Whatever it was, it made him miserable.

He returned to the Paso del Norte and tried the door to the room. To Cassie's great surprise Terence Sweeney was there in bed, alone.

"Shootin' all done, is it?"

"It's done."

"How was it?"

"Neat and clean. Oh, it was a fine execution. One of the best, I'd say."

"Ain't you goin' to tell me about it?"

"Nothing to tell. They just died. Three of them. Bandits. They picked the wrong general, is all."

"Suppose they must have."

"No dollies for you, then?"

The rider sat up in his bed. "You know, Texas women is *strange.* They travel in pairs and fear to be separated. I don't mind two on one, but they're scared of it. But now as you're back, the sky's the limit!"

Terence Sweeney got up and dressed and made Cassie come along with him. They stopped by the nearest saloon and drank Mexican beer. This was a benefit to Cassie's empty stomach.

Afterwards, they went hunting on Texas Street. There was plenty of quarry, but none that seemed interested in them. Cassie had left his Pullman cap in the room and now presented himself as a businessman in suit and vest. Terence Sweeney was still smart in his knee-high motorcycle boots. He was a year and two months older than Cassie and knew his way around the streets of any town of a Saturday night.

"Luck's bound to change!" cried Terence Sweeney. Like Rocks Mc-

Auliffe, he preferred to look on the bright side, and never mind the true situation. They turned off Texas Street and went north on Mesa. There were lots of pedestrians out taking the night air, but most were couples, man and woman. The saloons were peopled with cowboys and other rough characters; the streets showed a better class of citizen. Electrified lamps gave the place a prosperous and modern appearance. The town was not far different from St. Louis, as least in its better parts. They passed before the courthouse; a big clock told them it was nearly nine o'clock.

"Oh, well, it's early yet," said Terence Sweeney. "That explains it. You'll see—our kind o' female will show herself just minutes from now. Keep a sharp eye!"

They kept on north till the gravel ran out and the streets became dirt. Then they headed west and kept going almost to the river.

"I don't believe there's much town left out this way," Cassie suggested. The houses had gone from wood to adobe again.

"Well, there's lots o' time," said Terence Sweeney.

They worked up a good sweat; Cassie took to carrying his coat. They went back south, passing the Pullman Company offices, and came east on San Antonio Street. They were getting to know El Paso better than most residents, Cassie figured. Soon they had traveled five miles and were standing again in front of the Paso del Norte Hotel.

"It's Texas Street that's best," Terence Sweeney said. "I knowed it all along. Anyhow, there's no hurry about it—we got all the time in the world!"

"It's been a long day," Cassie replied, thinking to find some excuse for not marching another five miles.

At that moment, their luck changed.

"Look a' there!" cried Terence Sweeney. A carriage was then depositing its load in front of Freeman's Hotel across the street. "Only there's *three* of 'em, God bless! Wouldn't you *know* it! An' me hungrier than the devil, too!"

Cassie recognized them at once. The way they carried themselves—and smoked their cigarettes in the street—told him. For the moment, Cassie thought it the funniest of coincidences. But, thinking on it further, where else might such damsels be found of a Saturday night but in the streets?

"Let's go say hello," Cassie said.

"You *mean* it?" Terence Sweeney didn't look so cocksure as he usually did.

"Follow me," Cassie said, puffing his chest and marching forward. He was truly glad to see them: it was like meeting someone from home. "Well now," he called out, "isn't it a fine evening for a stroll?"

Miss Naomi, the Indian girl, was the first to know him. "It's dear Cassius hisself! Good evening, sir—and who's yer handsome friend?"

Miss Jolene and Miss Rita echoed these sentiments. Cassie was pleased to present Mr. Terence Sweeney of the Southern Pacific Railroad.

"Well now, what say you fine ladies to draft beer on ice?" offered Terence Sweeney. "Or champagne, if you prefer!"

They moseyed down Texas Street, looking to find a saloon that catered to females. Cassie worked it so that Miss Naomi and Miss Rita walked either side of Terence Sweeney while Cassie followed along with Miss Jolene on his arm. He told her of Rocks's plight, but she did not show much sympathy:

"We'd sure 'preciate supper more 'n beer, as we ain't had none yet. We was across to Mexico and saw men shot and missed our dinner, too. . . ."

They went back to the Paso del Norte Hotel and ate their supper there. The girls seemed much taken with Terence Sweeney, who offered a great line of stories when drinking whiskey. The three ladies were happy to drink whiskey, too; this came as some relief to Cassie, as whiskey was less dear than champagne. They ate beefsteaks and potatoes and ended up outside on the street around midnight.

Cassie knew he had had his limit of whiskey, and then some, so begged off when the girls asked to visit the famous gambling houses of the town, the Silver Dollar and Annie's Place and the Red Mill. After paying for supper, Cassie figured he had three dollars and change left in his pockets. He had no intention of bothering his grubstake upstairs in the Good Book.

"So I'll be saying good night to you ladies, and thank you most sincerely for your company."

The girls tried to make him come along, but Cassie stuck to his guns and felt better for it. Each one kissed him on the cheek, but he did not kiss back. He was sober as a judge, or just about.

"Then it's me an' the ladies on our own!" declared Terence Sweeney.

Cassie took out his last three dollars and stuffed them in his pal's pocket. "You'll be needing this, I suspect."

"Hallelujah!" cried the motorcyclist.

Cassie fell back on the bed, closed his eyes—heard a muffled rapping at the door. "Yes? What is it?"

No reply.

Wearily, he got up and stumbled to the door. "Miss Jolene!"

She brushed past him before he could think to hold her out. He was wearing only his skivvies. He retreated toward the bed, but she followed him. He slid between the sheets and pulled the blanket up to his neck. "Rocks'll sure be happy to see you!" he said stupidly.

She sat on the bed and removed her shoes. "Got anythin' to drink, dearie? Whiskey, maybe?"

"No, ma'am, sure don't!"

She undressed herself. He had seen her naked once before, in the second-section van. She seemed more naked now. She turned down the oil lamp and climbed in beside him.

"Here, sweetie, let me help."

She set to work on the buttons to his BVDs. He held back—then gave in.

PERSHING'S MEN FIND DESOLATE COUNTRY

Damon Runyon, in First Dispatch Permitted Out of
Headquarters, Details March and Hardships; No Men
Lost as Yet

By Damon Runyon,
Correspondent of the International News Service

WITH HEADQUARTERS, UNITED STATES ARMY IN THE FIELD
IN MEXICO—(Relayed by Army Wireless to Columbus, N.M.)—Slipping quietly and peacefully along the dusty roads of Northern Mexico,
General Pershing's flying columns are now covering a wide stretch of
territory in their pursuit of Villa.

No hostilities so far have been encountered anywhere along the line of
march. The Punitive Expedition has commenced buying fresh meat and
other supplies as it goes along and engages Mexican labor around the
camps, paying in American gold, which is mighty welcome to the natives.

Some mules and a few horses have been lost but no men. The only
shots fired in the Mexican republic by the expeditionary force, so far as
has been reported, have been fired by the cowboy scouts killing cattle.

Horses and mules died during the first couple of days, and were left to
the coyotes and buzzards that trail every column. The few Mexicans encountered stand at the roadside and view the long procession of Americans, that must seem to them interminable, in dumb amazement. They
offer no comment, however, but rush around hunting up eggs and other
articles to sell to the soldiers.

9

"ARE YOU GOING, THEN?" Cassie called out to the shadowy figure by the door. In the gloom, he supposed it was Jolene, taking her leave.

"Not goin' but comin'!" replied Terence Sweeney. "Missed yourself a fine night on the town, McGill—that you did!"

Slowly, Cassie came to his senses. His head felt cracked down the middle, his mouth dry as sagebrush, his eyes near to bursting. Sunbeams slanting past paper shades told him that dawn had come and gone. Distant church bells clanged out their Sunday greeting.

The motorcyclist had stripped naked and was giving himself a whore's bath out of the washbasin. "South Dakota women go straight to the top o' my list, McGill. And it's you I got to thank for it, nobody else!"

Some minutes passed before Cassie could sit up. He looked down to his privates and wanted the same bath as Terence Sweeney's. Besides a bath, he wanted Confession and Mass.

He got out of bed, crossed to the window, lifted the shade. An empty milk wagon clip-clopped down Texas Street following closely behind the electric trolley. El Paso was awake and lively; ladies' parasols already twirled in the hot sun.

The motorcyclist pulled on his boots again. "What say you to some ham and eggs, huh, McGill? And I believe I could down me a couple o' *cervezas*, I truly do. Only see to it I'm out to the aerodrome by one o'clock sharp. I'd sure hate to miss my ride!"

Cassie had taken over the basin. He soaped himself hard, then rinsed off in water so cold it made him gasp. "First, there's Mass," he said.

"Ah, Mass." The motorcyclist's eyes twinkled. "Sorry to say it, McGill, but the Sweeneys aren't practicing the Faith just now, for one cause and another. Sure'n I congratulate you, sir, on your own good deeds. Imagine it, readin' the Good Book when there was dollies to be had!"

Cassie was slow to take Terence Sweeney's meaning. When he did, his queasy stomach knotted into a ball of fear and dread. There on the chair beside the bed was the Gideon Bible. Surely he had left it where he found it, in the top drawer of the armoire. He grabbed it up and riffled through the pages.

Gone. She had missed nary a note.

"Say now, McGill," said Terence Sweeney, "is it a ghost you've seen?"
She had obtained the better part of $160.

"Might better have been a ghost," said Cassie, "than a lady."

Cassie revealed his sins, and Jolene's.

The motorcyclist doubled up with laughter. "Why then, she's surely the dearest woman you'll have in your lifetime!"

"I don't see the humor in it."

Terence Sweeney sobered up in no time at all. " '*Course* you don't! For the moment, I thought you was jokin'. Damn women! Tramps! Vagabonds! Come on now, we'll hunt the bitch down!"

Terence Sweeney led the way. They raced down to the desk in the lobby. None of the clerks remembered Jolene. In a big hotel like the Paso del Norte, she could come and go as she pleased.

"Ain't no shortage o' chippies hereabouts," said the bellman.

They marched across the street to Freeman's Hotel and found Naomi and Rita where Terence Sweeney had left them, in bed. The girls pleaded ignorance of Jolene's crime or where she might have gone.

"She's a high-and-mighty one," Rita said. "Ain't gonna share her earnin's wid us—not one dime!"

Cassie and Terence Sweeney swept through the hotels and boarding-houses on Texas Street and Mesa and San Antonio. Jolene Potts was not to be found. Any town of 50,000 inhabitants had more rooms for rent than the Army itself could hope to search out, so the job was hopeless from the start.

"That's it, then," Cassie declared finally.

They backtracked to the Pullman office and then Western Union. Still no sign of Rocks.

"You can forget that message you're holding," Cassie told both places.

"Hurts me to say it," said Terence Sweeney, "but if I'm to catch my ride, I'd best be heading out to the fort."

"Makes no difference," Cassie replied, " 'cause I'm going with you. The charm of this town just wore off. . . ."

It was no joy ride Cassie had in mind. His idea was to front Jacko Mudd and demand the return of their stakes, his and Rocks's, from the poker game at Dalhart. Maybe Cassie had cheated, but the troopers had cheated worse. Cassie meant to collect $100 and give half of it to Rocks.

"'But didn't you say you were singing Irish songs tonight for that millionaire o' yours?" Terence Sweeney reminded him. "Hachita's a long way from 'Paso!"

Cassie shook his head. "There's more important things in this world than damn 'Macushla.' "

They hoboed a ride out to the fort. While Terence Sweeney went to see the wheelwright, Cassie headed for the aerodrome. Standing by the Jenny were the same officers Cassie had seen at Hachita, Lieutenants House and Jeffers. He explained to them his need.

"It's railroad business," he lied. "The Pullman Company will be much obliged."

"And where'd you expect to ride, eh, boy?" asked Lieutenant House, the pilot. He was a tall blond gentleman with waxy eyebrows and mustache, penetrating blue eyes, and a wry smile. "With your pal and his load, we're a hundred pounds overweight now. Find yourself a train, why don't you?"

"I would, sir, only right this minute there's an Army scout lost in the desert, and I'm the only one who knows where he's headed." Cassie made up a quick story about Rocks's fleeing from savage Indians on the border.

Lieutenant House seemed dubious but fell for the tale anyway. "It's a good thing for you, boy, you're underfed and eager for discomfort!"

Terence Sweeney arrived with his newly spoked rims, and the Jenny was loaded. Cassie joined the motorcyclist flat on his belly in the cargo hold.

"Here now," said Terence Sweeney, "we'll have ourselves a look at the countryside." He used his pocketknife to cut a small hole in the canvas that covered the Jenny's wood framing. "Can't make it too big or the whole skin's liable to peel off in the breeze—then we're goners!"

The engine caught hold with a roar that made further talk impossible. Cassie didn't feel like talking anyway. His uneasy stomach performed several flip-flops as the aeroplane bumped along the landing strip and finally rose in the air. Cassie had ascended in a captive balloon at the Nebraska State Fair when he was ten years old, but that sensation was nothing to compare with this. For the briefest of moments, he contemplated putting Terence Sweeney's "window" to a different use from that which the motorcyclist intended. But luckily they had had no breakfast.

Even the tiny peephole made Cassie's eyes water. There was little enough to see. The countryside was as bleak from the air as on the ground. They followed the railroad tracks due west. The first place Cassie recognized was Columbus. Seeing it the way a buzzard did made a person realize what a lonesome and no-account place it was. Horse trails came into it from north and south, but neither amounted to much. Close to the train yards were the square black tops of fifty or more motorcars. These were to be used in speeding officers to the war, Cassie imagined. Or maybe war correspondents like Mr. Al Runyon expected to chase Pershing in them.

Cassie kept his eyes open but saw nothing of a lone horse and rider moving east.

"Please let me find him, Lord!"
But God did not see fit to answer Cassie's prayer.

They arrived over Hachita, swooped down, and circled the 4th Squadron's bivouac until a work party came out to corral the grazing horses. Wind-blown ruts in the desert made landing difficult. The Jenny set down amidst shrieks of protest from wood, wire, and canvas.

Terence Sweeney dove headfirst out the cargo hatch, then consulted his watch.

"One hundred thirty miles in one hundred nineteen minutes! A world record, I expect!"

The motorcyclist was a great friend to speed. He counted among his heroes the great race driver, Barney Oldfield, and the new champion, Eddie Rickenbacker, in his Dusenberg Special. Not wanting to spoil Terence Sweeney's fun, Cassie kept from mentioning that the Pennsy's *Broadway Limited* had reached 127 miles per hour back in '05 and carried a trainload of paying customers in the bargain. Aeroplanes would have to go some, Cassie decided, to match a fine express.

While the motorcyclist went off to assemble his machine, Cassie reported to Captain Bowles.

"Well now, McGill, I thought I advised you to stay clear o' this man's Army."

"Yes, sir, you sure did. Only—it's about my pal, sir. He's not yet shown himself in El Paso, and I was wondering—"

The captain's easy smile faded. "Patrols have gone east and west, boy, and there's still no sign o' the rascal. My guess is he's gone north to Deming an' is now makin' fools o' you and me both. Give it up, boy. You done your best for that fella. He'll turn up or he won't."

"I don't believe he's gone north, sir, or east or west either. I believe he's gone south."

The captain paused to consider Cassie's words. "Well then, boy, he's a bigger fool than ever I s'posed. 'Cause there's Mex raiding parties to the south, and renegade Injuns, too. If your partner's got a brain in his head, he won't go south."

"He's got brains, sir, but he uses them in a way different from most folks. I believe, sir, he's gone south to claim Colonel Slocum's reward."

Cassie explained Rocks's scheme.

The captain sat back, mouth open. "Such bloody-minded insolence! Takin' Villa all by his lonesome and claimin' the reward! I cannot believe it!"

"It's the truth, sir. Rocks will give it a fair try, too. He's not one to quit before the job's done."

"Without a compass?"

"He can read the sun, sir."

"Without an ounce o' food or a drop o' water?"

"He's been known, sir, to catch a rabbit in his bare hands. He's a short-stop, sir, and quick on his feet."

Cassie knew he was exaggerating but felt justified in stretching the truth on account of Rocks's predicament. Nor did Cassie reveal that Rocks was likely still manacled.

"Without a coat for night," the captain went on, "an' the temp'rature below freezin' on these plateaus?"

"He'll take heat from his pony, sir."

"I *know* that pony he stole—"

"*I* stole it, sir—not Rocks."

"—pony *you* stole, goddamit. It's high-spirited and short on manners both. Your pal most likely got tossed on his head a hundred yards south o' the perimeter!"

"He'd get back on, sir. He's that kind. If you could send a patrol south, sir—and let me go with it."

The captain glared at him. "I'm a fool, all right, Mistah McGill. But not so great a fool as that!"

"Then, if you'll lend me a horse, sir, I'll go on my own."

"I can't make you out, boy. What's your game?"

"He's my pal, sir."

"An' if I don't supply you with that horse?"

"Then I'll have to borrow one, sir, I suppose."

"An' if I lock your impudent ass in the guardhouse?"

"I'll break out, sir, first chance I get."

"Is there no *limit*, boy, to your conceit?"

The captain played with the curl on his forehead. Finally, he broke the uncomfortable silence that shrouded them. "Lucky for you, boy, there's a reconnaissance patrol goin' south within the hour. I've no authorization for a civilian scout, but I s'pose the rules can be stretched another inch or two."

"Thank you, sir!"

"Don't be thankin' me quite yet. You can go on one condition. Read this."

The captain handed Cassie a War Department circular. It bore the title "Emergency Enlistment Act." According to the document, there was a bill on President Wilson's desk authorizing the secretary of war to recruit the standing Army to its full strength of 120,000 men, up from the 100,000 men then in uniform. The bill would greatly increase pay in all grades and ranks. Privates would get $48 per annum, captains $500.

"Yes, sir?" said Cassie.

"Condition is," said Captain Bowles, "you sign a 'letter of intent' sayin' you mean to join up if an' when the President signs the bill. This way, 'case you're shot dead by some damn Mex who takes you for a trooper, my ass is covered. Return in one piece and we'll tear up the paper. What do you say, boy?"

"Where do I sign, sir?"

The proceedings took less than a minute.

"Report to Corp'ral Boniface," said the captain. "He'll give you a mount. After that, go see Lieutenant Van Impe—he's leadin' the patrol. Have a nice ride, *Private* McGill. . . ."

The mount they gave him was a mouse-colored mare, small and shy, called Sunshine. She was neither the best horse Cassie had ever seen nor the worst. The trooper who usually rode her, Private Frisko, a gaunt, tight-lipped New Englander, was dumbfounded that a mere recruit should be let up on her, and so was full of advice:

". . . She prefers a loose rein at the canter but needs to feel the bit at anything less. There's no use to jabbin' her—she'll not go quicker and will only take to sulking. . . . Say a kind word to her and stroke her head after a hard run—she's a smart girl and accustomed to easy treatment."

"I'll do my best, sir."

"See that you do, mister," said Private Frisko, "or you'll answer to me on your return."

The patrol was already waiting on him. Cassie let the troopers wait further. He had two jobs to do and, like Sunshine, did not go any quicker when jabbed.

First, he said his good-byes to Terence Sweeney. The rider was then wrenching up the wheels to his cycle.

"I'm soon off to Lordsburg, McGill. Sure you won't come along? Me an' my Indian, we could show you a thing or two 'bout travelin' overland!"

"I expect you could. But I've got business here. Thanks for showing me the ways of the aeroplane—I'd never have gone up without you to give me courage."

"It's the way of the future," said Terence Sweeney, "and I mean to follow it myself. There's a school for it in Phoenix, and I'm hopin' to go there an' swap this bike for lessons. You'll be hearing of me, McGill—that's the truth!"

"I expect I will. I'll keep my eyes peeled for your famous name in the *Lincoln Herald*."

Cassie's second task was harder: facing up to Jacko Mudd. He found the sergeant major in Headquarters tent. The trooper was having a chat with his cronies.

"So we've got ourselves a 'civilian scout,'" says the captain. "Well now, come forward, lad—let's have a look at you."

"What I've got to say is personal," Cassie replied.

Jacko Mudd's steady smirk deserted him for the moment. "Back to your posts," he said to his mates. "Personal, huh, Cassius? Well, spit it out, boy. Ain't nobody here to rat on you now."

Cassie steadied himself, then said his piece:

"I'm off to the desert to find my pal Rocks. When we get back, we'll be wanting the hundred dollars that's ours. That's our stake, Rocks's and mine, and you've no right to keep it. So either we get our money or else we go to Captain Bowles and tell him the true story of Dalhart. That includes your part and Corporal Binyon's part and Trooper Snivey's part, too."

"Now, hold on, lad—"

"No, sir, that's it. Cash money or a Western Union draft, either one. Otherwise, it's Captain Bowles and the judge advocate, too. . . ."

He joined up with the patrol. Seeing Lieutenant Van Impe again came as a shock. The redhead looked as ill-tempered as ever. Besides Van Impe, there was Corporal Boniface and eight privates from Troop B. They carried pistols and carbines but no sabers.

"*By the column of twos . . . forward . . . ho!*"

They rode out of camp at a fast walk. True scouts ordinarily ran at the head of a column, Cassie knew, but he was content to bring up the rear and eat troopers' dust.

"*. . . At the canter . . . ho!*"

They were on the trail to Culberson's Ranch, south and a few degrees west. It was from Culberson's Ranch that Colonel Dodd's 7th Cavalry, with Pershing himself leading the way in the rented Dodge automobile, had crossed over into Chihuahua. If Rocks went south, he went this way: there was no other trail a horse could follow.

Gusting winds soon arose, blowing grit and alkali in their faces. The patrol slowed, groped forward in the late-afternoon haze. Some of the veterans tied water-soaked kerchiefs over their mounts' eyes, but there was little relief to be had from the blinding sand. Dodd's column had cut the prairie trail to fine chalk: it parched the throats of men and animals alike, caked in their nostrils.

Cassie pulled his Pullman cap down and bowed his head until he could see nothing but the front of his own tunic and, infrequently, the rump of the horse ahead. How could Rocks have gotten far, he wondered, in such a hellish land? And how could a single Army patrol—or even a dozen—ever hope to find him?

They were nine or ten miles south of Hachita when the "point" man, a gangling private named Billy Muster, came back at a gallop and sounded the alarm:

"*Mex! Mex! It's them, all right—whole mess of 'em!*"

The trooper had spotted a campfire off to the west. Van Impe reined in and signaled for the men to halt.

"*Carbines at the ready! . . . By the right flank . . . ho!*"

The patrol moved off the trail at a walk, turning westward into the setting sun. There was little to see ahead but mesquite and chaparral and a distant grove of the giant saguaro cactus.

"*Prepare to dismount! . . . Dismount!*"

The troopers hobbled their horses, then formed a skirmish line and moved forward on foot up the arroyo. Cassie stayed close to the squad leader, Corporal Boniface, a nervous, wary sort of fellow, and imitated the trooper's every move.

Their boots sank deep into the sand, slowing their progress. A hundred paces farther on, they came upon a broad clearing in the mesquite. The ghostly saguaros stood like sentinels on all sides. A campfire still burned, its smoke white and misty. Even at a distance, Cassie could hear the fire. The oily mesquite branches used for fuel hissed and spit like a bevy of serpents.

The troopers left the arroyo and circled up the sandy banks to higher ground. Cassie followed along. There was one saguaro, taller than the rest, that caught Cassie's eye. At its center was a white patch. In Cassie's imagination, it looked to be a man, crucified like Jesus.

Van Impe, using hand signals, ordered the men to halt. Cassie continued forward.

O dear Virgin Mary, Our Lady of Chastity, don't let it be Rocks.

The troopers got down on their bellies, toes dragging in the sand, Krags trained on the clearing. Cassie kept his feet. Van Impe ordered him to get down, but Cassie paid no attention.

"Rocks, babe? Is that you?"

He went up and satisfied himself.

Thank you, dear Jesus, he's dead.

The shortstop still wore manacles. He had been roped to the tall cactus and his clothes cut off. The skin on his chest hung down in neat strips. The soles of his feet had been sliced free and replaced with slippers of cactus. His private parts were severed and stuffed in his mouth. He wore an awful grin in death.

Seeing it, troopers were sick on the ground. Cassie laughed out loud. A curious lizard crawled over Rocks's toes; the sand drank his blood; he wore cactus slippers. What was it that Rocks had asked for at Tucumcari —sand, cactus, even a lizard? Cassie had never heard a greater joke in his life!

Fifty yards farther up the arroyo, there was the glint of metal.

"There! By them rocks!" shouted Private Billy Muster.

"*Form defense perimeter!*" cried Van Impe. "*Fire on my command!*"

It was not the Mex at all. It was a small band of Indians, six or eight at most: Corporal Boniface had them fixed in his binoculars. They had been making their dinner on roasted jackrabbit and enjoying themselves over Rocks's corpse when Van Impe's patrol approached. Now they took refuge in the chaparral, which was their home.

Down a nearby ravine stood the renegades' horses: Boniface pointed them out. One animal stood out from the rest for its saddle, which bore the initials "U.S." burned into the skirt. It was cinched up the way Cassie had left it.

Poor damned shortstop: butchered for a stolen Army pony and cheap saddle.

Cassie started down the ravine. He wanted to touch Rocks's pony, finger that cinch again. He took two steps, then noticed puffs of sand erupting at his feet.

"*Down, you fool!*" cried Van Impe.

Only then did Cassie hear the gun shots, the whine of ricochets. The troopers did not wait for Van Impe's order, but began firing at will. One man had brought a Springfield: the muzzle blast from his weapon made twice the noise of the Krags. Corporal Boniface detailed two men to take turns running and firing until one of them reached the renegades' ponies and ran them off, wounding as many as he could with bullets in the rump so the Indians would have no means of escape.

It did not take any thinking at all. Cassie stooped to grab a Colt off a wounded trooper, then started up the slope toward the thicket that shielded the savages.

"*McGill! Get down, I say!*" cried Van Impe. The lieutenant sat hunched up with his back to a saguaro, his arms and legs pulled in lest they provide a target.

Cassie moved forward. Corporal Boniface, bolder than Van Impe, scampered to Cassie's side.

"Here, kid, take this—you're gonna need it."

He gave Cassie his machete. All the old Philippines hands still carried machetes on their belts.

The Indians began to shoot. A sudden blow dropped Cassie to his knees. He felt for his shoulder and brought away a blood-soaked hand. He thrust the machete into his trousers and kept the .45 in his shooting hand. He regained his feet and marched forward. Whenever he saw a muzzle blast in the mesquite, he turned toward it and fired the .45. He kept firing until the pistol was empty, then threw it down and went forward with Corporal Boniface's machete.

The troopers now followed. The Indians bolted from the chaparral; Army bullets cut them down. A young savage, fierce-eyed and naked, rushed at Cassie with a stone club. Cassie split his skull.

When the battle was over, the troopers roamed the chaparral, searching for wounded Indians. When they found one, they pierced his throat with a bayonet and left him to drown in his own blood. They tallied the score. There had been eight. Eight Indians had fought, eight had died. Besides Cassie, two troopers had taken bullets but regained their feet.

"Ya got three o' the bastards yerself, kid!" Corporal Boniface told Cassie. "That's mighty fine shootin', let me tell ya!"

Eventually, Lieutenant Van Impe came forward to inspect the corpses. "Leave them where they lie!" he ordered. "No sense to burden the horses. Dig a hole for that one," he said, pointing to Rocks.

In a rage, Cassie sprinted across the clearing and threw himself at Van Impe. The two of them tumbled through the fire pit and into cactus on the far side. The fingers on Cassie's good hand found the officer's windpipe. Van Impe, hard as nails, fought back, breaking Cassie's grip. Cassie only laughed—drove the officer's face into the sand. He was not satisfied until Van Impe's blood stained both their uniforms.

The other troopers, who had stayed back, now climbed on Cassie and pulled him off.

Van Impe blubbered like a girl:

"Arrest that man! *Arrest* him, I say! Don't stand about—*help* me, can't you? Bring the Red Cross kit! Don't you see I'm *bleeding* . . . ?"

Rocks's corpse swung lazily to the gentle gait of an Army mare.

They had checked Cassie's wound. A Mauser bullet had passed through the fleshy part of his shoulder and lodged in his tunic. They patched him up with the same Red Cross kit used on Van Impe, then tied him in the saddle of Private Frisko's Sunshine. Cassie did not resist; the bile had drained out of him. He fell asleep at once and missed the ride back to Hachita.

It was past 10:00 P.M. when they reached camp. They passed close enough to Miss Opal's to hear the girls' laughter and smell the bittersweet *cerveza*. Captain Bowles came out of Headquarters tent to greet them. Private Billy Muster had galloped ahead and given the captain a report on the action.

"Untie this man at once!" the captain ordered. His face was grave and pale. "Escort him to the infirmary—he's shot through!"

An orderly cleansed Cassie's wound and bandaged him. "If it turns bad," the fellow said, "you'll die o' blood poison, most likely."

Afterwards, Captain Bowles came to see him. "Can you talk, boy?"

"I can talk, sir."

"Y'all turned soldier on us for real, so I'm told."

"Sir?"

"Boniface says you're a fast man with a Colt. Still an' all, I'm tearin' this up." It was the "letter of intent" that Cassie had signed.

"Thank you, sir."

"If y'all was in uniform, we'd fetch you a medal. As is, you'll be lucky to 'scape the noose."

"I guess I'm a prisoner again, sir."

"Depends on the Dutchman. You gave him an awful beatin', boy."

"I can't exactly remember it, sir."

"Boniface says it was regardin' your friend."

Cassie remained silent.

"What would you have us do with the body?"

"Not leave him to rot in some hole in the desert!" Cassie's tears undid him; he was ashamed of himself.

The captain lighted his cigar. "Your pal deserves proper burial, boy—no argument 'bout that."

Cassie composed himself. "I'd like it to be in El Paso, sir, in a good cemetery. He's got no pa, and his ma's in the sanitorium, so there's no use to send him home."

"You know best, boy."

"There'll be expenses connected to it, I know. The Army needn't worry, sir—I'll settle up for him."

"The Army's not worried, son."

Cassie's tears started again. He hid his face in his hands.

The captain grew anxious. "Is your wound painin' you, boy? Is it morphine you're wantin'?"

Cassie shook his head—dried his eyes on the sleeves to his nightgown. "Sorry to be such a baby, sir. Only—Rocks'll be wanting a proper Mass, sir, and a Father to say a prayer by the grave."

"Well now, I s'pose we might persuade Father Tibbett to do it. The padre—"

"*No, sir!*" Cassie replied abruptly. "Not the padre. A Jesuit, sir—that's what's needed. Rocks deserves the best, though I guess there's few people who might think so. . . ."

Later that night, Cassie had another visitor to the infirmary tent: Sergeant Major Jacko Mudd.

"I'll be quick, boy. Your money's gone for good. Me an' Binyon, we had it stole from us in a game with the Sixth Infantry boys there at Columbus. Those fellas are the worst cheats in this world and not to be trusted past the lengths o' their noses.

"Thought you'd want your beads. They didn't mean nothin' to Ward—

he was just teasin' you. I guess he was a bastard, all right. Back in Philippine days, he was as fine a fella as ever lived. More'n one man in this outfit owes his life to Ward Snivey. But he turned bad after we come home. He had a girl out there, and she done him dirt. It changed him—cost him his stripes in the end. Still, he was one o' the best, and I can't help spillin' a tear or two over his passin'.

"Good-bye, boy, and thanks for what you done to the Dutchman. There's lots o' fellas in camp who'd kiss you for it, and that's the truth! Now be on your way home, lad, and learn somethin' from an old man's mistakes. . . ."

Cassie fingered Ma's rosary for the first time in days. The smooth wood beads eased his pain. He gave himself a heavy penance and started on it without delay. His prayers would be for Rocks and Ward Snivey both, he decided.

Next morning, Captain Bowles, using the Army's wire, arranged with the El Paso & Southwestern for the next eastbound train to stop at Hachita. The Squadron's carpenters ran up a box for Rocks. There being no fresh lumber to spare in the desert, the troopers used some planks salvaged from *Pullman's No. 3*, including remnants from the colonel's fancy painted signs: PANCHO VILLA EXPRESS. Rocks would have enjoyed that, Cassie knew.

Before the lid was nailed down, Cassie found Billy Joe Hardesty in C Troop and recovered Rocks's mitt. Cassie slipped the battered old glove over Rocks's stiff fingers.

There now, God, you got yourself a shortstop.

The lead locomotive hove into sight at noon. It was no regular freight but a four-section special, each section boasting a long string of parlors and horse vans. A proud banner on the first combination car proclaimed the outfit:

1st CAVALRY

"BEST IN THE WEST"

A detail from Jacko Mudd's Headquarters Platoon saw to the loading of Rocks's coffin into the combo. Despite the pain in his shoulder, Cassie stood by to make sure the box rode comfortably. When this was done, Captain Bowles ordered the detail to "Present arms!" and the Squadron bugler came forward on the platform and blew "Taps."

Afterwards, Captain Bowles shook Cassie's hand, gave him a quick hug, and told him to get on board. The captain had prevailed upon Lieutenant Van Impe to drop charges. The lieutenant needed some stitching, but he had kept his teeth.

Not looking back, Cassie climbed into the first-section van.

"Glad o' the company!" the smart aleck told him. "Cap'n McGill, is it? I'm Killeen, master o' *Pullman's No. 9*. Three days running out o' Monterey, California, we are, and bound for Laredo, Texas. . . . And what rig brung you here, eh, McGill? The devil's own, judgin' from the shape o' your tunic!"

Cassie set his tired eyes on the lanky trainman. The telltale words SPECIAL SERVICE graced his cap. The fellow looked to be Cassie's age and not the smartest brains ever to ride the rails.

"*Pullman's No. 3* out of Lincoln, Nebraska," Cassie answered.

"Oh, gosh! We heard talk o' you fellas back at Lordsburg! And that box you brung aboard—"

"Maybe you heard of him, too—Rocks McAuliffe, top shortstop in the Texas League and back in Nebraska before that. . . . He was my helper out of Lincoln. . . . Lost his life across the border. . . . He's to have Mass said over him at 'Paso."

"And he was a Pullman fella like us?"

"The best ever."

"Well now, make yourself to home, McGill! Take the super's bunk if you want—it's an honor to have you aboard! You carried real heroes whereas this lot o' mine is nothin' but gamblers and drunkards and damn women-chasers. . . ."

Cassie lay down on the super's bunk and pulled the curtains closed around him. He meant to ease the ache in his shoulder and think matters out—Miss Candace, the job in Webster's Machine Lubricant at Chicago, the promise of future studies at Rensselaer Polytechnic.

But he soon knew them all for what they were—a fool's dream—and he fell asleep even before Conductor Killeen could tug on the bell cord and signal his hoggers:

GREEN BOARD . . . FLAGMEN IN . . . MAKE SPEED.

Brown Meggs grew up in Los Angeles and Westport, Connecticut, spending his college years at the California Institute of Technology and Harvard. During the Korean War he served as special agent with Army Counterintelligence. After a brief stint as story analyst for Warner Bros. Pictures, Burbank, he worked as an industrial-film writer in Detroit. Thereafter, he spent eighteen years in the record industry, ultimately as chief operating officer and member of the board of directors of Capitol Records, Inc. In 1976 he resigned his corporate posts in order to commit himself to a second career as fiction writer. His other novels, which have also been published in England, Germany, Italy, Japan, and Spain, are Saturday Games (1974), The Matter of Paradise (1975), and Aria (1978). *Mr. Meggs makes his home in Pasadena with his wife, the former Nancy Bates Meachen. Their son, Brook, is presently a graduate fellow in English at Columbia University.*